SILENT NIGHT

SILENT NIGHT

by

Jack Sheffield

Magna Large Print Books
Long Preston, North Yorkshire,
BD23 4ND, England.

British Library Cataloguing in Publication Data.

Sheffield, Jack
    Silent night.

    A catalogue record of this book is
    available from the British Library

    ISBN   978-0-7505-4177-0

First published in Great Britain in 2013 by Bantam Press
an imprint of Transworld Publishers

Copyright © Jack Sheffield 2013

Cover illustration © mirrorpix

Jack Sheffield has asserted his right under the Copyright, Designs and
Patents Act, 1988 to be identified as the author of this work.

Published in Large Print 2015 by arrangement with
Transworld Publishers

All Rights reserved. No part of this publication may be reproduced,
stored in a retrieval system, or transmitted in any form or by any
means, electronic, mechanical, photocopying, recording or otherwise
without the prior permission of the Copyright owner.

Magna Large Print is an imprint of Library Magna Books Ltd.

Printed and bound in Great Britain by
T.J. (International) Ltd., Cornwall, PL28 8RW

This book is a work of fiction and, except in the case of historical fact, any resemblance to actual persons, living or dead, is purely coincidental.

For Lily Beth & Ava Grace
...may they always enjoy the magic of Christmas

Contents

Acknowledgements

I am indeed fortunate to have the support of a wonderful editor, the superb Linda Evans, and the excellent team at Transworld including Larry Finlay, Bill Scott-Kerr, Elizabeth Masters, Vivien Thompson, Bella Whittington, Brenda Updegraff and Lynsey Dalladay, not forgetting the 'footsoldiers' – fellow 'Old Roundhegian' Martin Myers and the quiet, unassuming Mike 'Rock 'n' Roll' Edgerton.

Special thanks as always go to my hard-working literary agent, Philip Patterson of Marjacq Scripts, for his encouragement, good humour and deep appreciation of Yorkshire cricket.

I am also grateful to all those who assisted in the research for this novel – in particular: Janina Bywater, neonatal nurse and lecturer in psychology, Cornwall; The Revd Ben Flenley, Rector of Bentworth, Lasham, Medstead and Shalden, Hampshire; Ian Haffenden, ex-Royal Pioneer Corps and custodian of Sainsbury's Alton; John Kirby, ex-policeman, expert calligrapher and Sunderland supporter, County Durham; Roy Linley, Lead Architect, Strategy & Technology, Unilever Global IT Innovation and Leeds United supporter, Port Sunlight, Wirral; Sue Maddison, primary-schoolteacher and expert cook, Harrogate, Yorkshire; Phil Parker, ex-teacher and Manchester United supporter, York; Gill Siddall, keen gardener and lover of flowers, Medstead, Hampshire; Linda Collard, education trainer and consultant, fruit-grower and jam-maker, West Sussex; and all the terrific staff at Waterstones Alton, including Simon, Sam, Kirsty, Louise, Fiona and Mandie; also, Sheena and Trish at Waterstones Farnham, and Kirsty and the team at Waterstones York.

Finally, thanks go to Richard and Trish Lord, owners of the excellent B&B in the Yorkshire Dales, Littlebank Country House, Settle, for their wonderful hospitality ... and their award-winning marmalade recipe!

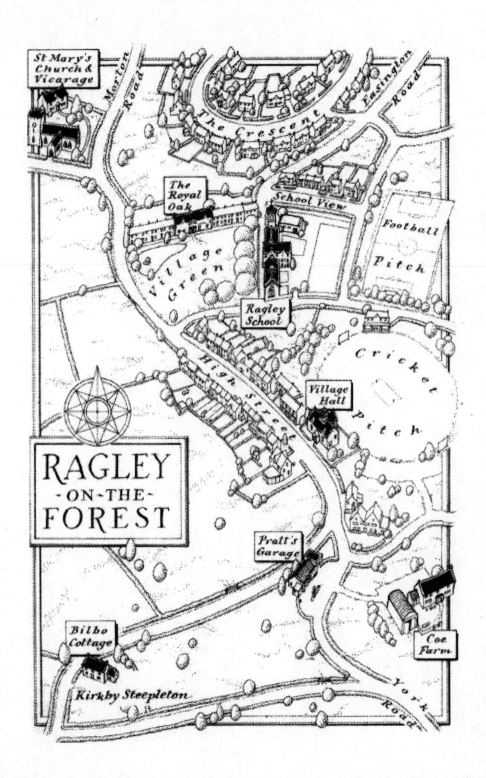

Prologue

Memories.

Some are sharp and clear like still cool water on a summer's day. Others, like tattered rags of cirrus clouds sweeping across a windswept winter sky, are lost for ever.

Years come and go, but some stay in the mind. 1984 was such a time ... and all because of a Christmas carol sung by a small girl. It was a song of innocence that touched the hearts of many, a poem of hope that resurrected a love that was lost, and set in motion the wheels of change.

The autumn term was always my favourite, with the gradual build-up towards Harvest Festival, Bonfire Night and finally the Nativity plays and coloured lights of Christmas. In contrast, the spring term was often one of coughs and colds, dark nights and freezing weather, before Easter arrived bringing new life to the hedgerows; while the summer term brought sunshine and sports days. This was the rhythm of our lives in the cycle of seasons.

For me, Christmas was always the best. Each year on the carousel of my teaching life I grew older, whereas the children at Ragley School were always the same – rising fives to eleven-year-olds, for whom the magic of Christmas filled their waking thoughts.

The academic year 1984/85 began quietly on a

perfect morning when late-summer sunshine slanted in through the windows of our Victorian school. It was Saturday, 1 September, and I was sitting at my desk in the school office. The beginning of the autumn term for the children of the village was two days away and I was responding to the many letters from County Hall. I sighed. It was the usual collection of Health & Safety regulations, budget cuts, curriculum reforms, a list of newly appointed advisers and even recommended room temperatures. Some things never changed.

I sat back and reflected on the school holiday that was now almost over. My wife, Beth, like me a village-school headteacher, had visited her parents in Hampshire the previous week for a short break with our year-old son, John William. She was returning that evening with the surprising news that her sister, Laura, had decided to leave suddenly for a new life in Sydney, Australia. Beth didn't want to discuss it over the telephone – apparently it was 'complicated'.

Meanwhile, on the office wall, the clock with its faded Roman numerals ticked on. In spite of the usual apprehension, I had always found the dawn of a new school year to be an exciting time, but little did I know what lay in store. The end of a world I had come to love was threatening like a far-off thundercloud. However, hope is an elusive companion, an invisible friend who occasionally taps you on the shoulder and leads you by the hand towards a better future. So it was that I viewed the coming days with optimism.

On that distant autumn day, all seemed calm as

my eighth year as headmaster of Ragley-on-the-Forest Church of England Primary School in North Yorkshire was about to begin.

Up the Morton Road the church clock chimed midday. I took a deep breath as I unlocked the bottom drawer of my desk, removed the large, leather-bound school logbook and opened it to the next clean page. Then I filled my fountain pen with black Quink ink, wrote the date and stared at the empty page.

The record of another school year was about to begin. Seven years ago, the retiring headmaster, John Pruett, had told me how to fill in the official school logbook. 'Just keep it simple,' he said. 'Whatever you do, don't say what really happens, because no one will believe you!'

So the real stories were written in my 'Alternative School Logbook'. And this is it!

Chapter One

The Last Earnshaw

93 children were registered on roll on the first day of the school year.
Extract from the Ragley School Logbook:
Monday, 3 September 1984

'She's las' one, Mr Sheffield,' said Mrs Julie Earnshaw sadly.

This tough Yorkshire lady had met me in the school entrance hall.

'Is she?' I asked.

'She is that – last of t'Earnshaws.'

I removed my black-framed Buddy Holly spectacles and polished them, wondering what was coming next. 'Oh, I see,' I said ... but I didn't.

Her sturdy four-year-old daughter, Dallas Sue-Ellen, was standing beside her. It was her first day at school and she was about to enter Anne Grainger's reception class. The little girl was wearing a Roland Rat T-shirt, a frilly multicoloured Toyah Willcox skirt, *Fame* leg warmers and white pixie boots. Her hairstyle resembled the fierce bristles of a blonde lavatory brush. She was chewing a liquorice shoelace and gave me a black-toothed smile.

'Y'see, Mr Sheffield, ah'd jus' like 'er t'be a good *effluence* on t'others,' said Mrs Earnshaw

20

with gravitas, "cause she's good at 'eart.'

'I'm sure she is, Mrs Earnshaw,' I agreed, but without conviction, while picking absent-mindedly at the frayed leather patches on my herringbone sports coat.

She looked down proudly at Dallas Sue-Ellen, who had finished her liquorice breakfast and was now picking her nose with a blackened finger.

'Dallas,' said Mrs Earnshaw firmly, 'go out t'play in t'yard.'

Dallas required no second invitation and hurried off.

Mrs Earnshaw leaned against the old pine display table and lowered her voice to a conspiratorial whisper. 'Y'see, Mr Sheffield, it's my Eric.' She looked quickly left and right. ''E's 'ad a *snip*.'

'A snip?'

'Yes, y'know – one o' them vivi-'ysterectomies.'

'Oh, I see,' I said ... and this time I did. The penny had dropped.

Mrs Earnshaw shook her head sadly. 'Poor sod's been walkin' round like John Wayne wi'out 'is 'orse this las' week.'

'I'm not surprised,' I replied with feeling.

She looked crestfallen. 'So no more little 'uns f'me.'

'Well, you've got three children to be proud of,' I said, trying to cheer her up.

'Ah 'ave that, Mr Sheffield,' she agreed. 'Our 'Eathcliffe an' Terry love t'big school an' they did well 'ere learning t'read an' write an' suchlike. It's jus' that ah'm concerned 'bout our Dallas.'

Anne Grainger, the deputy headteacher,

appeared suddenly from the stockroom carrying a box of infant safety scissors and some large sheets of card. Anne, a slim brunette in her early fifties, was our longest-serving teacher at Ragley and her reception classroom was always full of colour and activity. 'Hello, Mrs Earnshaw,' she said brightly. 'A big day for Dallas.'

''Ello, Mrs Grainger,' said Mrs Earnshaw. 'Ah were jus' tellin' Mr Sheffield 'ere that ah'm a bit worried.'

The first flicker of concern crossed Anne's face. 'And why is that?'

'Well, 'ow can ah put it?' said Mrs Earnshaw. 'It's *things*.'

'Things?' repeated Anne. She put the card and scissors on the table. 'What things?'

'Y'know, Mrs Grainger – all them *little things*.'

'Such as?' asked Anne.

Mrs Earnshaw took a deep breath. 'Well, ah were 'oping you'd teach 'er some table manners.'

'Oh, I see,' said Anne.

'An' she still needs 'elp goin' to t'toilet.'

'Does she?'

'An' she can't write 'er name an' ah'm flummoxed if ah know whether she's left or right 'anded.'

Anne nodded knowingly and said nothing.

'An' she won't do as she's told,' continued Mrs Eamshaw, gathering momentum, 'an' lately she's picked up some *words*, if y'get m'meaning, from 'er dad.'

'Oh dear,' said Anne.

'An' when she don't get 'er own way she starts fighting... But 'part from that, my Eric says she's gorra lot o' p'tential.'

I felt I ought to contribute, diplomatically of course, as I saw Anne's shoulders begin to slump. 'I'm sure she has, Mrs Earnshaw,' I said, thinking back to my teacher-training days, 'and it's up to us to help her *achieve* that potential ... with *your* help, of course.'

Anne gave me a glassy-eyed stare. 'That's right, Mrs Earnshaw,' she said, 'as always, we'll do our best,' and with a weary sigh she picked up the card and scissors and headed for her classroom.

In the school office our secretary, Vera Forbes-Kitchener, was sitting at her impeccably tidy desk having just labelled the new attendance and dinner registers, a pair for each of our four classes. When I walked in she was in conversation with Mrs Brenda Ricketts, who was clutching the hand of her four-year-old daughter.

Vera, a tall, slim, elegant sixty-two-year-old, stood up and smoothed the creases from the skirt of her immaculate Marks & Spencer two-piece pinstriped business suit. 'Good morning, Mr Sheffield,' she said. 'I've prepared the registers and I'm just completing some paperwork with Mrs Ricketts. Her daughter Susan is about to commence full-time education in Class 1.'

I smiled in acknowledgement and walked to my desk by the window. 'Hello, Mrs Ricketts,' I said.

'G'morning, Mr Sheffield,' she replied cheerfully.

Meanwhile Vera sat down again and studied her neat admissions register, completed in her beautiful copper-plate writing. 'So, Mrs Ricketts, you're William's mother.'

'Well, actu'lly, 'is proper name is *Billy*,' said Mrs Ricketts.

'We've got him down as *William*,' replied Vera.

'No, it's not William ... definitely *Billy*,' repeated Mrs Ricketts with emphasis. 'We christened 'im after m'favourite singer.'

'Oh,' said Vera, 'and who is that?'

'Billy Fury,' said Mrs Ricketts with a faraway look in her eyes. ''E were allus my 'earthrob.'

'Billy Fury?' asked Vera, who vaguely recalled the name.

'Y'know... "'Alfway to Paradise".'

'Pardon?'

''E 'ad that sexy voice an' a lovely quiff.'

'Did he?'

This was followed by a few seconds of synchronized swooning before normal service was resumed. Vera deleted the name 'William' with white opaque correction fluid and blew on it gently to encourage speedy drying.

'And this is Susan, is it?' asked Vera, looking down at the little girl.

'No, Mrs Forbes-Kitchener, it's Suzi wi' a "z".'

'Really?'

'Then one o' them 'yphens,' added Mrs Ricketts.

Vera was gradually losing the will to live. She put down her fountain pen. 'A hyphen?'

'Yes, it's Suzi, then a 'yphen, then Quatro.'

'Quatro?'

'Yes, Mrs F.' Vera understood that, after a while, parents tended to resort to this abbreviation. Having married the retired Major Rupert Forbes-Kitchener, as recently as Christmas 1982, Vera realized her new double-barrelled name had its drawbacks in rapid conversations. 'Y'see Suzi-Quatro is m'fav'rite *female* singer.'

'I can't say I know her,' said Vera. 'Is she from Spain?'

'No, y'must 'ave 'eard "Devil Gate Drive",' insisted Mrs Ricketts.

'Oh dear,' said Vera, wincing visibly. After all, she was also the sister of our local vicar. 'I really don't think I have.'

'Well, anyway, it's Suzi-Quatro Ricketts,' said Mrs Ricketts firmly and Vera added the name to her neat register with a heavy heart amid fleeting thoughts that the eighties and young mothers were quickly leaving her behind.

As Mrs Ricketts hurried out I looked at our ever-patient school secretary and knew I would be lost without her. 'Well done, Vera,' I said.

Vera stared at her admissions register in disbelief. 'Times are changing, Mr Sheffield.'

'I think I'll go out to the school gate and welcome the children and new parents,' I said.

Vera smiled. 'Well ... here's to another year,' she said and returned to her paperwork.

I glanced up at the clock on the office wall. It was 8.30 a.m. on Monday, 3 September 1984, the first day of the autumn term, and my eighth year as headteacher of Ragley-on-the-Forest Church of England Primary School in North Yorkshire had begun.

In the entrance hall Ragley's other two teachers were in conversation. Sally Pringle, a tall, ginger-haired, forty-three-year-old taught the eight-year-

25

olds and the youngest nine-year-olds in Class 3. Unlike Vera, Sally had an unconventional dress sense, no doubt influenced by her flower-power days; today she wore baggy purple cords, a magenta blouse and a vivid mint-green waistcoat.

'Hello, Jack,' she greeted me, waving a copy of the hall timetable. 'Just doing a deal with Tom about the use of the hall for my choir practices.'

'Fine,' I said. 'I'm just going down to the school gate.'

Next to her was Tom Dalton, appointed a year ago and our youngest teacher at twenty-five years old. He was in charge of the six- and seven-year-olds in Class 2. At five feet ten inches tall Tom was three inches shorter than my gangling frame, but he was significantly heavier, with broad, muscular shoulders and a rugby player's physique. He wore a crumpled blue denim suit, a white shirt, his old St Peter's School tie and slip-on Hush Puppies. His dark, shaggy hair flopped over his beetle brows and hung fashionably over his collar. According to Sally, he had 'film-star looks'. More to the point, he was in my eyes a good teacher who was making a positive contribution to the work of our school, particularly in the field of the new computer technology.

However, it was clear that many of our younger mothers also found him extremely attractive and there had been times when I had to warn him of the potential dangers of getting *too* close to parents. However, this advice counted for nothing when, earlier in the year, he had begun a brief but tempestuous relationship with an older woman. Normally this would have been none of my business, apart from the fact that the female in question happened to be my wife's single, dynamic and stunningly attractive sister, Laura. Consequently he gave me a slightly forced smile. 'I'll ring the bell at nine, shall I, Jack?' he asked.

I gave what I hoped was an encouraging 'water-under-the-bridge' smile. 'Thanks, Tom,' I said and pushed open the ancient oak door on its giant hinges.

As I walked across the tarmac playground, groups of children were leaning against the waist-high wall of Yorkshire stone topped with metal railings, sharing news of their summer holiday. Others, with sunburned faces, were running, skipping and bouncing tennis balls. It was a mixed lot from all walks of life. Our intake comprised the children of local farming families, others from the ever-expanding local council estate and some from the more prestigious dwellings up the Morton Road. The latter group included the sons and daughters of executives at the chocolate factory in York, one of the city's major employers. All of them waved as I walked down the cobbled drive to the giant stone pillars that flanked the wrought-iron school gate.

Seven-year-old Ted Coggins was in animated conversation with five-year-old Billy Ricketts. ''Ello, Mr Sheffield,' shouted Ted. 'Ah'm showin' Billy 'ow t'play conkers.'

'Well done, Ted,' I said with a smile.

'An' then ah'll teach 'im 'ow t'whistle.' Young Ted was famous for his ear-piercing whistle, achieved by putting the second finger of each hand in his mouth and blowing ferociously.

'Ah, yes, Ted,' I replied with caution and hurried on, recollecting that a whistle that resembled a high-speed train in a tunnel was not something to relish.

I stopped at the gate and drank in the view. Above my head an avenue of majestic horse chestnut trees, heavy in leaf, shaded the school wall and, at their feet, a group of small boys searched in the detritus of leaves and branches for the precious spiky fruits. Behind me our Victorian school of reddish-brown brick was bathed in the early autumn sunlight. It was a severe, striking building, with a steep grey-slate roof, high arched windows with pointed tops and a tall Gothic bell tower. For over one hundred years it had been the seat of learning for the children of the village and I felt proud to play my small part in its long history.

Suddenly a short, plump, expensively dressed lady I didn't recognize approached with two little girls. They were clearly identical twins, with golden ringlets, shining faces and cherubic smiles.

'Good morning, Mr Sheffield,' said the woman confidently. 'I'm Pippa Jackson. We've just moved in next door to the Dudley-Palmers on the Morton Road. They were full of praise for your school.'

'I'm pleased to meet you,' I said, reassured by the seal of approval.

'Yes,' continued this voluble lady. 'They mentioned the school's academic achievement and, of course, the emphasis on good behaviour, which is dear to my heart... So I'm enrolling my daughters today.'

'That's good to hear,' I replied. 'Welcome to Ragley School.'

'And these are my daughters, Honeysuckle and Hermione.' I looked down at her angelic offspring: they were dressed alike in matching pink gingham dresses, brown leather sandals and white ankle socks. 'Say good morning to Mr Sheffield, girls,' she instructed.

'Good morning, Mr Sheffield,' they said in perfect unison.

'Good morning,' I replied, 'and I hope you will enjoy your new school.' I smiled at Mrs Jackson. 'So perhaps you would like to go into the school office and register the girls with our secretary, Mrs Forbes-Kitchener?'

'Certainly,' she said. 'We've heard of your excellent secretary and we are delighted such an impressive Christian lady is on the staff.' She hurried off with her girls and I prayed they would have a good first day.

Meanwhile Ragley village was coming alive. Opposite the school was the village green with a duck pond that teemed with life. Under the shade of a weeping-willow tree stood an ancient wooden bench and on it sat some of the mothers with their rising fives, excited yet apprehensive at the thought of their children starting school. To my right was the white-fronted public house, The Royal Oak, standing in the centre of a row of cottages with pantile roofs and tall brick chimneys. Sheila Bradshaw, the buxom landlady, was watering the tubs of pelargoniums and trailing lobelia and she gave me a friendly wave before smoothing her tight, black-leather miniskirt and tottering back inside on her high heels.

Off to my left, down the High Street, was a row of shops. Miss Amelia Duff was outside her village Post Office, chatting with the love of her life, our local postman Ted Postlethwaite, while Diane Wigglesworth was Sellotaping a poster of Madonna to the window of her Hair Salon. In the doorway of Nora's Coffee Shop the assistant, Dorothy Humpleby, was swaying her hips in time to Stevie Wonder's 'I Just Called To Say I Love You'. It was playing at full volume on the old red-and-chrome jukebox and Timothy Pratt frowned at the noise as he arranged a neat row of garden gnomes on a trestle table outside his Hardware Emporium. Eugene Scrimshaw was sweeping the forecourt of the village pharmacy and Old Tommy Piercy was admiring the display of prize-winning sausages in his butcher's shop. Finally, Miss Prudence Golightly had already done over an hour's business in her General Stores & Newsagent and was discussing some of the popular topics of the day, including the price of bread and Arthur Scargill's hairstyle, with one of her regular customers, Betty Buttle.

I sighed, happy with my lot in this beautiful corner of God's Own Country. Our school was a focal point of the village, a centre of the community, and here I had found peace in my professional life. Finally, I breathed in the clean air and walked back up the drive. The first day of a school year was always special. It was a time of hope and expectation and I wondered what might be in store.

For this was 1984. It was the time of the miners' strike and the first Apple Macintosh computer. Virgin Atlantic had made its first flight and Trivial Pursuit was destined to become the most successful board game of all time. The one-pound note was to be withdrawn from circulation, moon boots would become a winter fashion and *Spitting Image* appeared on our screens. Band Aid's 'Do They Know It's Christmas?' was to be the year's bestselling UK single and countless children were destined to find happiness by adopting a Cabbage Patch doll. However, less happy was Michael Jackson, who had been burned while filming a Pepsi advert.

It was announced that O levels and CSEs were to be replaced by GCSEs, an IRA bomb shook the Grand Hotel in Brighton and Australia introduced the one-dollar coin. Meanwhile, L'Oréal introduced the first hair mousse and, in doing so, predicted an end to hair gel. It was also the year we said a sad farewell to Eric Morecambe, Richard Burton, J. B. Priestley and Tommy Cooper.

However, on this sunny morning, the villagers of Ragley-on-the-Forest were going about their usual business as the school bell summoned the children to their classrooms.

In Class 4 our main topic of conversation after registration concerned monitor jobs. For the oldest pupils in the school these tasks held a certain status and were valued. After asking for volunteers it was decided that Mo Hartley would follow in her elder sister's footsteps and become the official bellringer. Victoria Alice Dudley-Palmer, who

31

always prided herself on possessing the cleanest hands in school, became hymn-book monitor. Charlotte Ackroyd and Ben Roberts, both good at arithmetic and, significantly, both on the orange and most difficult box of workcards in our School Mathematics Project, were thrilled to run the school tuck shop. Louise Briers and Sam Borthwick, who spent most of their spare time reading, jumped at the chance to be library monitors. Harold Bustard, a happy little boy with a crew cut, sticking out ears and a constantly cheerful disposition, grinned when selected to be the pupil who hurried from one classroom to the next delivering messages. Finally, Danny Hardacre, probably the tallest ten-year-old I had ever taught, gave me a knowing look when he agreed to be blackboard monitor.

Soon we were under way. Each pupil had a reading record card, an *Oxford First Dictionary*, a library book, a Berol pen, a ruler, an HB pencil with a rubber on the end, a new tin of Lakeland crayons and a collection of exercise books.

Meanwhile, on the other side of the school hall, Anne's reception class was suddenly very busy. A group of mothers had brought their new starters into school and were helping them to hang up their coats on the labelled pegs. Mrs Ricketts made sure she had the chance to speak to Anne first. 'Ah've done t'paperwork wi' Mrs Forbes-Kitchener, so she knows about the 'yphen in Suzi-Quatro,' she explained with confident assurance.

'Thank you, Mrs Ricketts,' said Anne patiently. 'I'm sure Suzi will be fine.'

'An' she knows 'er manners, Mrs Grainger,'

announced Mrs Ricketts in a loud voice to the assembled throng of mothers. 'We brought 'er up proper.' She looked down at little Suzi-Quatro. 'Isn't that right, Suzi?' However, Suzi-Quatro had started hopping from one foot to another. 'Oh – do you need a wee-wee, my little chuckle-bunny?' asked Mrs Ricketts with affected politeness.

'No thanks, Mam,' said Suzi-Quatro, and Mrs Ricketts looked around her with a saintly expression. However, the agitated Suzi-Quatro hadn't finished, ''cause ah already did one in m'pants.'

Here we go again, thought Anne.

By mid-morning Anne's class was a hive of activity. Dallas Sue-Ellen Earnshaw was sitting at a table with a group of children including the Jackson twins, who were modelling identical farm animals. Dallas, meanwhile, was beating a lump of brown plasticine with her clenched fist into the shape of a substantial cowpat. Anne crouched down next to her. She noticed that the little girl was wearing an incongruous multi-layered skirt, a sort of tutu that had been rescued from an exploding paint factory. 'That's a pretty dress, Dallas,' said Anne softly.

Dallas didn't look up.

'It's all frilly,' added Anne with an encouraging smile.

'Yes, Miss,' she said, 'but it's a bloody pain to iron.'

There was an intake of breath from Anne and a puzzled look from the other farm-builders.

'Dallas,' said Anne firmly, 'you mustn't say that.'

'What – "bloody pain"?' asked Dallas, non-chalantly.

'Yes,' said Anne forcefully.

'OK,' agreed Dallas, unconcerned.

'So where did you hear that?' asked Anne.

Dallas looked up and smiled innocently at her frowning teacher. 'It's what m'mam allus calls m'dad.'

Out of the mouths of babes, thought Anne.

Later, when the bell rang for morning break, I called in to Tom's class where seven-year-old Charlie Cartwright was drawing a picture of what appeared to be a huge pig in a field. His left hand sported a heavily bandaged index finger and it was clear he was keen for me to see it. He held it upright in front of him as if it were an Olympic torch. 'It dunt 'alf 'urt, Mr Sheffield,' he said bravely.

I crouched down next to his desk. 'What happened to your finger, Charlie?' I asked.

'Ah broke it, Mr Sheffield,' he replied with a sad shake of his head.

'Oh dear,' I said, 'and how did you do that?'

'Cleanin' m'teef,' he said, pointing with the end of his crayon to his collection of wobbly teeth.

'Cleaning your teeth?' I asked in surprise.

'It were awful,' he said reflectively, 'it really 'urt.' Charlie was emerging as a master of pathos.

'But how did you break your finger while cleaning your teeth?' I asked, still perplexed.

'Ah fell off t'stool, Mr Sheffield,' he explained, picking up a pink wax crayon and colouring in the pig.

'Oh well, let's hope it gets better soon,' I said. I cast a glance at the bright pink pig in the field. 'Lovely drawing, Charlie,' I added supportively.

Charlie stood back to admire his creation. 'Thanks, Mr Sheffield,' he said proudly. 'It's m'mam sunbathin' in t'back garden.'

In the staff-room Vera had prepared five mugs of milky coffee and I hurried to collect mine as I had volunteered to do the first playground duty. Anne appeared from her classroom as I headed for the entrance door.

'How's it going, Anne?'

'Mixed,' she replied cautiously, but I could tell she had a lot on her mind. However, as the day progressed, in spite of the demands of making sure Dallas Sue-Ellen didn't wreck the classroom Home Corner, Anne found time for an occasional smile.

Just before lunchtime the children were gathered round her feet and Anne was showing them brightly coloured pictures from a book of farm animals. 'What sound does a cow make?' she asked.

'Mooo, Miss,' said five-year-old Julie Trickle-bank.

'Well done, Julie,' said Anne. 'And what sound does a sheep make?'

'Baaa, Miss,' volunteered Sam Whittaker.

Anne was on a roll. 'And what sound does a mouse make?'

'Click, Miss,' said Emily Borthwick. After all, only last night she had watched her father working on his new Apple Macintosh personal computer.

35

It was during lunchbreak when my wife, Beth, telephoned.

'How's your first day?' I asked. Beth was also a local village-school headteacher in Hartingdale Primary School.

'Busy, Jack, but fine,' she said. 'How about you?'

'The same,' I replied. 'We've certainly got some interesting new starters.'

There was a chuckle down the line. 'I know what you mean.'

'And how was John?' We had arranged for our year-old son to be looked after by a childminder in Hartingdale close to Beth's school. She had come highly recommended – caring, loving and completely trustworthy, with a teenage son at Easington Comprehensive School.

'Perfect, Jack. He looked happy enough and I can always nip out in an emergency.' There was a pause. 'Although it broke my heart to leave him.'

This was the downside of us both working, but we hoped it would work out. It certainly made the time we spent with him away from school even more precious.

'Well, have a good day,' I said.

'You too, Jack.' The line went dead and I was reminded that love can be a tough journey.

Meanwhile, on the playground two nine-year-olds, Sonia Tricklebank and Mary Scrimshaw, were twirling a long skipping rope and Hermione and Honeysuckle Jackson were watching Dallas Sue-Ellen as she jumped up and down. Dallas made sure there were no boys involved. 'Boys are

36

a bloody pain,' she had told the twins. Dallas had retained a deep mistrust of all boys ever since her brother Terry had carefully removed the silver foil from the back of her advent calendar and eaten the chocolates.

The twins were happy. They had skipped, fallen, skinned knees and elbows, and had followed Dallas everywhere. They had never come across a girl like her before at their ballet class or piano lessons.

Suddenly Mrs Earnshaw appeared on the other side of the school wall. She put down her bag of shopping and peered through the bars. 'Ah'm jus' passin' by,' she shouted to Dallas. ''Ow y'gettin' on?'

Dallas jumped out of the whirling rope and yelled back at her mother, 'Mam, Mam, what's a virgin?'

Mrs Earnshaw stared in astonishment and mouthed, 'Bloody 'ell.'

Sonia stopped turning the rope. 'Don't y'know what a virgin is?' she asked confidently.

'No, ah don't,' said Dallas.

'They sell records,' explained Sonia and resumed the skipping game.

That were a close 'un, thought a relieved Mrs Earnshaw and hurried home.

That afternoon I called into Sally's class.

'Cor, that's a big 'un!' exclaimed eight-year-old Hayley Spraggon in a loud voice, staring at her *Animals of the World* reference book.

'What is it, Hayley?' asked Sally, encouraged by the little girl's enthusiasm.

'It's a frickin' elephant, Miss,' said Hayley, full of awe and wonder.

'Pardon?' replied Sally, alarmed at the industrial language.

'A frickin' elephant, Miss,' repeated Hayley.

I looked at the picture. Under it were the words 'AFRICAN ELEPHANT' and I smiled and hurried back to my class.

It was near the end of the day when I opened Anne's classroom door to check all had gone well with her new starters.

I noticed the Jackson twins were making perfect hexagons from six coloured sticky-paper triangles and it appeared they clearly enjoyed the taste of the glue, as they licked each piece with obvious relish and stuck it down on the sheet of card. It was at times like this that I wondered about the Health & Safety at Work Act and the mass of documents that appeared in the post each day ... perhaps I had missed something important.

When the bell rang for the end of school, parents hurried into the reception class to collect their children while Ruby the caretaker arrived and retrieved her mop and bucket from the cleaner's store.

In the cloakroom area the Jackson twins, like mirror images, were helping each other into their coats. Close by, Mrs Earnshaw was chatting with Mrs Freda Fazackerly.

'Only seems five minutes since they were babies,' said Freda.

'Y'reight, Freda,' confirmed Mrs Earnshaw. 'They grow up too fast these days.' She nodded towards our caretaker. 'In fact ah 'eard Ruby's youngest is wearin' a bra.'

When Pippa Jackson arrived at the school gate she looked with an expression of alarm at the sticking plasters applied to Hermione's skinned knees and Honeysuckle's grazed elbow. However, that apart, they seemed healthy enough with their rosy cheeks and slightly grubby faces.

'So, girls, have you had a good day?'

'Yes, thank you, Mummy,' said Hermione.

'And we've learned a lot,' said Honeysuckle.

'That's wonderful,' replied Pippa.

'We've both got a reading book,' said Hermione.

'And we made hexagonal shapes,' said Honeysuckle.

'Well done!' exclaimed Pippa, clearly encouraged.

'And we modelled with plasticine,' continued Hermione.

'And made farm animals,' added Honeysuckle.

'Impressive,' said Pippa. 'So it sounds as if you like your new school?'

'Oh yes, Mummy,' said Hermione.

'And we've got lots of friends,' said Honeysuckle.

'New friends?' Pippa looked thoughtful.

'Yes, there's a big girl called Sonia and she let us play skipping,' said Hermione.

'And she told us what a virgin is,' added Honeysuckle.

Pippa's jaw dropped. 'Pardon?'

'But Dallas is our *special* friend, Mummy,' explained Hermione.

39

'Who's Dallas?' asked Pippa with a growing sense of dismay.

'She's over there with the frilly skirt,' said Hermione.

'Yes, and she says it's a bloody pain to iron,' said Honeysuckle with feeling.

Pippa's flushed face turned to deathly white.

Hermione spotted Ruby the caretaker by the boiler-house doors. 'Oh and that's the caretaker, Mummy.'

'Her daughter has started wearing a bra,' said Honeysuckle.

Pippa took a deep breath. 'Come with me, girls,' she said and turned to walk back up the drive towards the school entrance.

It took a good half an hour for a distinctly concerned Mrs Jackson to be satisfied that Ragley School was not a house of ill repute. Anne and Vera provided much-needed support and eventually she left with reassurances that tomorrow, hopefully, would be different.

Finally we stood by the office window and looked out.

'There's Dallas playing on the village green,' observed Anne.

'With not a care in the world,' said Vera.

'She's the last Earnshaw,' I added quietly.

'Thank God,' said Vera.

'And so say all of us,' replied Anne with feeling.

Chapter Two

Flowers Make Friends

The Revd Joseph Evans recommenced his weekly RE lesson. Miss Thyck visited school to seek support for the Harvest Festival at St Mary's Church on Sunday, 23 September. The headteacher forwarded the school's response to County Hall's discussion document 'A Common Curriculum for North Yorkshire Schools'.
Extract from the Ragley School Logbook:
Friday, 21 September 1984

Vera shuffled in her seat. She loved flower arranging, but this was the limit.

Shafts of early-evening sunlight flickered through the windows of the Ragley village hall as Miss Gardenia Rose Thyck, retired president of the North Yorkshire Federation of the Women's Institute and daughter of the celebrated gardener Samuel Thyck, droned on.

It was Thursday, 20 September, and the annual Harvest Festival at St Mary's Church was fast approaching. However, this year was destined to be different. It would include a Flower Festival with the Thyck Trophy to be awarded for the best arrangement – to be presented, of course, by Miss Thyck herself.

In her sixties, Miss Thyck was a short, portly woman in thick stockings, sturdy black shoes and

41

a two-piece tweed suit with a check so loud it was almost deafening. 'Ladies,' she said in a high-pitched voice, 'as we are aware, flower arranging is the most spiritually satisfying of the creative arts. It provides the opportunity for a gathering of sensitive souls within the happy sisterhood of the Women's Institute.'

With her best Mother Teresa smile, she surveyed benignly the ladies of the Ragley & Morton Women's Institute. 'Do remember, we must not simply share our blooms and foliage but also our knowledge and appreciation in a spirit of love and kindness.' Her shrill voice was rising to a crescendo. 'For we are a *sisterhood of sunshine,* spreading light in a dark world. So go forth and make your dreams come true, because, ladies, as it says in my bestselling book *The Thyck Guide to Flower Arranging* ... flowers make friends.'

Vera Forbes-Kitchener, as secretary of the Ragley Flower Committee, gave a brief vote of thanks and concluded with a rallying call: 'So good luck, everybody. Make sure your displays are in church by Saturday and, if you require any advice, please ask the committee.'

Hesitant applause followed except from the back row, where Deirdre Coe, a large lady with a double chin and a florid face, muttered, 'Stuff that for a bag o' monkeys.' She had her own ideas and they didn't include sharing and sisterhood.

There was much excited chatter as the groups of ladies dispersed to discuss their ideas for the forthcoming flower extravaganza. On her way out, Vera was aware that Deidre Coe was being particularly vociferous.

'What is it, Deirdre?' she asked. 'Can I help?'

'Ah don't need no lessons in flower arrangin' from no toffee-nosed secret'y,' sneered Deirdre in her own inimitable ungrammatical style.

For an instant Vera's eyes flashed fire. She had spotted the surfeit of negatives in the sentence but chose to refrain from considering it worthy of a reply. The more refined ladies gave a gasp of surprise, whereas Deirdre's little band of supporters grinned widely. Vera turned and walked away, satisfied in the knowledge that Judgement Day cometh.

On Friday morning the Harvest Festival was not uppermost in my mind when I arrived in the school car park to see a huge Mercedes-Benz 200 filling the space reserved for my Morris Minor Traveller.

However, my frown soon disappeared when seven-year-old Charlie Cartwright tugged my sleeve on the school entrance steps. ''Scuse me, Mr Sheffield,' he said politely.

I crouched down. 'Good morning, Charlie,' I said.

'Ah'm worried,' he confided forlornly.

'Why is that?' I asked.

''Itler's got 'iccups, Mr Sheffield.'

'Pardon?'

He looked upset. 'Would y'like t'listen?'

'Yes, please,' I said. The thing about being a teacher is that very little surprises you. Charlie was clutching a shoe box and the lid was perforated with holes. Tom Dalton was doing a 'Pets' topic with Class 2 and the children in his class

43

had been invited to bring in their small pets. Consequently, a motley collection of rats, mice, gerbils, budgerigars, rabbits and a noisy parrot were destined to appear that morning.

The ailments of hamsters had never been part of my training, but I crouched down and stared at the box. 'Is Hitler in there?'

Charlie nodded and lifted the lid. A hamster with a red-brown coat looked up at me with big soulful eyes. His white face and the black markings under his shiny nose gave him an uncanny resemblance to the German Führer. On cue, Hitler trembled slightly and made a noise like a squeaky toy.

'They're y'are, Mr Sheffield,' said Charlie. ''E jus' won't stop.'

'I'll tell Mr Dalton,' I promised reassuringly, 'and we'll see what we can do.'

'Thank you, Mr Sheffield,' he said, replacing the lid and going to show the hiccupping hamster to his friends on the playground. A melee of excited children soon gathered round. After all, a furry rodent with an unfortunate problem was definitely more interesting than chanting skipping rhymes or playing hopscotch.

When I walked into the school office, Vera looked agitated.

'This needs to be returned to County Hall *today*, Mr Sheffield.' She held up a bulky questionnaire entitled 'A Common Curriculum for North Yorkshire Schools'. The emphasis on *today* was noted. Suddenly the telephone rang. 'Oh yes ... and we have an important visitor,' added Vera

44

hurriedly, 'about the Flower Festival.' As she picked up the receiver she tore off a page from her spiral notepad, passed it to me and pointed towards the staff-room.

'Thanks, Vera,' I said, and I hurried through the connecting passageway from the office to our cosy little staff-room.

'Good morning, Miss, er, Thick,' I said, glancing down at the name on the paper.

She frowned. 'It's not *Thick*, it's *Thyck* ... rhymes with *bike*.'

'Oh, sorry,' I apologized.

'Granted,' she said abruptly. 'Now, Mr Sheffield, I've spoken to Mrs Forbes-Kitchener and she assures me your children will be supporting the Flower Festival in church on Sunday.'

'Yes, of course,' I confirmed.

Fortunately Vera came to the rescue at that moment. 'Excellent news, Gardenia,' she said.

'What's that, Vera?' asked Miss Thyck.

I gathered they were old friends.

'As you can imagine, the children are very enthusiastic and that last call was to say that the Cubs and Brownies will be making miniature gardens.'

'Oh, jolly good show!' said Miss Thyck. She gave me a hard stare. 'It is so important for children to experience the creative arts.' Then she stared out of the window, a far-off look in her eyes. 'Do you know, Mr Sheffield, I once had tea on a glorious autumn day in 1964 with Dame Sybil Thorndike.' She paused to let the significance sink in. 'We had a delightful discussion on the fine art of grinding powder paint with a mortar and pestle.'

'Really? That's wonderful,' I said, reflecting a little guiltily upon the boxes of ready-mixed poster colours in large plastic bottles in our stock cupboard.

'It should be an integral part of a child's education,' she continued in a voice of authority. 'In fact, I was only recently speaking of this to Mrs Finch-Larkins – of the *Surrey* Finch-Larkins, of course – and she agreed with me.'

'I see,' I said a little lamely.

I looked out of the window. In the far distance dark clouds were gathering over the Hambleton hills. 'Well, let's hope the weather forecast is wrong and it doesn't rain,' I said.

'Rain – rain!' she exclaimed. 'Don't even speak of it. Think *positive*. As I said to my dear friend Ms Beatrice Buttcock – author, *of course,* of *The Woman's Guide to Candles* – have faith: the day of the candle is returning.'

Her instant monologues had a remorseless quality to them. With each lengthy utterance I felt like a tent peg being beaten repeatedly into the ground.

'Well, lots to do,' she said, 'and I'll see you both on Sunday.' With that she shook my hand vigorously, made her exit and roared off down the drive while Vera and I watched from the staff-room window with some relief.

'Ah good,' said Vera as a little white Austin A40 pulled into the car park. 'My brother is here.'

Our local vicar and chair of governors, the Revd Joseph Evans, a tall, thin figure with a clerical collar and a sharp Roman nose, had arrived to commence his weekly religious education pro-

46

gramme. Joseph lived alone in the vicarage next to St Mary's Church on the Morton Road. He was a lovely, gentle soul who delivered wonderful sermons to his congregation but struggled when he entered the secret garden of primary-school children with their unique style of questioning. When he walked in, his elder sister sought immediately to reassure him. 'It will be fine, Joseph,' she said with an encouraging smile. 'All will be well.'

'Thank you, Vera,' he replied without sounding convinced. 'I hope so.'

'Come on now: "A merry heart maketh a cheerful countenance",' recited Vera.

'Proverbs, chapter fifteen, verse thirteen,' responded Joseph with a sigh and a wan smile. He squeezed Vera's hand and trudged off to Class 3 and his first Bible studies session of the new academic year.

By the end of the lesson Joseph was beginning to feel he would escape unscathed. However, the children in Class 3 were full of questions after his story of the Creation.

'Mr Evans, who was t'first baby?' asked an insistent Jemima Poole.

'Why do you ask?' said Joseph evasively.

''Cause it would 'ave to 'ave 'ad a mummy.'

The wonder of children's logic was lost as, at that moment, the bell rang for morning break and Joseph collected up the children's drawings and writing and trudged out. As they walked out of the classroom, eight-year-old Hayley Spraggon tried to cheer him up. 'Don't you worry, Mr

Evans,' she said. 'When ah grow up ah'll be rich an' ah'll give you some money.'

'That's very kind, Hayley,' said Joseph with a beatific smile and the reassuring thought that not all of his words of wisdom had fallen on stony ground. However, his curiosity was aroused. 'And why is that?'

''Cause my dad says you're t'poorest vicar we've 'ad.'

So it was that another little dent in Joseph's spiritual armour further eroded his confidence and he welcomed the mug of sweet, milky coffee provided by Vera.

Soon we were all gathered in the staff-room except for Tom, who was on playground duty.

'How did it go, Joseph?' asked Sally.

'Er, you have a lively class full of enquiring minds,' he said cautiously.

Sally grinned and the rest of us breathed a sigh of relief. Joseph had survived.

'Don't worry, Joseph,' said Vera, 'the Harvest Festival is always a triumph.'

'And the church will look especially beautiful this year with all the flowers,' added Anne by way of encouragement.

'And tomorrow will be a busy day,' continued Vera.

Anne nodded. 'Well, we shall all be there to support,' she said.

'Though I wouldn't say that flower arranging is exactly Jack and Tom's forte,' added Sally.

'I recall we're setting up some stage blocks at the back of the church to display the children's miniature gardens,' I said a little defensively.

48

'Well, bless you all,' said Joseph, and with a sigh of relief he walked out to the car park and drove off.

At the school gate he waved to Ruby the caretaker, who had arrived to put out the dining tables and chairs in the school hall for our daily reading workshop. It was always well supported by parents and grandparents, who came in to listen to children read and assist with our programme for reading development. Any words with which they had difficulty were written in their 'New Words' notebook and shown to their teacher on returning to class.

By eleven o'clock it was under way and seven-year-old Katie Icklethwaite was sitting next to her grandfather and reading from her Ginn Reading 360 book. Suddenly she broke off and stared thoughtfully up at the kindly face. 'How old are you, Grandad?' she asked.

He smiled benignly. 'I'm sixty-six,' he said.

Katie's eyes widened in astonishment. 'Flippin' 'eck, Grandad – did y'start at *one?*'

Grandad Icklethwaite, undeterred, pointed to the next line of the reading book.

The conversation on the next table was even more revealing. Eight-year-old Jemima Poole was reading her story book, entitled *Our House,* to her mother. The little girl stared at the picture of the bedroom. 'Mummy,' said Jemima with a troubled expression. 'What's it called when two people sleep in t'same room an'...' She struggled to complete the sentence. 'An' one sleeps on t'top of t'other?'

There was an intake of breath from Mrs Poole.

49

She had known this day would arrive, but not as soon as this. However, she quickly gathered her liberated self and decided to tell it how it was. After all, it had said in the article entitled 'The Family of the Eighties' in her *Woman's Realm* that it was important always to be frank and honest with your children 'Well, Jemima, it's like this...' She looked furtively at the nearby tables, took a deep breath and lowered her voice. 'It's called ... *sexual relations.*'

Jemima looked up, a puzzled expression on her freckled face. 'Axshully, Mummy ... ah'm not so sure, 'cause ah think Miss said it were called bunk beds.'

'Er, yes,' said Mrs Poole, her cheeks now a bright red. 'Mrs Pringle is quite correct. Do you know how to spell it?'

Jemima nodded, gripped her pencil tighter and printed out the words 'bunk beds' in her notebook, secretly wishing her mother would pay more attention.

At lunchtime our school cook, Shirley Mapplebeck, had served up Spam fritters, mashed potatoes, broccoli and gravy, followed by spotted dick and custard. I was sitting at the same table as Charlie Cartwright. 'How's Hitler?' I asked.

''E's still got 'iccups, Mr Sheffield, but Mr Dalton says 'e looks 'appy enough an' 'e's enjoying 'is food,' said Charlie. 'An' ah've promised not t'let 'im out o' my sight.'

'That's good to hear,' I said.

Across the table ten-year-old Charlotte Ackroyd was dispensing words of wisdom to nine-year-old Barry Ollerenshaw. The unfortunate Barry was clearly not keen on his greens.

'Problem is, Barry,' said Charlotte knowingly, and beginning to sound more like her mother every day, 'y'can't 'ide broccoli in y'custard, 'cause it's t'wrong colour.'

Barry resigned himself to the inevitable before Mrs Critchley, our formidable dinner lady, walked by.

After school dinner I took the opportunity to get some fresh air. It was always a joy to see the children at play. Mary Scrimshaw and Sonia Tricklebank were turning a skipping rope and chanting:

Pease pudding hot
Pease pudding cold
Pease pudding in the pot
Nine days old
O-U-T spells OUT!

On the school field, Sam Borthwick and Harold Bustard were fighting a dramatic *Star Wars* battle with imaginary light sabres, while eight-year-old Stacey Bryant and nine-year-old Lucy Eckersley were playing cat's cradle with a length of string while discussing how to complete the adoption certificate for a Cabbage Patch doll.

I smiled and, suitably refreshed, returned to the staff-room where Vera was filling the Gestetner duplicating machine with ink while Anne was reading Vera's *Daily Telegraph*. Anne was reassured to read that Harry, the newborn second son of Prince Charles and Princess Diana, was in good health.

Tom, as usual, was immersed in his computer magazine.

'How's Charlie Cartwright's hamster, Tom?' I asked.

Tom looked up. 'Hitler?' he said. 'Well, it's just a common hamster, Jack – *Cricetus cricetus*. They're certainly busy little creatures. They feed on seeds and grains and store them in underground burrows,' he added, recalling his O-level Biology. 'This one looks fine apart from his hiccups.'

'Perhaps it will pass,' I said.

It was indicative of our lives as teachers of young children that neither Vera, Anne nor Sally batted an eyelid at a conversation concerning Hitler and hiccups.

Soon Vera was turning the handle of our duplicating machine and then putting the copies on the windowsill so that the sticky black ink would dry. It was a letter to parents advertising, the Flower Festival. She knew the title 'Flowers Make Friends' would catch the eye and also appeal to Miss Thyck. As she counted out the copies she smiled in anticipation.

Meanwhile, in the county town of Northallerton, Deirdre Coe was staring at a magnificent floral display in the Blushing Blooms florist's shop. A thought had crossed her mind and she too smiled in anticipation.

Afternoon school went well and, while the children in my class were filling in their weather charts and making anemometers, I began looking through the programme of reading tests that would eventually be passed on to Easington Comprehensive School. I was pleased with Louise Briers, who now had a reading age of over eleven. Louise had read seventy-six correct words out of one hundred on the Schonell Word Recognition Test, finally failing on the line 'oblivion, scintillate, satirical, sabre and beguile'.

From Sally's classroom I could hear the strains of music. She was playing a cassette tape of Ludwig van Beethoven's *Piano Concerto No. 5 in F-flat major*. Although Beethoven had dedicated it to his patron, the Archduke Rudolf, it is unlikely that the archduke would have appreciated this stirring piece more than the eight- and nine-year-olds in Class 3. Sally had turned her ghetto-blaster up to full volume and the children were listening in awe and wonder.

When it came to an end and the windows ceased to rattle, nine-year-old Ryan Halfpenny put up his hand.

'Yes, Ryan?' asked Sally.

'It says 'ere,' said Ryan, looking down at his book of famous composers, 'that Beethoven was *deaf.*'

'That's right,' said Sally, pleased at Ryan's interest, 'he was.'

Ryan nodded with an air of authority. 'Mebbe that's why 'e wrote loud music, Miss,' and Sally recalled why she so enjoyed teaching this age group.

Suddenly everyone started talking at once about deaf grandparents, with, as usual, Damian Brown drowning out the others. Sally was annoyed with his ceaseless chatter. 'Damian, what do you call someone who keeps on talking when other people aren't listening?'

'A teacher, Miss,' said Damian, quick as a flash, and even Sally had to smile. She also made a mental note to phrase her questions a little differently in future.

At the end of school I was in the office completing the curriculum questionnaire for County Hall. The day of a common scheme of work for all schools in North Yorkshire, and maybe even the whole country, seemed to be drawing closer and I wondered if we would still be able to enjoy our camping trips, museum visits, pond-dipping and taking time out to watch Deke Ramsbottom ploughing Twenty Acre Field.

Finally it was done and ready for posting. At six o'clock I wrote in the logbook, 'The headteacher forwarded the school's response to County Hall's discussion document "A Common Curriculum for North Yorkshire Schools".' Then I locked up the school, climbed in my Morris Minor Traveller and drove the three miles home to Kirkby Steepleton, where Bilbo Cottage looked welcoming on this autumn evening.

In the hallway Beth was putting on her beige *Cagney & Lacey* coat. It had padded shoulders and a long belt looped in a casual knot at her waist, emphasizing her slim figure.

'John's been fed and he's fine,' she said. She glanced at her watch and anxiously pushed a lock of honey-blonde hair away from her forehead. With her high cheekbones and clear skin she looked the perfect English beauty and I stood back

54

to admire the view. 'Jack, I'm running late and it's my dissertation tutorial tonight.' Beth was in the final year of her part-time Masters Degree in Education at Leeds University. Her special study, 'Leadership in the Primary School', was well advanced and had received considerable praise from her tutor. It was clear my wife was a very bright and highly motivated lady.

'Drive safely,' I said. 'Love you,' and I kissed her on the cheek.

She smiled and her green eyes surveyed me steadily. 'You too,' she said, 'and there's a casserole in the oven.'

Not for the first time it occurred to me that I had clearly married an angel.

On Saturday morning Vera was reorganizing her kitchen and had cleared out a corner floor cupboard. The difficult task of rummaging in it's dark recesses for a casserole dish was destined to be a thankless chore no longer.

She had purchased a Marks & Spencer Revolving Storage System with nine plastic, air-tight containers on a cream-coloured carousel. It resembled a merry-go-round of Tupperware and provided a home for dried fruits, nuts, rice, pasta and cereals. At £14.99 it was a bargain and Vera spun it round in delight. These were small steps, but the beginning of a significant journey. Since marrying Rupert, Morton Manor was changing as Vera put *her* identity on their world.

Rupert had driven off to Pickering at the crack of dawn with Virginia Anastasia, his thirty-two-year-old daughter by his first marriage, in order to buy a new pony for her riding stables. Vera had the kitchen to herself and she luxuriated in her private space.

When the grandfather clock in the spacious entrance hall chimed nine o'clock she put on her coat and picked up her wickerwork trug basket. It was time to make preparations for the Flower Festival. There were occasions when Vera missed the vicarage where she had lived for so many years with her brother. However, one of the joys of Morton Manor was its magnificent hothouse, which increased the range of flowers available to her.

With loving care, she collected sunflowers, chrysanthemums, lilies, carnations and of course alchemilla, the florist's best friend, otherwise known as lady's mantle. Vera had always admired this acid green, fluffy-flowered plant and regarded it as one of the best foliage plants for the vase and garden. She would cut it back after its early-summer flowering and then feed it with potash so that its leaves always returned fresh and beautiful and ready to flower again in early autumn.

Then she collected a few yellow, fragrant floribunda 'peace' roses with their bronze and gold petals, along with some variegated ivy to add some greenery, and loaded everything into the back of her new Austin Metro, a gift from Rupert. Vera left nothing to chance and the flowers were carefully arranged in buckets of *hot* water so that they would last longer. Finally, after putting an aluminium watering can, a small roll of chicken wire and a pair of secateurs in the well of the front seat, she drove off very steadily for St Mary's Church and a weekend she would never forget.

It was mid-morning when I left Bilbo Cottage and set off for St Mary's. There was a special quality to the light at this time of day, a golden hue. September mists had descended again over the plain of York and on Ragley High Street the villagers appeared like wraiths in a Lowry mill scene.

The church was full of chattering ladies, with Vera leading the organizing. Other visitors had arrived to do their voluntary jobs. Albert Jenkins, one of our school governors, was there to wind the clock, and Lillian Figgins, our road-crossing patrol officer, known affectionately as Lollipop Lil, was polishing the pews. I never ceased to be amazed by the love of the locals for our church and their willingness to support its upkeep.

There were occasions when the Flower Committee and the Church Fabric Committee did not see eye to eye, particularly following the spillage of water on the faded carpets in the vicinity of the pulpit and, much worse, the pine needles that blocked up the vacuum-cleaner bag each Christmas ... but today was different. Everyone was working in harmony and soon Tom and I had erected a few stage blocks at the back of the church and Anne and Sally had covered them with oatmeal-coloured hessian.

Vera was supervising a floral display-in-a-toolbox at the base of the font prepared by the more green-fingered members of the Ragley Shed Society.

'The church looks magnificent, Vera,' I said.

'We work wonders daily, Mr Sheffield,' she

replied with a smile. 'However, miracles take a little longer.'

'The arrangements look ... well, just perfect,' said Sally.

Vera nodded in acknowledgement. 'There's a subtle difference between a florist and a flower arranger.'

'It's a gift,' said Anne, gazing around in admiration.

'Yes, we don't simply plonk them in a vase,' said Vera proudly. She didn't mention that she was a disciple of Constance Spry, the famous flower arranger whose book, *The Constance Spry Book of Flower Arranging,* was Vera's second Bible.

Soon she was offering encouragement to Anne and Sally while I worked with Tom. We were acting as willing but clearly hopeless assistants to create a display on behalf of the staff of Ragley School. I was sent to fetch a wrought-iron pedestal and a dish of water while Tom snipped pieces of chicken wire.

Sally began by cutting laurel to the required lengths to provide height and structure to our arrangement and Anne added trailing ivy, apparently to soften the base. With blooms in place, Vera walked halfway down the aisle to look back and assess our work. 'Excellent,' she said, 'and of course it's cool in church so the display will last longer.' For Vera, as the years went by, experience and wisdom had become steadfast companions.

Meanwhile the Cub pack had arrived and were lining up their shoe-box miniature gardens on the stage blocks like a long goods train. The Brownies were also busy. The girls had worked in pairs to make garden-in-a-cake-tins and these were arranged side by side on the shelf above the hymn books.

Eventually the work was done and we returned to our homes. The purple shades of evening had begun to caress the flanks of the distant hills and, where the rim of the earth met the sky, it was tinged with golden light. The sun was setting and the creatures of the night were emerging from their slumber. In the churchyard bats zigzagged with pulsing flight while the hedgerows were filled with the chitter of insects, and in the quiet kitchen of Morton Manor, as darkness fell, Vera was busy with one final task.

It was early on Sunday morning when Vera entered the quiet sanctuary of the silent church. She was carrying her own contribution – a small, elegant and unassuming, but very pretty, basket of flowers.

Before she reached the altar she stopped and looked to her right. There was an east window and the morning sun shone through the stained glass and lit up the lectern and the front pews. Beneath it was a corbel, a stone carving of a basket of flowers, with a wide stone shelf above it. *Perfect*, she thought. So with great care she placed her arrangement on the shelf and stood back to admire it.

It was then that she heard heavy footsteps.

'Well, that piddlin' little effort won't win, Miss 'Igh an' Mighty,' shouted Deirdre Coe. She was carrying the most magnificent flower arrangement, a bounty of blooms set to perfection in a large wicker basket.

Vera had to admit it outshone the humble efforts around her. 'It's lovely, Deirdre,' she said in true Christian spirit.

'It's more than that,' replied Deirdre disdainfully. 'It's a *winner.*' She thrust it triumphantly next to Vera's display and walked out.

At half past ten Beth put John in his car seat in her light blue Volkswagen Beetle and we drove off along the back road out of Kirkby Steepleton. Above our heads a skein of honking, frantic geese flew arrow-straight on their magnetic pathway against the darkening clouds and towards the spire of St Mary's. Ragley High Street was full of parents and children, a few carrying shoe boxes containing their tiny garden creations, as they made their way up the Morton Road. Charlie Cartwright was among them and he gave me a wave.

As was the custom, many of the villagers had brought in gifts for the display in front of the altar, including produce to be distributed around the village after the service. Vera had contributed a huge basket of Victoria plums from her garden, Deke Ramsbottom carried in a large sheaf of corn and this was flanked by a pair of George Hardisty's magnificent marrows.

We sang 'We Plough The Fields And Scatter' at a brisk pace. However, Elsie was playing the *new* tune she had rehearsed and the congregation was determined to sing the one they knew. It was a close-run thing but it was generally acknowledged that our sparky organist had won by a short head.

During the offertory hymn the collecting plate

was passed along the pew. 'Y'don't 'ave t'pay f'me, Mam,' said Alfie Spraggon, "cause ah'm under five.'

After the service Joseph introduced Miss Thyck, who placed a shiny trophy on the lid of the font. 'Ladies and gentlemen, boys and girls, our festival of flowers has certainly brought the village together,' she said proudly. 'Flowers are part of our journey towards perfect harmony. They bring peace and contentment. So see your work as an act of creation, a perfect juxtaposition of natural forms.'

The adults nodded politely and the children looked puzzled. Deirdre Coe, sitting in the pew alongside her floral masterpiece, gave a smug grin.

'First of all,' Miss Thyck announced, 'congratulations to the children. Your miniature gardens are simply splendid,' and all the children beamed with pleasure. 'And well done to all the grown-ups. While some of us are simply born with the gift of flower arranging,' she added without a hint of modesty, 'these are worthy efforts.' She turned towards Deirdre's arrangement. 'Who brought this display?' and Deirdre's hand shot up eagerly. 'It is, of course, *magnificent* and an example to us all.' Deirdre relaxed, content in the knowledge that the trophy was as good as hers. 'You will probably not be aware that I own the Blushing Blooms florist shop in Northallerton,' Miss Thyck continued, 'where the window displays are created by the internationally renowned flower arranger Anthony Cleaver CBE. This is from his prize-winning "Harvest Gold" collection ... so thank you for including it as an example to us all.'

Deirdre Coe's florid face turned to grey. The stares of reprimand from the members of the Women's Institute were like daggers to her heart and the craven Deirdre appeared to wilt visibly under the crossfire. Vera tried hard not to smile.

Miss Thyck's voice had reached a crescendo. 'So, in conclusion, it gives me great pleasure to present the trophy to *both* the Cubs and the Brownies for their imaginative gardens.' Everyone applauded except Deirdre.

Charlie Cartwright in his Cub uniform and Jemima Poole in her Brownie outfit walked to the front of the church and, to huge cheers from the children, held aloft the Thyck Trophy.

Joseph gave a vote of thanks and, as his hobby was wine-making, he offered Miss Thyck a bottle of his 'Cowslip Creation'. Miss Thyck appeared genuinely pleased with the gesture, whereas the rest of us believed the pretty cowslips should have remained in their natural habitat and not been transformed into a concoction that more often than not resembled rotting seaweed.

As everyone left the church Charlie Cartwright picked up his shoe box. 'Is that your garden?' asked Miss Thyck.

'No, Miss, it's 'Itler.'

'Hitler?'

'Yes, Miss – my 'amster.'

He removed the lid and Miss Thyck stared in surprise. 'What a delightful hamster,' she said. 'When I was your age I had a hamster and he was my best friend.'

''Itler's *my* best friend,' said Charlie with a

sincerity that was almost heartbreaking. 'But 'e's got 'iccups.'

Right on cue, Hitler squeaked.

'No, young man,' explained Miss Thyck kindly. 'Never fear – it simply means he's happy and greeting a new day. It's actually related to something called the "oestrus cycle" which occurs every four days, so no need to worry.'

'Thank you, Miss,' said Charlie and he put the lid on the box and set off home.

Vera had heard the conversation. 'That was very thoughtful of you, Gardenia,' she said.

Miss Thyck surveyed the church and breathed in the fragrance of a thousand flowers. 'Well, Vera ... flowers really do make friends,' she said.

Vera looked down the path outside where Deirdre Coe was staring at them with thoughts of retribution in her heart. 'Yes, Gardenia,' she said with a smile, 'I agree.'

Chapter Three

Ronnie's Bench

The Parent Teacher Association and school governors have bought a bench to commemorate the life of Mr Ronald Smith, late husband of our caretaker Mrs Ruby Smith. The presentation will take place on the village green at 10.00 a.m. on Saturday, 6 October. County Hall requested copies of our Health & Safety policy in preparation for their working paper.
Extract from the Ragley School Logbook:
Friday, 5 October 1984

'So, on behalf of the Parent Teacher Association and the governing body of Ragley School,' said the Revd Joseph Evans, 'it gives me great pleasure to declare Ronnie's bench well and truly open.'

There was loud applause, especially from the Ragley Rovers football team. Our caretaker's late husband, Ronnie Smith, had been their manager prior to his untimely death last New Year's Eve. The team captain and local refuse collector, six-feet-four-inch Big Dave Robinson, shouted, 'Three cheers f'Ronnie.'

''Ooray!' yelled his diminutive five-feet-four-inch cousin and fellow binman Little Malcolm Robinson, accompanied by the rest of the football team.

It seemed that everyone had come to support

64

this special event. All the High Street shop-keepers had recruited temporary staff to enable them to attend and they were lined up next to the Ragley School staff, along with Don and Sheila Bradshaw from The Royal Oak. The rest of the crowd included the majority of the villagers plus the members of the Easington & District Pigeon Club, along with Lucky Lennie the bookmaker from York, who had been sad to lose one of his favourite customers.

It was Saturday, 6 October, a morning of autumn mists, amber hues and fragile shadows. The distant fields were still, waiting for the sun to burn off the droplets of dew on the corn stubble. However, on Ragley's village green russet leaves were falling like countryside confetti and, after the cheering, the large crowd stood in silence for a few moments as Joseph gestured our caretaker to-wards a beautiful, solid oak, hand-crafted bench.

So it was that Ruby Smith, with her six children gathered around her and her granddaughter on her lap, was the first to sit on Ronnie's bench.

Ruby was a popular member of the Ragley community. At twenty stone and in her extra-large bright orange overall she had always been a cheerful sight skipping round the school with her mop and galvanized bucket and singing songs from her favourite film, *The Sound of Music*. That was until Ronnie's death; since then she had often remained very quiet, as if she was hanging on to the past. Throughout her married life, with six children to clothe and feed, the beer-swilling, chain-smoking, regularly unemployed Ronnie had been little help. Life had always been a struggle for Ruby but she had faced it bravely ... never more so than now.

Ruby was fiercely proud of her children. Thirty-three-year-old Andy was a sergeant in the army and thirty-one-year-old Racquel was the proud mother of Krystal Carrington Ruby Entwhistle who at two years old was the apple of Ruby's eye. Her other four children shared Ruby's home on the council estate at 7 School View. Twenty-nine-year-old Duggie, nicknamed 'Deadly' as he worked for the local undertaker, had a bed in the attic; twenty-four-year-old Sharon was engaged to Rodney Morgetroyd, the Morton village milkman; and twenty-two-year-old Natasha worked part-time in Diane's Hair Salon. Finally, the youngest in the family, eleven-year-old Hazel, was in her first year at Easington Comprehensive School. As Ruby often said, 'First an' las' were an accident – but ah love 'em all.' For Ruby it had proved a sad moment when, last summer, Hazel had left Ragley School, as all her children had attended there. It was the end of an era.

When Ruby sat on the bench surrounded by her family there was another round of spontaneous applause from the crowd. It was a poignant moment and a scene that will live with me for ever. Anne Grainger's husband, John, a burly, bearded man, stepped forward and took a photograph that Ruby was destined to put in a frame and treasure for the rest of her life. John, the local craftsman, looked on with satisfaction. He was quietly pleased with the bench he had created, and the carved acorn that adorned each armrest was his unique signature.

The finishing touch was a shiny brass plaque attached to the backrest. It read:

In memory of
RONALD GLADSTONE SMITH
1931–1983
'Abide With Me'

Up the Morton Road the church clock struck ten o'clock.

'For whom the bell tolls,' said Tom Dalton quietly. The words of John Donne seemed particularly appropriate at that moment and I nodded in acknowledgement. I looked around me at the faces I knew so well, all deep in their own thoughts. We had lost one of our own and for Ragley village this was an event that affected everyone. In a small community it touched all our lives.

Suddenly the raucous cries of rooks in the high elms shattered the silence, the crowds dispersed and everyone returned to the business of the day.

Ruby immediately shooed off her children. 'Ah want a bit o' peace,' she said, 'on y'dad's bench.' Then she looked up to where I was standing with Beth under the weeping willow tree while, at our feet, John was stretching up to grasp the green leaves. 'Come an' tek weight off y'feet, Mr Sheffield.'

Beth gave me a gentle nudge. 'Go on, Jack – you talk to Ruby and I'll get some shopping done with John.' She lifted him into his pushchair and they set off down the High Street.

I sat down. 'A special day, Ruby,' I said and touched the brass plate. 'It's a wonderful tribute to Ronnie.'

'Ah were jus' thinkin' about 'im.'

I nodded. 'I'm sure you have a lot of happy memories.'

'Well, ah did enjoy m'courtin' days,' said Ruby wistfully. ''E bought me a Babycham an' a bag o' crisps an' ah were smitten. An' 'e 'ad that lovely Bill 'Aley kiss-curl.'

I recalled Bill Haley and His Comets singing 'Rock Around The Clock' in my distant youth and the lead singer's distinctive hairstyle, which incorporated a lock of hair on his forehead in the shape of an inverted question mark. For me, it had never caught on.

Hazel Smith was playing with little Krystal on the grass. 'Good to see them playing together, Ruby,' I said.

'They're good girls, Mr Sheffield, never any bother – tho' it's been a bit of a struggle t'mek ends meet with our 'Azel needing a uniform an' 'xpensive stuff for t'big school. An' ah think our Krystal might 'ave one o' them *elegies*. She were sneezing summat rotten in church.'

I recalled studying Thomas Gray's 'Elegy Written in a Country Churchyard' for A level but guessed we were talking about something completely different.

'Anyway,' continued Ruby, 'Mrs F says Dr Davenport knows a lot about *elegies* so it'll be fine.'

'Here she comes now,' I said and got up to leave. 'Good to talk to you, Ruby. I'll go and find Beth and John.' I waved to Vera as she walked across the green towards Ronnie's bench.

Ruby patted the space next to her. 'Come an'

join me, Mrs F,' she called out. 'It's a comfy seat.'

'And a lovely reminder of Ronnie,' said Vera as she sat down.

'Thank you, Mrs F,' said Ruby. 'Ah'm so grateful you're 'ere.'

Vera looked down at Ruby's dumpy, work-red hands and thought she noticed the first signs of arthritis. She stretched out her long, cool, elegant fingers and gently laid a hand on them. 'Ruby,' she asked softly, 'how are you?'

'Ah'm all cried out, Mrs F,' replied Ruby, '...all cried out.'

'I'm sure you are,' said Vera soothingly.

'Ah keep thinkin' o' daft things – like when 'e said he'd tek me abroad t'foreign places, t'that Cistern Chapel an' that leanin' tower o' Pizza ... but 'e never did. 'E were like that wi' promises were my Ronnie.'

'Perhaps he meant well,' said Vera.

There was a long silence as Ruby stared at her two sons sitting outside The Royal Oak and swapping stories. 'Our Andy's spittin' image of 'im but, as true as ah'm sittin' 'ere, 'e'll turn out a better man.'

'I'm sure he will,' agreed Vera.

'But ah'm still worried, Mrs F, 'bout our Duggie goin' out wi' that *mature* woman.' Ruby removed her favourite straw hat and stared at it. There were six pressed roses attached to the headband. She touched her chestnut curls and, as the morning sun broke through the gauze of mist, Vera noticed the first signs of grey. 'She prances up an' down like t'Queen o' Sheba – an' she won't see forty again,' complained Ruby.

'Perhaps it will simply come to a natural conclusion, Ruby,' said Vera without conviction.

'Ah thought it were jus' one o' them *phrases* 'e were goin' through an' 'e'd o' got over it by now. Problem is, one flutter o' them false eyelashes an' 'e goes runnin' after 'er. Then it's goodnight Vienna.'

'I'm sure it will workout, Ruby. Douglas is still a young man finding his way in the world.'

'An' there's another,' said Ruby. Tom Dalton had waved a hurried farewell as he climbed into his rusty royal blue Renault 4 and roared off home down the High Street towards York. 'Ah reckon there's summat up wi' that Mr Dalton, you mark my words. 'E's like a cat on a 'ot tin roof,' continued Ruby.

Vera kept her own counsel and remained silent.

On the far side of the village green George Dainty was talking to Old Tommy Piercy. 'An' what do you think o' George Dainty, Mrs F?'

'He appears to be a very polite and considerate man,' said Vera.

"E's certainly a diff'rent kettle o' fish t'my Ronnie,' said Ruby, 'an' that's a fact.'

'Yes, he is ... but we're all different, Ruby.'

Suddenly Dr Davenport limped by, clearly in some discomfort. His wife, Joyce, was one of Vera's dearest friends in the Women's Institute.

'Richard,' Vera greeted him, 'whatever is the matter?'

'I tripped over the cat, Vera,' said the good doctor forlornly.

Vera looked suitably concerned. 'Oh dear, how is it?'

'Well, I'm trying not to put too much weight on it,' he replied with a brave smile.

'No, Richard,' said Vera a little sharply, 'I meant Tibbles.'

'Oh, I see,' he said as understanding dawned. 'He's fine, I think,' and with a nervous smile he struggled away to find his wife.

Ruby chuckled. 'Men,' she said.

'Very true,' said Vera, glancing at her watch, 'and I have some shopping to do, Ruby, so I'll see you later.'

George Dainty saw the opportunity to sit with Ruby. A short, rotund man with a ruddy face and a gentle smile, he stepped forward and raised his flat cap. ''Ello, Ruby,' he said. 'May ah sit down?'

'O' course, George,' said Ruby.

George had retired from his lucrative fish-and-chip shop in Alicante in Spain and had returned to his home village of Ragley, where he had bought a luxury bungalow on the Morton Road.

He sat down and removed his cap. 'So, Ruby, 'ow's it goin'?'

Ruby sighed. 'Ah were jus' telling Mrs F that ah don't know if ah'm comin' or goin' wi' our Duggie,' she said forlornly. ''E's still goin' out wi' that *mature* woman. Ah don't know what 'e sees in 'er.'

George kept his thoughts to himself. He could guess *exactly* what Duggie saw in the curvaceous, confident, worldly-wise assistant from the shoe shop in Easington. She was definitely a head-turner.

'So ... are y'thinkin' about Ronnie?'

Ruby sighed. 'M'mother used t'say, "What the

eye don't see, the 'eart don't grieve for", but ah'm not so sure, George – ah still miss 'im.'

'Ah'm sure y'do, Ruby,' replied George quietly. 'Don't fret.'

'You needn't be so polite, George Dainty,' said Ruby. 'We all know 'e were a useless article, 'xcept ah did love 'im in spite of 'is ways.'

George smiled. 'Thing is, Ruby, you always did tell t'truth.'

Ruby nodded in acknowledgement. 'Speak t'truth an' shame t'devil, my mother used t'say – an' she were right.'

'Ah well,' said George and he shuffled a little closer, 'least said soonest mended.'

'Ah reckon 'e did love me, George ... in 'is own way. An' 'e gave me six children an' ah worship t'ground they walk on.'

'Ah'm sure y'do, Ruby.' And he patted her hand very gently.

'It's jus'...'

'Jus' what, Ruby?' asked George.

Ruby wiped away a tear with one of Vera's beautifully embroidered lace handkerchiefs. 'Ah feel as though ah'm wastin' m'life.'

'Surely not,' said George.

'An' ah'm wond'rin' what comes next.'

'It's what y'*choose*,' said George.

'But there's a pain that won't go away,' said Ruby.

'Don't worry – it will one day.'

'When, George?'

'When you decide.'

'But what about *t'milk o' 'uman kindness*, ah used t'ask m'self,' said Ruby, ''cause it never seemed t'flow on me – jus' on other folks.'

'C'mon, Ruby,' said George firmly. 'No more ifs or buts. It's not end of t'world. Let's get on wi' life.'

Ruby gave a faint smile. 'Mebbe so, George.'

'Look 'ere, Ruby, remember when you were May Queen? Well, ah won t'bakin' prize for m'wholemeal loaf. Ah can still mek a fine loaf ... ah'll mek one f'you if y'like.'

'Ah'd like that, George,' replied Ruby.

George was wearing his expensive duty-free wristwatch. He glanced at it. ''Ow about we 'ave a nice cup o' tea in Nora's?'

Ruby smiled and together they walked down the High Street with George keeping a respectful distance.

Beth was shopping in Prudence Golightly's General Stores and I took advantage of Ronnie's bench. I relaxed in the sunshine as John played on the grass at my feet and stroked the recently cut grass with great interest.

Meanwhile, I indulged in the gentle art of people-watching. Stan Coe, local pig farmer, itinerant bully and elder brother of Deirdre, was berating Lillian Figgins, our road-crossing patrol officer, about her supervision of the zebra crossing during the week. 'Y'like a little 'Itler on that zebra, 'olding up us workin' folk,' shouted Stan from his grime-covered Land Rover. Lillian responded with an icy smile. You messed with Lollipop Lil at your peril. You could see it in her eyes – *the day of judgement is nigh*.

Ruby's daughter Racquel was sitting on the

village green with her daughter Krystal, and she beckoned to John to toddle over to join them. I smiled as John and the little girl developed an early concept of sharing as a handful of new-mown grass was passed from one tiny hand to another. They were a new generation, born in the eighties, and I wondered how life would turn out for them.

Suddenly Beth appeared carrying a bag of shopping in one hand and John's comfort shawl over her other arm. She sat down next to me. 'John looks happy,' she said. It was a welcome change to see Beth looking relaxed. Our lives had moved on from nightly vigils and we were both getting a good night's sleep again. Occasionally I wondered about a second child, but Beth's life seemed so full with her headship, university work and caring for John that I decided to leave that discussion for another day.

Beth rummaged in her handbag and brought out a newspaper cutting. 'Jack, I've been thinking,' she said.

'About what?'

'Financial planning,' she said with a stare that meant 'pay attention'.

'Financial planning?' I asked. 'I thought we were doing fine on two salaries again.'

'No, Jack, I'm thinking *long-term.*'

'Really?'

'Yes. There's an article here about pensions. They're being reviewed again. It says the basic state pension is £35.80 per week and £57.30 for married couples from the end of next month.'

'Pensions – but that's a lifetime away.'

Beth sighed. 'Jack, *someone's* got to think about

planning for the future – and it's never too early to think about boosting our pensions.' She held up the cutting. 'So, I'm going to check this out. It's a Barclays Personal Pension Plan and we could build up an investment.'

'How about a sandwich in the Coffee Shop?' I suggested suddenly.

Beth smiled in recognition that financial planning was not on my immediate agenda. We collected John and strolled into Nora's where Tina Turner was belting out 'What's Love Got To Do With It' on the jukebox.

Diane the hairdresser had slipped out between appointments for a quick break and she headed for Ronnie's bench. Diane had spent eighteen pence that morning on a *Daily Mail* at Prudence Golightly's General Stores. She sat down, lit up a John Player King Size Extra Mild cigarette, took a contented puff and opened her newspaper.

October was proving a busy month. In the world beyond Ragley village there were now three and a quarter million people out of work. Also, Neil Kinnock had taken Norman Tebbit's advice and arrived on a bicycle at the Labour Party Conference in Blackpool. The debate was dominated by Arthur Scargill and the miners' strike, so it proved not such an easy ride for the ginger-haired Welshman. The miners had put their own peace plan to the Coal Board boss, Ian MacGregor, for bringing an end to the seven months of the miners' strike, but in the meantime the Home Secretary, Leon Brittan, was considering making picketing by more than six people an illegal act.

Something had to give.

Diane smiled when she saw a photograph of David Gower, the golden boy of English cricket, relaxing with his fiancée, Vicki Stewart, in the Seychelles. *Lucky girl,* she thought. Then she skimmed through the article on Julie Tullis, a forty-five-year-old mother of two from Sussex, who was the first woman to attempt to climb Everest and, not for the first time, Diane considered giving up smoking.

Meanwhile, on the television page, *Coronation Street* was experiencing the usual ups and downs of northern life. Fate was being unkind to Jack Duckworth while his wife, Vera, was having all the luck. In *To the Manor Born* Peter Bowles had surprised Penelope Keith by moving his multi-million-pound business to the manor.

Diane thought the best story was undoubtedly the one about Carol Thatcher, the Prime Minister's daughter. The thirty-one-year-old journalist was on a three-week press trip to the Far East and was reported to have gone on stage in a Bangkok sex show. However, she did not admit to holding a green balloon between the thighs of a naked woman prior to it being burst with a popgun. The undeterred Mrs Thatcher had commented, 'Carol is a hard-working journalist and behaves accordingly.'

'Oh yes?' murmured Diane to herself as she pinched the end of her cigarette, put it in the pocket of her overall and set off to give Margery Ackroyd a Bonnie Tyler with blonde highlights.

Margery was standing outside the hairdresser's

and sharing the local gossip with Betty Buttle.

'Good send-off f'Ronnie,' said Betty.

Margery nodded. 'Mind you, 'e were allus a useless article.'

'Neither use nor ornament,' added Betty for good measure.

Personal affairs are laid bare in a small village and Miss Duff, the Ragley postmistress, had set a few tongues wagging over her passionate affair with our popular local postman, Ted Postlethwaite. Eyebrows were raised when Amelia ordered a huge double bed for delivery from the Cavendish furniture store in York. Whenever Ted finished his round and called into the Post Office, the ladies in the queue nodded knowingly as Amelia invited him to call back for a cup of tea. When Ted replied, 'Yes please, Amelia – with milk and two sugars,' the euphemism did not go unnoticed.

The two ladies exchanged glances when they saw Ted walking into the Post Office.

''Bout time she 'ad a bit o' 'appiness,' said Margery.

'Y'reight there, Margery,' agreed Betty.

'An' what 'bout that dishy Mr Dalton at t'school?' continued Margery. ''E could leave 'is slippers at t'end o'my bed any time.'

'Mine as well,' added Betty and she set off to the General Stores to buy a fresh crusty bloomer.

Diane appeared. 'Come on, Margery,' she said.

'Ah've changed m'mind, Diane,' said Margery. 'Ah'd prefer a Tina Turner.'

'No problem,' said Diane. A delivery of hairspray had arrived only that morning.

On the other side of the village green twelve-year-old Heathcliffe Earnshaw and his eleven-year-old brother Terry were leaning against the school wall and watching the world go by. The two boys had attended Ragley School and were both now at the comprehensive school in Easington. These sons of Barnsley in South Yorkshire were inseparable friends.

'That's a good bench, Terry,' commented Heathcliffe.

'It's f'Mr Smith,' said Terry. 'Mam said he'd gone to 'eaven.'

They both stared up at the sky.

'Thing is,' said Heathdiffe, ever the leader of this dynamic duo, 'if we stood on it we could reach that branch.'

The boys stared at the weeping willow arching gracefully over the bench and the duck pond.

'Y'reight, 'Eath, we could – at least *you* could 'cause y'taller.'

''Old on, Terry, copper's coming,' said Heathcliffe with urgency as PC Pike, the local bobby, drove past in his little grey van. A dog was barking in the back, banging its muzzle on the rear window.

'Terry, did y'see that dog in t'back o' t'police van?' asked Heathcliffe.

Terry looked perplexed. 'Yeah – ah wonder what 'e did wrong?'

Heathcliffe looked at his brother in dismay. 'Sometimes, y'daft as a brush.' Terry smiled innocently at his hero of a brother, Batman to his Robin. Heathcliffe ruffled his brother's spiky

78

blond hair and grinned. 'C'mon, our kid, let's climb a tree.'

It was late afternoon when Hazel Smith was sitting on Ronnie's bench with her mother.

'Hiya, Freckles,' said Ben Roberts as he sped past on his BMX Raleigh Burner. Ben was wearing his new National Health spectacles.

'Shurrup, Four Eyes,' shouted Hazel at his back as he headed for the butcher's, shopping bag swinging madly from the handlebars. 'Ah don't like boys, Mam,' said Hazel. 'They're all rude an' rotten.'

Ruby repressed a smile. 'Now then, our 'Azel,' she said sternly. 'If y'can't say owt nice, then don't say nowt at all.'

Hazel pondered this response. 'Mam – that's 'xactly what Grandma said t'you when y'said Deirdre Coe were as crooked as a corkscrew.'

Ruby looked at her daughter and realized she was growing up faster than she had thought. She gave her a hug, rummaged in her purse and handed her a five-pence piece. 'Go get y'self some sherbet lemons from Miss Golightly,' she said and added as an afterthought, '...an' give one t'Ben Roberts f'good luck.'

Ruby looked around her at the village that had been her home for over fifty years. Down the High Street the villagers were lighting their first fires and trailing gossamer spirals of woodsmoke drifted from a hundred tall chimney pots into a steel-blue sky. Ruby sighed and her thoughts drifted up into the heavens to join those of Ronnie.

It was a time of silent tears and broken dreams, and thoughts of the few happy times in her life. She recalled a Christmas card signed by all six of her children; a long-ago summer when she had been crowned May Queen; the day Vera had recommended her to be the school caretaker; winning the village Pancake Race; and an old cracked vase with six precious roses.

She looked down at her work-red hands, tugged at her wedding ring and gave a sad smile ... it was a band of memories. She twisted it a little further up her finger away from the swollen knuckle to ease the pain. It was a little habit that was becoming more frequent, almost a nervous need.

A few minutes later Hazel reappeared with a bag of sweets. She waved cheerily to Ben as he cycled by. 'Ah'm off 'ome now, Mam,' she said.

'OK, luv,' said Ruby, 'ah'll jus' sit 'ere for a little while longer.'

Hazel looked thoughtfully at her mother. 'An' don't worry, Mam, 'bout our Dad, 'cause ah know where 'e is now. Ben Roberts told me.'

Ruby looked up at her youngest daughter silhouetted against the setting sun and saw herself as a young girl again ... so long ago. 'And where's that, luv?' she asked quietly.

Hazel moved closer to her mother, held her hand and looked up with bright eyes at the darkening sky. 'Mam, 'e's sleeping with the angels.'

Then she stretched down, gave Ruby a kiss and wandered off home.

It was late evening when Ruby put on her warmest coat, closed her front door quietly and walked back to the village green. Above her head, syca-more keys were falling like a spiral of wishes, each one on an unknown journey. When she reached Ronnie's bench she sat down and reflected on the day. She stared up at the vast stardust sky. ''Usband,' she murmured to herself, 'ah miss you.'

The glowing orange lights of The Royal Oak shone brightly and George Dainty walked out with a group of local farmers. He saw Ruby and sat down beside her. ''Ello, Ruby,' he said gently.

The temperature was dropping quickly and George shivered. 'Ruby, ah don't like leavin' you on yer own like this.'

'Ah'll be fine,' said Ruby. 'Ah jus' needed a bit o'peace. Wi' six kids ah've never 'ad much o'that.'

George took a slip of paper from his pocket and wrote something down. 'This is m'phone num-ber, Ruby. Just give me three rings when y'get 'ome an' ah'll know you're safe 'n sound.'

Ruby stared at the paper. 'Ah will, George.'

Later Ruby looked up. Above her the crescent of a cornflower moon hung in an indigo sky, and a shooting star briefly split the firmament with a spear of white light, only to fade suddenly and disappear ... life and death in ethereal juxta-position.

Ruby simply smiled, recalling her life with Ron-nie, and rose from the bench, the glitter of starlight in her eyes. 'Well, ah s'ppose it wasn't bad while it lasted,' she said to herself. The house was dark when she returned. Ronnie's bobble hat no longer hung on the hook on the back of the bedroom door. It had been placed on the lid of his coffin and Ruby smiled as she recalled that

Hazel had said he could wear it in heaven on cold nights.

Ronnie's bench was empty now and, as the temperature continued to drop sharply, it became covered in a white frost that sparkled in the moonlight. Above it a barn owl swooped like a pale ghost of the night and flew up the Morton Road towards the vicarage. The church clock chimed the midnight hour as Ruby clambered into her empty bed. 'Ah well, that's life,' she said. But of course she meant quite the opposite.

Chapter Four

The Binmen of Benidorm

School closed for a one-week half-term holiday and will reopen on Monday, 7 November.
Extract from the Ragley School Logbook:
Friday, 26 October 1984

The spacious cobbled square in Easington was a perfect place for a market and a meeting place for the folk of the local villages. Lively stallholders announced their wares, occasionally drowned out by the town crier in his three-cornered hat and ceremonial frock-coat. He resembled an old-fashioned Mayor of London as he rang his bell and chanted, 'O Yea, O Yea, O Yea!'

It was Friday morning, 26 October, and Big Dave Robinson and Little Malcolm Robinson, the two cousins and lifelong friends, had parked their refuse wagon outside Grimsby Gerry's mobile refreshment caravan. They were sitting on plastic garden chairs while enjoying mugs of sweet tea and doorstep-sized bacon butties. 'This is jus' what we needed,' said Big Dave ... and he didn't mean the sandwiches.

'Y'reight there, Dave,' said Little Malcolm. 'Let's 'ave a look.'

They had purchased a half-price Polaroid One-Step 600 camera for £10 from Shady Stevo's

83

market stall. Stevo had been persuasive. 'It teks *cheapest* instant pictures ... twenty poun' in York, so it's a reight bargain.'

'Nothing's too good f'my Nellie,' Big Dave had announced.

'An' my Dorothy an' all, Dave,' added Little Malcolm.

So the deal was struck. They had each chipped in with five pounds, Stevo put it in a plastic bag and handshakes had been exchanged. While they supped the last of their tea they decided to ask Clint Ramsbottom to be the official wedding photographer as he was clearly the most artistic member of the Ragley Rovers football team.

It was all coming together nicely and tomorrow's joint wedding day beckoned. Big Dave was to marry Fenella Lovelace, known as Nellie, the football-wise Barnsley fan, and Little Malcolm was to marry Dorothy Humpleby, the Coffee Shop assistant.

They returned their mugs to the counter. 'Where y'goin' for yer 'oneymoon?' asked Grimsby Gerry.

'Benidorm,' said Big Dave.

'Bloody 'ell, lads,' exclaimed Grimsby Gerry, 'y'mus' be in love.'

'No, we gorrit cheap,' said Big Dave.

However, Little Malcolm didn't immediately agree with his giant cousin as he usually did. He really *was* in love.

In Ragley School it was morning break and a few of the children in Tom's class were standing by the wall and staring out through the railings at the passing traffic.

'Binmen are gettin' married tomorrow,' said seven-year-old Ted Coggins as Big Dave and Little Malcolm roared past in their refuse wagon from the Easington Road and on to the High Street.

'Ah know,' said six-year-old Patience Crapper, sounding bored.

'What's special 'bout gettin' married?' asked Ted.

'Don't y'know?' said Patience, whose opinion of boys was already very low.

'No ah don't,' said Ted.

'It's t'*dress*, silly.'

''Ow d'you mean?' said Ted.

'You 'ave t'look like a *princess*,' explained Patience. *'Ev'rybody* knows that.'

Ted thought about this incomprehensible response for a while. Eventually he spoke up. 'Would y'like to 'ear me whistle?' ... but Patience had already gone to show Katie Icklethwaite her new pink pixie boots. Ted stared after her, looking puzzled; a lifetime of not understanding the opposite sex had begun.

In Nora's Coffee Shop on the High Street Dorothy Humpleby, the twenty-seven-year-old, five-feet-eleven-inch assistant and would-be model was standing behind the counter. Little Malcolm approached her while Big Dave waited at his favourite table.

'We can't stop,' said Little Malcolm as he craned his neck to look up at the woman of his dreams. 'We've already 'ad us mornin' break but ah wanted t'check y'were all right.'

Dorothy stopped filing her nails and sat on the

85

stool behind the counter so she was on the same level as Little Malcolm. She had been having second thoughts about her going-away dress. It was a bold creation with black and white horizontal stripes that resembled a liquorice allsort. 'Malcolm, do ah look fat in stripes?'

Little Malcolm thought for a millisecond too long.

'So ah do then?' retorted Dorothy sharply.

'No, y'don't,' insisted Little Malcolm. 'It'll show off yer *assets*.'

Dorothy was intrigued, completely unaware this was a line taken from a recent episode of *Bergerac*. 'Do y'think so, Malcolm?'

'Ah do,' said a very relieved Little Malcolm.

Meanwhile, ten miles away in York, above the local newspaper office, Nellie was saying goodbye to her flat and had packed her case for Benidorm. She had included a pair of new Chris Evert trainers plus *two* Barnsley football shirts, a long-sleeved one for during the day and a short-sleeved one for sleeping in. It had been agreed that Nellie would live with Big Dave in Dave and Malcolm's council house while Little Malcolm would move in above the Coffee Shop with Dorothy.

Nellie glanced up at her bedroom wall and the huge poster of Ryan O'Neal and Ali McGraw in *Love Story* and thought she might have to change it to something more cheerful, maybe a calendar of the beauty spots of Barnsley. That would fit in more appropriately with the decor of her new home.

She stretched out on her double bed and wondered what life would be like when she moved in with her great hulk of a Yorkshireman. Big Dave didn't actually do *finesse* and she thought about her collection of pottery zoo animals lined up on the mantelpiece. She couldn't imagine the long-necked giraffe lasting very long.

At lunchtime in the staff-room Vera was reading her *Daily Telegraph* and frowning at the news. Investigations were still continuing into the recent Brighton bombing which was a direct attack on the British government by the IRA. A long-delay time bomb had been planted and people had died. However, much to Vera's relief, her political heroine Margaret Thatcher had escaped unscathed and declared a day of defiance and sorrow.

She moved on to the article about the Ethiopian famine, which earlier in the week had captured the hearts and minds of the country when television journalist Michael Buerk had presented a harrowing report of a starving people. In particular, the photographs of the children had tugged at Vera's heartstrings and she wondered what she could do to help. Meanwhile, a pop singer she had never heard of was thinking along the same lines. Bob Geldof had turned to his friend, the Ultravox singer Midge Ure, and composed a song to be released on 29 November with sales destined to exceed one million in the first week. However, on that October morning in our quiet corner of North Yorkshire it was merely a ripple, a gentle flap of butterfly wings in a far-off place, but destined to have an effect on the lives of many.

Meanwhile, in her state-of-the-art conservatory in their luxury bungalow on the Morton Road, Petula Dudley-Palmer, the wealthiest woman in the village, was reading her *Woman's Realm* and had come across an advertisement for a twenty-one-piece Danish kitchenware set. Her husband, Geoffrey, a high-ranking executive at the local chocolate factory, had one of the new popular Mastercard credit cards and Petula was fingering it thoughtfully.

After the usual lunchtime trade, Nora Pratt, a short, portly lady in her mid-forties, turned the sign on the door of her Coffee Shop from OPEN to CLOSED.

'Well, Dowothy,' said Nora, for whom the letter R had always proved elusive, 'y'mus' be weally excited.'

Dorothy was staring at her reflection in the chrome jukebox while Madonna sang 'Like A Virgin'. 'Actu'lly, Nora ... ah'm worried.'

'Wowwied?' said Nora. 'What about?'

'*Protection*, Nora,' said Dorothy. 'Y'know ... when ah'm on 'oneymoon wi' my Malcolm.'

Nora smiled knowingly. 'No, Dowothy, it'll be no twouble. In a twopical climate y'jus' 'ave to avoid them ultwa-violet ways.'

''Ow d'you mean?'

'Well, y'need a weally good pwotective sun cweam from t'chemist shop ... Eugene'll put y'wight.'

Dorothy wasn't sure Nora was on the same wavelength. However, there was still last-minute work to be done on her wedding dress, not least

88

the chunky plastic signs of the zodiac that needed to be sewn on the waistband.

Big Dave had borrowed Little Malcolm's 1250cc bright green, two-door 1973 Hillman Avenger Deluxe to collect Nellie and her cases from her flat in York. Nellie was staying overnight at the Coffee Shop.

'Let's 'ave some tea, Dave,' suggested Nellie. She switched on the kettle and took the milk out of the fridge.

Big Dave looked puzzled and picked up the milk. 'Nellie – what's this when it's at 'ome?' The label read 'SKIMMED MILK'.

'It's skimmed milk,' said Nellie.

'*Skimmed* milk ... *skimmed!*' exclaimed Big Dave. 'Y'mean they've tekken all t'goodness out?'

'It's to 'elp wi' slimming,' explained Nellie.

'It looks diff'rent,' said Big Dave dubiously, 'sort o' more grey than white.'

'Jus' try it, Dave,' said Nellie patiently. 'We're gettin' married soon so we've got t'get used to each other's little foibles.'

Big Dave didn't know what foibles were. He decided not to mention it, even though it occurred to him that whatever they were he would have had big ones. 'All reight, luv,' he agreed cautiously.

'An' we'll 'ave t'*share* 'ouse'old jobs,' continued Nellie, 'like washing-up.'

Big Dave looked surprised. 'No, ah allus did 'eavy jobs an' Malcolm did little 'uns like washin'-up an' suchlike.'

'What 'eavy jobs?' asked Nellie.

89

Big Dave thought for a moment. 'Ah put t'bins out on Thursdays.'

Little Malcolm had called into the chemist's shop on the High Street. As usual, the pharmacist, Eugene Scrimshaw, was wearing his Captain Kirk uniform under his white coat. Eugene had never missed an episode of *Star Trek* and had converted his attic into the flight deck of the *Starship Enterprise*.

'Ah got one o' them stomach aches, Eugene,' said Little Malcolm. 'Y'know t'type; it flared up this morning.'

'It's probably nerves,' said Eugene sympathetically. Little Malcolm had the constitution of an ox and hadn't missed a day's work in his life.

Eugene selected a packet from the shelf behind him. 'These'll 'elp you relax, Malcolm,' he said kindly.

Little Malcolm looked dubious. 'Thing is, Eugene, ah don't want summat t'mek me *sleepy* tomorrow night ... if y'tek m'meanin'.'

Eugene nodded knowingly and replaced the tablets. 'Try these instead, Malcolm,' he said, 'an' go forth an' prosper.' As Little Malcolm walked out of the shop and the bell rang madly, Eugene raised his hand and gave his version of Mr Spock's Vulcan salute while his wife, Peggy, glanced up from stacking Johnson's Baby Cream and shook her head sadly. It was tough being married to a dedicated Trekkie.

Towards the end of the lunchbreak I was at my desk in the office completing a Yorkshire Purchasing Organization order form for A4 paper and rubber glue. Vera had made me a mug of black tea with a slice of lemon and Shirley the cook had handed round a plate of homemade ginger biscuits. The sound of the children playing drifted through the window. Some were skipping and chanting a rhyme:

One man went to mow,
Went to mow a meadow,
One man and his dog,
Spot, bottle o' pop, fish an' chips,
Ol' Mother Riley an' 'er cow,
Went to mow a meadow.

Tom tapped on the door and walked in. 'Sorry to disturb you, Jack, but can I have a word?'

I glanced at the clock and drank the last of my tea. 'Come on, let's get some fresh air,' I said.

Outside on the playground we leaned against the school wall. It took a while for Tom to break the silence. 'I'm thinking of my future at Ragley,' he said.

I was surprised. 'Why, Tom? I don't want to lose you. You're a good teacher ... respected by children and parents alike.'

'It's Laura,' he said simply.

I nodded and sighed. 'She's in Australia now.'

'I know,' said Tom, 'but life's just not the same without her.'

I weighed my words. 'Tom ... she wanted a fresh start. You must know that.'

'I do,' he said, 'but it's difficult.' He shuffled and stared up at the horse chestnut trees above our heads. A stiff breeze was tugging at the last of the curled brown leaves. Then he surveyed the school and the children playing. 'I do like it here, Jack, and I appreciate the opportunity you gave me.'

'So what are you saying?' I asked.

'Ragley holds too many memories.' He looked down at his thick brogues and shuffled amidst the decaying, skeletal leaves at our feet. 'So I've decided to spend half-term with my sister in London and then maybe later get a teaching job down there.'

'I see,' I said.

'I haven't made up my mind yet, but I just wanted you to know.'

I patted him on the shoulder. It was meant to be a reassuring gesture for a young man who was clearly troubled. 'I appreciate you sharing this with me, Tom, and I do understand. I know that Laura going away was a bolt out of the blue for you.'

He smiled and shook his head. 'It was much more than that, Jack.'

I was curious. 'What do you mean?'

He pushed himself away from the wall and turned to face me. Then he looked me squarely in the eyes and said softly, 'Laura thought she might be pregnant with our child.'

During the summer holiday Beth had confided in me and shared this story, but I remained silent.

'It turned out to be a false alarm,' continued Tom, 'but it made me realize what I want out of life. I'm unsure what to do next, whether in London ... or even one day in Australia.'

Suddenly the bell rang for the beginning of afternoon school. 'I'm sorry, Jack ... but I'm just a little confused at present.'

We walked back into school for the beginning of afternoon lessons, both deep in thought.

Later that afternoon in St Mary's Church, Joseph Evans was leading the wedding rehearsal. Derek 'Deke' Ramsbottom, local farmworker, occasional snowplough driver and singing cowboy in The Royal Oak, was the joint best man for both Big Dave and Little Malcolm. Nellie's proud father, Billy, was giving his only daughter away, while Nora Pratt was doing the honours for orphan Dorothy. Local teenagers Claire Bradshaw and Anita Cuthbertson were the bridesmaids, while Deke's three sons, Shane, Clint and Wayne, were the ushers.

Joseph took them step by step through the service he knew so well – where to stand, when to kneel – and confirmed their choice of hymns; namely, 'Praise My Soul The King of Heaven' and Big Dave and Little Malcolm's favourite, 'Fight The Good Fight', which they always sang with gusto.

All went well. Finally, Big Dave and Little Malcolm took Billy and his wife, Audrey, to The Royal Oak, where they were staying overnight, while Nora, Nellie, Dorothy and the bridesmaids returned to the Coffee Shop.

At the end of school the children were excited. Darkness was already falling as they scampered down the drive with thoughts of a one-week holi-

MERTHYR TYDFIL PUBLIC LIBRARIES

day, Halloween, bonfires and fireworks on the near horizon.

In the cloakroom area of Anne's reception class the youngest children were putting on their coats while a few parents were checking the Lost Property box for miscellaneous socks and wellington boots.

Six-year-old Mandy Kerslake looked up at her mother and suddenly asked, 'What's sex, Mummy?'

The enlightened Mrs Kerslake was a nurse at the hospital in York and considered herself to be a modern eighties woman. She crouched down and said quietly and precisely, 'It's what mummies and daddies do to make babies.'

At that moment the heavily pregnant Mrs Freda Fazackerly walked past with her daughter Madonna.

'Look, Mummy,' Mandy shouted at the top of her voice. 'Mrs Fazackerly 'as 'ad sex!' and Mrs Kerslake hurried out, considering that perhaps in future there was a time and a place to be enlightened.

It was late in the evening when the women in the Coffee Shop finished the last of Nora's home-made champagne-and-brandy cocktails, the champagne direct from one of Shady Stevo's trips to the Carrefour hypermarket in France.

Later, Nora and Dorothy were sitting on the bed in Dorothy's bedroom next to her bulging suitcase. 'Ah'll 'ave y'room weady f'y'when y'come back,' said Nora tearfully, 'an' y'can 'ave t'upstairs bathwoom all t'y'selves. Wuby's son,

94

Duggie, an' 'is mate are weawangin' m'dwessin' table an' wa'dwobe in t'big bedwoom an' ah'm tweating m'self to one o' them en suites.'

'Thanks, Nora, you're a true friend,' said Dorothy. 'You've been like t'mother ah never 'ad.' Since her parents had been killed in a road accident, Dorothy had spent ten years moving from one home to another until Nora had taken her in at the age of eighteen. 'An' ah love this room,' she went on. 'It's nearest ah've ever 'ad to a proper 'ome.' She looked round at the peeling wallpaper and posters of Shakin' Stevens. 'An' when ah go away wi' Malcolm, ah'll miss you, Nora.'

Nora wiped away a tear. 'But you'll be back soon ... an' it'll be good 'aving a man about the 'ouse,' she said. 'An' don't forget – t'bathwoom is all f'you now.'

Dorothy didn't know the term 'symbolic gesture', but she understood it in her own way and gave Nora a big hug.

The following morning the Coffee Shop was full of life and chatter and hairspray. Diane had come in early to do their hair and make-up.

Nellie had chosen a curly Irene Cara while Dorothy had finally decided on an Agnetha Fältskog, while giving the benefit of her make-up advice to the very excited bridesmaids. She held up her magazine. 'It sez 'ere, girls, that y'can "slim millimetres off y'features wi' artfully applied blushers", so ah'm gonna 'ave a go. Ah definitely want t'look like 'er in Abba.'

Meanwhile, on the radio, Dave Lee Travis had just introduced the all-girl trio Bananarama and

Claire and Anita were singing along to 'It Ain't What You Do It's The Way That You Do It'.

Life was a little more tranquil in St Mary's churchyard, where the silk of spiders laced the shrubbery and the rooks cawed and wheeled above the high elms.

As Beth and I drove up the Morton Road the early arrivals were already milling around the church grounds. Mrs Jackson and the twins were taking the shortcut past the vicarage along the winding path bordered by ancient gravestones.

'Remember, girls,' said Mrs Jackson, 'we need to be quiet and respectful in the graveyard.'

'Why is that, Mummy?' asked the inquisitive Hermione.

'Yes, what for, Mummy?' added the logical Honeysuckle. 'No one can hear us because they're all dead.'

What do they teach them these days? was the thought that passed through Mrs Jackson's mind, although it was with a smile that she held their hands and joined the crowd at the front of the church.

Beth was carrying John, eager to select a seat at the back in case our lively son became over-exuberant. Big Dave and Little Malcolm were standing in the ancient porch, smart in their new suits, about to walk in and take up their positions in the front pew.

'Thanks f'coming Mr Sheffield,' said Big Dave.

'You've got a good day,' I replied, looking at the cloudless sky. 'And how are you feeling, Malcolm?'

'Ah'm shittin' bricks, Mr Sheffield,' he blurted out and then glanced nervously as Vera had suddenly appeared and was pretending not to hear. 'Beggin' y'pardon, Mrs F,' he added quickly.

'Time to come in, gentlemen,' said Vera with a knowing smile.

The two brides arrived together in the back of Rupert Forbes-Kitchener's Bentley and the crowd of villagers gave a collective cheer of appreciation as they stepped out.

Dorothy looked like a tall, slim meringue in a dress with lots of horizontal frills. It was in a daring off-the-shoulder-style, with a plunging neckline that showed off her substantial cleavage to great effect. While the large Aquarius symbol on her Wonder Woman headband appeared at first sight a little incongruous, it did blend in with the signs of the zodiac surrounding her waist and the huge sparkly earrings in the shape of silver horse-shoes.

The short, compact, unfussy Nellie was relatively plain in comparison, with a simple, ivory-white dress designed to hang loosely from her prodigious bosom straight down to the ground. The overall impression from a distance was of a shiny Thermos flask.

Soon Elsie Crapper was playing the Wedding March on the organ. Nellie led the way, accompanied by her father in his best suit and Barnsley FC tie, followed by Dorothy, with Nora at her side in her new royal blue hat with a brim like a flying saucer.

By coincidence, Beth and I were sitting in a pew next to a small brass plaque in remembrance of a distant relative of Big Dave and Little Malcolm. It read:

In loving memory of
REGINALD ARTHUR ROBINSON
Beloved son of Herbert and Charlotte Robinson
Killed in action September 25th 1915
Age 17 years and 6 months
'THY WILL BE DONE'

'Let us pray,' announced Joseph, and Big Dave and Little Malcolm knelt down on the beautifully decorated kneelers, a gift to the church from the local Cross-stitch Club.

He opened his Book of Common Prayer and recited the words that were so familiar, knowing deep down that they would never be addressed to him. 'Dearly beloved, we are gathered here in the sight of God, and in the face of this congregation, to join together this man and this woman in holy matrimony.' As the ceremony progressed Joseph kept repeating himself as he turned first to one couple and then to the other.

'Wilt thou have this woman to thy wedded wife?' he asked.

'Ah will,' replied Big Dave in a commanding voice.

Joseph turned to Little Malcolm. 'Wilt thou have this woman to thy wedded wife?'

'Ah will an' all,' added Little Malcolm nervously.

Joseph smiled reassuringly at Nellie and Dorothy. 'Wilt thou love him, comfort him, honour and keep him in sickness and in health...'

Little Malcolm sneezed and Big Dave rum-

98

maged in his pocket and brought out a spotted handkerchief the size of a tea towel. He handed it to his diminutive cousin with a smile and Little Malcolm blew his nose loudly.

'Who giveth this woman to be married to this man?'

Nora stepped forward and the members of the congregation recalled that Dorothy had no family. 'Ah do,' said Nora, 'an' 'ere's the wing.'

Billy Lovelace also stepped forward. 'Ah do an' all, y'reverence,' he said, 'an' ah've got a ring an' all.'

The two couples were asked to join their right hands, over which Joseph draped his white stole. 'With this ring – I thee wed,' he said.

And so it was that on this special day Ragley's favourite refuse collectors were married and the sun shone down on the two couples as they emerged from the church. Clint Ramsbottom was taking his role of official photographer very seriously and was urging Big Dave and Little Malcolm to hurry up and concentrate on standing still and smiling.

'C'mon, Malcolm,' said Dorothy, 'it's not 'xactly *Krypton Factor.*'

'M'face is 'urtin' wi' smilin',' pleaded Little Malcolm.

'Stay there an' try t'look 'appy, y'great lump,' said Nellie. 'You an' Malcolm 'ave been faffin' about like Pinky an' bloody Perky.'

Big Dave looked lost. The significance of being likened to a television puppet meant nothing to this son of Yorkshire.

In the crowd Margery Ackroyd, the local gossip,

was enjoying the moment. 'Thing is, Betty,' she said to Betty Buttle, 'Malcolm's ent'ring into 'oly wedlock wi' someone a lot younger than 'im.'

'Mind you, Margery,' said Betty, 'so did Charlie Boy wi' Princess Di.'

'Mebbe so,' conceded Margery.

'An' 'e's been courtin' that lass for a few years now,' added Betty for good measure.

Margery had kept her *pièce de résistance* until last. 'Yes, Betty,' she whispered, 'ah shouldn't be tellin' you this, but ... they've 'ad more 'ot nights than ah've 'ad 'ot dinners.'

The two couples left the church grounds in style. All the refuse collectors in the Easington area had lined up on either side of the path all the way to the lychgate to provide a guard of honour. Each man proudly gripped the metal handle of a dustbin lid as if they were Viking warriors holding aloft their shields. It was a dramatic send-off and Big Dave and Little Malcolm beamed in delight, while Vera looked on thinking, *It takes all sorts.*

On the Morton Road outside the church, white ribbons and streamers were festooned on the Ragley dustbin wagon and the two teddy bears tied to the front bumper were both wearing frilly white dresses. In addition, one wore a Barbie doll tiara while the other looked the part in a Barnsley Football Club bobble hat. Big Dave and Nellie climbed in and led the procession of cars, with Little Malcolm and Dorothy in the gleaming Bentley close behind.

The wedding breakfast in the village hall was a relaxed and lively affair with a few incoherent speeches on the stage, followed by loud music.

Don and Sheila Bradshaw from The Royal Oak had set up a makeshift bar with a trestle table creaking under the weight of a barrel of Tetley's Bitter and another of Chestnut Mild.

I bought an orange juice for John, who seemed to enjoy playing under the refreshment tables, a white wine for Beth and a half of Chestnut for myself.

'Y'know what they say, Mr Sheffield,' said Sheila coyly. 'Y'don't know 'appiness 'til y'married,' she glanced across at the massive frame of Don, 'an' then it's too late.'

Meanwhile Clint Ramsbottom, the resident Ragley village disc jockey, was playing Wham!'s 'Wake Me Up Before You Go-Go' as he drank a bottle of Budweiser.

Old Tommy Piercy came over to pay his respects. 'Y'lookin' a fair treat, Mrs Sheffield,' he said.

Beth, in an elegant two-piece cream suit with her hair in a French pleat, smiled. 'Thank you, Mr Piercy.'

'And young John is comin' on grand,' he added as our son munched on a soggy crisp.

'A good wedding, Mr Piercy,' I said.

Old Tommy puffed on his pipe and pondered. 'Fair t'middlin', Mr Sheffield ... fair t'middling.' This was the ultimate accolade from this blunt, rugged Yorkshireman and I smiled at his reluctance to heap a surfeit of praise on the proceedings. 'Gi' me t'old days back again,' he continued with

101

feeling. 'Y'knew where y'stood then wi' a pint in yer 'and an' a shillin' in y'pocket. Ah've no time f'these fancy compooters an' all them little plastic cards that'll get yer int' debt. Mark my words – no good'll come o' them.' He frowned in the direction of Clint Ramsbottom. 'An' we didn't 'ave none o' this so-called *music* ... an' *German* beer.'

It was late in the afternoon when the two married couples finally tied their suitcases on to the makeshift roof rack of Little Malcolm's car and drove down the High Street with assorted balloons tied to the back bumper for the start of their honeymoon.

Eight days later they returned from Benidorm.

None of them had a suntan ... but they were all smiling.

Chapter Five

A Surprise for Sally

The new music adviser, Miss Sarah Mancini, visited school to discuss a Christmas carol event in York in December.
Extract from the Ragley School Logbook:
Monday, 12 November 1984

'How do you spell that, please?' asked Vera. She was scribbling notes in perfect shorthand on her spiral-bound pad. 'Yes, I've got that, Miss Mancini – and we shall look forward to meeting you.'

It was Monday morning, 12 November, and outside the office window the first harsh frosts heralded the coming of winter. Vera was already busy behind her desk as I hung up my duffel coat and old college scarf.

'Exciting news, Mr Sheffield,' said Vera. 'We have a new music adviser and she sounds delightful.'

Vera printed out a name on a paper off-cut and passed it to me. It read: 'Miss Sarah Mancini, County Hall'.

'Thanks, Vera,' I said. I had seen the announcement regarding Miss Mancini in the recent North Yorkshire circular. She had been appointed from one of the London authorities and was clearly making her mark.

Vera opened the desk diary and made an entry. 'And she's calling in this morning to introduce herself.'

Just before 10.15 a.m. I was working with Charlotte Ackroyd, Ben Roberts and Victoria Alice Dudley-Palmer. They were calculating the volume of spherical shapes when suddenly Charlotte, without appearing to look up from her equation, announced, 'Three-door Vauxhall Chevette coming up t'drive, Mr Sheffield.' Charlotte knew her cars.

A few minutes later, Vera tapped on my classroom door. 'Our visitor, Mr Sheffield,' she said quietly.

A confident woman in an open-necked cream blouse and a striking grey pin-striped trouser suit walked in. She took in the bowed heads of the children and the hum of activity. 'Hello, Mr Sheffield,' she said in a hushed whisper. 'What a busy classroom. I'm Sarah Mancini, the new music adviser from Northallerton. I hope I'm not disturbing you.'

At close to six feet tall, her dark brown eyes were almost on a level with mine. Her high cheekbones were flushed from the cold air and her raven-black hair was tied back in a flowing ponytail. I guessed she was about the same age as me, perhaps in her late thirties. We shook hands.

'Good to meet you,' I said, 'and you're welcome in the classroom at any time. The children are proud of their work, so do have a look if you wish.'

Charlotte Ackroyd raised her hand. 'Finished, Mr Sheffield – and ah've got it right,' she announced with a confident smile.'

104

'This is Charlotte, Miss Mancini,' I said. 'She loves her mathematics ... and she is in our school choir.'

'That's wonderful,' Miss Mancini said, radiating enthusiasm. 'Actually, that's why I'm here.' She looked at the children again as if she wished to soak up the atmosphere. Most of them were busy completing their School Mathematics Project workcards, while others were finishing off a vocabulary exercise using their dictionaries. 'I've heard so much about your wonderful choir from the chair of the Education Committee.'

'Miss Barrington-Huntley?' I said in surprise.

'Yes,' replied Miss Mancini with a wry grin, 'I've discovered there's not much Miss Barrington-Huntley *doesn't* know.'

'Well, that's good to hear,' I said. 'So ... welcome to Ragley School, and I hope you may have time to meet our music specialist, Mrs Pringle. It's Sally who teaches the choir.'

She considered this for a moment. 'Perhaps I could have a word with *both* of you,' she said quietly. 'You see, I have an interesting project in mind.'

Intrigued, I glanced at the clock. 'Well, it's time for morning break so we can go to the staff-room if you wish.' I looked at the eager Harold Bustard. 'Harold, please ask Mrs Pringle to come to the staff-room as we have a visitor who would like to meet her.' Harold was gone in the blink of an eye, while Mo Hartley went to ring the bell, Charlotte and Ben set off to open up their tuck shop and Danny Hardacre cleaned the chalk-board. Sarah Mancini nodded in approval as, like

105

a well-oiled machine, the children tidied away their books and walked out to the cloakroom to put on their coats before going out to play.

We strolled across the hall together and Sarah Mancini paused by each display of work. 'You have a lovely school, Mr Sheffield,' she said.

'Please ... call me Jack.'

She smiled. 'And I'm Sarah, of course.'

The formalities were over and my curiosity was aroused. 'And, if I may say, Mancini is an interesting surname.'

'Yes, an English mother and an Italian father – and they both *love* music,' she added with a smile.

I nodded in appreciation. She was a striking woman, an Italian beauty but with the fair skin of her mother.

The staff-room was welcoming on this cold day. Vera had prepared mugs of milky coffee and turned on the gas fire. Introductions were completed and Sally, Vera and Anne sat down while Tom was on playground duty.

'So, Sarah, I'm intrigued,' I said. 'What's the project you mentioned?'

Sarah Mancini opened her black leather shoulder bag and took out a printed sheet of A4 paper with an impressive letterhead. 'Let me explain,' she said. 'My brother, Phil Mancini, works for Yorkshire Television, based in Leeds. He's in charge of an outside broadcast team for a project entitled *Christmas Voices*. It comprises five short items of no more than ten minutes each to go out next month, featuring children's school choirs in Yorkshire. He's busy recording the fourth in the series at present in Harrogate. The last one will take place at St Michael le Belfrey Church in York.'

'Right next to the Minster,' said Sally.

'A beautiful church,' said Anne.

'And it's thriving these days,' added Vera.

'Yes, it really is the perfect venue,' said Sarah, glancing down at the typed notes, 'and we're recording on Friday, 7 December for proposed transmission during the early evening on Friday, 21 December.'

'Our last day of term,' I said, looking at the calendar on the staff-room noticeboard.

'Yes,' said Sarah. 'The intention is that the series will go out towards the end of the local evening-news slot from Monday to Friday – a sort of feel-good Christmas finale to the programme. Here's the preliminary running order.' She handed over a photocopied sheet and we passed it round. The list included a ten-minute slot with the heading 'School Choir' and an empty box alongside. 'It's simply a Yorkshire Television mini-version of *Songs of Praise*.'

'I love that Sally Magnusson on *Songs of Praise*,' mused Vera. 'She takes after her father ... lovely clear diction.'

'And Cliff Michelmore,' added Anne, who was another avid viewer. 'I loved his programme from Clifton Cathedral. He's always so elegant and calm.' For Anne, the perfect man had the voice of Cliff Michelmore and the body of David Soul, but she kept this latter thought to herself.

There was a short silence as we gradually took in all the information we'd been given. Finally, Sally asked the question on everyone's lips: 'Sarah ... where do *we* fit in?'

Sarah surveyed our expectant faces. 'Well, before making a *definite* commitment, I should like to hear *your* choir first, with a view to Ragley School taking part. I've heard such great things from colleagues at County Hall.'

Everyone seemed to react at once.

'What a surprise!' exclaimed Sally. 'Fame at last!'

'How exciting!' said Anne.

'Well,' added Vera cautiously, 'if selected, the children will be thrilled.'

The bell rang for the end of morning break. 'So, Sarah,' I asked, 'when would you like to hear the choir?'

Sarah Mancini looked at her wristwatch. 'I have a meeting in Northallerton at twelve, so is it convenient to call back this afternoon?'

'What do you think, Sally?' I asked.

Sally glanced at the hall timetable on the noticeboard. 'Well, I could do a choir practice at two,' she said, 'if you take the rest of the children, Jack.'

'We could come in and listen,' I said. I looked at Sarah Mancini. 'All the children in the choir are in the top two classes,' I explained. 'The oldest children.'

'How many are in the choir?' asked Sarah.

'Thirty-six, including the recorder group,' said Sally. 'I take anyone in the top two classes who would like to join.'

'And how many are in the two classes?' asked Sarah.

'Twenty-five in mine and twenty-three in Class 3,' I said.

'Why not include them all?' she suggested. 'It

seems a shame to leave a dozen children behind.'

Sally grinned. 'Well, as long as the other forty-seven can drown out Damian Brown we should be fine.'

I considered the implications. 'We would need to give the children the choice,' I said.

'Good idea,' agreed Sally.

'And we would have to send a note home to parents to ensure they want their child involved,' I added and everyone agreed.

'Well, that sounds fine to me,' said Sarah as she collected her coat from the little cloakroom area between the staff-room and the office.

'Just a thought,' said Sally, 'but I also have a truly gifted little girl who will be singing a solo at the Christmas Crib Service in church.'

'You mean Rosie Sparrow?' asked Vera.

Sarah Mancini paused in buttoning up her coat, clearly interested. 'Rosie Sparrow?'

'Yes, a lovely girl,' I said. 'She arrived here two years ago.'

'How old is Rosie?' asked Sarah.

'She's not nine yet,' said Sally, 'but, as I said to Jack when she first arrived, she has the voice of an angel.'

'It's *my* turn to be intrigued,' said Sarah as she picked up her shoulder bag. 'So until this afternoon – and I'll aim to be back shortly after two o'clock.'

At lunchtime in the staff-room Vera was reading the front page of her *Daily Telegraph* and smiling.

The handsome ex-movie star Ronald Reagan had recently won his second term as President of the USA with a landslide victory. The slogan 'It's morning in America' had reflected the mood of the nation and he had settled once again into the Oval Office and enjoyed another friendly chat with Margaret Thatcher in Downing Street. Vera studied the two photographs and was pleased to see that Margaret was wearing a blouse with a large flamboyant bow that suited her so well. Meanwhile, cowboy Ronnie was looking his usual dapper self, although his hair was suspiciously darker than usual.

Eternal youth, thought Vera as she touched her carefully permed hair.

Meanwhile Sally and I were in the school office discussing the events of the morning.

'I've been thinking, Jack,' she said thoughtfully, pointing out of the window towards a group of girls.

'What about?' I asked as I followed the direction of her gaze.

'Rosie Sparrow,' she said.

Rosie and her best friend, Jemima Poole, were turning a skipping rope and the twins, Hermione and Honeysuckle, oblivious to the biting wind, were jumping in and out. Rosie and Jemima were chanting:

Make friends,
Make friends,
Never ever break friends.
If you do, you'll catch the flu
And that will be the end of you.

'What about Rosie?' I asked.

'I was just thinking how well she had settled in given the difficulties she faced before she came here.'

At two o'clock Charlotte Ackroyd announced, 'That posh car's comin' up t'drive again, Mr Sheffield.' It was Sarah Mancini, on time, and by ten past two all the children in the top two classes had carried their chairs into the hall.

'Now, boys and girls,' said Sally. 'Please would the recorders sit here,' she pointed to her left, 'and choir – sit in your usual places in the middle of the hall.' Sally smiled at me. 'And would those of you not in the choir sit here with Mr Sheffield.' She pointed to her right.

She set up her music stand and picked up her guitar. 'Boys and girls, we have an important visitor here today. Her name is Miss Mancini and she loves music and has come to hear you sing and play your recorders.' The children stared with interest at our visitor. 'So would anyone like to choose a song?'

Ryan Halfpenny and Sonia Tricklebank put up their hands. 'Yes, Ryan?' asked Sally.

'"Kumbaya", Miss,' he said.

'Good choice,' said Sally, 'and what would you like, Sonia?'

'"Bright Eyes", Miss,' said Sonia.

'Excellent choice,' said Sally as she fixed a capo in place and then took a plectrum from the pocket of her waistcoat. She strummed a chord. 'So let's warm up with "Kumbaya", and the children who are not in the choir do join in. Recorders, you know your part. So ... all stand.'

The children sang with their usual gusto and I watched Sarah Mancini as she relaxed in her seat and began to smile.

'Now for "Bright Eyes"' said Sally. She opened her new *Jukebox* song book, selected number 29 and strummed an F chord. 'Let's really *concentrate* and show Miss Mancini just how good we are.'

The children stood up straight. All the faces of the choir were visible as they were arranged in three rows in order of height.

'So ... we'll have the recorders first, then those of you in the middle sing the tune and the rest of the choir please sing your usual descant.' She paused for a moment. 'Rosie,' she said quietly, 'you often sing a solo here. Would you mind doing it for Miss Mancini?'

Rosie's cheeks flushed slightly. She looked at Sarah Mancini, who gave her an encouraging smile. 'Yes, Mrs Pringle,' she said confidently.

The children performed superbly, the recorders held their notes beautifully and little Rosie Sparrow sang as she always did – with a purity that stirred the soul. I watched Sarah Mancini as she leaned forward on her chair, her hands as if in prayer against her lips, still, statuesque, a picture of concentration. Finally, there was an imperceptible nod of the head.

'Well done, everybody,' said Sally and looked towards Sarah, who stood up and applauded.

'Thank you so much, children,' she said. 'That was simply wonderful.'

It was afternoon break and when the children had gone out to play Sarah asked if she could use

112

the telephone in the office and then for us to join her in a few minutes.

When Sally and I walked in she was sitting at Vera's desk and studying some scribbled notes in her spiral-bound notebook. 'Well, that exceeded expectations,' she said. 'Congratulations, Sally – you've obviously worked very hard with the choir and the recorders were excellent.'

Sally beamed in delight and we sat down.

'I've just telephoned my brother and he's as excited as I am about the Ragley choir. So we should *definitely* like to arrange for you to come into York for the recording session next month.'

'I'm sure that can be arranged,' I said.

'My brother suggested you rehearse *two* carols, beginning with a lively one of your choice and including the recorder group.'

Sally nodded in appreciation. 'That's fine,' she said. 'We'll practise a few and come up with a favourite.'

'But for the *second*,' said Sarah with gravitas, 'I told Phil about Rosie. It's obvious she has a wonderful voice and she sings with confidence ... a definite *presence*. You really do have a gifted pupil.'

I thought back to my teacher-training days of the sixties when my tutor, Jim Fairbank, had discussed the fact that so-called 'gifted' children in the creative arts could go unnoticed in the busy day-to-day life of a primary-school classroom. He gave us examples of the creative thinking tests of the American psychologists Getzels and Jackson and the lateral thinking tests of Edward de Bono. At the time they meant little to me, but gradually the reality dawned. 'Jack, *all*

113

children have talent,' he had said to me during a teaching practice. 'It is up to you to identify that talent and nurture it.'

'So, Sarah, what have you in mind?' I asked.

'He said he would like a first-verse solo for the big finish.'

Sally looked at me thoughtfully. 'We could do with having a chat with her mother, Jack.'

'I agree,' I said. 'Let's see if we can catch her at the end of school when she picks up Rosie.'

'And what carol were you thinking of, Sarah?' asked Sally.

'This one,' said Sarah. She took some sheet music from her shoulder bag and put it on the desk.

We leaned over and read the title ... 'Silent Night'.

Maggie Sparrow, a slim woman in her twenties with long fair hair and sea-grey eyes, was standing by the school gate when Sally walked across the playground with Rosie. A look of concern crossed her face, but Sally's warm smile put her at ease again.

'Ms Sparrow,' said Sally, 'I've got some good news to share with you about Rosie. Can you spare a few minutes?'

Maggie Sparrow looked puzzled but pleased. 'Of course,' she said.

'Mr Sheffield was hoping to have a word in the school office. Perhaps Rosie could help me clear up in my classroom?'

'Yes, go on, poppet,' said Maggie, 'you go with Mrs Pringle and I'll see you soon.'

Maggie walked into the school office. 'Hello, Mr Sheffield,' she said. She was clearly confused by the invitation.

'Thank you for calling in, Ms Sparrow,' I said, 'and please don't be concerned: it's good news ... in fact, quite *exciting* news.'

'Really?' said Maggie Sparrow, looking relieved.

We chatted for five minutes and I described the events of the day, including the proposal for Rosie to sing a solo.

'So, you can see why we wanted to discuss it with you first,' I said. 'All the children in my class and Mrs Pringle's class are involved and a note will go out to parents tomorrow.'

'Wonderful news, Mr Sheffield,' she said, 'and we're always singing at home. In fact, her father was a good singer...' She stared down at her hands as if it was a painful memory.

Vera had filled in the background long ago. As a teenager in Leeds, Maggie Sparrow was a fan of a local rock band. Rosie was the result of a relationship with the lead singer. There were problems and it hadn't worked out. Eventually she had met a new partner, a drifter who had proved abusive and violent and, two years ago, he had abandoned her and social services had picked up the pieces.

However, Maggie and her daughter were now happily settled in one of the old rented dwellings in Cold Kirkby, a tiny hamlet between Ragley and Kirkby Steepleton which was just in our catchment area. Each day they arrived at school on William Featherstone's Reliance bus and Maggie continued on to Easington, where she had regular part-time employment in the library. Life had moved on from the dark days of her past. 'My mother deserted me and put me into foster care. I don't want that to happen to my Rosie,' she had said when she first arrived at Ragley.

Now Maggie stared out of the window. 'She's always been a determined child ... just like her father.' She sighed and smiled. 'I suppose she's like me, nursing an unspoken need in her heart.'

I was captivated by her honest flow of words, thoughts that came from the very soul. She got up to leave and we shook hands. I had always admired this young woman. She bristled with fierce determination, and she exuded the strength of a mother.

Maggie collected Rosie and as they walked down the drive hand in hand she looked at her watch. It would be half an hour before the next bus. 'Let's call in at Mrs Poole's house,' she suggested. This had become a regular event, particularly as Jemima Poole and Rosie were best friends.

'Jemima said her great-grandma had died, Mummy,' said Rosie.

'I know. Mrs Poole told me,' replied Maggie.

There was a thoughtful pause. 'Where did her great-grandma go, Mummy?'

'She went to heaven, my poppet,' said Maggie softly.

'Why?'

'Because she was poorly.'

'How did she get to heaven?'

'Jesus took her.'

'Can we go to see her?'

'No ... she's sleeping now.'

'When she wakes up, will she be better?'

'Yes, she will.'

'Well, that's all right then.'

Maggie smiled. 'I heard you were singing today.'

'Yes, Mummy, a tall lady came to hear the choir.'

'And did you sing well?'

'I think so, Mummy ... because she smiled at me.'

When I got home Beth was in the kitchen using her Moulinex Multi Chef – an inspired gift for Christmas last year – to prepare some homemade carrot and parsnip soup.

I put my arms around her and nuzzled her neck. 'That smells good,' I said.

'Me or the soup?' she asked with a tired smile.

'How's John?' I asked.

Beth cut a crusty slice off the fresh loaf, spread a generous portion of Lurpak and offered it to me. 'He's asleep – nodded off after his tea.'

'I'll pop up and see him,' I said, biting hungrily into the fresh bread.

Beth tugged my sleeve. 'So how did *your* day go?'

'Perfect,' I said and hurried up the stairs.

John was sleeping peacefully and I leaned over and kissed his soft cheek. He would soon be too big for his cot. Not for the first time it occurred to me that children proved expensive.

When I came down two steaming bowls of soup were on the table.

'Sounds as if you had a good day,' said Beth.

117

I smiled. 'Guess what?'

Beth looked up. 'Go on, then – I know you're dying to tell me.'

I picked up my spoon. 'The new music adviser came to Ragley today.'

'And?'

'We're going to be on television!'

A mile away the hamlet of Cold Kirkby comprised six terraced dwellings and a few farm buildings. Maggie Sparrow had worked hard during the past two years and the house was snug and warm, with cheerful curtains, simple furniture and a warm log fire.

After supper, Maggie had read a story to Rosie, watched her fall asleep and was sitting downstairs when the telephone rang. She was expecting the call – Rosie's father, Mark, ringing from Leeds.

The conversation ebbed and flowed in a stilted way until they finally reached the subject of Rosie.

'Mark, you *should* see her.'

'Ah jus' didn't think it was fair 'avin' *two* fathers in 'er life.'

'The guy's gone now and he'll never come back.'

'Ah 'ope not.'

'It's a fact, Mark. I made a mistake and, if you recall, things weren't good between us.'

'We were young.'

'Why don't you come and see her?'

'Well, ah 'aven't wanted to confuse 'er.'

'You're still using that as an excuse.'

'Well ... ah might come.'

'I'm not telling her you *might* come, Mark. That

wouldn't be fair.'

'Ah'm not sure, Maggie ... she might not want t'see me.'

'Mark ... she's saved all your letters and post-cards. She *does* want to see you, and I don't mind, really I don't.'

'But ... what if she doesn't *like* me?'

'She will, Mark. Don't be scared of coming to see her.' There was a long silence.

'Ah'll see, Maggie.'

Sally had enjoyed tea with her babysitter and at six thirty her daughter was ready for bed. Grace Alexandra Pringle, a bonny, ginger-haired little girl, was now three years and nine months old. She was shaking her wristband of bells and sing-ing 'Three Blind Mice' when Sally's husband, Colin, walked in. As a reformed smoker he was sucking a sherbet lemon as if his life depended on it.

'Hello, my little princess,' he said to Grace, picking her up.

He kissed Sally on the cheek, then stopped and looked more closely at her. 'I know that look,' he said. 'Come on – out with it!'

Sally smiled. 'I had a surprise today,' she said.

Colin was curious. 'And are you going to tell me about it?'

'Let's just say that, very soon ... you'll be buy-ing me a new dress.'

Chapter Six

A Date for Nora

County Hall sent the document 'A Vision for the implementation of Computer Technology within a Core Curriculum for Small Schools in North Yorkshire' to all village schools in the Easington area and requested responses from all headteachers. Preparations were made for the PTA Quiz Night in the school hall tomorrow evening at 7.00 p.m.

Extract from the Ragley School Logbook:
Friday, 30 November 1984

Nora Pratt looked thoughtfully in the mirror. It was early morning on Friday, 30 November, and a special day awaited the owner of the village Coffee Shop. Nora had a date.

However, first of all she had decided to do something about her sagging facial muscles. Her face looked lined and tired. Since Little Malcolm and Dorothy had moved into the bedroom next to hers, their energetic and vociferous lovemaking had necessitated the purchase of earplugs from Eugene Scrimshaw's pharmacy. Even so, a good night's sleep was a luxury she no longer enjoyed.

Since reading an article in last month's *Woman's Realm* magazine while in Diane's Hair Salon, she was determined to do a series of exercises every day. The first was to blow gently

120

as if on a dandelion clock. This was not difficult; however, the second task was a little more involved. The intention here was to stretch the mouth and surrounding muscles and it involved repeating the sounds 'Oooh, Aaarh, Eeee' at regular intervals. Little Malcolm and Dorothy often wondered what Nora got up to when she made these apparently erotic sounds in her newly installed en suite, but thought it better not to ask.

Finally, Nora brushed her teeth with Gordon Moores toothpaste for a brighter, whiter smile'. At least that's what it said on the packet, *and they should know,* she thought. Nora stared at her reflection. It was a long time since she had been out with a man and she wanted to look her best.

It was morning break when I walked into the school office and Vera had just completed her late-dinner-money register.

'Soon there won't be any more of these,' she said wistfully, taking a pound note out of her metal lock-up money box, holding it up to the light by the office window and staring at it.

'Sad in a way,' I said, 'and more holes in my pockets from all the loose change.'

'I wonder where it will all end,' she murmured as she put the pound note back in the box. As usual, she would complete the dinner register in her immaculate cursive writing and deposit the money in the local bank in Easington.

Chancellor Nigel Lawson had recently announced that the English green pound note was due to be phased out after one hundred and fifty years. The pound note had replaced the gold

121

sovereign during the First World War, but it had served its purpose and men in sharp suits on the recent television news had informed us that the new pound coins introduced last year would last fifty times longer.

'The end of an era,' said Vera as she closed the lid and locked the box. 'And I've put a copy of the reminder to parents about the Quiz Night on your desk, Mr Sheffield.'

'Thanks, Vera,' I said and picked it up. It read:

PTA Quiz Night
Saturday, 1 December, 7.00 p.m.
Teams of four.
£2.00 per team.
Tea & Cake on sale.
Raffle.

Over coffee, I chatted with our supply teacher, Miss Flint, who was working in Class 3 during the morning session. Sally had gone to York for a meeting with Sarah Mancini regarding the *Christmas Voices* television programme. Miss Flint was a loyal colleague and a dear friend of Vera. She regarded herself as 'old school'.

Earlier, I had called into her classroom to check all was well. The children were working their way through a mathematics test in complete silence. Their faces were the picture of concentration as they completed a series of mental arithmetic problems. In Miss Flint's classroom, a calculator was never in sight.

Meanwhile, in Nora's Coffee Shop the lunchtime

rush hadn't yet begun and Nora and Dorothy were chatting by the Breville sandwich toaster.

'So what's the panto this year, Nora?' asked Dorothy. Nora always had the star part in the annual New Year's Eve village pantomime on account of her having had a non-speaking part in *Crossroads* many years before.

'It were either t'*Sound o' Music,* Dowothy, or *Dick Whittington,*' said Nora.

'Ah like t'*Sound o' Music,*' said Dorothy, 'wi' all them nuns an' leather shorts an' mountains.'

'Pwoblem were a wimple,' explained Nora, 'so we picked *Dick Whittington.*'

'A wimple?' said Dorothy, puzzled. 'Couldn't y'rub some cream on?'

'No, y'soft ha'po'th, it's what y'wear on yer 'ead an' it'll spoil me 'airdo.'

Dorothy nodded in acknowledgement and began to sway in time to Nik Kershaw's 'I Won't Let The Sun Go Down On Me' on the jukebox. 'What y'wearin' tonight, Nora?' she asked.

Nora picked up a copy of an old *Cosmopolitan* magazine from behind the counter and pointed to a photograph. 'It sez 'ere, Dowothy, "the gwace of lace", an' all y'do is…' Nora read it out loud, '"pin a piece of pwetty lacy matewial on to y'plungin' V-shape neckline".'

'What for, Nora?' asked Dorothy, who considered it would hide one of Nora's best assets, namely her substantial bust.

Nora studied the text carefully. 'It sez "for that sexy touch of class".'

'It'll look lovely, Nora,' said Dorothy. 'So … do y'think you'll 'it it off?'

123

'Ah dunno, Dowothy. 'E sounds t'be weally bwainy an' ah'm, well, y'know … av'wage.'

Dorothy looked down at the short, plump Coffee Shop owner with deep affection. 'No y'not, Nora. You're much better than that. An' in any case, 'e'll prob'ly like other things about you, such as y'personality,' she said generously.

Nora pondered this for a moment. 'Mebbe y'wight,' she said thoughtfully. 'They do say opposites attwact.'

After Mrs Mapplebeck's warming and welcome school dinner of stew and dumplings, Tom and I went into the office to complete an important task.

'Thanks for your help with this, Tom,' I said. A weighty document had arrived from County Hall with an equally weighty title: namely, 'A Vision for the Implementation of Computer Technology within a Core Curriculum for Small Schools in North Yorkshire'. The Education Committee had demanded a prompt response and it had proved a difficult task. It was clear that computer technology was advancing at a remarkable rate and would play a significant part in future curriculum planning.

By 12.45 p.m. it was finished and ready for Vera to post on her way home. There was time for a breath of fresh air before afternoon school, so we put on our coats and walked down the drive to the school gate.

'I'm pleased about the Computer Club,' I said. 'Great idea.' Tom had started an after-school club and it was proving very popular.

124

He gave a sheepish grin. 'Just trying to keep up with the children, Jack,' he said. 'There's at least half a dozen of them who have got their own computer at home now.'

I leaned on the wrought-iron gate and shook my head in disbelief. On a teacher's salary I couldn't imagine owning one of my own. 'By the way, Tom,' I said, 'Vera took a call from County Hall today about the school getting a *colour* monitor.'

His eyes lit up. 'That would add a new dimension, Jack ... and I guess the black-and-white ones will soon be phased out anyway.'

New technology was moving so fast that it was hard to keep up.

We stood there in silence for a while as a cold wind sprang up and rustled the branches of the trees above our heads. It was a morning when the sun had forsaken the land and dark clouds hung like a mantle of gloom over the plain of York.

'Penny for them, Tom,' I said quietly.

He looked up nervously with the pale shadow of a smile. 'Sorry, Jack ... miles away.'

'So what's on your mind?' I asked.

There was a long silence. 'A few problems.'

I sipped my coffee and looked out at the excited children running and sliding on the frozen playground. 'Can I help?'

He breathed out long and slow. 'I was just thinking I'd made a mess of things.'

I looked at him; he was clearly troubled. 'We're presumably not talking about *work*, because all your children in Class 2 are making terrific progress.'

He sighed. 'Thanks, Jack ... but it's not work. It's life.'

'Life?'

He looked me square in the eyes. 'And Laura.'

'I guessed as much.'

Above our heads a solitary rook cawed in the skeletal branches of the high horse chestnut trees. It was a sonorous, brittle cry ... the sound of winter.

'She's gone now, Tom. Time to close that chapter in your life.'

'And move on,' he added.

'Move on?'

'Yes, Jack, a fresh start. Get my life back together again.'

'You mean leave Ragley? You've only been here a year.'

He shifted his feet. Anxiety was etched on his face. 'They are still just thoughts, Jack ... nothing more at present.'

'I understand,' I said. I glanced at my watch. 'Time for the bell.'

He nodded and straightened up. I put my hand on his shoulder. 'Let's talk again when you feel ready. Just don't do anything in haste.'

He nodded but said nothing, and we both walked slowly back into school.

It was early afternoon when Dorothy took over in the Coffee Shop and Nora went next door for her appointment with Diane the hairdresser.

''Ello, Nora,' said Diane. ''Ow's Dorothy?'

'Weally 'appy,' said Nora as she settled in the seat in front of the large mirror. 'She's walking about like love's young dweam.'

Diane nodded knowingly. 'Well, that's good to 'ear, Nora, 'cause we both know she's not 'xactly sharpest knife in t'drawer. In fac', las' time she were in, she thought t'capital o' New Zealand were Bishop Auckland. But ah'll say this for 'er – she's picked a winner wi' Little Malcolm.'

'Vewy twue,' said Nora.

''E's 'onest as t'day is long,' said Diane, a far-away look in her eyes, 'an' 'e'll never be un-faithful,' she added with feeling.

'So ... what's it t'be, Nora?' she went on, staring in the mirror at Nora's tangled hair, which resembled a rook's nest in a hurricane.

Nora passed over a copy of Dorothy's *Smash Hits* magazine and pointed to a group photograph of the stars of *Fame*. 'Ah fancy an Iwene Cawa, please, Diane,' she said confidently. 'Ah want t'look special.'

''Ow come?' asked Diane.

Nora took a deep breath. 'Ah've gorra date.'

'A date?' said Diane. She stared into the mirror. This really was news.

'Wi' a man,' added Nora for good measure.

'A man?'

'Yes, an' 'e sounds jus' wight,' said Nora.

'Why's that then?'

Nora smiled contentedly. ''E's single, fifty-thwee an' weally bwainy.'

'What's 'is name?'

'Tywone Cwabtwee.'

'Ah like Tyrone ... very manly,' mused Diane.

'Ah'm meeting 'im outside Wowntwee's t'night at seven o'clock,' said Nora.

'So, what's 'e look like, this Tyrone?' asked Diane.

'Ah don't know,' admitted Nora with a first hint of concern.

'So 'ow did y'get a date with 'im?'

'From that Dateline in t'*Easington 'Ewald.'*

'Y'mean that computer test?' asked Diane. 'Ah saw that.' In fact, Diane had considered filling in the questionnaire but, as every man she had ever dated turned out to be an unfaithful two-faced so-and-so, she had decided to give it a miss.

'Yes,' said Nora, 'an' ah'm weally excited.'

Diane nodded thoughtfully, walked away to the shelf unit by the window and checked the box of giant plastic rollers. It was common knowledge that, many years ago, Nora's previous and only boyfriend had been Frank. She had loved him but he had left her for someone else.

Diane was determined to give her neighbour the best Irene Cara she could possibly manage. It was clearly a big night for Nora and the Ragley hairdresser was determined to do her bit.

Meanwhile, in the village Post Office, the post-mistress, Amelia Duff, also had a date. There were no customers, so she popped into her tiny kitchen.

She had purchased a copy of *Woman's Realm* for twenty-four pence from Prudence Golightly and was studying the recipe for Marrow au Gratin. Amelia was making a special dish for Ted the postman. She was sure he was building up towards discussing marriage. Making love with him on her double bed after the second delivery on a

128

Friday was the highlight of her week. However, they didn't exactly talk a lot. A Friday-evening candlelit meal might encourage the quiet postman to open up. The fact that they had grown the marrow together had proved in itself a labour of love.

As a young woman, Amelia had read the novels of D. H. Lawrence and often wondered about the earthy embrace of a gamekeeper. However, the Ragley village postman had eventually proved just as intoxicating. As she grated the large slice of Wensleydale cheese her thoughts wandered and she smiled.

At the end of the school day I was reading the J. R. R. Tolkien classic *The Hobbit* to my class and they sat there in wonderment. I hoped that some of them would be inspired sufficiently to read *The Lord of the Rings* trilogy for themselves in the coming years. However, when the bell rang Charlotte Ackroyd had other things on her mind. 'Mo Hartley's coming to our house tonight, Mr Sheffield,' she said. 'We're gonna make some parkin pigs and then watch *Blue Peter* at five o'clock.'

When you're ten years old life is for living.

Vera popped her head round the door. 'Mrs Phillips to see you, Mr Sheffield.'

Staff Nurse Sue Phillips, a tall, blue-eyed blonde, was waiting in the entrance hall holding a large box. Sue was the chair of the Parent Teacher Association and a wonderful supporter of Ragley School.

'All sorted for tomorrow evening,' she said breathlessly. Sue was always in a hurry and lived her life at breakneck speed. 'I've got Albert Jenkins to be question master.'

'Perfect,' I said. Apart from being a school governor, Albert was probably the most knowledgeable resident in the village.

'And look at this,' said Sue. 'I've just bought it in York. It's a Trivial Pursuit game. It's all the rage. Apparently everyone is buying one for Christmas.' She put the box on the old pine table. The label read 'Genus Edition'.

She took out a stiff cardboard container that resembled a box of After Eight mints but was filled with small cards. 'There are six categories of questions,' she explained. 'Geography, Entertainment, History, Art & Literature, Science & Nature and Sport & Leisure. It's a board game, but we only need these question-and-answer cards, so Albert can use them for the quiz.'

'Well done, Sue,' I said.

'We've got posters in the High Street and teams can be two couples, so we should have a full house. Members of the committee are bringing raffle prizes and I've spread the word that all the proceeds will go towards new books for the school library.'

'Brilliant,' I said, admiring her energy. *If you want something doing ask a busy woman,* Vera had once said.

Sue glanced at her watch. 'Must rush, Jack ... on duty in York,' she said and hurried out.

It was 6.30 p.m. and Nora was ready. Dorothy had inspected the dubious lace attachment, hastily stitched to Nora's best dress, and Little Malcolm had insisted on driving her into York. As the man of the house he felt it was his responsibility and, in any case, Dorothy was adamant she wanted to be one of the first to hear about what the mysterious stranger was like.

'Where shall ah drop you off, Nora?' he asked.

'Wowntwee's Theat'e, please, Malcolm – next to t'factowy. Tywone is tekkin' me t'see t'Opewatic Society. They're doin' *Songs from the Shows*.'

'Ow will y'know it's 'im?' said Little Malcolm as they approached the local chocolate factory and the smell of cocoa drifted in the air.

''E'll be weawing a *wed* wose and ah'm weawing a *white* wose,' said Nora.

Tyrone Crabtree was standing outside the entrance to Rowntree's Theatre, looking expectantly at the traffic coming in from the north of the city. He was a short, tubby, balding man with a Bobby Charlton comb-over and a checked sports coat that should have come with a government health warning. The knife-edge creases in his cavalry twills, black shoes polished to a mirror shine and bright red tie with the yellow initials RQM completed the ensemble. Now in his fifties, he had finally begun to wonder about companionship.

He spent most of his time reading, particularly the *Encyclopædia Britannica*, and, of course, watching every *Mastermind* programme. He recalled three lady friends, as he called them, in his life. Two of the relationships had lasted less than a week. Michelle, the usherette from the Odeon Cinema, said he didn't come up to expectations in the daylight and Mabel, one of the secretaries in the accounts department at Rowntree's, told him he was utterly boring. The liaison that did last was with Audrey Gawthorpe, who worked in the reference library in York. Audrey was an authority on the history of the French Revolution. It was her fascination with guillotines and whether a severed head retained the capacity to utter a last word that finally persuaded Tyrone to have his library card stamped elsewhere.

Little Malcolm pulled up just past the theatre where the road widened out before the railway bridge and looked in his nearside wing mirror. 'That's 'im, Nora,' he said. ''E looks smart.'

'An' on t'questionnaire it said 'e's two inches taller than me,' said Nora.

Little Malcolm did a quick calculation and beamed. He was an inch taller than Nora's new boyfriend. For a vertically challenged binman this was manna from heaven. 'Looks all reight t'me, Nora,' he said then drove off back to Ragley.

Nora touched her white rose and smiled.

'Hello, Nora,' said Tyrone. 'Thank you for coming. These Smarties are for you. I didn't want anything too ostentatious with us going to the theatre,' he added.

I like a man who uses big words, thought Nora. 'Thank you, Tywone,' she said. 'That's weally kind.'

Tyrone noticed Nora's difficulty with the letter R but thought it wise not to mention it. After all, *not many of us are perfect,* he thought.

'I like y'wed tie,' said Nora.

'I'm the Rowntree's Quiz Master,' said Tyrone proudly and pointed to the initials. 'One of the

132

managers had this made up for me. He supports my monthly quiz night for the retired employees of Rowntree's and provides the prizes.' Tyrone was suddenly animated. 'We had a bumper box of Lion bars last month ... mis-shapes, mind you, but still – it's the thought that counts.'

He's intelligent as well, thought Nora and she smiled.

She was still smiling when Little Malcolm collected her from outside the theatre at 10.15 p.m.

Early on Saturday morning in Ragley High Street, Harold Bustard looked at Ben Roberts riding past on his Raleigh BMX Burner and wished he still believed in Father Christmas and recalled a time when Christmas wishes came true.

Ben pulled up at the kerb. "Ello, 'Arold, what's matter? Y'look fed up.'

Harold sighed deeply. 'My girlfriend doesn't like me.'

'What's 'er name?' asked Ben, suddenly full of interest.

'Ah don't know,' said Harold mournfully. 'She goes t'Morton School an' she comes t'Brownies in Ragley ... an' she won't tell me 'er name.'

Ben was a good-hearted little boy and he recognized a soul in torment. 'D'you want to 'ave a go on m'bike?' he offered.

'Cor, yes please,' said Harold.

Ben dismounted. 'Jump on an' ah'll give you a push,' he said. 'In fac', let's go in t'schoolyard an' do wheelies.'

Harold set off with Ben in hot pursuit. Thoughts of girls were forgotten. After all, *what do girls know*

133

about bikes? thought Harold.

Beth had fastened John in his car seat, put two large shopping bags in the boot of her VW Beetle and we set off for Ragley to do our weekly shopping. Loyalty to the local shopkeepers prevented us going to the new supermarket on the ring road. Even so, we were beginning to feel the days of our village shops were numbered.

As we approached the school car park Harold Bustard appeared, cycling for all he was worth, with Ben Roberts running behind. They disappeared up School View, so all was quiet when we drove through the school gate. Tendrils of mist hung like ghostly cobwebs in the bare branches of the horse chestnut trees and behind them, against a wolf-grey sky, the school lay still like a house of secrets.

'I'll go to the General Stores if you post this parcel to Laura,' said Beth.

It was a Christmas present for her sister in Australia. *Post early for Christmas* it said on the poster on the door of the Post Office. Betty Buttle and Margery Ackroyd were walking out as I went in. 'She's gettin' a bit scatterbrained is that Miss Duff,' said Betty in frustration. 'She got m'savins book mixed up.'

'Ah blame that postman,' said Margery knowingly. ''E's turned 'er 'ead.'

This sounded decidedly painful, but I made no comment and hurried into the Post Office to get the parcel weighed.

As it disappeared behind the wire grille I wondered what Laura might be doing for Christmas... Perhaps a beach barbecue with her new friends, whoever they may be.

Meanwhile, Nora had invited Tyrone to sample the delights of her Coffee Shop and he was standing at the counter sorting out some change. 'I save fivepenny coins in my Coronation mug,' he said proudly. 'It used to be threepenny bits ... I was sad to see them go,' he added forlornly.

''Ere's y'fwothy coffee, Tywone,' said Nora.

A poster advertising the Ragley Amateur Dramatic Society's annual pantomime, *Dick Whittington and His Cat,* was on the wall behind the counter.

'Ah'm playing t'lead wole,' said Nora proudly.

'That's wonderful,' said Tyrone. 'I can't wait to see it.'

Nora frowned. 'Ah'm weally wowwied, Tywone, 'bout wemembewing m'lines.'

'Nora, it takes more muscles to frown than to smile,' said Tyrone knowingly, 'so smile.'

Nora smiled.

'We're *synoptic,*' said Tyrone with gravitas.

'Weally?' said Nora.

'Yes, my dear,' said Tyrone.

Nora looked puzzled. 'But what does it mean, Tywone?'

Tyrone raised his cup of coffee as if proposing a toast. 'It means we see with the same eyes.'

Nora's eyes were like saucers. 'Oooh, Tywone,' she said breathlessly.

Nora was not a sports fan, but she always tried to take her Saturday break when *Grandstand* was introduced by her heart-throb, Des Lynam, on BBC1. She loved his sexy moustache, second only to Omar Sharif's, and when he kissed her in her dreams ... it tickled.

However, Nora's thoughts were elsewhere. When Tyrone had heard about the quiz night at the school his eyes had lit up. Malcolm and Dorothy had agreed to join them to make up a team of four. Life had suddenly become exciting for Nora and she switched off Des Lynam in full flow.

After all, there was a *new* man in her life.

Albert Jenkins was one of the wisest men I knew. He had always done his best for the school and the village community and had taken over as the bellringer at St Mary's Church following the death of Archibald Pike. Ragley born and bred, and now in his seventies, he was well respected and the perfect quiz master. The school hall was full by the time he was testing the microphone.

He looked at the school clock. Albert liked punctuality.

'Well ... it's seven o'clock, Albert,' I said.

'Procrastination is the thief of time, Jack,' he said with a gentle smile.

'Charles Dickens?' I ventured, thinking hard and recalling my English studies at college.

'Well done,' he said. 'In *David Copperfield* ... but originally the eighteenth-century poet Edward Young.'

It occurred to me that I could learn a lot from this modest, well-educated man who ploughed a quiet and lonely furrow through this life.

'Pity that's not one of the questions,' I said with a grin.

Sue Phillips introduced the evening and I sat down with my team. Ruby's daughter, Natasha, was babysitting for us and Beth and I were joined by Sally Pringle and her husband Colin.

'I hope we don't come last, Jack,' said Sally, looking around at all the other eager teams, pencils poised and waiting for the first question. 'We'll never live it down.'

'Number one is a Science and Nature question,' said Albert. 'Who invented the arch?'

Sally smiled. 'The Romans,' she said with confidence. Around the hall discussions broke out and the first heated argument of the evening began.

'Number two is a Sport and Leisure question,' said Albert. 'What board game is called "checkers" in North America?'

'Draughts,' whispered Colin.

'That's right,' said Beth and, as I had been voted to be team scribe, I wrote 'Draughts' next to No. 2.

'Geography now,' continued Albert. 'Where is the Marianas Trench?'

'No idea,' I said. There was silence. Everyone shook their heads. I looked around the room. No one was responding with the exception of Nora's new boyfriend, Tyrone, on the next table, who had been welcomed with significant interest by the other villagers. 'I heard him say "The Pacific Ocean",' I said.

'We can't put that down,' said Beth. 'It's cheating.'

137

Reluctantly I left it blank.

'Art and Literature,' said Albert. 'Where was King Arthur's Court?'

'Camelot,' said Beth and the two women exchanged a smile.

And so it went on. Nora's boyfriend was a little distracting as, after each question, he not only appeared to know the answer but also provided an encyclopaedic summary of additional facts.

We did reasonably well. Sally knew that the Paul McCartney album cover on which the actor James Coburn appeared was *Band on the Run* and I knew that 'Agatha Christie' was the answer to 'What mystery writer's disappearance in 1926 prompted a nationwide search?'

Half an hour later we reached the final two questions.

On Nora's table Tyrone looked quietly confident and Nora was proud he knew all the answers.

'Science and Nature,' announced Albert. 'What's the best way to pick up a rabbit?'

Tyrone went grey. He knew everything about rabbit feeding habits, burrow-engineering and had seen *Watership Down* three times, but he had never handled a rabbit.

Little Malcolm smiled. 'Y'pick 'em up by t'scruff of its neck,' he said. 'Not by t'ears, like them magicians.'

'Well done, Malcolm,' said Nora.

'Y'can rely on my Malcolm for t'difficult ones,' said Dorothy.

Malcolm beamed. He loved it when Dorothy said *my* Malcolm.

Tyrone wrote down the answer, much relieved.

'Last question,' said Albert. 'What did the Wicked Witch of the West write in the sky over the Emerald City?'

Tyrone was silent. He didn't know the answer.

Dorothy suddenly became animated. 'It were "Surrender Dorothy",' she said. 'Nora was in t'*Wizard of Oz* in t'las' panto an' she shouted it out loud. Ah remember 'cause it were my name.'

Tyrone felt as if he had just won the Pools as he wrote down the answer and Malcolm looked at the woman he loved with pride.

Sue Phillips collected all the answer sheets and we enjoyed tea and cake while the marking was completed.

Finally Sue thanked everyone for their support and announced the results. My team got a cheer for coming third and won a bag of KitKat bars, provided by Ruby. Vera and Joseph had teamed up with the doctor and his wife and they were delighted to come second, but not too thrilled with their prize – a bottle of Joseph's homemade wine. 'And the winning team, to receive this magnificent hamper donated by Prudence Golightly,' announced Sue, 'is the one led by the owner of Ragley's favourite Coffee Shop – Nora Pratt.'

There was tumultuous applause for a popular winner.

Raffle prizes were distributed and, much to everyone's amusement, Vera won the Barbie's Mansion that Mrs Ackroyd had cleared out of her loft that morning.

The crowd dispersed, we locked up the school and Tyrone walked Nora back to the Coffee Shop.

'So what's your job at Wowntwee's Factowy?'

asked Nora.

'I'm in charge of cardboard boxes – thousands of them.'

'Weally?'

'Yes, Nora, it's an important job,' replied Tyrone.

'An' you've got a good memowy, Tywone,' said Nora. 'You must do a lot o' weading.'

Tyrone pulled himself up to his full height. 'I'm known in the packaging department as a master of trivia,' he said proudly.

'Twivia?'

'Yes, Nora,' said Tyrone, 'but it's *interesting*.'

'Intewestin' twivia?'

'Yes, Nora ... an' ah want *you* t'share my world of trivia with me.'

'Oooh, Tywone,' said Nora. Her cheeks flushed and she felt like a teenager once again.

Chapter Seven

Little Sparrow

All the children in Classes 3 and 4, including the school choir and recorder group, travelled by coach with Mrs Pringle and Mr Sheffield to St Michael le Belfrey Church in York for the television broadcast recording of Christmas Voices, *a celebration of music and carols. Miss Flint and Mrs Forbes-Kitchener accompanied the party.*

Extract from the Ragley School Logbook:
Friday, 7 December 1984

It was early morning on Friday, 7 December and, outside the bedroom window of Bilbo Cottage, the world looked different. The first snow of winter had settled on the distant land and the ploughed fields had been transformed into a washboard of smooth white folds. Nature had gripped the frozen earth in an iron fist and no life or sound penetrated its hardness. It would be a tough journey to school on this special day, but it had to be made. A television recording in York awaited the children and in Ragley village the excitement was building.

Beth and I were busy with our usual routine and John was sitting in his high chair polishing off a hearty breakfast of juice, cereal and buttered toast soldiers. At sixteen and a half months our

141

son was a sturdy and energetic toddler and he yelled 'Ma-ma' and 'Da-da' with insistent regularity. Beth tried to eat her bowl of porridge at the same time and I sipped a steaming mug of black tea while jotting down a few notes for the day ahead.

'Good luck, Jack,' said Beth with a tired smile. Her workload was beginning to tell and I thought that Christmas couldn't come soon enough to give her a well-earned break.

I washed the breakfast dishes as Beth put on her coat and scarf in the hallway. There were curve-stitching patterns of frost on the windowpanes. 'Drive carefully, Beth,' I shouted from the kitchen.

'Deke Ramsbottom will have been out with his snowplough, Jack, so don't worry.'

After she had wrapped John up like an Eskimo and strapped him into the child seat in her car she hurried back to give me a reassuring peck on the cheek. 'Hope it goes well, Jack.'

'Love you,' I said, '...and keep safe.'

I felt that familiar sadness as they drove off.

Soon it was my turn and I breathed on my key and inserted it into the frozen lock of my Morris Minor Traveller. My trusty little car, although beginning to show signs of age, never seemed to let me down and soon I was on the back road from Kirkby Steepleton. The world was silent and cold, and a patchwork of bitter snow covered the hedgerows on this bleak morning. As I entered Ragley village I peered through my misty windscreen, pulled up on to the forecourt of Pratt's Garage and stopped by the single pump.

Victor Pratt, elder brother of Nora and Timothy, lumbered out covered in grease and oil and wearing a multicoloured balaclava, presumably knitted by a colour-blind aunty keen to use up the leftovers in her spare-wool basket.

'Fill her up please, Victor,' I said cheerily, hoping to lighten the aura of gloom that always seemed to surround our local garage owner and car mechanic.

'M'chilblains are back, Mr Sheffield,' he said wearily as he removed my petrol cap and shoved in the nozzle of the pump. Then he rested a greasy, oil-covered hand on the window and I pretended not to notice. 'They come ev'ry winter,' he added forlornly, '...ah blame t'government.'

I was curious to ask him why but refrained, as I knew it would provoke a lengthy diatribe regarding his recent ailments. He glanced down at his steel-capped footwear. 'An' bunions in y'boots is no fun either,' he added as a parting shot.

In Ragley High Street I pulled up outside Prudence Golightly's General Stores & Newsagent. The frost-hardened snow crunched beneath my feet as I crossed the forecourt and my breath steamed in the freezing air. The villagers hurried by, wrapped in scarves and heavy coats. Winter had come to Ragley village and plumes of woodsmoke from a hundred log fires drifted into a steel-grey sky that promised more snow.

The bell over the door jingled cheerily as I walked in and the diminutive Miss Golightly stepped up on to a higher wooden step behind the counter to serve me at something of a comparable height. 'Good morning, Mr Sheffield,'

143

she said brightly and handed me my newspaper. 'A little chilly this morning.'

I had grown used to the tough locals who didn't seem to feel the cold. 'Good morning, Miss Golightly,' I replied with difficulty. My jaw seemed to have frozen during the short walk from the car.

Miss Golightly was animated. 'Everyone is talking about the choir being recorded for the television, Mr Sheffield. How exciting! You must call in tomorrow and tell me how it went.'

'It will be a pleasure, Miss Golightly,' I said.

'And Jeremy will be watching, of course, when the broadcast goes out,' she added, glancing up at her lifelong friend.

'Good morning, Jeremy,' I said. It always pleased Miss Golightly when her customers treated Ragley's best-dressed teddy bear as something other than an inanimate object. He was sitting on his usual shelf next to a tin of loose-leaf Lyons Tea and an old advertisement for Hudson's Soap and Carter's Little Liver Pills. Prudence took great pride in making sure he was always well turned out. Today, appropriately, he was dressed in a purple choir robe with a frilly white collar and on his feet he wore smart black leather shoes. 'Jeremy wanted to be part of the occasion,' explained Prudence. 'He was thrilled with his new outfit.' She looked up at him with deep affection. 'I think he's a baritone,' she mused.

I smiled at this remarkable lady and wondered about her life. The slightly stooped figure was that of a tiny grey-haired lady, but the eyes were those of a young woman, bright, alive ... and still in love. For Prudence, the memories of that magical time

144

in 1940 were still sharp and clear: a clasping of hands, a walk in a Kentish orchard, a seat of tree roots and a final conversation. The young Spitfire pilot had never returned ... but he lived on.

For Prudence, years would come and go but Jeremy's words would last for ever, undiminished, set in stone.

Ragley's favourite bear wasn't the only one sporting a new outfit. When I arrived at school Anne and Vera were in the entrance hall admiring Sally's new dress.

'Terrific!' exclaimed Anne.

'I thought I'd treat myself to something special for the occasion,' said Sally.

'It's just right, Sally,' said Vera, 'absolutely perfect.'

This was the first time I could recall Vera praising Sally's very individual dress sense. The long velvet skirt, flattering with unpressed pleats, plus a matching round-necked bolero bound with a matching satin trim, was just right for her television debut. The plain blouse with baggy sleeves and neat cuffs completed the ensemble to perfection.

'So elegant,' added Anne approvingly. 'You really look the part.'

'Classical – and yet artistic, with a certain *joie de vivre*,' said Vera thoughtfully.

Sally was moved by the unexpected praise and she gave her a hug. 'Thanks, Vera.'

'It's *your* day, Sally,' said Vera, 'so *live* it.'

No one mentioned my outfit.

I had put on my best suit for the occasion and

my old St John's College tie. However, I was relieved it wouldn't be *me* in front of the camera. My grey three-piece was beginning to look a little baggy around the knees and threadbare at the cuffs. Any links with sartorial elegance were tenuous to say the least.

During morning assembly the children were excited and those in my class and Sally's had all dressed for the occasion. They looked smart in their school uniform of blue polo shirt, V-neck sweater, with a grey skirt for the girls and trousers for the boys. Their faces were well scrubbed, many of the girls wore pretty ribbons in their hair, shoes had been polished and, surprisingly, Damian Brown appeared at long last to have discovered the customary use of a handkerchief.

Sally had restrung her guitar and the first carol seemed to be going well until I heard Billy Ricketts recalling his alternative version. He was singing 'While shepherds washed their socks by night' and I frowned in his direction. He responded with an impish grin and I had to look down at my carol sheet to avoid smiling.

When all the children had settled and were sitting cross-legged on the floor, I outlined the arrangements for the day. 'Classes 3 and 4 will leave by coach from outside school at 12.45 p.m., and I'm pleased to say Miss Flint and Mrs Forbes-Kitchener will be coming along to support.'

The careful supervision of the children in York was paramount and two extra adults were required for such a large party, particularly for our walk from the coach to the church and back again.

'Remember, boys and girls, you are Ragley School *on display* so you must be on your *best behaviour.*' The children nodded as if to say *we've heard it all before.* 'And, while I'm away, Mrs Grainger will be in charge, supported by Mr Dalton.'

Tom suddenly smiled and whispered to Anne, 'That makes me Acting Deputy Head for the afternoon,' and throughout the morning he kept reminding us of the fact.

Joseph Evans had called in to wish us luck, but also to take Class 2 for a religious education lesson. The theme was 'Prayers' and this promoted some interesting discussion at the end.

The six- and seven-year-olds began to chatter.

'What is it, Zoe?' asked Joseph.

Little Zoe Book looked puzzled. 'Please, Mr Evans – why do we *have* to pray?' she asked politely.

'So we can talk to God,' said Joseph.

Scott Higginbottom put up his hand. 'But, Sir … why can't we use t'telephone?' he asked.

Joseph realized he was having another of his alternative universe experiences. For a moment he was lost for words.

More conversations broke out. 'You'd think that God would have telephones in heaven,' said Jeremy Urquhart.

'Stand t'reason,' said Katie Icklethwaite, eager to support the indisputable logic.

'They'd 'ave t'be one o' them new mobile phones that they 'ave on t'telly,' added Rufus Snodgrass, ''cause y'can't 'ave telegraph poles on clouds.'

An animated discussion continued, with the children staring out of the window and up at the sky and, once again, Joseph was grateful for the sound of the bell for morning break.

While I was shivering on playground duty and the children were charging around as if it were a summer's day, in the staff-room Tom was reading my *Times*, mainly for the rugby articles, and Anne was flicking through Tom's *Daily Mail*. Sally was reading her *Guardian* and complaining about the typing errors, while Vera was immersed in her *Daily Telegraph*. The miners' strike was still continuing and she was concerned that, in spite of her faithful support for the Prime Minister, many of the mining communities were enduring severe hardship.

Difficult times, thought Vera, *and Christmas is coming.*

At the end of break I dropped into Anne's classroom and recalled that the beauty of being a primary-school teacher is that you get two Christmases, one with the pupils and one at home.

Two four-year-olds, Alfie Spraggon and Karl Tomkins, were making coloured paper-chains as if it were a matter of life and death. It was a veritable factory of industry on their table. Meanwhile, in the wet area near the sink, five-year-old Julie Tricklebank was standing in front of a paint-splattered easel. She had painted a picture of a robin on a landscape-format A3 sheet of white sugar paper. It had a huge, fat red body and no legs.

'That's a lovely robin,' I said.

'Thank you,' replied Julie as she stood back to admire her masterpiece.

'It hasn't got any legs,' I added helpfully.

'Paper weren't tall enough, Mr Sheffield,' explained the logical Julie.

As an afterthought, she added two rapid horizontal brushstrokes, one on each side of the body. 'There y'are, Mr Sheffield – it's a sitting-down robin.'

I was reminded that problem-solving comes easy to five-year-olds.

Something else obviously occurred to Julie and she put down her bristle brush, wiped her hands on her back-to-front painting shirt and looked up at me. 'Mr Sheffield, our Sonia says she's goin' t'see Santa in Easington Market. Are you going?'

Posters advertising the Easington Christmas Market, including Santa's grotto, sponsored by the local Rotary Club, were everywhere in the village.

'Yes, I am,' I said. 'Are you?'

Julie considered this carefully. 'No, Mr Sheffield, ah'm goin' t'wait and see 'im on Christmas Eve ... when 'e comes down t'chimney.'

It was shortly before midday and in my class you could hear a pin drop. I always loved story time and the children were completely immersed in *The Box of Delights,* the classic novel by John Masefield. They had been watching the series each week on BBC television and the discussion was fascinating. Their view of this fantasy drama reminded me that childhood is often a magical world of make-believe that sadly seems to

149

disappear with the onset of adolescence.

Lunchbreak was a hurried affair. I attached a checklist of the children on a wooden clipboard and the experienced Sally put a couple of sick bags in her music case with that *be prepared* look.

After a warming school dinner of fish pie, mashed potatoes and carrots, followed by jam roly-poly and lurid pink custard, the children pulled on their coats and we trudged through the snow down the school drive. William Featherstone had parked his cream-and-green Reliance bus next to the village green and the children clambered aboard, clutching their recorders, bags of throat lozenges and clean handkerchiefs. Our driver was his usual polite and smart self in his collar and tie and navy blue jacket. 'Grand day for a bit o' singin', Mrs Pringle, Mr Sheffield,' he said, touching the neb of his cap.

We left on time, with a few excited mothers waving us off as William double de-clutched into first gear and we set off down the High Street and then along the B-road towards York. It was a steady journey as we travelled south over the railway line and towards the huge redbrick Rowntree's factory with its familiar smell of cocoa. I sat at the front next to Vera, while Sally was at the back with Miss Flint, who sought out any signs of inappropriate behaviour with a gimlet eye.

Vera, as always, filled me in on the local knowledge regarding our destination, the church of St Michael le Belfrey. Apparently, in recent years it had grown in prominence thanks in the main to David Watson, who, according to Vera, had led a

150

remarkable life. 'He was one of the great Christian leaders of our time,' she said. 'He became curate-in-charge of the nearby St Cuthbert's Church in 1965 and at that time there were only a dozen people attending services. However, David attracted so many new followers that they moved to the larger St Michael le Belfrey, where the congregation grew to many hundreds.'

It was then that Vera gave a deep sigh and stared out of the coach window. 'Sadly, David died of cancer earlier this year,' she said quietly. 'He wrote a wonderful book entitled *Fear No Evil* concerning his fight against the disease. I'll loan it to you if you wish.'

'Thank you, Vera,' I said, 'I should like that.'

We parked on Lord Mayor's Walk and then escorted the crocodile of children up Gillygate with its eclectic collection of shops, including a tattoo parlour with the incongruous sign in the window: 'Tattoos while-u-wait'.

As we turned left into Duncombe Place the carved stone West Towers of York Minster, the largest medieval cathedral in Britain, reared into view, etched against a winter sky. The Anglican church of St Michael le Belfrey occupied a broad plot of land on the southern side of Minster Yard, immediately alongside the Minster itself. It was a spectacular building, built between 1525 and 1536 during the period of the English Reformation, and was the largest parish church in the city. Guy Fawkes was baptized there in 1570 and I wondered what he would have made of the scene today.

Large vans were parked outside and long

electrical cables stretched everywhere, while bearded technicians in jeans, woolly jumpers and lumberjack boots hurried around. A large sign, 'Christmas Voices – Recording Today', had been pinned to an easel next to the doorway.

It was with a feeling of awe and wonder that I stepped into this special place. However, inside it didn't feel like a church – more a film set with lighting engineers hurrying here and there and cameras being wheeled into position.

'Jack, Sally – you made it on time, well done.' It was Sarah Mancini, looking flushed with excitement. She gestured towards a handsome, denim-clad man who was issuing orders. He looked like a swarthy Bob Dylan with a Doctor Who scarf draped round his neck. 'And that's my brother Phil,' she added.

'We appreciate you coming,' said Phil, 'and we're all ready for you.'

'Well, thanks to Sally, the children are well rehearsed,' I said.

Phil turned to Sally. 'I've heard great things from my sister. You've obviously worked hard with your choir.'

'I'm new to all this,' said Sally, somewhat over-awed as she looked around at the production crew.

'Just do what you normally do, Sally,' said Phil gently, 'and ignore us. We'll start with "Ding Dong", which is bright and lively, and then do some shots of the church interior. We've got tiered stage blocks for the children and you're centre stage, so to speak. They need to look at you, not the cameras.' He stood back and studied Sally for

152

a moment. 'And by the way ... your outfit is terrific.'

Sally blushed visibly and Vera, sitting on the front pew, nodded in approval.

'All set?' I said to Sally.

She smiled. 'I must say, Jack, I'm really looking forward to this ... a new experience.'

'Good luck,' I whispered and took a seat in the darkness, away from the bright lights.

The children lined up in position, the recorders tried out a few notes, Sally took her guitar out of its case and Phil Mancini told the cameras to roll.

Sarah Mancini, in a stunning black dress, looked confidently into the camera lens. 'Here we are in the city of York in the beautiful church of St Michael le Belfrey. Our final school choir of the week is from Ragley Church of England Primary School and is led by their teacher, Sally Pringle. The children are all between eight and eleven years old and their first carol is "Ding Dong Merrily On High".'

Sally strummed the first line, nodding in time, and the children came in at precisely the right moment. *Practice makes perfect,* thought Sally as the children sang their hearts out. Phil Mancini asked for the final verse to be repeated as one of the cameras focused on the stained glass, and the children performed like professionals. I had rarely felt so proud.

'Now for "Silent Night",' said Phil and there was a discussion involving Phil, Sarah and Sally. The children were rearranged so that Rosie Sparrow was now centre stage. She would sing the first verse and then everyone would join in.

Sally moved to a raised stool at the side, next to the recorder group. She placed her *Carol, Gaily Carol* Christmas songbook on a music stand and opened it to 'Silent Night'.

Sarah Mancini introduced our second carol and then came the moment I shall never forget. The cameras rolled again, Sally strummed a chord and Rosie Sparrow, bathed in bright light and with a red ribbon in her hair, began to sing.

Silent night, holy night,
All is calm, all is bright...

Sarah Mancini looked at her brother curiously – she had never seen him react like this before. He was standing in the semi-darkness next to a camera as if hit by a thunderbolt. When it was over there was a stunned silence among the crew and then someone began to clap, then another and another, Phil Mancini gave his sister a hug and I heard him say, 'You were right, little sister ... the voice of an angel.'

Sarah Mancini told the children how proud she was of all of them, then she crouched down next to Rosie. 'Well done, Rosie,' she said. 'That was simply wonderful,' and the little girl smiled.

When the children had donned their coats and Phil Mancini had given a vote of thanks, Sally lined everyone up to leave the church, with Vera and Miss Flint bringing up the rear.

I was standing in the darkness of the church entrance when, to my surprise, I saw Maggie Sparrow standing there.

'Mr Sheffield, hope you don't mind.' She sounded out of breath. 'I know there was no room for parents, but I thought I would come into York and collect Rosie ... so long as it's all right with you. I wanted to give her a treat and take her round the shops.'

'Of course, Ms Sparrow,' I said. 'And she sang beautifully. You'll be so proud when you see her on television.'

I thought she was going to burst into tears. 'Thank you for saying so, Mr Sheffield.' She stared into the darkness at the crowds of shoppers and the Christmas lights beyond. I collected Rosie from the line of children and took her to her mother. 'Well done, my poppet,' said Maggie.

'The nice man said I was good, Mummy,' said Rosie and, hand in hand, they walked into the gathering dusk as snow fell on their shoulders.

Late that evening Beth and I were sitting by a log fire in Bilbo Cottage. Beth had put aside her dissertation and we were sharing a bottle of Merlot.

'Vera rang just after I got home, Jack, and said all went well.'

'And you'll love Sally's new outfit when you see the programme,' I told her with a grin.

'Yes,' said Beth with a smile, 'Vera filled me in with the details.'

We sipped our wine and stared at the dying embers in the fire grate.

'What about the little girl, the soloist?' asked Beth.

'You'll see for yourself,' I said. 'She's very special.'

'I'm really looking forward to the programme,' she said.

'So am I,' I replied.

But of course I didn't know then the impact it would have on the lives of others.

One mile away, the bright moon illuminated the hamlet of Cold Kirkby with sharp white light. A barn owl flew over the silent cottages and the high elms creaked ominously in the gusting wind.

Rosie Sparrow was in her bed and Maggie was stroking her daughter's hair, caressing elusive sleep.

'Who were you talking to on the phone?' asked Rosie.

'Your daddy,' said Maggie.

There was a pause. 'Did you love him?' asked Rosie.

'Yes I did,' said Maggie softly.

'And do you still?'

'Yes.'

'Why?'

'I just do.'

'And is he coming back?'

'I don't know, darling.'

'Why did he go away?'

'Sometimes some things are too big to understand, but I think he was looking for something.'

'What was that?'

'Himself,' Maggie murmured to herself.

A few minutes later Rosie Sparrow at last fell into an exhausted sleep after the excitement of the day. Maggie tiptoed to the bedroom door and turned out the light.

She looked for a long time at her sleeping child. Finally, as she closed the door she smiled and whispered, 'Goodnight and God bless ... my little sparrow.'

Chapter Eight

Do They Know It's Christmas?

School closed today for the Christmas holiday and will reopen on Thursday, 3 January 1985.
This evening children and parents have been invited by the PTA to come into the school hall to watch the live television broadcast of Christmas Voices. *The programme features the Ragley School choir.*
Extract from the Ragley School Logbook:
Friday, 21 December 1984

Overnight snow had covered the vast plain of York and left behind a morning of silence and light. It was Friday, 21 December, the dawn of a new white world, and the last day of the autumn term beckoned.

When I walked into the school office Vera was adding a manila folder to our large metal four-drawer filing cabinet. 'Good morning, Mr Sheffield,' she said. 'Mrs Phillips has been in and confirmed the arrangements for the television broadcast this evening. The PTA will come in at six to set out the chairs round the back of the hall, then put benches in front for the top two classes and, finally, the little ones can sit on the floor at the front. She asked if you would wheel out the television set at 6.15 p.m. and tune it in.'

'Thanks, Vera, I'm looking forward to it,' I said.

158

Vera glanced down at her pad. 'And Mrs Map-plebeck has offered to serve tea and mince pies afterwards.'

'Excellent,' I said and hurried off to help Joseph prepare his assembly.

Morning assembly was a bigger event than usual, with readings and carols. Sally's choir sang:

Baby Jesus sleeping softly
On the warm and fragrant hay
Children all the wide world over
Think of you on Christmas Day.

Then Joseph told the story of the Nativity and, after a final prayer, the children filed out for morning break. A group of them approached our friendly vicar in the entrance hall. 'That were a good story, Mr Evans,' said Charlie Cartwright, 'speshully them wise men – but ah were jus' thinkin'...'

'What about?' asked Joseph. He was pleased that his talk had promoted interest in the birth of Jesus.

'Well,' said Charlie, 'were there any wise *women?*'

Joseph paused, perplexed for a moment.

'They'd 'ave prob'ly brought some nappies,' contributed Rosie Spittlehouse helpfully.

'An' a flask o' tea,' suggested Ted Coggins.

'An' a nice slice o' cake,' added Katie Ickle-thwaite for good measure.

As the conversation gathered momentum, Joseph sidled out for his welcome cup of coffee.

When the bell went for the end of morning break

Vera put down the Christmas edition of *Good Housekeeping* and began the washing-up. As always, she washed the glasses first, then the mugs and finally the saucepan in which she had heated the milk. In Vera's world even the contents of the kitchen sink had a pecking order.

However, the tea towels had been taken away by Ruby to be washed. Only a Princess Diana tea towel remained and Vera shook her head in dismay. She held it up and looked lovingly at the image of the young princess. For Vera it would have been unthinkable to use it to dry pots and subject the face of royalty to such indignity. She hurried into the kitchen to borrow a spare one.

As the morning progressed I called into Tom's class. The children were writing Christmas poems and prayers and Tom was going from one table to another to help with spellings.

He grinned at me. 'You'll love these, Jack,' he whispered and I peered over the heads of the children at their neat printing.

Seven-year-old Siobhan Sharp had taken her Christmas prayer very seriously. 'Please God,' she wrote, 'don't make me have any sprouts this Christmas.'

Meanwhile the children who were writing Christmas poems were sucking the ends of their pencils in complete concentration. Scott Higginbottom had shown compassion for Santa with four lines written from the heart:

Santa comes every year
He always brings his sack

It must be very heavy
I bet it hurts his back.

Charlie Cartwright was rather more specific:

I sent a letter to Santa
I asked him for a bike
I hope it is a red one
Cos green I do not like.

Whereas Rosie Spittlehouse used the opportunity to reveal her opinion of boys:

Santa comes every year
To leave us presents and toys
I hope he leaves some for me
And none to all the boys.

It was a busy day and when it drew to an end the children were excited as they pulled on their coats, with thoughts of Christmas stockings, parties and playing in the snow.

Anne was saying goodbye to the children in her class. 'And I'll see some of you at the carol service,' she said.

'Who's Carol?' asked Madonna Fazackerly and Anne sighed. As an experienced teacher, she supposed she should have known better.

In the cloakroom area Anne was aware of Dallas Sue-Ellen Earnshaw staring at her. Dallas tugged the sleeve of her friend, Suzi-Quatro Ricketts. 'What does Mrs Grainger do in the 'olidays?' she asked.

'I know,' said Suzi-Quatro confidently. 'She

stays 'ere 'til we come back.'

Anne smiled. It was good to know one's place in the world.

Meanwhile, in my class, I was aware that presents had certainly changed since I was a boy. My pupils were discussing the imminent arrival of Atari Space Invaders in their pillowcases on Christmas Day.

By 6.20 p.m. the school hall was full of children, parents and grandparents and I had wheeled our giant television set to the front. There was an air of anticipation as we waited for the programme to begin.

Ruby's daughter, Natasha Smith, was our regular babysitter now, so Beth had been able to come in with me. It was always reassuring to see John look relaxed and happy when Natasha arrived and then play contentedly with her. She had her mother's smile and clearly loved children.

Beth looked fashionable in a velvet skirt and a plain blouse with baggy sleeves and padded shoulders. However, the *pièce de résistance* was an elegant sleeveless bolero. Her hair was longer now, just how I liked it. She looked sensational. She was sitting in the back row talking to Sally Pringle and Sarah Mancini but, to my surprise, they had been joined by Miss Barrington-Huntley, the chair of the Education Committee at County Hall in Northallerton. This powerful, straight-talking lady had always appeared to admire Beth's professionalism and was keen to offer advice whenever the opportunity arose.

They were in animated conversation when I

stood up to thank Sue Phillips and the PTA for organizing the event. Then I turned up the volume control, Tom turned down the lights and quiet descended as we all watched the flickering screen.

In the Fforde Grene public house in north-east Leeds, Rosie Sparrow's father, Mark Appleby, ordered a pint of John Smith's Best Bitter after repairing his last gas boiler of the week. He stared up at the blank television screen above the bar.

'Ah'm s'pposed t'be watchin' a local news programme,' he said to Doris, the barmaid. 'My ex said ah'd be interested.'

'What's on then?' asked Doris as she pulled a frothing pint.

'Dunno,' said Mark, glancing up at the clock. 'She said it were on ITV at half past six.'

'Ah'll turn it on.' She looked at the other men propping up the bar. 'Jus' quiet though.'

The Fforde Grene had become Mark's favourite place on a Friday night after work. He had paid his £2 admission to listen to live bands such as the Groundhogs and Dr Feelgood while he played snooker in the back room. There was company here and music ... and an opportunity to forget what might have been.

Mark supped his pint and stared at the screen. Suddenly, a smart Italian-looking woman was introducing the Ragley School choir. He put down his drink. 'Can y'turn it up, please?' he asked.

The camera panned in to the centre of the front row where a little girl was singing a solo. 'Turn it up, Doris,' shouted one of the drinkers at the bar.

163

'It's nice to 'ear little 'uns singin' at Christmas.'

Doris turned up the volume knob. When Rosie had finished singing 'Silent Night', Doris turned to Mark. 'That lass 'as a lovely voice.'

Mark smiled knowingly. 'She should 'ave,' he said as he put down his glass on the bar. 'She teks after 'er dad,' and he picked up his coat and walked out.

It was the first time Doris could remember Mark leaving a half-filled glass.

'Congratulations, Jack – an absolute triumph,' said Miss Barrington-Huntley as she sipped a cup of tea. 'And wasn't the little soloist a delight?'

'That's kind of you to say, Miss Barrington-Huntley,' I said, 'but it's all down to the hard work of Mrs Pringle, our music teacher, and Miss Mancini for setting it all up.'

'Of course. I must speak to them and express my appreciation.' She looked over my shoulder. 'And I must have a word with Beth before I leave.' Then she bustled off in that busy style of hers.

Half an hour later the crowds had dispersed and Anne and I did our familiar locking-up routine of windows and doors. Then we dropped her off at her home on The Crescent.

'See you at the Crib Service on Sunday,' said Anne with a wave.

As we drove off I noticed that Beth was strangely quiet when we turned on to the back road to Kirkby Steepleton.

'What did Miss High-and-Mighty have to say?' I asked.

'She was very encouraging as always, Jack,' said

Beth quietly.

'We're lucky to have her in North Yorkshire and she's always been fond of you.'

'Yes, I suppose so,' said Beth. 'She suggested I ought to consider a bigger headship at some time.'

'I see... Well, why don't you?'

Beth seemed surprised. 'But I thought we were concentrating on *you* going for a larger school, not me.'

'Beth ... you know how happy I am at Ragley School. I'm a *teacher*, not a manager. It's a much better idea for *you* to progress your career, not me. Then we'll both be fulfilled.'

Beth pondered this for a moment, and smiled.

Eventually the lights of Bilbo Cottage beckoned.

'Well ... it's worth thinking about, Jack.'

Late on Saturday afternoon all roads led to the Easington Christmas Market and, like most of the local villagers, I set off in search of a Yuletide bargain. As I drove up Ragley High Street Ben Roberts gave me a wave. He was on his Raleigh BMX Burner, practising a few new stunt tricks on an icy patch outside Timothy Pratt's Hardware Emporium.

When I parked in one of the side roads, our local market town was lit up brightly, with stalls set up around the edge of the large cobbled square. Coloured lights on a tall Christmas tree shone brightly, and the number-one Christmas record, Band Aid's 'Do They Know It's Christmas?' was blasting out on the tannoy system, with the shoppers singing along. Bob Geldof, the

Boomtown Rats' singer, and Midge Ure of Ultravox had decided to enlist the help of friends in the music fraternity to raise money for the starving people of Ethiopia and so Band Aid had been formed. It had proved an inspirational idea that had captured the imagination of the nation.

I bought a bag of roasted chestnuts and leaned against the picket fence that surrounded Santa's grotto, which was in fact a large wooden shed covered in polystyrene snow. Outside, the six members of the Ragley Handbell Society were playing 'All I Want For Christmas Is My Two Front Teeth' slightly out of tune. This was partly because they hadn't practised and also because the chromatic order was severely impaired as the leader of the group had sprained his wrist on the one-arm-bandit fruit machines in Scarborough.

Once again Gabriel Book had volunteered to be Santa and had donned his red suit, big black boots and cotton-wool beard. The grotto was a charitable contribution from the local Rotary Club and the president had, as usual, persuaded his two unwilling daughters to act as Santa's little helpers. Predictably, Good Fairy and Busy Elf did not live up to their names. Good Fairy had gone outside for a smoke and Busy Elf had replaced the bright-red twenty-watt bulb on Rudolph's nose with a clear sixty-watt bulb so that she could read her *Smash Hits* magazine.

Mrs Brenda Ricketts came in with her son, six-year-old Billy.

'Ho, ho, ho,' said Santa. Gabriel was proud of his 'Ho-ho-ho'.

''Ello, Santa,' said Billy cheerily. 'D'you

remember me?'

'Santa remembers all good girls and boys,' said Gabriel cautiously.

'Ah'm one o' t'good 'uns, Santa,' replied Billy confidently. 'An' ah'm six now, Santa – ah've jus' 'ad m'birthday.'

'That's lovely,' said Santa. 'And what would you like for Christmas this year?'

'Same as las' year, please.'

'Oh, and what was that?'

'Don't y'remember, Santa? It were a rat.'

'A rat!' exclaimed Santa.

'It were *Roland* Rat, Santa,' explained Mrs Ricketts. "Im off t'telly.'

'Ah, yes,' said Santa dubiously. 'Well, I'll look in my toy cupboard at the North Pole.'

'Or in m'mam's catalogue,' suggested Billy helpfully, getting off Santa's knee and walking over to get his gift from Good Fairy, who had just stubbed out her cigarette on Santa's sleigh.

'By the way,' asked Santa, 'what happened to the rat I gave you last year?'

'Jimmy Poole's dog ripped 'is 'ead off, Santa,' said Billy sadly.

Next in the queue was nine-year-old Sonia Tricklebank with her five-year-old sister Julie.

'So what y'gonna ask Santa for?' asked Sonia.

Julie looked up at her big sister. 'Ah'm gonna ask for a kitten.'

Sonia considered this as they walked in. 'Well, start by askin' for a pony ... an' work y'way down.'

Julie didn't like being told what to do and by the time she peered up at Santa an argument had begun.

167

'Sorry, Santa,' said Sonia. 'M'mam'll be 'ere in a minute.' She frowned at her sister. 'An' our Julie won't do as she's told.'

'Now, now,' said Santa. 'Remember, Santa's elves are watching.'

Sonia sighed deeply and looked around suspiciously. 'Well ... 'ow about ah tell 'er off be'ind t'curtain?'

And so it went on. His last customer was Rufus Snodgrass, who asked for a Hasbro Transforming Robot. As they left Gabriel muttered to himself, with a hint of sadness, 'So we've moved on from Meccano.' He still had vivid memories of making a working crane from a box of Meccano 2B. As he took off his boots and wiggled his toes in his extra-thick socks he pictured a warm fire, a cup of tea and a slice of Christmas cake accompanied by a generous chunk of Wensleydale cheese. *The world is changing,* he thought, *but some little pleasures remain.*

I walked over to a nearby stall and joined the crowd behind Ragley's binmen, Big Dave and Little Malcolm. A swarthy character was selling a variety of merchandise at knock-down prices.

'Ladies,' he shouted, 'in them posh shops in Hoxford Street down in London this state-of-the-art alarm clock would knock y'back fourteen poun' ninety-nine.' He held up a battered-looking box with the label Braun Voice-Controlled Alarm Clock. 'This is a wonder of t'modern age. Y'don't 'ave t'shout at yer 'usbands in t'morning, ladies. Y'can shout at this little beauty instead. It beeps until y'tell it t'shut up an' it does as it's told.' I could sense the interest. 'So gather roun'', 'cause 'ere t'day, 'speshully f'you, ah'm not askin' ten poun' ... in fac' ah'm not askin' seven.' You could almost hear the drum roll: the big sell had arrived. 'Ah'm almost givin' 'em away... So ... who'll be first t'give me a fiver?'

Betty Buttle pulled a five-pound note from her purse and held it up in triumph. 'Ah'll 'ave one,' she shouted. He cleared his stock in seconds and then held up a Swatch watch. 'Now then ... 'ave a look at this little beauty. It's shock-resistant, y'can swim underwater wi' it an' it tells t'time in fifteen different countries.'

''Cept not in this one,' shouted Big Dave.

'C'mon, Dave – y'know a bargain when y'see one,' the stallholder said.

'D'you know 'im, Dave?' whispered Little Malcolm.

'It's Fast Eddie.'

'Fast Eddie?'

'Yes,' said Big Dave. 'Eddie Ormonroyd from Scarborough. 'E buys and sells owt 'e can lay his hands on an' 'e's allus too quick for t'police.'

'Ah see what y'mean, Dave ... so 'e's fast then?'

'Fast ... fast!' exclaimed Big Dave. ''E's like shit off a shovel.'

Little Malcolm nodded in appreciation. 'Well, y'can't get faster than that.'

Meanwhile, Fast Eddie was getting into full swing. 'C'mon, ladies,' he yelled. ''Ere's y'chance t'spice up y'sex life.'

There was a stunned silence. Fast Eddie held up a video and on the cardboard sleeve was a photograph of a nubile woman under the title

Lyn Marshall's Everyday Yoga. 'It works on VHS, it works on Betamax and ladies,' Fast Eddie lowered his voice to a stage whisper, 'it works in t'bedroom.'

Before he could say how much he wanted, Betty Buttle shouted, 'Ah'll 'ave one,' and everyone laughed.

I decided to give Fast Eddie a miss. More often than not, I had picked up a bargain at the slightly more reputable Shady Stevo's stall so I wandered over and stood next to Mrs Earnshaw, who smiled in acknowledgement. She was holding on to Dallas Sue-Ellen while Heathcliffe and his brother Terry were in earnest conversation.

'Ah've asked for an Eric Bristow Darts Game,' said Heathcliffe. He'd seen them in Woolworths for £7.99. Stevo was selling them for a fiver.

'But we 'aven't gorra dartboard,' said Terry.

'No, ah know we 'aven't. So that's why you've got t'ask our mam f'one.'

'OK, 'Eath,' agreed Terry.

'An' another thing,' said Heathcliffe sternly. 'Don't tell Mam 'er diet isn't working ... else y'll get nowt.'

After some deliberation, I bought a box of four Memorex C90 videotapes to record some of the Christmas Day and Boxing Day programmes, including *The Man with the Golden Gun* with Roger Moore as James Bond; the ballet *Giselle* – a special request from Beth; *Elton John in Central Park* and *A Tribute to Eric Morecambe*.

There were many contented shoppers. Nora Pratt was showing Tyrone Crabtree a gift she had bought for Dorothy. She held up the box on which was printed the words 'Elizabeth Arden – Eye Fix Primer', read the small print and smiled. 'An' it's fwagwence fwee, Tywone ... Dowothy will love it.'

Mrs Coggins gave me a wave. She had been into York and had bought a Batman playsuit from British Home Stores and was wishing she had come to the market first. She bought a Remington Popcorn Maker for £15, an MB Pac-Man game for a fiver and an Etch-a-Sketch for £3.50.

That evening Little Malcolm was wrapping his Christmas gift for Dorothy. As far as he was concerned, it was the perfect gift for the love of his life and, at half price from Fast Eddie, definitely a bargain.

He picked up the box and studied it carefully. It was a Clinique with Love set. He removed the lid, stroked his stubbly chin and nodded in appreciation at the extravaganza of beauty products. They included protective shampoo, nail-treatment cream, a wide-tooth comb, soft-beige extra-help make-up, pink berry-stain semi-lipstick, and moisturizing lotion. He finished the wrapping with copious strands of Sellotape and wrote in neat printing on a piece of card 'to my wunderfull wife from yor Malcolm x' and stood back in satisfaction. He was proud of his neat printing.

Sunday morning dawned clear and cold, and a crowd of parents and grandparents trudged through the snow towards St Mary's Church for the annual Crib Service. It was one of the high-

171

lights of the festive calendar, and Beth and I bumped John's pushchair over the crushed ribbon of frozen footprints through the church gates to the haven of the entrance porch.

The Crib Service was different this year, with a request from the Ragley Playgroup to perform their Nativity play. It made a change from Anne's class and we were all looking forward to the spectacle of seeing much younger children performing.

Fiona Shaw was the playgroup leader and prided herself on being an innovative free-thinker. In consequence, the children had chosen their *own* parts, so we were treated to five Marys, three Josephs, six kings, one Snow White pulling a toy lamb on wheels and an ominous and strangely incongruous Darth Vader. The explanation for the latter was that it was his birthday and he was keen to wear his present.

Mrs Spraggon was sitting in front of me with her three-year-old daughter, Kirsty. The little girl was wearing cardboard donkey ears and grey furry pyjamas. 'You'll be on soon,' said Mrs Spraggon.

Kirsty looked up at the wooden cross mounted on the wall. 'What's that, Mummy?'

'Jesus's cross, darling,' she said softly.

Kirsty looked concerned. 'Why is he cross, Mummy?'

Suddenly, Fiona Shaw gave the signal. 'Donkey and Mary please.'

The first bars of 'Little Donkey' were played by Elsie Crapper on the organ and the children began to sing.

172

Unfortunately, Kirsty chose that moment to hop from one leg to the other. 'Oh dear,' said Mrs Spraggon. 'Sorry everyone – the donkey needs the loo,' and she hurried out to the church hall.

'I wonder if they understand what's going on?' whispered Beth as an eclectic group of children wandered aimlessly towards the bale of straw and cardboard manger placed in front of the altar.

'It'll be John's turn next year,' I said.

Beth looked down in horror. 'Lord help them,' she said. John was ripping up a carol sheet with his strong little fingers and chewing the pieces.

At the end there was an unexpected treat. Fiona Shaw had asked Sally if she would accompany Rosie Sparrow on her guitar at the end of the Nativity scene. So it was that, after Fiona had arranged the children in preparation for parents to take photographs, Sally strummed the first few chords and Rosie sang 'Silent Night'. It was a perfect conclusion and applause rang out as cameras flashed.

When Rosie went back to her pew she sat down next to her mother and a man I hadn't seen before. As we left the church, I asked Vera who it might be.

'It's Rosie's father, Mr Sheffield,' said Vera quietly. 'He's come home.'

We stood for a moment and watched the three of them walk down the path towards a small van with a gas logo on the side. Rosie was being held aloft by her father and she was smiling.

Vera tugged my sleeve and whispered, 'Jack...' It was rare for her to call me by my first name. 'Winter is the darkest season,' she said, 'but there is *light* in the world.' It was at times like this that I realized that Vera was not just the voice of Ragley School but also the soul.

I looked back at Rosie Sparrow and her parents.

It was a lasting image of a family who would share Christmas together.

Chapter Nine

Dick Whittington and His Pratt

Mrs Grainger and Mrs Pringle, with children from the reception class and the school choir and orchestra, will be supporting the Ragley annual village pantomime, Dick Whittington and His Cat, *in the village hall on 31 December.*
    Extract from the Ragley School Logbook:
        Monday, 31 December 1984

'He can't crouch down all the time,' said Felicity Miles-Humphreys. She was desperate. As artistic director and production manager of the Ragley Amateur Dramatic Society, life was always tense during the dress rehearsal for the annual village pantomime.

It was Monday morning, 31 December, and the production of *Dick Whittington and His Cat* was experiencing problems. Felicity ran her fingers through her long, frizzy, suspiciously jet-black hair, adjusted her scarlet headband and hurried towards the stage with her flowing white kaftan billowing like a spinnaker. 'After all, darling, he is showing wonderful feline grace.'

Felicity's son, Rupert, a shelf-stacker in the local supermarket with delusions of theatrical stardom, was playing the part of Tommy, Dick Whittington's cat. At six feet four inches tall he towered over the diminutive Nora and their partnership appeared incongruous to say the least.

'But ah can't weach is 'ead,' pleaded Nora Pratt, 'an' ah 'ave t'pat it when ah sing "Anothe' Wock and Woll Chwistmas".'

'Let's take five,' announced Felicity and she hurried to the kitchen to check her handbag and the diminishing supply of Valium.

Three miles away in Kirkby Steepleton, life was more peaceful. I stared out of the kitchen window of Bilbo Cottage at a desolate monochrome snowscape. A blanket of snow covered the bone-hard land and all sound appeared to be absorbed in this frigid world. There was no wind, just lazy swirling flakes of snow drifting down from a grey sky. On the radio Paul Young was singing 'Everything Must Change' and I wondered what the New Year might bring.

Beth's parents, John and Diane Henderson, had driven up from Hampshire to spend a week with us. They had arrived the day after Boxing Day and moved into our second bedroom. John's cot was now at the foot of our bed, so everything felt a little cramped.

While I was enjoying a cup of tea and a slice of toast in the kitchen, Diane, a slim, attractive blonde, was kneeling on the carpet in the lounge, spending precious time with her grandson. She had bought a jar of Matthews' Fullers Earth Cream to help reduce John's nappy rash and our son was rolling about on his changing mat, enjoying the extra attention. 'He'll be fine now, Beth,' said Diane. She picked him up, sat down in an armchair and rocked him gently.

'I don't know how you do it,' said Beth. 'He never plays up with you.'

Diane gave an understanding smile. 'I had plenty of practice with you and your sister.'

'Would you like a coffee?' asked Beth, wanting to feel useful.

'Yes please,' said Diane, kissing John gently on his forehead. 'I just wish you lived a little closer, then I could do this more often.'

Beth walked into the kitchen and stepped over my outstretched legs. As she filled the kettle she stared at the cluttered worktops and sighed. 'We need a new kitchen, Jack,' she said, shaking her head. 'You can't swing a cat in here.'

'Yes, it is *compact*, I suppose,' I said, looking around unconcerned.

The first hint of annoyance flickered across Beth's face. She shut the kitchen door and spoke quietly. 'Eventually we have to either build an extension or move house. We can't go on like this. It's *impossible* when we have visitors.'

'It's a lovely cottage, Beth. We've had some good times here.'

Beth sighed as she added milk to Diane's coffee. 'I know ... but we need to move on – and maybe talk about a bigger headship in the New Year.'

It seemed we had gone from new kitchens to new jobs in a trice. The forces that shaped our world no longer appeared to be in my control. I put my hands on her shoulders and kissed her. 'Beth ... a village-school headteacher can be a difficult job, but it's the life I love. A headteacher of a large school becomes a *manager*. First and foremost, I'm a *teacher*. Ragley School is perfect for me. So maybe the headship of a large school has to be *your* goal, not mine, and if it is I'll support you.'

Beth picked up the mug of steaming coffee and paused by the door. 'Thanks ... but do you really want to be a village headteacher for the rest of your career?'

The simple answer was yes, but I decided on another tack. 'I did think that one day I might train teachers – perhaps at the college in York – so that I could pass on the knowledge I've gained.'

Beth looked at me quizzically. 'Well, both suggestions may well be for the best, I suppose.' It seemed faint praise, but a possible altercation had been avoided. I could see her slip into a quiet reverie of private thoughts and I wondered where her ambition might take us. Beth was clearly a very determined lady. She opened the door as John Henderson appeared in the hallway.

'The Land Rover's warming up, Jack, so we can go when you're ready,' he said, blowing into his hands for warmth. 'It's right what they say,' he added with a grin. 'It's cold up north.'

John Henderson was tall and lean with steel-grey hair and a relaxed, laid-back manner. I liked my father-in-law, who always seemed at peace in his world. He was dressed in a country-checked shirt, warm Aran sweater and thick cord trousers, tough brogue shoes and a heavy woollen overcoat. He looked much younger than his sixty-one years.

'Thanks, John,' I said. 'Maybe you can give me a hand with King Neptune's Kingdom.'

'I'd rather have a bacon sandwich in that nice

little coffee shop,' he whispered in my ear.

I had volunteered to help out with the scenery for the Ragley pantomime and John appeared keen to get out of the house for a while. His Land Rover was an ideal vehicle for the journey into Ragley on this bitter morning and I enjoyed the drive and his companionship. It was a grey world and the skeletal branches of the high elms were coated in frost.

'Lovely part of the country, Jack,' said John, staring out at the dramatic North Yorkshire landscape. The back road out of Kirkby Steepleton was a snowy ribbon of light as, gradually, a pale winter sun emerged from the high cirrus clouds.

'Yes, John,' I said reflectively.

It's my home, I thought.

A few miles away, Sally Pringle wasn't admiring the spectacular scenery. As she pulled on her coat and picked up her guitar case prior to helping out with the dress rehearsal, she stared at the biscuit barrel on the kitchen worktop.

Sally had begun her post-Christmas 'Thinking Woman's Diet'. She had started the day with a Kellogg's Special K breakfast at 250 calories per serving, having been swayed by the strapline 'You'll end up sliding into your jeans and pinching nothing but compliments'.

However, there was a problem: it wasn't working.

Sally grabbed her car keys and, as an afterthought, selected a couple of custard creams and put them in her pocket. She set off for the Crescent to pick up Anne en route to the village hall.

Up the Morton Road, Petula Dudley-Palmer was eating her breakfast alone. Like Sally, she had selected Kellogg's Special K and she stared at the text on the box of cereal. It was described as the 'Thinking Woman's Diet' and it occurred to Petula that she did a lot of thinking these days, mainly about her life with Geoffrey and why he spent so many evenings away from home ... on business.

'It goes with the territory,' he often said. Then she looked around at her beautifully furnished conservatory and the carefully manicured lawns beyond the double glazing and thought, *This is my territory ... and it's lonely*. Although, of course, she had her girls; they were the light of her life.

She glanced through her latest catalogue and noted the Dreamland Electric Underblanket. Perhaps that would encourage Geoffrey to share their double bed on these bitterly cold nights.

'Come on, girls, time to go to the village hall,' she shouted, 'and bring your turbans for the Sultan's Palace scene.'

Meanwhile, Anne Grainger was keeping her figure-conscious thoughts to herself.

Before Christmas she had posted a cheque to a company with an impressive-sounding name: Needletrade International in Surrey. She had purchased a B-Slim Pantie Corselet that included double extra-front supports. It claimed to flatten the tummy by up to four inches, smooth bulges and give the wearer a trim bottom. Sadly, Anne realized it came at a cost. When she had

180

crouched down to admire the cover of her David Soul LP something had definitely twanged and the substantial cheeks of her shapely bottom had taken on a life of their own in an attempt to escape their corselet prison. So Anne had bowed to the inevitable that morning and put on the baggy tracksuit she wore for her housework.

After all, she thought, *I'm only fixing safety pins on a dozen rats' tails and making the tea.*

John parked outside Prudence Golightly's General Stores. Diane had given us a shopping list and we bought a few groceries for the New Year's Day holiday. As we left I held the door open for Mrs Tricklebank and her two daughters, Sonia and little Julie.

'We're looking for a present for my great-grandma,' announced Sonia.

'That's a kind thought, Sonia,' said Prudence. 'And how old is she?'

Sonia thought about this for a moment. 'Well, *really* old,' she said.

Julie peered up into the kind face of the Ragley shopkeeper. 'But not as old as you,' she added as a helpful afterthought.

Mrs Tricklebank blushed profusely as she bought a box of lace handkerchiefs and a card that read '70 years young'.

Prudence, with true Christian spirit, gave each of the girls a gift of a tiny stick of barley sugar and a kind smile. However, after mother and daughters had hurried out and the jangling bell became silent, she looked in the mirror hanging on the back of the stockroom door and remembered the

181

younger woman that used to stare back at her.

Outside, peering in the window at the jars of liquorice torpedoes, sherbet lemons and coconut whirls, were the two Earnshaw brothers.

''Eath, ah'm not gettin' married,' said Terry thoughtfully. 'Ah'm gonna stay single.'

'Well, ah'm not,' replied Heathcliffe decisively.

'Why's that then?' asked Terry.

'Ah want someone t'tidy up after me.'

Terry nodded. He knew if you listened to your big brother you could learn a lot. They walked in to buy two ounces of aniseed balls and Terry hoped there would be an even number in the bag.

Two hours later, after bacon sandwiches in Nora's Coffee Shop and the hectic construction of a slightly shaky Sultan's Palace, John and I drove back to Kirkby Steepleton. He seemed strangely quiet as the wipers of his Land Rover cleared the berms of snow in slow, lazy sweeps.

Suddenly he broke the silence. 'I still worry about Laura,' he said and his brow furrowed. 'She writes from Australia but I can't imagine her settling there.'

'How is she, John?' I asked.

'Fine, according to her letters ... but who knows with Laura? She never seems to settle and the fling she had with that young teacher on your staff was the final straw.' He took a deep breath. 'She had words with her mother – *strong* words.'

'I didn't know,' I said quietly.

'Within a week she had packed her bags and gone.'

As we drove back to Bilbo Cottage, the vast

stillness of winter descended like a silent shroud.

At six o'clock Beth and I were ready to leave. As a treat we had decided to have a drink and a bite to eat in The Royal Oak before the pantomime.

'Don't hurry back,' said Diane. She was about to give our son his bath.

'Have a good time,' said John.

'Dad, it's the *Ragley* pantomime – not exactly the West End,' said Beth.

'Well, good luck, Jack. Let's hope your Sultan's Palace survives the stampede of rats,' said John with a smile.

The bright orange lights of The Royal Oak were a welcome sight as we parked in the High Street. The bar was filling up with villagers seeking a pre-pantomime drink and some hot food and when we walked in the evening's entertainment was warming up in the corner. The sign above the dartboard read: 'The Troy Phoenix Trio' but, sadly, it had been severely depleted. Troy, also known as Norman Barraclough, the local entertainer who sold fish from a white van, wasn't happy. His lead guitarist had to work late cleaning toilets in York and his drummer could only use one stick after trapping his fingers in the door of his girlfriend's Reliant Robin.

Beth sat down at a bay-window table while I went to the bar. 'A glass of white wine and a half of Chestnut, please, Sheila.' I glanced up at the menu chalked on the blackboard. 'And two giant Yorkshire puddings with beef and onions, please.'

'An' plenty o' my special gravy, Mr Sheffield, jus' 'ow y'like it,' added Sheila with a flutter of her false eyelashes.

Old Tommy Piercy was sitting on his favourite stool by the bar next to the autographed photograph of Geoffrey Boycott. He was wearing his faded baggy suit and was proudly displaying his war medals on his chest. Old Tommy always made an effort for the New Year's Eve pantomime. 'And a pint of Tetley's for Mr Piercy as well, please, Sheila,' I added.

Old Tommy was incorrigibly content with his life. After all, his sausages were now famous across North Yorkshire and his lifetime of endeavour seemed complete. 'Good evenin', Mr Sheffield, and, if ah may say, Mrs Sheffield is lookin' reight bonnie t'night,' he said.

'Thank you, Mr Piercy, and good evening to you,' I replied.

'It's a fine night for t'village panto,' he said.

'Y'love this village, don't you, Tommy?' said Sheila as she pulled his pint.

'Ragley village,' he murmured wistfully, tamping the bowl of his briar pipe with a gnarled thumb. 'Ah were born 'ere an' ah'll die 'ere. Best place on God's earth. In t'scheme o'life ah were blessed, Mr Sheffield.' He stood up and patted me on the shoulder. 'Enjoy it while it lasts, 'cause there's folk out there who thrive on change ... change for change's sake.'

I kept my thoughts to myself.

Half an hour later Beth and I walked down the High Street to the village hall. Our local bobby, the recently qualified PC Pike, was standing at the door smiling at everyone as they walked in. It

184

was his intention to get to know the locals. 'Hello, Mr Sheffield, Mrs Sheffield,' he greeted us as we walked in and gave Elsie Crapper our fifty pences.

As we took our seats it ocurred to me that, as each year went by, policemen were beginning to look younger.

The pantomime was up to its usual standard, which wasn't saying much. Nora was playing the part of Alice. According to the programme she was the beautiful, young, lissom daughter of Alderman Fitzwarren, played by Peter Miles-Humphreys, the stuttering bank clerk. The fact that her Alpine corset was straining at the seams was overlooked by the partisan audience. Likewise, when Nora sang 'You Can't Huwwy Love' it was almost un-recognizable as the Supremes' classic, but she received generous applause.

Ruby, as always, was in the front row with her daughters. However, this year she occasionally dabbed her eyes as she recalled the dreadful con-clusion to last year's pantomime when Ronnie died.

During the interval Scott Higginbottom was sitting next to Ted Coggins and complaining bitterly while indulging in one of his favourite occupations, picking his nose with a grubby fore-finger.

'What's matter, Scott?' asked Ted.

'Ah'm fed up wi' m'grandad,' said Scott.

'Why's that?'

'Well, 'e makes me wear 'is old gas mask from t'Second World War when ah pick m'nose.'

'Does it work?' asked Ted.

Scott considered this for a moment and shook his head. 'No, ah can get m'little finger up t'side.'

The second half was marginally better than the first half, even when Nora sang 'I Have A Dweam'. Dick Whittington, played by a thigh-slapping Claire Bradshaw, the daughter of Don and Sheila in The Royal Oak, was by some distance the star of the show. Claire had her mother's confidence and was cheered to the rafters in the underwater scene in King Neptune's Kingdom. Her battle in almost total darkness with Kenny Kershaw's octopus was dramatic to say the least. The fact that one of his mother's tissue-filled tights had torn off in the dress rehearsal did not diminish the enjoyment.

'S'only got seven legs,' observed Big Dave in the back row.

'Y'reight there, Dave,' agreed Little Malcolm.

'Nice tights though,' said Dorothy.

Alderman Fitzwarren tended to delay the proceedings owing to his unfortunate stutter. However, the audience showed considerable support.

'Yes, D-Dick, you c-can marry my d-d-d–'

'Daughter!' shouted the football team in the back row. After all, good drinking time was being wasted.

The comic figure Idle Jack, played by Young Tommy Piercy, Old Tommy's grandson, was cheered throughout, while Stan Coe, appropriately cast as the villainous King Rat, was booed so loudly no one could hear a word he said. His sister, Deirdre, was equally booed in spite of her playing the part of the Dame – according to the script 'the endearing and friendly Sarah the Cook'.

At the end a relieved audience clapped Nora, who received the traditional three curtain-calls and a huge bouquet of flowers, while Tommy the Cat went home in a huff after the audience had cheered the rats instead of him throughout Act Two.

Before we left, Ruby gave Beth a short lecture on 'gripe water' and how to prevent thumb-sucking in young infants. She was clearly returning to normal. However, one regular aspect of her character had sadly departed: namely, her wonderful singing. I had not heard any of her favourite songs from *The Sound of Music* for a long time now ... in fact, since Ronnie's funeral.

I took one last look at my Sultan's Palace and was pleased it had survived intact, but not as pleased as Fairy Bowbells, played by Amelia Duff, who received a large bunch of flowers from Ted Postlethwaite, followed later by a night of unrestrained passion.

As the crowds disappeared into the night and parents collected their children, Beth and I stayed to help clear up with Joseph and Vera, plus various members of the cast. Finally, Vera ushered Felicity out of the door with instructions to have 'a good lie-down' and we turned out the lights.

There was a new notice on the inside of the door, but in the darkness it was impossible to read.

'Could be important,' I said anxiously.

'Bother,' said Vera. 'We shall have to go back to put the lights on.'

187

I felt my way back, found the light switch and, once again, the entrance was bathed in light.

The notice read:

PLEASE TURN OUT THE LIGHTS BE-FORE YOU LEAVE.

'Which nincompoop put that there?' asked Vera.

There was a nervous cough behind us. 'Actually, it was me,' confessed Joseph.

We said goodnight and I walked hand in hand with Beth up the High Street and across the village green to my car. Under a frozen sky we walked together, the brittle grass cracking beneath our feet.

'You're quiet,' I said.

'Just thinking, Jack,' replied Beth softly.

'I wonder what the New Year will bring,' I said.

I looked at her classic English beauty and held her in my arms as we reached the car. We kissed and her hair was soft against my face. Ours was a love forged in fire, set in stone. Her journey was also mine, and I knew I was destined to follow in her footsteps.

When we arrived home I stared up at the cold night sky. A pallid moon shone down on Bilbo Cottage and the north wind created a sibilant whispering in the eaves of the pantiled roof. It seemed to be saying 'Change is coming'.

We walked into our home and I closed the floral curtains and shut out the night ... but not my thoughts.

Chapter Ten

Viva Las Ragley

The school sound system was loaned to the village hall committee for their Elvis competition on Saturday, 5 January.

Extract from the Ragley School Logbook:
Friday, 4 January 1985

It was Friday, 4 January, our second day of the spring term, and on the morning news the Education Secretary, Sir Keith Joseph, announced that another six thousand teaching jobs would go this year. Life at the chalkface at the outset of 1985 was getting tougher.

However, that wasn't uppermost on Deke Ramsbottom's mind.

Ragley's singing cowboy had parked his snow-plough by the village green and was waiting for me in the school entrance hall. He removed his cowboy hat as I walked in.

'Mornin', Mr Sheffield. Sorry t'trouble you, but ah was wond'rin' if y'could see y'way to 'elpin' us out.'

'Of course, Deke.'

'It's for t'Elvis night,' he said.

'Yes, all the staff will be there to support,' I assured him, 'and it's for a good cause.' I nodded towards the poster on the General Notices board:

Viva Las Ragley
Elvis Presley – the King of Rock 'n' Roll
Talent Competition
Ragley Village Hall
Saturday 5th January 1985
Entry 50p
Proceeds towards the Ethiopian Famine Relief Fund

It was the weekend before the fiftieth anniversary of Elvis's birth and the village hall committee had decided to celebrate it in style. Deke was the chairman and he was determined it would be a successful evening. It was also one of many village events planned to support the starving people of Ethiopia.

'We're struggling f'speakers,' explained Deke. 'We've got our Clint's microphone but we need plenty o' volume, if y'get m'meanin'.'

I took Deke into the school hall. 'You're welcome to use these, Deke.' I pointed to the two large speakers underneath the record deck on our Contiboard music trolley.

'Champion,' said Deke. 'Ah'll send our Shane an' Clint t'collect 'em after school if that's all right.'

'That's fine, Deke, and I'll let Ruby know.'

He shook my hand, absent-mindedly polished his sheriff's badge, replaced his stetson and walked out. At the door he paused and grinned. 'Word 'as it Malcolm's 'aving a go – 'e's been practisin'.'

An hour later Little Malcolm Robinson was in

190

Eugene Scrimshaw's village pharmacy.

'What's wrong, Malcolm?' asked Eugene. 'Y'lookin' a bit peaky.'

'It's Dorothy,' said Little Malcolm, rubbing his stubbly chin thoughtfully and sinking deeper into his donkey jacket. 'She wants me t'sing tonight.'

'You'll be fine,' said Eugene by way of encouragement.

Little Malcolm shook his head sadly. 'Thing is, Eugene, ah'm 'usky.'

''Usky?'

'Yes – an' coughin' an' suchlike.'

'This is best f'coughs,' said Eugene. 'It'll clear y'tubes an' it won't mek y'drowsy.' He handed over a bottle of Covonia Original Bronchial Balsam with menthol.

'Thanks, Eugene, yer a pal,' said Little Malcolm.

'What y'singing?'

Little Malcolm looked sheepish. 'It's Dorothy's fav'rite – "Burning Love". She said it were 'is biggest hit of t'seventies.'

'Could be a winner,' said Eugene.

'No, likely as not that'll be Lionel 'Igginbottom,' said Little Malcolm.

'T'Prudential Insurance man?'

'Yes, an' 'e's a proper Elvis lookalike – a dead ringer.'

'Well, do y'best, Malcolm,' said Eugene. 'Ah'll b'rootin' for yer.'

'Thanks, Eugene,' said Little Malcolm, and he picked up his medicine and went out to join Big Dave in their refuse wagon.

It was morning break and Sally picked up her

January issue of *Cosmopolitan* magazine and smiled. 'So, everyone, would you like to hear what's predicted to be in and out in 1985?'

Everyone looked up in expectation.

'Well, this is what's *in* ... styling mousse, Jackie Collins, condoms, Escort XR3, expense accounts and older men.'

'Oh dear,' said Vera. 'What's the world coming to?'

'It's very *direct*,' added Anne cautiously.

'Not sure about older men,' said Tom with a smile in my direction.

'So what's out?' I asked.

Sally read on. 'The pill, Joan Collins, Roland Rat, water biscuits, chocolate mousse and leg warmers.'

There was silence as we weighed the perceived enormity of these changes in our lives, then with a sigh we returned to the Yorkshire Purchasing Organization catalogue and the price of HB pencils.

Just before lunchtime I called in to Class 1. Anne had clearly had a mammoth art session and all the children had completed a painting of their family, each on a sheet of thick cream A3 paper.

The result was that the wet paintings were now hanging, like a Monday wash day, on a length of baling twine. It stretched from the door frame that led to the toilets, diagonally across the class-room to the Home Corner. In this carpeted area Madonna Fazackerly was ironing a soft toy monkey and Julie Tricklebank was acting out the preparation of a full Sunday roast dinner on the plywood worktops.

At lunchtime Sally and Anne had given the school dinner a miss and, while the smell of cabbage lingered, they were still sticking to their January diet plan. Anne was boiling the kettle for their packets of Batchelors Slim a Soup. Sally had selected Beef and Tomato while Anne had gone for Chicken and Leek.

'Only forty calories per serving,' said Sally with forced enthusiasm.

Meanwhile Tom was reading his *Daily Mail* and pondering the fate of soccer star George Best. He had been moved to Ford Open Prison in Sussex and was hoping to get in the prison football team. *How are the mighty fallen*, thought Tom. Then he frowned while reading about the dreadful accident that had befallen the Def Leppard rock drummer, Rick Allen. After crashing his sports car his left arm had been severed and he was fighting for his life.

Seeking relief from the gloom he looked around the staff-room to check no one was looking over his shoulder and opened his newspaper to June Penn's horoscope page. His stars looked promising. June had announced that 'a new friend plays an important part in your life' and he wondered who it might be.

Meanwhile, Vera was reading her *Daily Telegraph*. 'Oh dear,' she said out loud. 'It can't be ... Margaret will never believe it.' Arthur Scargill had been voted 'Man of the Year' on Radio 4's *Today* programme and Vera closed her newspaper in disgust.

At afternoon break I was on playground duty

and, nearby, Stacey Bryant and Hayley Spraggon were in conversation.

'Do you know what *love* is?' asked Stacey.

'Dunno,' said Hayley. ''Cept my mummy and daddy are in love.'

'Why?'

''Cause they can't 'elp it,' retorted Hayley.

''Ow come?'

'Ah think it's like cabbage.'

''Ow d'you mean?'

'Well, when Mrs Mapplebeck serves it f'school dinner, you've no choice.' And they ran off to play 'What's the Time, Mr Wolf?' near the welcome shelter of the boiler-house doors.

I stood by the school wall and surveyed the children playing contentedly in the snow. Dazzling shards of light lanced between the scurrying clouds and lit up the school building, with bright white snow curving gently against the bell tower.

Suddenly I spotted Tom Dalton walking out to join me. He waded through excited children who were apparently impervious to the bitter north wind. A scattering of snowflakes had settled on his long black hair and the shoulders of his Barbour jacket. He stood beside me and leaned against the wall. Behind him the metal railings, topped with decorative fleurs-de-lis, looked like candles on a birthday cake. He wrapped his hands round his coffee cup as if he wanted to borrow its warmth before giving it back to the world.

Eventually Tom spoke quietly. 'Jack ... she wrote to me before she left.'

'I didn't know that,' I replied guardedly.

'Yes,' said Tom. 'So maybe there is some hope.'

194

I thought I would start the afternoon with a few simple general knowledge questions just to blow away the cobwebs. 'What's the capital of France?' I asked.

To my surprise, Harold Bustard's hand shot up. 'Yes, Harold?'

'F, Mr Sheffield – it's F,' he said excitedly.

'Er, yes, Harold. Well done,' I said hesitantly.

I noticed his hands looked grubby. 'Have you washed your hands?' I asked.

'Yes, Mr Sheffield,' said Harold quick as a flash. He held up his hands. 'They're quick-dry.'

Sometimes, as a teacher, you just had to smile.

When the bell finally rang for the end of school, Harold came up to me with a big smile on his face. 'Guess what, Mr Sheffield,' he said. 'Ah'm gettin' a bike jus' like Ben's.'

The bestselling bicycle in the January sales was the BMX at £39.99 and Mr and Mrs Bustard wanted to reward their son for trying hard at school.

'That's great news, Harold,' I said.

I recalled my first Raleigh bicycle in 1955 and the feeling of freedom it gave me. As he ran off, it reminded me that when you're ten years old life is an adventure waiting to happen.

In the entrance hall Deke's two eldest sons, Shane and Clint, had arrived. The two farm-workers were very different. Shane was a skinhead psychopath with the initials H-A-R-D tattooed on the knuckles of his right hand, while Clint was a fashion-conscious young man with a

195

liking for David Bowie haircuts, frilly shirts and, on special occasions, eyeliner.

'We're 'ere for t'speakers, Mr Sheffield,' said Shane.

'In the hall,' I said. 'Help yourselves.'

'Thanks, Mr Sheffield,' said Clint, glancing at his reflection in the window and carefully checking that his spiky orange hair was in place.

They collected the speakers, put them in the back of Deke's pig trailer and drove off.

Meanwhile, in the staff-room, Vera was chatting with Anne and Sally. 'Joseph's sixtieth birthday is in a few weeks,' she said. 'I'm thinking about a gift for him.'

'And we must get him something from the staff,' said Anne.

'Or maybe a book on wine-making,' said Sally.

Vera gave us all a quizzical look over her steel-framed spectacles. 'Yes, I bought him a beginner's guide a while ago. It didn't go down well.'

I nodded. 'A bit like his wine, Vera.'

We all saw the funny side and laughed, just as Joseph walked in.

'Well, they say laughter is the best medicine,' he said with an encouraging smile. He looked puzzled as we burst out laughing again.

That evening in Bilbo Cottage, Beth and I had settled down after getting John off to sleep. Our son was an energetic little boy and growing fast. It was always comforting when he finally closed his eyes and we had time together.

Beth was in a reflective mood. 'Do you recall that chat I had with Miss Barrington-Huntley? It was in your school hall after Rosie Sparrow's "Silent Night" on television.'

I put another log on the fire and knelt on the hearth-rug. 'Yes, I remember.'

'She mentioned that a few larger headships were coming up in North Yorkshire.'

I glanced at the fireplace as the log crackled into life. 'So ... are you thinking you might try for one?'

'Well, I should be in a stronger position once I've got my Masters degree.'

'You know I'll support you,' I said.

'Thanks – but I'll have to be cautious about the size of the school.'

'How do you mean?'

Beth smiled. 'Well, being a *woman* doesn't help. We both know in this day and age women simply aren't considered for the larger headships.'

'Sadly, you may be right... In fact, I can't think of one in North Yorkshire.'

'So ... would *you* think of a larger headship?'

I sighed. This was familiar ground. 'I'm happy where I am as a village-school teacher – and we earn enough to be comfortable. I'd rather be in a job where I'm happy than one where I'm bombarded with daily problems.'

Beth looked at me curiously. 'Is that how you see it?'

'Maybe... But, either way, I'll support you if that's what you want.'

She smiled and got up to search for something in the Welsh dresser. 'Left over from Christmas,' she announced, opening a bottle of Royal Mint Chocolate Liqueur, and we sipped it like contented kittens in front of a roaring fire.

It was Saturday evening and Natasha Smith was child-minding for us again. Beth and I left early for the Elvis night and called in at The Royal Oak. On the jukebox Paul McCartney and the Frog Chorus were singing 'We All Stand Together'. As we approached the bar, the conversation turned to Ian Botham, who had been arrested on a drugs charge. However, the cricket star's fall from grace didn't concern Ragley's favourite binmen.

'We've supped some stuff t'night, Mr Sheffield,' said a bleary-eyed Big Dave.

'Dutch courage, Mr Sheffield,' said Little Malcolm. He sounded as if he had a sore throat.

'Good luck tonight, Malcolm,' said Beth. It was well known that Malcolm was entering the competition.

'Thanks, Mrs Sheffield, ah'll need it,' he spluttered.

Big Dave and Little Malcolm took their drinks back to the bench seat under the dartboard where Nellie and Dorothy were sharing the news of the Rolling Stones. Ronnie Wood had married his lover Jo Howard and had given her a pair of gold pistols as a wedding gift. Apparently, best man Keith Richards had arrived in his Rolls-Royce eating fish and chips and swigging light ale.

'An' what about Barbara Windsor?' said Nellie.

The forty-seven-year-old *Carry On* star had divorced her husband, Ronnie Knight, who lived in Spain and was wanted for questioning regarding two robberies.

'She's gonna marry her boyfriend,' added Nellie. ''E's a chef an' 'e's only twenty-nine.'

198

'Good luck to 'er,' said Dorothy.

'Ah've allus liked 'er since 'er bra bust in *Carry On Camping*,' said Big Dave.

Little Malcolm was about to agree but wisely kept quiet after a warning glance from Dorothy.

Beth had found a table near the bay window while I ordered drinks at the bar. Sheila was pulling pints and Don the barman was talking to Old Tommy.

'They said there would be ten centimetres of snow,' said Sheila.

'That sounds deep,' said Don.

'What's that in *real* money?' asked Old Tommy.

'Four inches, Mr Piercy,' I said.

Old Tommy considered this for a moment. 'Ah prefer inches,' he said. 'It doesn't sound as deep.'

'Are you going to the village hall, Mr Piercy?' I asked.

'Ah'll go t'support them little bairns in Africa but not t'see t'so-called talent, 'cept for m'grandson o'course,' said Old Tommy. 'If Elvis were alive 'e'd be turnin' in 'is grave.'

'That's a bit 'arsh,' said Sheila.

'Ah speak as ah find an' ah say it as it is,' stated Old Tommy with a contented puff of his old briar pipe. According to our local butcher, as a straight-talking Yorkshireman, this was the mantra of his life.

'Well, ah don't rate that Clint Ramsbottom's chances,' shouted an inebriated Lionel Higginbottom from further down the bar. ''E can't sing a note.'

'Oy, button y'lip,' shouted Shane. He raised his

199

fist. 'No one calls my Nancy-boy brother names.'

Clint looked dubiously at his brother. After all, he meant well.

Old Tommy took a thoughtful puff on his briar pipe. 'Y'know what they say, Clint – a friend in need is a pain in the arse.'

Everyone laughed, the conversation resumed and Don pulled a pint of Chestnut.

''E couldn't knock t'skin off a rice pudding, Mr Piercy,' said Shane disdainfully, 'but 'e's m'brother.'

'Think on, young Shane,' advised Old Tommy, 'an' listen t'one what knows ... fighting gets y'nowhere, but *loving* does. So find y'self a nice young woman.'

'That's not easy, Mr Piercy,' said Shane.

'That were allus my problem when ah were young like you,' said Old Tommy.

'What were that then, Tommy?' asked Don.

Old Tommy's eyes twinkled as he replied. 'Slow 'orses an' fast women.'

Don glanced at Sheila in her fluorescent pink boob-tube. 'Ah know what y'mean.'

Shane looked up at the clock. 'Oy, drama queen!' he shouted to Clint. 'Shape thissen – we're off.'

At 7 School View Sharon Smith looked at the clock. 'C'mon, Mam, let's go to t'village 'all. It'll do y'good. It's a bit o' culture.'

Ruby sighed. ''E were never int' culture were y'dad. Ah remember ah wanted t'go t'that A an' E museum in London what Queen Victoria built ... but 'e never took me.'

200

Our school caretaker seemed to spend all her evenings now watching television with her daughters. She had enjoyed the most recent episode of *Dallas,* although she was concerned that Miss Ellie was haunted by her dead husband ... and Ruby thought of Ronnie. She had also admired Judith Chalmers showing off her permanent suntan on the island of St Lucia in the Caribbean in *Wish You Were Here* and she reflected on the holidays she had never had. Even the escapades of Benny Hill couldn't cheer her up.

But perhaps an evening in the village hall would, and Sharon helped her into her warmest cardigan and coat.

The evening was a lively affair.

The local entertainer Troy Phoenix, in his sparkly flares, was the Master of Ceremonies. He had plugged in Timothy Pratt's famous 'clapometer' – a peculiar invention that the fastidious owner of the Hardware Emporium had knocked up in his shop. It responded to the sound of the audience clapping and measured a reading on a shaky dial. Backstage, Wayne Ramsbottom was in charge of the backing tracks on his brother Clint's ghetto-blaster.

By midway through the contest, Grimsby Gerry was emerging as the favourite with his version of Elvis's 1962 hit 'Return To Sender'.

'It's about a poor lad an' 'is girlfriend's not comin' back,' explained Troy. 'Y'know t'feeling lads, don't you?' He winked at Claire Bradshaw in the front row. ''Cept it's never 'appened t'me.' He looked down at his list. 'An' now we 'ave another Ragley favourite – Young Tommy Piercy, singin' t'second single Elvis released after returning from t'army. It sold more than twenty-five million copies. So let's 'ear it f'young Tommy wi' "It's Now Or Never".'

Sadly, it turned out to be *never* for the young butcher, although he received a generous round of applause from all his customers, particularly those who had received a free box of Paxo stuffing at Christmas.

Chris 'Kojak' Wojciechowski, the Ragley Rovers' Bald-Headed Ball-Wizard, caused some debate among the audience. Troy had done his homework and told us that the 1961 *Blue Hawaii* track 'Can't Help Falling In Love' was probably Elvis's greatest love ballad.

Kojak started singing about wise men rushing in, sadly completely off key.

'Y'can't 'ave a bald Elvis,' shouted Big Dave. 'It jus' ain't right.'

'Y'reight there, Dave,' agreed a nervous Little Malcolm as his big moment approached.

Next was Clint Ramsbottom. 'Clint's gonna sing the 1957 song, "All Shook Up", that topped the pop, country an' R&B charts,' said Troy.

'That's weally special, Tywone,' said Nora Pratt in the third row.

Tyrone gave Nora his *trivia* look. 'That's known as a *trifecta*,' he whispered into her ear. Then he edged a little closer and held her hand.

'It's t'favourite now, Tywone,' said Nora, 'that Pwudential Insuwance man. 'E's singin' "Jailhouse Wock".'

'An 'ere we go again wi' a 1957 classic,' said

202

Troy, 'and t'name of Elvis's third film. It's "Jail-'ouse Rock" an' t'Elvis lookalike, Lionel 'Igginbottom.'

The problem was that Lionel was no longer a lookalike. His beautifully styled Elvis wig was missing and he was sure he had put it on top of his executive briefcase before leaving home. Unknown to Lionel, it had slipped on to the kitchen floor and his deaf and increasingly short-sighted mother had thought it was next door's kitten. It was only after Lionel had left for the village hall that she noticed it hadn't touched its saucer of milk.

Lionel began to sing about a party in the county jail, but his heart just wasn't in it. The wig had been the crowning glory of the complete ensemble, right down to his Cuban-heeled sequinned shoes, and he received muted applause.

'Ah've told 'im 'til cows come 'ome t'check 'is case,' said Lionel's mother, 'but does 'e tek any notice? Does 'e 'eck.'

Finally it was Little Malcolm's turn. 'So put yer 'ands t'gether for Little Malcolm Robinson who will be singin' Elvis's biggest 'it of t'seventies, reachin' number one in 1972 – 'is twentieth number one and 'is fortieth Top Ten 'it, "Burning Love".'

Little Malcolm walked on in his Elvis outfit and picked up the microphone.

'Ah'm dedicatin' this song t'my beautiful wife,' he said and there wasn't a dry eye in the house.

'C'mon *my* Malcolm!' shouted Dorothy.

'Gi' it some welly!' yelled Big Dave.

Little Malcolm puffed out his chest and began

to sing in a throaty, husky voice that had the ladies of Ragley swooning in the aisles as he informed them that he was a hunk of burning love.

It was a foregone conclusion before he reached the end. The dial on the clapometer went nearly off the scale and Little Malcolm was declared the winner.

When Beth and I drove home the moon was a broken crescent, cracked like porcelain, as scattered clouds hurried across the sky.

'Wasn't Malcolm really good?' said a surprised Beth.

'And what a voice!' I said.

'They say good things come in little packages,' said Beth and then smiled. 'Pity you're six feet one!'

Outside the village hall Eugene Scrimshaw was congratulating Little Malcolm.

'Well done, Malcolm,' he said. 'Medicine must 'ave worked.'

Little Malcolm, deep down, was a kindly soul and he didn't want to upset Ragley's Captain Kirk. 'Y'reight there, Eugene,' he agreed.

However, when he got home he threw the cough mixture in the bin. *Ah like bein' 'usky,* he thought.

'Ah we gettin' up t'bed,' said Malcolm, 'or d'you want a coffee?'

'Oooh Malcolm, y'voice is *real sexy,*' swooned Dorothy. 'Let's f'get t'coffee.'

Half an hour later Nora was looking for her earplugs.

Chapter Eleven

Just Another Day

County Hall requested responses to their questionnaire 'A Policy for the Efficient Heating of Village Schools'. The school optician carried out eye tests. Repairs were completed to the roof above the school office. Boiler repairs were arranged for next week. School closed today for the half-term holiday and will reopen on Monday, 25 February.

Extract from the Ragley School Logbook:
Friday, 15 February 1985

A bleak and bitter day had dawned. When I peered through the bedroom window of Bilbo Cottage, the stillness of winter lay heavy on the countryside. It was as if we were frozen in time in an everlasting Narnia winter. It was Friday morning, 15 February, and the world was still as stone under its smooth white blanket. The temperature in North Yorkshire had dropped to minus ten degrees on the high moors and the land was held fast in the grip of winter. In the distance, over the Hambleton hills, dark clouds were rolling towards us and the rooks squawked their danger cries as the wind began to rattle the branches where they nested.

In the garden of Bilbo Cottage, sparrows and chaffinches were busy in the hedgerow while a solitary robin, its feathers ruffled in the stiff breeze, perched forlornly on my garden seat, looking hopefully for a few crumbs.

'I think I've got a cold coming on,' said Beth.

She looked tired. It occurred to me that it must be serious as, like most women I knew, she battled on through coughs and colds without mentioning them.

'Well, you'll have time to recover during half-term,' I said in an attempt to be positive.

'Sadly, I've got to complete my dissertation, so I'll be busy,' she said with a sigh and a sneeze.

We were both weary after a sleepless night, as our son had been awake for most of it. I helped her strap John into his car seat. 'Good luck and have a good day,' I said.

'You too,' she replied and kissed me lightly on the cheek. 'Is there anything special today?'

'Thankfully, no,' I said. 'Just a quiet day ahead.'

I should have known better.

On my journey from Kirkby Steepleton the wind gusted around me and my Morris Minor shook in protest. The fuel gauge showed nearly empty so, reluctantly, I pulled in at Victor Pratt's garage.

Victor looked more weary than usual as he lumbered out to meet me.

'Ah've gorra problem, Mr Sheffield,' he said, as his hand holding the petrol pump turned purple with cold.

'Oh dear, Victor,' I replied, 'and what might that be?'

'Ah've got that insom – insom–'

'Insomnia,' I said.

'That's it, Mr Sheffield,' he said, wiping his

hands on a greasy cloth and taking the ten-pound note from my hand. 'In fac', ah can't sleep f'worryin' about it.'

I know the feeling, I thought.

As I pulled up outside the General Stores I recalled it was my turn to replenish the staff-room biscuit tin.

'And some biscuits for the staff-room please, Miss Golightly,' I said.

'Garibaldi, Mr Sheffield?' asked Prudence.

Barry Ollerenshaw was standing in the queue behind me. 'My gran calls 'em "flies' graveyard" biscuits, Mr Sheffield,' he said with an encouraging smile.

Prudence paused and we both looked at this popular biscuit with a new appreciation. 'Perhaps a packet of digestives,' she said with a smile.

When I arrived at school Ruby was pouring salt on the steps of the entrance porch. She didn't look pleased. 'We've gorra problem, Mr Sheffield,' she said. The fierce north-east wind was freezing the side of my face, whereas Ruby's only concession to the weather was an old headscarf double-knotted beneath her chin.

'What's that, Ruby?' I yelled above the gale.

She pointed to the grey slate tiles on the roof above the office. 'Couple o' tiles 'ave shifted wi' t'wind. Weather'll get in if we don't gerrit fixed sharpish. Ah've told Mrs F.'

'Thanks, Ruby,' I said and hurried up the steps.

In the shelter of the entrance porch Hayley Spraggon and her little brother, Alfie, had brought in their pets for our morning assembly. Sally's theme was 'Kindness to Animals' and eight-year-old Hayley had volunteered to contribute.

Alfie was holding a shoe box which had been filled with miscellaneous vegetation and ripe fruit. 'This is Boycott, Mr Sheffield,' he said proudly, 'an' 'e can poke 'is 'ead out of 'is shell.'

I peered in. 'That's a fine tortoise, Alfie,' I said. Boycott, named presumably after the Yorkshire and England cricketer who accumulated runs at his own steady pace, looked content in his box.

'An' would y'like t'see my gerbil, Mr Sheffield?' asked Hayley. She was holding a wire cage and staring at her small furry friend.

'Is it a boy or a girl?' I asked.

'It's a girl, Mr Sheffield,' said Hayley. 'She's called Sparky the Second.'

'What happened to Sparky the First?' I asked ... then wished I hadn't.

'M'dad 'it 'er wi' a shovel, Mr Sheffield.'

'Oh dear,' I said.

'She got out an' 'e thought it were a rat.' Hayley sighed at the memory. 'But 'e said 'e were sorry so, like m'mam says, no 'arm done.'

It struck me that some children were old before their time. 'I see,' I said, wincing at the image that had come into my mind.

I decided not to mention this conversation to Sally prior to her 'Kindness to Animals' assembly. It was then that Sparky the Second looked up at me sadly and I wondered if she had heard the bit about the shovel.

The school office was like an ice box and Vera, seemingly undeterred, was wearing a warm coat and scarf.

'Good morning, Mr Sheffield,' she said. 'I've rung John Paxton about the loose tiles.' She pointed to the ceiling. 'Fortunately they're above this wing of the school and not a danger to the children.'

John Paxton was the village handyman and could repair hinges, fix broken desks, unblock gutters, replace broken windows and mend fences and gates. He was a reliable Jack-of-all-trades and honest as the day is long.

'Thanks, Vera,' I said with relief.

'I've telephoned the office, but there is a new and exceedingly irritating administrator answering the telephone at County Hall and redirecting calls,' said Vera testily. 'He is not proving helpful.'

'Don't worry, I'll have a try,' I said, blowing into my hands to get some feeling back into my fingers.

'Also,' continued Vera, glancing down at her notepad, 'the school boiler is playing up, which is why the office is so cold. However, Ruby says she can keep enough heat in the classrooms for us to be able to survive today.'

'Oh well, that's something,' I said.

'The engineer will come in during half-term,' said Vera, 'and to top it all we have to respond to this today.' She held up a smart, spiral-bound laminated booklet with the North Yorkshire Schools crest; it was titled 'A Policy for the Efficient Heating of Village Schools'. 'There's a questionnaire in the back.'

I shook my head in disbelief. 'Well, at least it will be warm in the staff-room,' I said, trying to find a ray of comfort.

'Oh yes,' said Vera, 'almost forgot ... we can't go in the staff-room today as the school optician will be in there using it for eye tests.'

I smiled while groaning inwardly, then sat down at my desk and dialled the number for County Hall in Northallerton. It was picked up immediately, which was encouraging.

'Good morning, Jack Sheffield here from Ragley Primary School,' I said.

'Jeffrey Stank here,' was the chirpy reply. 'Jeffrey-with-a-J,' he added.

Undeterred by the irrelevance, I pressed on. 'I simply need authorization to replace a couple of roof tiles – it's urgent,' I explained.

'Ah well, Mr Sheffield – there are *procedures*,' he said. 'You'll need to complete an SW909 for the Small Works Department.'

Jobsworth, I thought.

'Well, can you send one out to me?'

'Yes,' said Jobsworth, 'and you should receive it within five working days.'

'I need to get it fixed *now*,' I said.

'As I said, Mr Sheffield, we have to have procedures.'

When I first arrived at Ragley in 1977 I had found a useful ally in County Hall. He could authorize these simple jobs without recourse to the North Yorkshire County Council secret police. In consequence, no one would knock on my door and seek an explanation for the lack of paperwork to support the payment of two pounds and fifty pence for the repair of a broken desk. This, in turn, would avoid the need to purchase a new desk at a vastly inflated price.

However, I guessed the days of completing any simple human activity such as this without the need for a trail of half a tree's worth of paper were numbered. The completion of official forms was becoming a significant and unwelcome aspect of my professional life and I wondered where it would end.

'Fine,' I said, unable to hide my irritation. 'So please could you put one in the post?'

'Have you got a pencil, Mr Sheffield?' asked Jobsworth. 'You need your reference number.'

'Reference number?'

'Yes, every call has a reference number.'

The bell rang. 'Sorry, must go, I'm teaching now,' I said and replaced the receiver. An appropriate expletive came to mind but, as Vera was the vicar's sister, her presence curtailed any profanity.

The fact that it was colder than usual in school didn't seem to deter the children. As the morning progressed, the excitement in my class was growing.

'It's snowing again, Mr Sheffield,' Dawn Phillips called out as the pattering against the window increased in volume.

'Looks like that proper snow that meks good snowballs,' said Frankie Spraggon.

'An' snowmen,' said Sam Borthwick.

'An' igloos,' added Danny Hardacre with the ambition of youth.

The children stood up and looked out of the windows.

'It's definitely settling Mr Sheffield,' observed

Mo Hartley.

'It'll be good at dinner time,' said Harold Bustard. 'That's if you'll let us go on t'field, Mr Sheffield.'

'Please can we, *please?*' begged Ben Roberts. He had learned long ago that a double helping of please often produced positive results.

'Finish your SMP and we'll see,' I said.

As if I had flicked a switch, the children all bowed their heads and gave full concentration to their School Mathematics Project workcards.

Meanwhile, in Class 3, Joseph Evans was pleased the discussion about 'Heaven' had gone so well. As playtime approached the children packed away their exercise books and gathered near the door to file out to the cloakroom.

However, Damian Brown had stuck out his tongue at Jemima Poole. 'How do you think you'll go to heaven behaving like that?' asked Joseph light-heartedly.

Damian gave this some thought. 'Well, Mr Evans, we could run in an' out o' t'pearly gates reight fast an' keep slammin' 'em.'

'Oh dear,' said Joseph, 'and why is that?'

'Well, St Peter will say, "Mek y'mind up – come in or stay out," jus' like our mam says.'

Suddenly the children were gathering around Joseph, full of questions.

'Mr Evans,' asked Jemima Poole brightly, 'is Sunday a day of rest?'

'Yes, Jemima, it is,' said Joseph benignly.

Jemima considered this for a moment. 'So why do we 'ave t'go t'Sunday School?'

'An', Mr Evans, does God 'ave a las' name?' shouted Stacey Bryant.

'An' what about dead people, Mr Evans?' added Ryan Halfpenny, going off at a tangent.

'Dead people!' exclaimed Joseph. He was rapidly losing the will to live.

'Yes,' said Ryan. 'Why doesn't God stop lettin' people die, 'cause then 'E wouldn't 'ave t'mek new ones?'

The logic of young children never ceased to amaze Joseph. 'That's a good point,' he conceded with good grace.

At morning break Mrs Fazackerly was waiting for me in the school entrance hall.

'It's our Madonna, Mr Sheffield,' she said. 'She's at 'ome wi' a rash an' it's a sight t'be'old.'

'I'm sorry to hear that, Mrs Fazackerly,' I said. 'That's a shame, because she was fine yesterday.' Mrs Fazackerly had a reputation for keeping her daughter at home for a wide variety of reasons.

'Well, ah'm tellin' y'straight, Mr Sheffield, it's as true as true can be,' she protested. 'An' may I be struck down dead in m'best shoes if it's not.'

I found myself glancing down at her footwear, presumably to gauge the quality, but the downtrodden heels and scuff marks suggested she would live another day.

The office was freezing and all the teachers called in to collect a warm mug of coffee from Vera. Just above our heads, John Paxton, known locally as Whistling John, was hammering to his heart's content while whistling Johnny Tillotson's 1960 hit, 'Poetry In Motion'.

I glanced at Vera's *Daily Telegraph*. There was a photograph of Sir Clive Sinclair, who had recently launched his C5, a battery-powered electric tricycle with a top speed of 15 mph. On the same page it mentioned that the BBC proposed to launch a new soap called *EastEnders* next week. Like the tricycle, I couldn't see it catching on.

'This cup of coffee is for the optician,' said Vera, putting it on a tray with two digestive biscuits. 'She said it was a bit stuffy in there but she'll manage.'

Meanwhile, I had lost all feeling in my toes.

'I'll take it in, Vera,' I offered. I thought I would check to see if the eye tests were going to plan.

As I popped my head round the door the heat hit me like a welcome sauna and for a few moments it was bliss. 'Is everything all right?' I asked politely, putting the tray on the coffee table.

The optician gave me an abrupt nod. 'A little too warm in here,' she said, 'so I turned the gas fire to the LOW setting.'

I smiled through gritted teeth. 'Fine,' I said, 'just see Mrs Forbes-Kitchener in the office if you need anything.'

She nodded curtly and carried on. Zoe Book was staring at a large chart of assorted letters in descending order of size. The optician pointed to the third line from the bottom. 'And can you read this line?' she asked.

'Yes, thank you,' said Zoe politely.

The optician looked up at me with a *why-are-your-children-like-this?* smile and she didn't say thank you for the coffee.

After break I called in to Anne's classroom, where Billy Ricketts was standing by the number apparatus cupboard. He had pushed two wooden Cuisenaire counting rods up his nostrils and was pretending to be a walrus.

I suggested he take them out, wash them under the tap in the art corner and put them back in the box, while secretly admiring his convincing mime.

Meanwhile Anne appeared much more active than usual. It later emerged that she had sent off for a Multi-Exerciser from a mail-order address in Melton Mowbray in Leicestershire. It promised to 'reduce tummy flab and trim your figure' and it appeared to be working.

By lunchtime the temperature was dropping fast and in the school office a cruel wind rattled the wooden casements as we gathered to share news.

'Jack, have a look at this.' Tom had a computer magazine open at a page with a photograph of young children using computers as if they had been born to it. 'There's some new educational software and it's compatible with Commodore 64, Spectrum 48K and BBC B Computers.'

Anne gave me that familiar wide-eyed smile she assumed whenever Tom seemed to speak in a different language.

'It's all there, Jack,' he said, pressing home the point. 'Numbers, letters, shapes, measuring money, reading and telling the time.' He looked across at Anne. 'It's perfect for our two classes, Anne, and I'm happy to help you until you get the hang of it.'

Anne smiled again. 'Thanks, Tom. I realize I have to move with the times, but you might need some patience with me.'

Tom grinned shyly. 'Don't worry, we'll be fine,' he said. 'I'll pass on all I know.'

Anne looked at Tom with curiosity.

There was silence as we considered the meaning at different levels until Vera broke the spell. 'Tea anyone?' she asked.

I decided to put on my coat and scarf and go out on to the playground to check all was well. John Paxton gave me a friendly wave from the rooftop and, like the children, seemed oblivious to the sharp wind and gusting snow.

'Y'can't beat a bit o'snow, Mr Sheffield,' shouted an excited Billy Ricketts. His bare knees looked purple with cold and his cheeks were the colour of rosy apples.

On the other side of the school wall Old Tommy Piercy walked by and waved.

'Windy day, Mr Piercy,' I shouted as another gust bent the branches of the horse chestnut trees.

'Wind?' retorted Old Tommy. 'This is nowt. When ah were a lad we 'ad winds that'd tek fleece off a sheep's back. Now that were *proper* wind.'

'Oh well, have a good day,' I said.

'Any road, ah'm off to T'Royal Oak for a bit o' food,' he said. 'It's one o' Sheila's specials – venison pasty.' To my surprise, he passed a parcel to me through the school railings. 'It's an 'ot pie, Mr Sheffield, for John on t'roof. One o' my prize-winning growlers,' he added without a hint of modesty and wandered off.

I smiled. These were the small gestures of

216

friendship I had learned to know and appreciate in our village community – a helping hand here, a kind word there and a warm pie on a cold day.

On the other side of the village green a familiar Rolls-Royce moved smoothly from the Morton Road into the High Street. Petula Dudley-Palmer looked preoccupied as she pulled up outside Piercy's butcher's shop. She had just spoken to her husband Geoffrey on the telephone but he hadn't ended the call by saying 'Love you' as he usually did and Petula was thinking about their early courtship when they used to laugh and hold hands.

Old Tommy Piercy was a member of the SAS – the Sausage Appreciation Society – and was very proud of his prize-winning sausages. His grandson, Young Tommy, was gradually taking over and he had just displayed a tray of the famous sausages in the window next to the pigs' trotters and speciality black pudding.

Young Tommy had grown into a handsome man and he treated his lady customers with polite grace and charm. When he served Petula she felt that thrill again – the kind she recalled when Mr Parkinson, the student science teacher, had let her and Emily Poulton use a Bunsen burner. He would pass round a box of Swan Vesta matches and tell them to use only one ... one match, one chance, one opportunity to light the blue flame. She and Emily had professed undying love for the young, slender Mr Parkinson, while he was entirely oblivious of their teenage passion and racing hormones. However, unknown to them, he went home each evening to a nurse from Wythenshawe who knew a lot more about sex than he did about copper sulphate crystals.

The last time Petula had visited the shop Old Tommy had said knowingly, 'In a village like Ragley there are no secrets.'

Oh yes there are, thought Petula.

When she returned home she closed the curtains and the measured ticks of the clock counted out the heartbeats of her life.

Back in school, Scott Higginbottom and Patience Crapper were standing in the dinner queue. 'Would you like to be my girlfriend?' asked Scott.

Patience looked at him with disdain. 'No,' she said firmly.

'Ah've gorra tortoise,' said Scott, as if this would seal the engagement.

'Still no,' said Patience.

'Why not?' asked Scott.

''Cause ah'm not like a tortoise.'

''Ow come?'

'Ah can choose.'

Conceptually, this left Scott on the starting line in the art of wooing.

After school dinner a commotion on the playground attracted my attention and I hurried out. Ben Roberts and Harold Bustard had made a slide in the frozen snow outside the boiler-house doors. Harold had fallen and cut his head and the dinner lady, Mrs Critchley, was tending him as I stepped through the crowd to see what was happening.

''Arold 'as split 'is 'ead open, Mr Sheffield,'

shouted Ben.

'Will 'e die, sir?' asked Scott Higginbottom.

'It's a lot of blood,' added Rosie Spittlehouse, fascinated by the small cut on poor Harold's forehead.

'There won't be much left,' said Ted Coggins knowingly.

'Will 'e lose 'is memory, Sir?' asked Barry Ollerenshaw.

'An' would 'e know 'e'd lost it, Sir?' added Damian Brown.

'Is 'e con-shush?' Rufus Snodgrass wanted to know, and so it went on until normal service was resumed. We contacted Mrs Bustard and kept a careful watch on Harold until his mother came in to collect him.

Afternoon break proved a little more encouraging. Shirley appeared from her kitchen and surprised us with a plateful of piping hot buttered crumpets that provided the perfect accompaniment to Vera's excellent milky coffee. Much refreshed, we all returned to our classrooms.

In Class 1 Anne opened her illustrated copy of *Squirrel Nutkin*. 'Where did we finish the story yesterday?' she asked. 'Do you remember, Billy?'

'Give us a minute, Mrs Grainger,' said Billy Ricketts, screwing up his face in concentration. 'My 'ead's trying t'tell me.'

In Class 2 you could have heard a pin drop. Tom was reading *Charlotte's Web* to his children and they were spellbound as Wilbur the pig continued his magical journey through life on the farm.

Meanwhile, up the Morton Road in her state-of-the-art conservatory, Petula Dudley-Palmer was reading an article in her *Woman's Realm* under the headline 'Where the quality of family life matters most'. She wondered if there might be answers here to bring back a little romance into their marriage. Geoffrey had seemed very distant lately and she didn't know why. She sipped her coffee and reflected on her life. She had taken her daily dose of Vykmin multivitamin capsules to ensure good health ... but she still felt depressed.

Then she chose her favourite wicker chair and settled down to read *The Growing Pains of Adrian Mole* and found that the author, Sue Townsend, cheered her up a little. Later she coated four pieces of chicken with Crosse & Blackwell Southern Style seasoning, so a tasty evening meal was in store. In the fridge was a Black Forest gateau that she had been saving for an intimate soirée with Geoffrey.

It was then that the telephone rang and Geoffrey told her he would be late and not to worry about dinner.

Oh well... The girls will enjoy the gateau, she thought.

It was five o'clock and I was in the school office, wading through paperwork, when the telephone rang. 'We don't appear to have received your completed questionnaire on school heating, Mr Sheffield,' said a strident voice. It was Jobsworth.

'Ah, yes,' I said, searching in the in-tray on my desk. 'I have it here.' It comprised four sides of small printing on a folded A3 sheet of paper – a sort of mini Domesday Book. 'I'm busy with it now,' I said unconvincingly.

'Make sure it's posted back to us immediately,' instructed Jobsworth. 'We can't complete our records without it. You must appreciate, Mr Sheffield, that this information is important.'

'I'm sure it is,' I said, without, I hoped, a hint of sarcasm.

There was a riffle of papers. 'And it would appear the chief culprits are most of the village schools in the Easington area.'

'Where the headteachers have a full-time teaching commitment, I expect,' I said with feeling.

Jobsworth was unimpressed. 'And your reference number is NYCC 85/607,' he added.

'Reference number?'

'Yes, for the roof repair you mentioned this morning,' he said. 'You will need to fill this in and send it back to us for authorization,' and the line went dead.

I didn't mention that Whistling John had completed the job for the price of a hot pie.

Then I picked up the form and wrote 'Ragley Church of England Primary School' on the top line before my pen ran out of ink.

An hour later I had completed the questionnaire and, wearily, I locked up the school and drove down the cobbled drive. A baleful crescent moon emerged from behind the tattered rags of clouds and the shadows of the giant horse chestnut trees draped the frozen playground.

I posted the questionnaire in the post box on

the High Street and drove home. When I walked in, Beth was standing at the kitchen table making marmalade.

'My mother's recipe,' she said with a grin. 'Never fails.'

She had chopped twenty Seville oranges and six lemons in half and squeezed the juice into her largest pan. While I went to see John she added four bags of sugar and, after cutting the oranges into quarters and trimming off the ends, she sliced every segment really finely. Everything that was left on the chopping board, including the pith, pips and bits of rind, was put in a muslin bag along with some pectin. The bag was then tied up and put in the pan. When I returned the mixture was boiling.

'So how did your day go?' I asked.

'Fine,' said Beth. 'I got home early, so I thought I would do something completely different.'

'Did you complete that wretched heating questionnaire?' I asked.

Beth thought for a moment. 'Oh, that... I delegated that to my caretaker.'

Feeling slightly crushed that I hadn't thought of that, I put the kettle on.

Beth looked up. 'So, how was it for you?'

I reflected on the hole in the school roof, boiler trouble, freezing conditions, the demise of Sparky the First, Harold's cut head and Jobsworth's questionnaire, and I sighed.

'Just another day,' I said.

Chapter Twelve

Thatcher's Children

Final repairs to the school boiler will be completed on Saturday, 2 March. A new floor polisher will be delivered tomorrow morning and Mrs Smith has agreed to take delivery.

Extract from the Ragley School Logbook:
Friday, 1 March 1985

The weather had changed dramatically in the last few days. The snow had gone and warmth began to spread over the land. On the high moors the clacking of grouse and the high-pitched call of curlews sought attention and announced the first signs of a distant spring.

It was Saturday morning, 2 March, and in Ragley the village green was waking from a long winter. The pond was full of new life and the willow was turning green. On the grassy bank outside the village hall the first signs of the blue-grey bullet heads of daffodils had begun to spear through the hard, frozen earth and lift the spirits. It was a morning full of optimism and a time for the entrepreneurs of the future to begin their journey ... perhaps even the Earnshaw brothers.

'Mam, please can we 'ave some pocket money?' asked Heathcliffe Earnshaw plaintively.

'No, y'can't,' said Julie Earnshaw. She was

standing by the stove frying bacon. 'Ask y'dad.'

Heathcliffe looked at his brother Terry. 'You ask 'im,' said Heathcliffe quietly. 'Ah broke that window las' week.'

Mr Earnshaw was reading his *Racing Post* while Dallas Sue-Ellen was playing with a Barbie doll behind the sofa.

'Dad,' said Terry, 'please can we 'ave a bit o' pocket money?'

Mr Earnshaw didn't look up.

'It's t'go to t'pictures, Dad,' added Heathcliffe. 'Everybody else is goin'.'

'It's *Gremlins*,' continued Terry. 'It's on in York this afternoon.'

'Bus goes at one o'clock, Dad,' said Heathcliffe with a sense of urgency.

Mr Earnshaw peered over his paper. 'Ask y'mam,' he said curtly.

The television was chattering away in the corner. A lady standing outside the Houses of Parliament was announcing that the miners' strike might be close to an end after almost a year of struggle. Then they moved smoothly back to the studio and a brief cameo of some of Margaret Thatcher's famous speeches.

'You turn if you want to. The lady's not for turning,' said the Prime Minister to thunderous applause.

'She said that a few years back,' said Mrs Earnshaw knowingly as she turned the rashers in the spitting fat. 'Ah voted for 'er.'

'Well ah didn't,' said Mr Earnshaw in disgust. 'Ah'm unemployed 'cause of 'er.'

'Well get off y'backside then an' find a job,'

snapped Mrs Earnshaw.

Mr Earnshaw winced under the verbal assault and buried himself further in his paper.

'Human dignity and self-respect are undermined when men and women are condemned to idleness,' said the Prime Minister in a strident voice.

'There y'are,' shouted Julie Earnshaw above the spitting fat of the frying pan. She looked at her two boys. 'Heath', Terry – listen t'yer mother. Money doesn't grow on trees.' She turned off the gas and began to cut thick slices of bread. 'Y'need t'work 'ard jus' like that plumber in t'village. Luke Walmsley started 'is own business an' 'e's doin' well for 'imself. 'E's jus' got a new van.'

On the television Margaret Thatcher was saying that she wanted council tenants to have the chance to buy their homes.

'One day 'e might own 'is own 'ouse,' continued Mrs Earnshaw.

'Y'mean not payin' rent?' asked Heathcliffe in surprise.

'That's right. An' you an' Terry could do that.'

Margaret Thatcher began to talk about a 'free economy'.

'Turn it off!' yelled Mr Earnshaw.

Mrs Earnshaw pointed the spatula at her husband. 'Ah don't want you boys t'grow up like 'im,' she said with feeling. 'Now, 'ere's y'breakfast,' she went on as she put the bacon sandwiches on the table. 'An' if y'want money y'need t'go out an' *earn* it. You 'ave t'provide a service that other folks want an' will pay for.'

This was a new concept for Heathcliffe, and

225

thoughts began to stir in this son of Barnsley. He bit hungrily into his bacon sandwich. "Urry up, Terry,' he said. 'We're goin' out.'

Vera looked from her kitchen window at the magnificent grounds of Morton Manor. Snowdrops and crocuses lifted the spirit and, against the Yorkshire stone walls of the stable block, japonica buds were waiting to burst into life.

Her life had changed since she had married Major Rupert Forbes-Kitchener and moved into her new home. Her three cats, Treacle, Jess and Maggie, the latter named after her political heroine Margaret Thatcher, had soon settled in, but for Vera it had been a trying experience. Her twice-weekly Cross-stitch Club, church flowers and Women's Institute meetings kept her busy, but she was slowly making her mark on her new home. The kitchen had proved to be the biggest challenge. She was writing a shopping list when her attention was drawn to the television set on the worktop. A news programme featuring Margaret Thatcher's famous speeches had begun with one of Vera's favourites about the lady's not for turning. She remembered it well. It was about the time she recalled noticing Rupert. She heard his footsteps approaching the kitchen door.

'Any plans today, my dear?' he asked as he sat down at the kitchen table and Vera poured him a cup of Earl Grey tea.

A tall, imposing man in his mid-sixties, Rupert was immaculate as ever in a tweed suit, crisp white shirt, East Yorkshire regimental tie and brown heavy brogues polished to a military shine.

'Yes,' said Vera, 'I've got some shopping to do in Boots in York.'

'Jolly good,' said Rupert vaguely.

'It's for that microwave we discussed.' Vera showed Rupert her list. It read 'Sharp 541 microwave oven – £159.95 – Boots Credit Card'.

Rupert was completely unconcerned about the cost but frowned when he saw the reference to the credit card. 'A credit card, Vera?'

'Yes, dear,' said Vera. 'Don't concern yourself... They are useful to have and I won't be getting into debt.'

Rupert smiled and kissed her lightly on the forehead. 'Of course.' Then he sipped his tea thoughtfully. 'Virginia didn't come home last night.'

'I think she went off with her current boyfriend,' said Vera. 'It's that Timmy Farquharson from that horsey set near Pickering.'

Rupert frowned. 'My daughter can do better than that,' he said firmly.

Vera nodded. 'I agree ... but she's a young woman now and she has to make her own choices.'

Rupert always admired Vera for her wisdom and her elegance. It was also apparent that Vera's hair was no longer grey. The silver strands at her temples had changed subtly over a period of time to a more youthful brunette since Diane the hairdresser had begun to make more frequent home visits. 'You know best, my dear,' he said.

Vera picked up the list and stood up. 'And on my way home I'm calling in with some flowers for Dot Howard. I heard she'd been burgled again.'

'Bad business, what?' said Rupert, shaking his

head in annoyance.

'Yes indeed,' agreed Vera.

In Bilbo Cottage I was in the kitchen finishing an appetizing bowl of hot porridge while Beth was reading *Jack and the Beanstalk* to John. The school boiler had proved problematic, but the repair man was making his last visit this morning and I needed to call in and check all was well.

The television was on and a news reporter was explaining that Thatcher's free market economics had strengthened the overall economy and created a growing middle class, but had widened the gap between rich and poor. In the same breath he mentioned that social unrest was growing and I wondered where it would all end.

I looked at my watch. 'The boiler man said he'd be in mid-morning.'

'Can you pick up some groceries?' asked Beth. 'Your son eats like a horse,' she added with a grin and pointed to a list on the table. Beth looked more relaxed. She had just finished her dissertation and was due to hand it in to her tutor the following week. It was a huge weight off her shoulders. She was the carefree Beth again that I knew so well and for a brief moment I daydreamed. The silent music of our love echoed throughout our tiny cottage and the memories of our time together were vivid.

I washed my porridge bowl in the sink. 'I don't know how long I'll be, so I'll see you later,' I said, kissing her on the cheek.

The newsreader had moved on to an item about the new BBC twice-weekly soap. 'You were wrong about *EastEnders*,' said Beth with a smile. 'It seems to have been well received.'

Last month seventeen million viewers had tuned in to the new series in order to share the daily lives of people living in Albert Square in the London borough of Walford. It had caught the imagination of the villagers and in the local shops it was a source of gossip and anticipation.

Gossip was certainly the order of the day in Nora's Coffee Shop – along with a good helping of anticipation. Chaka Khan's 'I Feel For You' was on the jukebox and Nora was writing a special offer on the chalkboard. Dorothy was serving frothy coffees to eighteen-year-olds Claire Bradshaw and Anita Cuthbertson at a corner table – and they were discussing sex.

The two girls saw Dorothy as an experienced woman. 'Dorothy – I'm getting a thing for older men,' whispered Anita.

'We both are,' added Claire knowingly.

'Ah know what y'mean,' said Dorothy. 'Shakin' Stevens'll be thirty-four nex' week an' 'e's jus' dishy.'

The teenagers had moved on from 1978 when they left my class to attend Easington Comprehensive School. They had fallen in love with the American pop idol David Cassidy. After his boyish good looks had appeared on the side of their breakfast Weetabix box, they had worshipped the ground he walked on. However, with experience came a new beginning.

'I'm thinking of going on t'pill,' confided Claire.

'Flippin' 'eck!' said Dorothy and began wiping

the table with a tea towel to stall for time.

'Y'mother'll kill you,' said Anita, suitably aghast but secretly envious.

'Ah know, but ah fancy Kenny.'

'But 'e's only eighteen.'

'Ah know,' said Claire.

'So what 'appened to *older* men?' asked Dorothy.

'Well, you've got t'start somewhere,' protested Claire.

The bell above the door jingled and Claire looked up expectantly, hoping it might be Kenny Kershaw, but it was only the Earnshaw boys. With a sigh they returned to studying Anita's fold-up poster of Tears for Fears and discussing new techniques for ironing their hair.

The brothers walked confidently to the counter, where Nora was admiring her neat printing on the 'Today's Specials' board.

''Ello, Miss Pratt,' said Heathcliffe politely. 'We've started a business.'

Heathcliffe and Terry pointed to their cardboard badges, which read 'Earnshaw Delivery Services'.

'So what y'delivewin'?' asked Nora, replacing the stick of chalk in her apron pocket.

'Food,' said Heathcliffe, ''cause *everyone's* got to eat. If you mek t'food, Miss Pratt, we'll deliver it … and we've got transport.'

'Twanspo't?'

'Yes,' said Terry, 'Ben Roberts 'as lent us 'is bike an' we've gorra basket on t'front.'

Nora smiled. 'Good idea, Tewwy – but ah jus' pwepare food an' people eat it in t'shop.' She

230

studied the two eager faces. 'Why not twy Miss Golightly?'

'We will, Miss Pratt. Thanks f'list'ning,' said Heathdliffe and they hurried out.

In the General Stores Prudence Golightly was more receptive. She was a kindly lady and always willing to support young people and their initiatives.

'Take this to Mrs Poole, please, boys,' she said. 'She forgot her tins of dog meat for Scargill.' She pointed to four tins of PAL with marrowbone jelly. 'Here's five pence each.' She looked up at Jeremy the bear. 'And Jeremy says you can have a barley sugar.'

'Thanks, Miss Golightly,' said Heathcliffe.

'...an' Jeremy,' added Terry as they hurried out to make their first delivery.

In the school boiler house Jim the boilerman stroked the black oven doors with affection. Jim loved his boilers and he had travelled over from Harrogate to complete the final repairs.

'That'll see y'reight, Jack,' he said. 'It'll las' you a few more years.' He looked at his watch. ''Ow about a coffee in Nora's?'

'Good idea,' I said. 'I'll just check that Ruby will lock up.'

Ruby had taken delivery of a new floor polisher and she was trying it out in the hall. Meanwhile, Vera had called in and they were in conversation as we washed our hands and set off across the High Street for some refreshment.

Heathcliffe and Terry had arrived at Mrs Poole's

house and Scargill the Yorkshire terrier was about to enjoy a good meal. Heathcliffe explained to Mrs Poole about their new business while Terry waited outside the front gate with the precious bicycle. It was widely known that there had been a few burglaries in the area and Heathcliffe had instructed Terry to stand guard. Jemima Poole walked down the path to talk to Terry. She was holding a half-eaten sugar mouse by its string tail after Scargill had bitten off the head and slavered over the rest of its pink sugar body.

Terry looked apprehensively at Jemima. After all, she was a *girl*. Terry was in the Ragley Scout Troop and what he didn't know about birds' eggs, clove hitches and how to cook sausages using a primus stove wasn't worth knowing – but he didn't understand girls.

Jemima stared at a worm in the hedgerow. 'If you eat that worm ah'll give you this mouse.'

Terry loved sugar mice, even half-eaten ones. Without hesitation he picked up the worm, popped it in his mouth, crunched it to pieces and swallowed quickly. Then he opened his mouth wide so Jemima could see it had gone.

Jemima was impressed and repulsed at the same time. She handed over the decapitated mouse and Terry ate it, including the string.

Heathcliffe appeared and shut the garden gate behind him. He stared suspiciously at Jemima. 'What y'talking to 'er for?' he asked. 'She's a *girl.*'

'Sorry, 'Eath,' said Terry and they returned to the High Street to seek out their next delivery.

When Jim and I walked into the Coffee Shop the jukebox was on full volume. Pete Burns of Dead or Alive was singing the new number one record, 'You Spin Me Round'. Dorothy was sitting on a stool behind the counter. She had just spent forty pence on the latest *Smash Hits* magazine and, after reading an article on Alison Moyet, she was trying to memorize all the words of Madonna's 'Material Girl'.

She looked up. ''Ello, Mr Sheffield.'

'What's it to be, Jim?' I asked.

Jim scanned the menu. 'Scrambled eggs on toast an' a mug o' coffee, please.'

'And the same for me, please, Dorothy,' I said.

We sat at a corner table as Big Dave and Little Malcolm walked in. Big Dave reacted with surprise. 'Why 'ave y'changed y'counter?' he asked. 'That's where y'pork pies used t'be.'

'We're movin' wi' t'times, Dave,' said Dorothy.

''Ow come?' asked Little Malcolm. 'An' why 'ave y'changed t'menu?' he added, staring up at the chalkboard. In big letters it read:

TRY OUR NEW VEGGIE ROLLS.

Nora was scrambling eggs and toasting bread. 'Ah'm makin' it vawied,' she said.

Big Dave peered suspiciously at a plate of what looked like sausage rolls but had a different label. 'But what's them?' he asked.

'Veggie wolls,' said Nora.

'Veggie rolls?' said Little Malcolm. He looked dubiously at the log cabin of pastries. 'So ... is there any meat in 'em?'

'Don't be daft, Malcolm,' replied Dorothy, 'o' course there's no meat in 'em.'

MERTHYR TYDFIL PUBLIC LIBRARIES

'We've made 'em f'*vegetawians*,' said Nora defiantly.

'Well, don't tell Old Tommy,' said Big Dave. ''E'll 'ave 'eart attack.'

'Y'reight there, Dave,' agreed Little Malcolm.

Nora served up our scrambled eggs on toast and put the plates on a tray on the counter.

'What's that?' asked Big Dave, pointing a grubby finger.

'Parsley,' said Dorothy.

'We put a spwig on top,' said Nora.

'It's t'mek it look posh,' added Dorothy for good measure.

Big Dave stared at it in disgust. 'Ah don't want no green stuff on m'breakfast – it's not nat'ral.'

'So what's it t'be then?' asked Dorothy.

'Two pork pies an' two mugs o' tea,' said Big Dave defiantly. 'We need energy t'shift bins.'

'Y'reight there, Dave,' added Little Malcolm, 'an' we need some *protein* t'keep us 'ealthy.' He had been reading one of Dorothy's diet books.

'Y'can get pwotein in my veggie wolls,' retorted Nora as a parting shot, but Dave and Malcolm had retired to their usual table.

Heathcliffe and Terry were doing well. Old Tommy Piercy had given them a list of deliveries and at five pence for each one they had enough for a visit to the cinema plus bus fare and some to spare.

''Ere's y'las' delivery, boys,' said Old Tommy. 'Tek these pig's trotters t'Mr Tup'am an' then go t'Mrs 'Oward wi' these sausages. Tell 'er it's a gift. Poor lady got burgled again by all accounts an'

234

she's all on 'er own now 'er 'usband passed on.'

'Mrs 'Oward?' said Heathcliffe.

'Chauntsinger Cottage,' said Old Tommy, 'jus' pas' Virgil the blacksmith ... gorra red door.'

'Thanks, Mr Piercy,' said Heathcliffe.

The church clock struck eleven o'clock and Heathcliffe made a strategic decision. 'You go t'Mr Tup'am while ah tek t'bike and go to Mrs 'Oward. Then ah'll meet y'back 'ere before we go 'ome an' tell Mam we've earned some money. Then we'll go an' see *Gremlins*.'

Heathcliffe cycled up Chauntsinger Lane and walked his bike to the red door.

In the past year, since her husband died, Dot Howard had been targeted by an unscrupulous thief not once but three times. Finally, in despair, she had pinned a postcard to her front door. It bore a poignant message:

COME IN
THERE'S NOTHING LEFT BUT
MEMORIES

Heathcliffe read it without understanding and knocked gently on the door.

An elderly, careworn lady answered and gave him a gentle smile. 'Hello, young man,' she said.

'Mr Piercy sent y'these, Mrs 'Oward,' said Heathcliffe. ''E says no charge ... it's a gift.'

Heathcliffe thought the old lady was about to burst into tears.

'Would you like a drink of orange juice?' she asked with a tearful smile.

'Ah 'ave t'get back,' said Heathcliffe.

'Oh well, another time.'

But Heathcliffe had a good heart and recognized loneliness when he saw it. 'All right, jus' a quick one, thank you.'

Vera and Ruby were standing by the school gate. Ruby was delighted with her new North Yorkshire County Council floor polisher and Vera was now the proud owner of a microwave.

Ruby's son Duggie drove past speedily after finishing his morning shift at the funeral director's in Easington. "E's allus been an erotic driver, 'as our Duggie,' said Ruby. "E thinks 'e's James 'Unt.'

'How is he these days?' asked Vera.

"E's fit as a fiddle an' twice as 'andsome, is my Duggie,' said Ruby proudly. Then she frowned. 'Jus' a shame 'e can't find a nice girl 'is own age 'stead o' courtin' that *mature* woman.'

'Have you met her yet?' asked Vera.

'Yes, an' she's a strange one,' said Ruby, lowering her voice. 'She's told 'im she's got that *Gloucester-phobia* an' she wouldn't cope in a small coffin wi' nowhere t'move or breathe.'

'Oh dear,' said Vera.

'So my Duggie said 'e'd make sure she were *cremated* – an' 'e'd do it at cost price. She were ever so grateful.'

Vera recalled the bunch of flowers on the passenger seat of her car. 'Well, Ruby, I must go. I wanted to call in to see Dot Howard.'

'Give 'er my best, Mrs F,' said Ruby.

'Very well, Ruby.'

'Poor lass is like me now,' said Ruby, '...a widow.'

Vera simply nodded and gave Ruby a hug. 'I think I'll walk. It will do me good.'

Heathcliffe was standing by the mantelpiece and sipping his beaker of orange juice. It was clear Dot Howard was enjoying the company.

'It wasn't just a robbery – it was a violation of the soul,' she said.

Heathcliffe didn't fully understand but he knew the lady was upset.

She picked up a broken picture frame. Next to it was a photograph of Mr and Mrs Howard smiling in the sunshine while on holiday in Portmeirion in Wales. 'They even trod on my favourite picture,' she said.

Heathciffe finished his drink and departed; he had a lot on his mind as he cycled back to the main street. Terry was waiting for him outside the General Stores.

Heathcliffe parked his bicycle, took the coins from his pocket and counted their earnings.

'What we gonna do nex', Heath'?' asked Terry.

Heathcliffe took a creased school exercise book from his back pocket and jotted down some figures.

'Well ... we've got one poun' an' five pence. We could buy a lolly f'Dallas, a posh 'anky f'our mam, a box o' matches f'Dad, go to t'pictures an' invest t'rest into t'company.'

'That sounds good, 'Eath,' said Terry.

Heathcliffe sighed and shook his head. 'But we're not gonna do that. Ah've gorra better idea,' and he walked back into the General Stores.

In Chauntsinger Cottage, Vera and Dot Howard were sitting in the kitchen drinking tea. 'I was listening to the wireless this morning, Vera, and Margaret Thatcher was talking in that strident voice of hers.'

Vera restrained herself. She knew Dot Howard wasn't a fan of the Prime Minister. They moved on to talking about the younger generation.

'Children today aren't what they used to be,' said Dot reflectively.

'Oh, I don't know,' said Vera. 'There are some lovely boys and girls at the school.'

'Perhaps,' conceded Dot grudgingly.

Suddenly there was a knock on the door.

'Another visitor,' said Dot in surprise. 'They're like buses today.'

Heathcliffe was standing there. His face was red after a speedy cycle ride. He took a small parcel out of his pocket. 'This is f'you, Mrs 'Oward,' he said simply, then jumped back on his bicycle and rode off.

Dot walked back into the kitchen. She removed the brown paper and stared in delight. It was a picture frame. 'It's beautiful,' she murmured to herself and removed the glass to put her precious photograph in place. When she turned it round she noticed a small sticky label on the back. 'The kind boy forgot to take the price off,' she said with a smile. It read '£1.00'.

At one o'clock William Featherstone's bus left the top of the High Street for York. Heathcliffe and Terry were sitting on the back seat.

'It was good of Mam t'give us t'money,' said

238

Terry. 'Ah wonder why she changed 'er mind?'

'Dunno, Terry,' said Heathcliffe. 'Mebbe summat t'do wi' Mrs F calling round t'talk to 'er.'

'What are we deliv'rin' t'morrow, 'Eath?' asked Terry.

'Dunno ... but t'business did well t'day,' said Heathcliffe proudly. 'We might try summat else, then maybe one day we'll own our own 'ouse, jus' like t'Prime Minister said.'

This was too complicated for Terry. He stared out of the window as the medieval city of York came into view. "Eath ... what's gremlins?'

'Bit like you only better lookin',' said Heathcliffe and he ruffled his little brother's spiky blond hair. Then he settled back in his seat and smiled ... and dreamed of big houses and flashy cars.

Chapter Thirteen

A Decision for Tom

Our Senior Primary Adviser, Richard Gomersall, visited school this morning. School closed today for the Easter holiday and will reopen on Monday, 15 April.
Extract from the Ragley School Logbook:
Friday, 29 March 1985

It was the pre-dawn of a day when the first breath of spring hung in the air, tenuous and tantalizing, the merest hint of a new season. The promise of light and colour and warmth stretched out before us. It had been a long, cold winter and life had come full circle, but now the season had changed. It was Friday, 29 March, the last day of term, and spring had returned once more to Ragley village.

I opened the bedroom window of Bilbo Cottage. The first light of a pale sun gilded the distant hills and the scent of wallflowers was in the air. The new season that lay ahead filled my thoughts and I turned to look at Beth. She was asleep and I stood there listening to her soft breathing. The sibilant sounds brought comfort to my soul. I loved this woman with a fierce passion, but recently she had seemed *different* somehow. There was a new energy within her, vibrant and visible. Beth's work filled her waking

240

hours. She clearly revelled in the daily challenge of her professional life.

When I arrived at school it was clear that Easter was in sight. It was a farewell to dark nights and runny noses.

The entrance hall looked welcoming. Anne and Sally had draped the large pine table with mint-green hessian and created a wonderful display of spring flowers. Children's poems had been carefully mounted on the noticeboard alongside. Vera was there adding the final touch – a bunch of catkins brought in by Sonia Tricklebank and she arranged them expertly in a brown earthenware vase.

Sally and Anne had also agreed to help Vera with the Lenten lunches during the holiday by providing bread and cheese. This was a very special annual event that took place in the church hall and was always well supported. While religion played a significant part, it didn't go unnoticed that the soup was prepared by Mary Hardisty to her own special recipe handed down through generations of the wives of Yorkshire hill farmers. It was scrumptious.

Our English lesson to start the day reminded me why I loved teaching. Some of the children had brought in primroses and pansies and we carried these to the display in the entrance hall. While we were there, we discussed the distinctive shape of the petals and why they heralded the coming of spring. Chalk drawings, poems and paintings followed and the writing and artwork showed me once again just how creative young children can be. It also occurred to me that, while it was demanding to be a headteacher with a full-time teaching commitment, on occasions such as these it was the best job in the world.

'Smart Ford Sierra coming up t'drive, Mr Sheffield,' said Charlotte Ackroyd suddenly.

It proved an opportune time for our Senior Primary Adviser, Richard Gomersall, to call in. He looked round my classroom with its inviting carpeted book corner, stories written in neat handwriting, our nature table teeming with life and information books, the colourful displays and vivid artwork ... and he sighed. 'Jack,' he said, shaking his head in resignation, 'I hate to say this but the educational world as we know it will change in the next few years. This common curriculum idea is gathering political momentum at County Hall and in London. I'm not sure you'll be doing your wonderful pond studies and visits to the local farm in quite the same way ever again.'

I reflected on his words. 'It's been coming for some time now,' I said. 'Let's hope it doesn't prevent us from encouraging children to love learning.'

'I agree,' said Richard, 'and by the way, corporal punishment was on the agenda this week and looks as though it's on the way out as well. Eventually, they'll make it a law – and that will appeal to the European Parliament.' He surveyed the well-behaved, responsible children who were busy getting on with their various tasks. They were sharing, discussing their work and using dictionaries to look up new words. He smiled and shook his head. 'Not entirely relevant in Ragley,

Jack, but it was different in my day.' He put his hand on my shoulder and grinned. 'In fact, a good thrashing was considered to be character building!'

I looked at my wristwatch. 'Richard, morning assembly is in a few minutes if you'd like to stay.'

'Sorry, Jack, I'm doing the grand whistle-stop tour so must dash. I'll just check out Mr Dalton's class before I go. How's he doing, by the way?'

I considered my response. 'He's an excellent teacher but has been a little unsure about his future,' I said cautiously. 'Although he seems more settled now.'

'Fine, Jack. See you next term,' and we shook hands as he hurried off to Class 2, where Tom was reading to the children. When Richard walked in you could have heard a pin drop such was the intense interest, and he smiled in appreciation.

As a Church of England Primary School, it was the norm for Joseph to lead our Easter assembly and he was soon imparting his wisdom. 'The annual feast of Easter isn't just a single day,' he said, 'but rather fifty days from Holy Saturday until the feast of Pentecost.'

Danny Hardacre in my class suddenly looked interested at the sound of the word 'feast'. Joseph went on to tell the story of 'doubting' Thomas, the apostle, who represented recurrent scepticism and I recalled Richard's words about the school curriculum.

There was a sudden change in the weather and heavy rain began to fall, so a wet playtime was announced and the children would return to their classrooms. As they walked out of the hall Joseph was surrounded by eager faces. 'That were a good story, Mr Evans,' said Ryan Halfpenny cheerfully. A flurry of hailstones battered against the hall windows and Ryan smiled. 'Y'can't beat a bit o' Jesus on a wet playtime.'

'My mam would 'ave soon sorted out that doubting Thomas, Mr Evans,' said Frankie Spraggon. 'She would've said mek y'mind up sharpish else you'll get no pudding.' He wandered off, pleased to have imparted such wisdom, and began to whistle loudly.

'Frankie – why are you whistling in school?' Joseph called after him.

'Well, Mr Evans,' replied Frankie cheerfully, 'ah asked God t'teach me t'whistle jus' like Ted Coggins – an' 'E did!'

Outside, the fierce hailstone shower fell from the heavens like a shimmering steel curtain. The children pressed their noses to the windows and stared at its frightening ferocity.

'Is God angry, Mr Evans?' asked Lucy Eckersley.

Before he could reply, Damian Brown chipped in. 'No,' he said with the confidence of youth. ''E's jus' 'aving a quick clean-up.'

Joseph smiled. Damian had a point. Dust, debris and twigs were cascading from the sloping tarmac playground down the cobbled drive and away to the High Street.

By lunchtime the shower had passed and a fitful sun was trying to pierce the iron-grey clouds. I picked up a plastic tray and joined the school dinner queue.

It was an appetizing hot meal: braised local beef, boiled potatoes and cabbage. This was followed by pink sponge pudding and bright yellow custard – a technicolor sweet course that almost required a pair of sunglasses!

After lunch I spotted Mrs Spittlehouse with her six-year-old daughter in the entrance hall. She had called in with Rosie's wellington boots.

The little girl smiled up at me. Her front teeth were missing.

'The tooth fairy came last night, didn't she, luv?' said Mrs Spittlehouse with the smile of a caring mother.

'She left me a note, Mr Sheffield,' said Rosie.

'And what did it say?' I asked.

'Dunno,' said Rosie, 'ah couldn't read t'squiggly writing. Ah reckon t'tooth fairy needs t'practise 'er 'andwriting like we do.'

Mrs Spittlehouse blushed furiously and I was reminded why teaching young children had its moments.

When we gathered in the staff-room Vera was reading her *Daily Telegraph*. The miners' strike had ended after almost a year of industrial action. Many had returned to work marching behind brass bands while their wives stood at the pit gates and distributed carnations as a symbol of returning heroes.

Vera was saddened to read that during the hardship, some families had resorted to scavenging for coal on the very dangerous spoil heaps and this had resulted in the deaths of three children. Arthur Scargill had the last word: 'We face not an employer but a government aided and abetted by the judiciary, the police and you people in the media.' The conflict had ended, but you sensed another was about to begin.

Meanwhile, Sally was flicking through the pages of her March issue of *Cosmopolitan*. Under a heading 'The Bran-Slim Diet Plan' a particularly happy lady was reported to have said, 'I lost thirteen pounds in four weeks,' and the rebellious Sally selected a second custard cream. She moved on to Irma Kurtz's agony column where problems were dearly rife among her readers. They included a twenty-year-old who was madly in love with Michael Jackson and a woman whose husband kept naked photos of his first wife and she wondered if she should be concerned.

Perhaps my life isn't quite so complicated after all, thought Sally.

After lunch Ruby came in to stack away the dining tables. She was carrying a metal bucket. Another little ritual for our good-hearted caretaker was to collect all the metal foil tops from milk bottles in the school kitchen. After rinsing them clean she passed them on to her daughter Racquel to take to the charity shop in York.

'What are y'doin' that for, Mrs Smith?' asked Charlie Cartwright.

'It's f'blind dogs, luv,' explained Ruby and hurried off with the precious bucket.

Ted Coggins looked puzzled. 'Seems a shame, Charlie,' he said.

'Why's that?' asked Charlie.

'Well, they won't be able t'see 'em,' said Ted.

With another problem solved in their young lives they ran off with a stick of chalk to see who could take a running jump at the boiler-house wall and make the highest chalk mark.

To everyone's surprise, the sun came out and a bright rainbow split the sky to the wonderment of the children. It was a perfect opportunity for a nature walk and some fresh air for the boys and girls in my class.

Vera and Ruby were called upon to help with the supervision and soon we were walking down the High Street towards the woods near the cricket pitch. A few villagers waved as we went by. They looked busy and it seemed that the folk of Ragley had begun to do their spring cleaning. The children were full of interest. In the hedgerows, honeysuckle and primroses were bursting into life and birds were building nests with frantic activity.

We stopped under the shade of a huge, graceful ash tree.

'We found a dead squirrel just 'ere, Mr Sheffield,' said Callum Myler.

'Oh dear,' I said.

'Ah were wi' m'dad an' we buried it,' said Callum.

'Oh well, that was thoughtful,' I said.

'After 'e'd cut 'is tail off.'

'And what happened to the tail?' I asked in bewilderment.

''E stuck it on m'nan's fur 'at.'

'Why did he do that?'

''E said it made a perfec' Davy Crockett 'at, Mr Sheffield.'

'Davy Crockett?'

'Yes, Mr Sheffield, then 'e put it on an' started singing "Davy, Davy Crockett, King of the wild frontier", an' m'mam said 'e were a sandwich short of a picnic an' closed t'kitchen door.'

'Will t'squirrel 'ave gone to 'eaven yet, Mr Sheffield?' asked Mo Hartley, 'or will 'e 'ave t'wait 'til 'is body's all decomposed?'

I was impressed with the word 'decomposed' and was about to attempt a reply when everyone seemed to be speaking at once.

'Y'wouldn't get squirrels in 'eaven,' declared Harold Bustard.

'Why not?' asked Victoria Alice Dudley-Palmer.

''Cause there's no trees for 'em t'swing on,' said Harold with conviction.

''Ow d'you know?' interjected Sonia Tricklebank.

'Stands t'reason,' said Harold and pointed to the sky. 'There's nowt but clouds.'

And some of them look dark, I thought.

'Come on, boys and girls,' I said. 'It's going to rain again. Let's get back to school.'

It was only another brief shower and by afternoon playtime spring sunshine lit up the bright faces of the children as they ran and chased on the playground. Their conversations concerned the forthcoming two-week holiday ... but mainly Easter eggs.

Tom was on duty and I noticed he was standing in the shade. He looked preoccupied. When the bell rang for the end of break he approached me as I left the staff-room.

'Jack,' he said, 'can I have a word after school if you can spare the time?'

'That's fine, Tom,' I said. 'See you then.'

Meanwhile, Sally hurried out and in her haste she left her copy of *Cosmopolitan* open on the coffee table. Vera glanced down at the article as she cleared away. The heading in bold letters read: **'How to Have a Multiple Orgasm'** and, with flushed cheeks, she closed it quickly, put it under the pile of *Art & Craft* magazines and proceeded to rearrange the tea cups on the tiny worktop.

At the end of school there was much to do. After saying goodbye to the children I called into the office and telephoned Beth. I told her I would be later than usual as we had a staff meeting. Also Tom wanted to see me.

'Well, don't be *too* late,' she said. 'I'm preparing something special to celebrate the end of term.'

The staff got to work and we cleared our classrooms, updated the children's records and then settled down to discuss forthcoming events for the summer term. We planned dates for sports day, parent-teacher interviews and class visits. Sally suggested a trip to Hornsea for the children in her class and mine and we pencilled in 7 June.

Finally Vera and I were in the school office and Vera was putting the cover on her typewriter and leaving her desk in its usual immaculate state of tidiness.

'Have a good holiday, Mr Sheffield,' she said as she put on her coat.

'You too, Vera,' I said, 'and, of course, we won't

see you at the Easter service.'

Vera smiled. 'Yes, enjoy Oxford,' she said. Beth and I had planned a short holiday.

I glanced up at the clock. 'Tom wants to see me.'

Vera looked concerned. 'I do hope he finds some peace in his life. He's a lovely young man, but clearly troubled. I hope he's all right.'

'Yes, so do I.'

It was almost seven o'clock and I had completed a mountain of paperwork for County Hall and updated the school logbook when there was a tap on the door. It was Tom.

'Sorry to keep you waiting, Jack,' he said. 'I'm going to London first thing tomorrow and I wanted to get the children's reading records up to date ... I've got lots to do during the holiday.'

Then he went strangely quiet. It seemed that, for Tom, conversations had become strangers in a lonely world of silent thoughts. I glanced at the clock and made a decision. 'I'll lock up, then let's walk across to The Oak. We can have half an hour over a drink.'

'Thanks, Jack,' he said, 'good idea,' and I was encouraged by his response.

When we walked in I asked Tom to find a table while I bought the drinks.

Behind the bar Sheila only had eyes for Ragley's youngest teacher. ''E's a proper looker, that Mr Dalton,' she said appreciatively.

I smiled. 'Two pints of Chestnut please, Sheila,' I said.

'I'll bring 'em over, Mr Sheffield.'

250

Tommy Piercy was propping up the bar from his usual seat. 'Mixed weather today, Mr Piercy,' I said.

'We breed 'em tough up in t'North tha knaws,' said Old Tommy proudly. 'Three months winter an' nine months bad weather,' and he chuckled loudly.

Sheila delivered the drinks and made sure Tom Dalton had every opportunity to assess her curvaceous figure. She put down the tray, smoothed her black-leather miniskirt and tugged the top of her pink boob-tube a little lower. Then she leaned over and placed our drinks in front of us and for a brief moment Tom was treated to an eye-watering glimpse of Sheila's magnificent chest. Then she winked at him. She always believed in giving full value.

However, Tom's mind was elsewhere and she tottered off on her high heels.

'Jack,' he began hesitantly, 'you know how much I appreciated you giving me this job.'

'You've done well,' I said guardedly.

He nodded. 'Thanks. Ragley's a great school and everyone has been supportive.'

I sensed there was a *but* coming. 'Well, we're a good team,' I added quietly.

'And I'm proud to be part of that team,' he said, '...and I've only been here just over a year.'

'It's important you're happy in your work,' I said.

He smiled and ran his fingers through his long, black, wavy hair. 'That's the point, Jack. I love teaching – and I'm looking forward to the future.'

We were skirting round the subject and we both

251

knew it. 'You need to explain,' I said.

He stared at the ceiling trying to find the right words. 'You know why.'

'So tell me.'

Finally he looked at me squarely and said simply, 'Laura.'

When we parted woodsmoke was creeping down Ragley High Street like a grey wolf while the drizzle was on the cusp of turning to steady rain. Tom drove off in his rusty royal blue Renault 4 and headed up the Morton Road rather than towards his flat in York.

Silver strands of fleeting clouds drifted across a pale crescent moon like wraiths in the night and I reflected on our short conversation.

When I arrived home Beth was preparing her speciality dish – pork chops in wine with herbs. She was preoccupied, chopping green apples and slicing spring onions. A generous glass of white wine was on the worktop and she paused occasionally to take a sip. I stood in the doorway admiring her slim figure while mischievous thoughts flickered through my mind.

The cassette player was plugged in and she was playing her favourite double-cassette collection of fifty love songs featuring Barry Manilow, Elton John, Michael Jackson, Cliff Richard, Abba, the Carpenters, Diana Ross, Gladys Knight, the Everly Brothers, the Three Degrees, Stevie Wonder and Lionel Richie.

'Happy holidays,' she said with a smile. I wrapped my arms around her and nuzzled her neck. It was good to be home. 'Had a good day?'

she asked.

'Just had a chat with Tom.'

She paused, turned and looked at me and, as always, she understood me better than I knew. 'And I presume there are decisions to make.'

I sighed and nodded. Beth's world appeared to be driven by ambition and achievement, whereas mine meandered in the here and now.

'Jack, people don't need to stand still to live – there are challenges out there for everyone, a new world to explore.' She kissed me gently. 'Now, pour me another glass of wine and make yourself useful.'

We were relaxing by the fire after a wonderful meal when the telephone rang.

'Bit late,' I said to Beth.

It was Joseph. 'Sorry to trouble you, Jack.'

'Not a problem, Joseph. How can I help?'

'I'm ringing as the chair of governors,' he said.

'Oh, that sounds very formal.'

'I suppose it is,' said Joseph quietly.

'So what is it?'

'I regret to inform you that I've received an official correspondence from Mr Dalton.' There was a hesitant silence over the telephone. 'Jack ... it's a letter of resignation.'

Chapter Fourteen

Oxford Blues

School will reopen on Monday, 15 April.
Extract from the Ragley School Logbook:
Friday, 29 March 1985

I parked my Morris Minor Traveller just outside
Oxford and paused to drink in the spectacular
view. It was Good Friday, 5 April, and a holiday
weekend beckoned in one of the great university
cities of the world.

'It's wonderful,' said Beth.

Our son was with her parents. It was John and
Diane's fortieth wedding anniversary and they had
decided to visit Woodstock, a place of happy
memories for them. We had agreed they would
take our lively toddler with them, leaving us free to
wander the streets of Oxford and meet up again at
their home in Hampshire on Easter Sunday. A
couple of days of complete freedom stretched out
before us.

I smiled and squeezed her hand. 'Perfect,' I
said. 'It feels like being on honeymoon again.'

The expectation in my voice was not lost on
Beth as she gave a whimsical look. 'Not far now
to the hotel,' she said.

John and Diane had surprised us with the gift
of two nights at their favourite hotel, the pres-

tigious Randolph Hotel in the centre of Oxford. They explained it was partly a birthday present for Beth and would also give them precious time with their grandson. Whatever the case, it was welcome and there was a hint that they recognized we could both do with a break away from schoolwork and childcare.

So it had been fun to sit down and plan our mini-break. We were determined to sample the many colleges with their quadrangles of manicured lawns and honeyed stone, along with the galleries, bookshops and roadside cafés. It was an opportunity simply to wander along the cobbled streets where the domes, rotundas, bell towers and slim spires formed a skyline of ancient beauty.

The sun was low as we drove into this wonderful city and drank in its history. Many centuries had passed since a Saxon princess, Frideswide, established a monastery where teams of oxen could cross the River Thames at 'Oxenford'. By the twelfth century it had become a seat of learning and in the thirteenth century halls of residence had been built for the students along with the first of the great colleges, University College, Merton and Balliol. However, for now the Randolph beckoned and we soon realized why John and Diane had spoken so highly of this very special hotel. Built in 1864 to a grand design, it was the perfect base for our holiday.

After settling into our room, we showered, changed and went downstairs to the dining room for a welcome meal. Beth knew Oxford well and soon, refreshed and relaxed, we left the hotel and walked hand in hand up St Giles'.

We stopped outside The Eagle and Child public house, known locally as The Bird and Baby. 'A famous landmark,' said Beth. 'You're treading in the footsteps of your favourite author.' We walked in, bought a bottle of local beer and a glass of white wine and squeezed into a little booth of dark wood in a smoky corner. It was where a group of Oxford writers, known affectionately as the Inklings and including J. R. R. Tolkien and C. S. Lewis, used to meet – no doubt to discuss Middle Earth and Narnia. This was precious time, just the two of us, anonymous among the tourists and, so it seemed, without a care in the world.

It was very late when we returned to the hotel. Our room was spacious and I sat on the bed. 'Nice and soft,' I said expectantly and Beth just smiled.

Early on Saturday morning Beth's naked body was lying beside mine and she was breathing deeply. I slid quietly out of bed and explored the tea-making facilities. Beth stirred as the kettle boiled.

'Good morning,' she said sleepily.

'Tea?' I asked.

'Lovely,' she replied, leaning on one elbow and looking up at me, '...unless of course you want to come back to bed.'

I didn't need asking twice.

When we finally opened the curtains the sun was shining and Oxford was waking to a new day. After a magnificent breakfast we walked out of the hotel into Beaumont Street. Beth's father had given us a local guide book and a street map.

'I know this place well,' said Beth, taking in the

wonderful architecture around us. 'My parents brought us here when we were children. I've so many happy memories. I remember Laura saying the buildings were like fairy castles.'

'How is she?' I asked.

'Fine, by all accounts,' said Beth. 'Dad says they love her in Australia and she's enjoying her new lifestyle in the Sydney fashion world.'

Laura had rushed off to Australia like a moth to a new flame and for a moment I reflected on the lovestruck Tom Dalton. I had been saddened when he confirmed that he had decided to leave Ragley and I wondered if one day he would follow Laura to the other side of the world. I recalled the effervescent and enigmatic woman I had come to know so well. Her departure had been sudden, impetuous and typical of my dynamic sister-in-law.

Meanwhile, across the road, the grand neo-classical Ashmolean Museum and its collection of art and antiquities beckoned. 'So where shall we start?' I asked.

Beth had made up her mind. She was eager to see the Sheldonian, so we walked hand in hand up Broad Street. I could understand her enthusiasm when we arrived at this early Christopher Wren masterpiece. Beth's green eyes were alive with excitement. She loved her history. 'Isn't it spectacular, Jack?' she said as, above our heads, the April sunlight lit up the bearded faces of the carved statues that stared out like imposing Roman Caesars.

'A timeless world,' I said as I relaxed at last and enjoyed this private cocoon of space I shared with the woman I loved. I had brought my camera and had just put in a new roll of film with thirty-six transparencies, enough for a full day of photography, and Beth posed for the first one.

Across the road was the famous Blackwell's Bookshop. It was one of the largest in the world and, for me, a literary heaven. Beth immediately recognized my interest. 'Come on,' she said with a smile, 'I know you love your books.'

After half an hour of browsing, Beth purchased a book of poems by Robert Browning as a gift for me and a brightly illustrated copy of *Alice in Wonderland* for her school library. We walked out again into the sunshine and stopped by the bridge across New College Lane that linked the Old and New Quads of Hertford College. A passing student happily agreed to take our photograph standing under the 'Bridge of Sighs', aptly named owing to the close resemblance to its Venetian namesake.

'Happy?' I asked and Beth kissed me on the cheek as the young man clicked the shutter.

Beth's historical knowledge far exceeded mine and she gave an informative commentary as we meandered into Radcliffe Square. It was dominated by the domed, circular Radcliffe Camera, the great rotunda built to hold the unique library of Dr John Radcliffe, the learned physician to Queen Anne. Then we followed a party of American tourists across the Old Schools Quadrangle outside the world-famous Bodleian Library, said to contain a copy of every book published in Britain.

When we reached Brasenose College we stared in amazement. Steven Spielberg was filming *Young Sherlock Holmes* and had arranged for huge quantities of magnesium sulphate to be sprinkled on the windowsills to represent snow. Sadly, there was no sign of the talented American film director, perhaps wearing an 'ET Phone Home' T-shirt. So we continued to the High Street, or simply The High as the locals appeared to call it, where we bought two newspapers, an *Oxford Times* for me and a *Times Educational Supplement* for Beth.

'How about a coffee?' suggested Beth.

'Good idea.'

'I know just the place,' she said, taking my hand and leading me into Oriel Street towards three more of Oxford's beautiful old colleges. We passed Oriel with its Gothic-style front quad and Corpus Christi. It was as if we had stepped back in time as our footsteps echoed on the ancient cobbled stones outside Merton College. The Grand Café beckoned and we stopped for refreshment in this elegant, historic coffee house.

We ordered rich ground coffee and Beth read her paper while I flicked through the entertaining and diverse articles in the *Oxford Times*. It was certainly nineteen pence well spent.

House prices had shot up again and first-time buyers could now expect to pay the exorbitant sum of £34,000 for a three-bedroom semi. In the local council elections the Tories were defending a slender lead and that, Energy Secretary Peter Walker confirmed, was the Conservative Party's top priority.

However, under the advertisements for the local Easter Bonnet Parade with its Easter eggs, bunnies and daffodils was undoubtedly my favourite article. It related to the urgent request for 'TOAD

259

WARNING' signs on the local roads after a reported 522 squashed toads had been found, many in the act of mating! A local biology teacher explained that the male toads prefer to stand on the road as it makes their voices carry further to attract females. The deeper the male toad's voice, the more attractive it is to the female. It appeared they had just come out of hibernation and were raring to go. Sadly, in a multitude of cases, their pleasure was short-lived! In the meantime, the Berks, Bucks and Oxon Naturalist Trust had already put up signs and were leading the way in this vital lifesaving initiative.

Across the table, Beth was engrossed and blowing gently on the surface of her coffee, in that familiar way of hers, prior to sipping it thoughtfully. She had turned her copy of the *Times Educational Supplement* to the headteacher appointments page. Something had caught her interest and she took a pen from her handbag. 'Look at this one, Jack,' she said. She had circled one of the advertisements. It read:

Forest Lodge County First School, Scarborough, Group 5. NOR 235. Required for 1st September 1985. Full details from the Area Education Office, County Hall, Northallerton.

'Look at the salary,' she said. It was printed in bold type: **'Salary Scale £10,572–£11,784'**.

I gasped. 'Five figures – it's a fortune!' and I recalled my first salary slip in 1967 informing me I had earned £48.00 for my first month's work as a teacher. Life, salaries and the cost of living had moved on. The world around me was changing and it appeared I hadn't quite caught up. It occurred to me that I knew a lot about teaching children to read and write but, unlike Beth, I knew little about financial planning.

We stirred our coffee in endless revolutions, each waiting for the other to speak, but words were few and thoughts were many. Finally I looked again at the advertisement and Beth broke the silence. 'It would be tough competition,' she said quietly.

'Are you thinking of giving it a try?'

'Why not?' she asked with a nonchalant wave of the hand.

'Well, if you want to give it a go, I'll support you of course ... but don't be too disappointed if you don't get an interview.'

Beth stretched across the table and squeezed my hand. 'Thanks,' she said. 'I'll send for an application form.' She took out her pocket diary and scribbled down the details as we finished our coffee.

I looked at our elegant bone-china cups, empty now. 'Another?' I asked.

Beth didn't hear. She was too engrossed in the advertisement. I attracted the attention of the waitress and ordered another pot of coffee. Then I looked back at Beth. She was twirling a lock of honey-blonde hair around her finger, deep in thought. Her profile was sheer elegance, with fair skin, high cheekbones and lips pursed in concentration. I felt a moment's sadness. Aspiration is one thing, realism is another. In our world of education women were rarely promoted to higher office and, rather selfishly, I reflected that my life at Ragley School was secure for a few more years.

Finally, Beth looked up with a knowing smile. 'Jack, think about it ... I've nothing to lose and if I was fortunate enough to get an interview it would be really good experience for the future.'

I was reluctant to state the obvious, but as it turned out Beth had read my mind. 'I know what you're thinking ... as a woman I've no chance of a big headship.'

'I think there's a lady headteacher of a Group 5 school in Hertfordshire,' I said in an attempt to offer some encouragement. 'I read an article about her.'

She looked at me coolly. 'Perhaps I'll be the next.'

Her words were soft yet sure, like silk and steel.

By mid-afternoon, after a light lunch by the River Cherwell, we decided on a leisurely conclusion to our tour and I found myself staring at an un-wieldy flat-bottomed boat next to a sign advertising 'PUNTS FOR HIRE'.

As a confident Yorkshireman who misguidedly thought he could turn his hand to any new skill, I was willing to try to propel one of the punts by means of a traditional long pole. Fortunately, Beth had a wiser head and we paid a young man, who steered us expertly from the flat platform at the back of the boat. It was a relaxing way to unwind after our intensive sightseeing tour.

'So what are you doing about a replacement for Tom?' asked Beth.

'I've spoken to Joseph, as chair of governors, and to Richard Gomersall at County Hall, and Tom's post will be advertised next week. Then we'll shortlist and have interviews, probably in early June prior to a September start.'

'Let's hope whoever you select stays a little longer,' said Beth.

'Yes, it's an important decision. I really didn't think he would leave.'

Beth trailed her fingers in the cool water and stared at the branches above us.

At six o'clock we were back at the hotel and while Beth was in the bathroom I switched on the television.

An animated Church leader was standing in front of a poster emblazoned with the words 'HANDS OFF OUR DAY OF REST' as a warning to Sunday traders. It was suggested that the noise would intrude on family worship and families would be split. This was followed by the news of high prices for vegetables after the bitterly cold winter and a reminder of the government's spending restrictions and their pledge to keep inflation down by limiting public spending. The programme ended with a survey that suggested the compulsory use of seat belts was turning drivers into reckless road-users and encouraging high speeds.

Just as I was about to switch off, we were asked to stay tuned to *The New Adventures of Wonder Woman* followed by *The Noel Edmonds Golden Easter Egg Awards* and I wondered where the cheerful and stylishly coiffeured presenter bought his outlandish shirts.

We had decided to have a light meal in the city and then go to the cinema. The curiously named Ultimate Picture Palace was showing *Romancing the Stone*, a comedy adventure with Kathleen Turner and Michael Douglas, and *Local Hero*, with its haunting music by Mark Knopfler. We settled for *Local Hero*, with Burt Lancaster as the stargazing head of a giant oil corporation, and I finished up whistling the theme tune all the way back to the hotel.

Over a late-night drink in the bar Beth's thoughts returned to the cluster of large-school headships that she'd noticed in the *Times Educational Supplement*.

'Jack, they were all five-figure salaries,' she said. 'It would make such a difference to our future if it eventually came about.' She leaned forward and held my hand. 'Think about it – a larger house with an extra bedroom for a start.'

'You mean for when your parents come to stay?' I said. I recalled the congestion in Bilbo Cottage whenever we had visitors. 'I suppose so. As you said, you can't swing a cat in the kitchen.'

'Exactly,' said Beth forcefully, 'and we may have an addition to our family one day ... when the time is right.'

I smiled, recalling last night. A little brother or sister for John sounded a good idea to me. 'Perhaps you're right.' Then I thought back to the view from our leaded bedroom windows at home. 'But I'd be sad to leave Bilbo Cottage.'

'Jack, we can't stand still. We've to move with the times. It's the eighties and the world is changing.'

I sighed. 'My mother brought me up to believe in *society*, and then to leave it better than I found it. "Make a contribution," she used to say. I suppose that's what I'm doing in my own small way – teaching children to write, compute, share, be confident and to love learning.'

'I know, Jack, and I respect you for that. But can't you see what's coming? The teaching you're enjoying now is destined to change. All the signs are there, and if some of the government's proposals come to pass then the work you love will change. One day it could take away your very soul and I would hate to see that. You can't stand still for ever. We have to start making plans for the future.'

It was an impassioned plea and I knew deep down that she was right.

Tired after a long day of fresh air and sightseeing, not to mention the Irish coffee nightcap, we went up the elegant staircase to our room. The weather had changed and there was the sound of soothing rain pattering fingertip softly on the panes. There was a chair and small circular table by the window. I tugged the curtains shut a little and sat down. While Beth was undressing I picked up the book of poems she had bought for me and began to read. It was a familiar poem by Robert Browning:

Grow old with me!
The best is yet to be...

And I hoped it would be so.

Chapter Fifteen

Belly Dancing for Beginners

The Revd Joseph Evans visited school to teach Class 4.
Extract from the Ragley School Logbook:
Friday, 19 April 1985

It was early morning and a cloud of mist formed a gauze of droplets over the sleeping land. Outside Bilbo Cottage a thrush was pecking at the tilled soil of my bed of raspberries and the scolding cries of a blackbird pierced the air as it tried to crack a snail's shell. Beth had carried John into the garden to hear the first cuckoo of the year and yellow-orange tulips brightened the tubs in our entrance porch.

It was a lovely morning and we had arranged for Natasha Smith to babysit for us that evening so that we could have a relaxing meal together. I had a meeting after school at St John's College in York, where I had agreed to provide a series of lectures to final-year students. A programme needed to be arranged, so we had decided that I would drive back from York and meet Beth at seven forty-five for dinner in The Royal Oak.

All seemed well until, during breakfast, we heard the patter of the morning mail falling on the mat. After that, life wasn't quite so serene.

One of the letters for Beth had a Northallerton postmark and she opened it quickly.

'It's the Scarborough headship,' she said, shaking her head. 'I haven't got an interview.'

'I'm sorry,' I said and gave her a hug, '...but there'll be others.'

I could see her mind ticking over. The disappointment was palpable, but her jawline was firm as she read the letter again. 'Yes, I'm sure there will be,' she said. 'It's just frustrating that we live in a world where some people clearly don't believe a woman can do a job as well as a man – better in some cases.'

I knew what she meant. It seemed as if, in terms of promotion, there was a glass ceiling, for talented women such as Beth. 'Let's talk tonight,' I said.

A busy day was in store, hopefully with a relaxing conclusion.

The journey to school was always a delight at this time of year. On Ragley High Street creamy-white almond blossom was bursting from the tight buds on the trees outside the village hall. It was a bright image of hope, while on the village green a canopy of new green leaves on the weeping willow provided dappled shade over Ronnie's bench.

It was Friday, 19 April and the end of the first week of the summer term. As I drove into the school car park bright yellow forsythia beside the school gate lifted the spirits. By the time I had parked my car it was a crystal-clear morning and every detail of the Hambleton hills was sharp and defined. There were no clouds, just a vast blue sky over the plain of York.

I met Mary Scrimshaw on the entrance steps. She had brought an armful of tall stalks of almond blossom for the nature table and a bunch for Vera for church. She smiled and hurried in to knock on the door of the office, where Vera was already hard at work.

Half an hour later Mary, along with the rest of my class, was reciting the eleven times table and I noticed Sam Borthwick looking puzzled. 'What's the matter, Sam?' I asked.

'Ah were jus' wond'rin' why we do tables ev'ry day, Mr Sheffield.'

'They're very useful in life, Sam,' I said.

'But why don't we use calculators?' he pleaded. 'Ah got a Casio f'Christmas.'

'Well, we use those as well,' I said, 'but one day your calculator might not work and then you'll appreciate knowing your tables.'

Unconvinced, he carried on chanting, number perfect.

Meanwhile, in Anne's class the twins were doing a sixteen-piece jigsaw together, 'Flowers of the Hedgerow'. Hermione was left-handed and Honeysuckle used her right. In perfect harmony, piece by piece, they worked together. The final piece of cow parsley was slipped into place as I approached their table.

'Well done,' said Anne.

'Shall we…?' said Honeysuckle.

'…do another one?' finished Hermione.

Billy Ricketts had brought in a bottle of milk and *two* straws. The spare one was to demonstrate his new skill each morning playtime when he would lie on his back on the school field and blow through the straw to levitate a single spherical chocolate Malteser on a cushion of air. Meanwhile his admirers, Dallas and Madonna, would watch this scientific phenomenon with open-mouthed amazement. They also hoped one day he might offer them a Malteser. However, in Billy's view girls were girls and in the currency of life their support did not equate to the gift of a precious sweet.

In Class 4 Joseph had arrived for a short lesson on the New Testament but was soon explaining to Frankie Spraggon that it wasn't 'Father, Son an' Holy Goat', though Frankie had his mind on other things.

'Ah saw a dead badger this morning, Mr Evans,' he said.

'Oh dear,' said Joseph.

''As 'e gone t'badger 'eaven, Mr Evans?' yelled Harold Bustard excitedly.

'Don't shout, please, Harold,' said Joseph.

'Do animals 'ave a diff'rent 'eaven, Mr Evans?' asked Sonia Tricklebank.

'An' is it t'same as 'uman 'eaven?' enquired Ben Roberts. The debate was gathering momentum and Joseph was becoming a little flustered.

'There wouldn't be enough room, would there, sir?' said Victoria Alice Dudley-Palmer quietly.

'Stands t'reason,' agreed Sam Borthwick.

'Ah 'ope there's no rats in 'eaven, Mr Evans, 'cause ah 'ate rats,' said Mo Hartley mournfully.

'An' spiders,' added Mary Scrimshaw for good measure and wincing visibly.

Conversations broke out everywhere concerning beetles, bee stings, the force-feeding of sprouts at Christmas and how do clouds support your weight.

The bell for morning break came as a blessed relief for Joseph and not for the first time he wondered if he would ever understand how children's minds worked.

When I walked into the staff-room Vera was boiling a small pan of milk 'I don't know quite what to make of it,' she said. 'I walked to school this morning because it was such a lovely day and I noticed a crowd of ladies outside the Coffee Shop. Nora has a large poster on the window advertising a "ladies only" night tomorrow.'

'That sounds interesting,' said Sally.

'And what did it say?' asked Anne.

'You'll never believe it,' said Vera as she poured the hot milk into our mugs. '"Belly Dancing for Beginners"!'

'I saw it once on holiday,' said Tom and then considered it best to leave it at that.

'Well, we've not had *that* before in the village,' said Anne cautiously, sensing Vera would disapprove.

'Yes, not quite the done thing,' said Vera, 'but it is 1985 and I suppose young women are *different* these days.'

And those in their forties have still a bit of life in them, thought Sally.

Across the High Street in the Coffee Shop, Nora was excited.

'Ah saw a big cwowd looking intewested, Dowothy,' she said, 'so well done.'

It was Dorothy who had come up with the idea. 'Ah knew they would be, Nora,' she said. 'Brenda said belly dancing would bring new romance into m'life wi' Malcolm.' Nora considered there was already enough romance in the adjoining bedroom but kept this thought to herself. 'An' she *knows* things, does Brenda,' continued the animated Dorothy, '''cause 'er 'oroscopes are always right.'

Brenda Crackett, a muscular, big-boned forty-year-old with a different boyfriend every week, worked in the bread shop in Thirkby. Brenda's claim to fame was that she had won the Gawthorpe World Coal Carrying Championship by carrying a sack of coal two thirds of a mile to the finish at the maypole on Gawthorpe's village green. Also, for a little extra cash, she wrote the weekly horoscope article in the *Easington Herald & Pioneer* under the pseudonym Gypsy Fortuna. Dorothy's star sign was Aquarius and she was always thrilled when she read that Malcolm, as a vertically challenged Gemini binman, had cause for optimism in his otherwise mundane life. However, Brenda also gave occasional but highly memorable belly-dancing performances in The Pig and Ferret. It had proved another source of income and an opportunity to entertain a vigorous young farmhand for the weekend. Brenda definitely lived life to the full.

Outside in the High Street, Betty Buttle was in the mobile library van perusing the Mills & Boon section. She had just returned a well-thumbed paperback. The write-up on the back cover had spoken of lust and betrayal in the Belgian Congo. Betty thought it was likely to be a sort of Hercule Poirot with a few suspender belts thrown in but, sadly, that hadn't proved to be the case and she had given up by page six.

Now Betty was selecting a book for Elfrida, her sister-in-law. Elfrida was in bed having succumbed to 'what was going round'. She had decided to miss her weekly visit to the library as she didn't want to spread whatever it was. This made sense to everyone and demonstrated a level of community spirit that always went down well among Ragley's literary set. After selecting *Chances* by Jackie Collins, Betty walked to the Coffee Shop and stared at the bright poster.

'Well, ah'm definitely goin' t'that,' she said.
It read:

The Coffee Shop will be hosting
a <u>ladies only</u> night
Friday 19th April at 8.00 p.m.
Belly Dancing for Beginners
Tuition by Yorkshire's leading belly dancer
Brenda Crackett of Thirkby
No previous experience necessary
Good for your health and keeping slim
Followed by coffee and cakes
Admission £1.00

Then Betty walked into Prudence Golightly's General Stores and rummaged in her purse. 'An' a packet o' that Typhoon tea,' she said.

'That should blow the cobwebs away,' said Prudence lightly, but the attempt at a joke was lost on Betty. The farmer's wife was wondering what to wear for an evening of belly dancing.

At lunchtime in the staff-room Sally had boiled some water for her Batchelors Chicken and Leek Slim a Soup. 'Only forty calories,' she reminded us yet again with forced enthusiasm. Meanwhile, Vera had brought in a packet of McVitie's Cherry and Coconut Country Cookies and we all revelled in the pleasure of our secretary's superior biscuits. After a split second of soul-searching, Sally selected one. 'Not quite in my diet regime,' she said with a wry smile, 'but lovely anyway.'

Ted Coggins was having similar concerns about *his* diet. In the dinner queue he was looking dubiously at his plate of cold ham and salad. The lettuce had been carefully shredded by Mrs Mapplebeck.

'But ah don't like grass, Miss,' he said, 'jus' *proper* food.'

At the end of school I left Vera and Sally chatting in the school office and drove to my meeting in York. I was looking forward to it. The notion of passing on my knowledge of the primary curriculum and classroom management to students appealed to me.

Ruby came into the office to empty the bin. It was clear that she needed cheering up.

'How are you, Ruby?' asked Sally.

'Ah'm not 'xactly full o' t'joys o' spring, Mrs P,' said Ruby, shaking her head of chestnut curls, 'but y'could say ah'm gettin' there,' she added as an afterthought.

273

'I've got the weekly bags of groceries for your mother,' said Vera.

'Thank you, Mrs F,' said Ruby.

The food was supplied by the Church Support Group, organized by Vera and aimed at helping old folk in need in the village. Ruby's mother, Agnes, was an appreciative recipient.

Sally decided to take the initiative. 'If you give them to me, Vera, I could deliver them on my way home.'

'That's kind, Sally,' said Vera. 'They are in my car.'

'Perhaps Ruby would like to come along with me,' suggested Sally.

Ruby smiled. 'Ah'm reight grateful, Mrs P.'

Later, when Ruby had finished her cleaning and Sally had marked a pile of topic folders, they set off to Ruby's mother's house.

Agnes was sitting in her battered armchair. Ruby's mother had spent the afternoon knitting dishcloths. These were regarded with genuine awe and wonder among the villagers of Ragley. Commercially produced dishcloths from the new supermarket on the York ring road were fine, but lacked the substance and cleaning power of Agnes's rugged, close-knit marvels.

'Mrs Pringle from school 'as give me a lift, Mam,' said Ruby as she unpacked the groceries.

'And how are you?' asked Sally.

'M'legs 'ave gone all funny,' said Agnes.

However, there was nothing humorous about arthritic knees and Dr Davenport was doing his best for her with a course of painkillers. Even so, Agnes firmly believed her steady improvement was down to Ruby's regular application of goose grease.

'So y'won't be goin' to t'belly dancin' at Nora's t'night, Mam?' said Ruby with a smile.

'M'belly dancin' days are over,' she said forlornly. Ruby flushed noticeably with embarrassment as she guessed her mother was recalling other activities in her youth.

'It should be good fun,' said Sally, but Agnes was going down another track. She looked sternly at Ruby. 'Well, ah told 'er straight when she were a teenager. If y'go out wi' boys ... allus wear a vest.'

When they left, Sally parked outside 7 School View.

'Thanks, Mrs P,' said Ruby.

Sally studied Ruby for a moment. 'What are you doing tonight, Ruby?'

'Nothing, ah s'ppose,' said Ruby. 'Mebbe a bit o' telly.'

'Right,' said Sally with conviction. 'I'll pick you up at ten to eight and we'll go to the belly dancing. It should be fun.'

Ruby's eyes lit up. 'Thanks, Mrs P,' she said. 'Ah'll be ready.'

In the Spraggon household young Alfie was reflecting on an interesting conversation with the relatively worldly-wise Dallas Sue-Ellen Earnshaw.

'Dad,' he said, 'where do babies come from?'

'Ask y'mam,' answered Mr Spraggon without raising his head from the paper.

'Mam, where do babies come from?'

'Ask y'dad,' said Mrs Spraggon while she

275

flipped over the fish fingers in haste.

'That's no good, Mam,' said Alfie, shaking his head, "cause 'e dunt know either.'

Mr Spraggon looked up from his paper at his wife as she slapped the plates on the table. 'What's all t'rush?' he asked.

'Ah 'ave t'get ready,' said Mrs Spraggon.

'What for?'

'Belly dancin',' said Mrs Spraggon.

In the Earnshaws' house Mr Earnshaw was more phlegmatic about his wife going out.

'Where's Mam goin', Dad?' asked Terry.

'She's off to summat t'do wi' dancin' in t'Coffee Shop. Ah s'ppose it's a change from them Tupperware parties she goes to,' said Mr Earshaw.

'What's a Tupperware party, Dad?' asked Terry.

'Well, women all go t'someone's 'ouse an' they look at plastic boxes an' mebbe buy 'em.'

Terry smiled. He knew when his dad was pulling his leg. 'Go on, Dad,' he said, 'tell us what they *really* do.'

Meanwhile, in The Royal Oak, Big Dave and Little Malcolm had decided on a night in the pub as both Nellie and Dorothy were involved in the belly-dancing event. However, at that moment they had some serious news for Deke Ramsbottom, the Ragley cowboy.

'Deke, we need a word,' said Big Dave sheepishly, while Little Malcolm shuffled uncomfortably.

'What's that, lads?' asked Deke as he supped the last dregs from his tankard and wiped his mouth with the back of his hand.

Big Dave looked left and right and, satisfied no one was within earshot, spoke quietly. 'It's *personal*, Deke.'

'An' a bit *awkward*,' added Little Malcolm.

Deke put his empty tankard on the bar and frowned. ''Ow do y'mean?'

'It's 'bout Duggie,' said Big Dave.

'That's reight,' added Little Malcolm.

Big Dave sighed, clearly in difficulty. 'Malc, get another pint in f'Deke.'

Little Malcolm took Deke's tankard to the far end of the bar and Don pulled on the handpump to produce another frothing pint of Tetley's bitter.

'Spit it out then, Dave,' said Deke. 'What about Duggie?'

'Well,' said Big Dave, 'since Ronnie passed – God rest 'is soul – your t'nearest thing to a dad to 'im.'

'Ah s'ppose,' said Deke with an assured nod devoid of all modesty.

Big Dave coughed, searching for the right words. 'So y'need t'know what we saw this morning on us rounds.'

'An' what were that then?'

Little Malcolm placed the full tankard in front of Deke.

''Ave a sup first,' suggested Big Dave.

The enormity of this conversation was beginning to dawn on Deke and he took a nervous sip. 'Go on then ... 'it me with it.'

'We were outside that woman's house that 'e's seein',' said Big Dave.

277

'An' ah could see in t'window,' said Little Malcolm.

'An' we saw 'im,' said Big Dave.

'But 'e couldn't see us,' added Little Malcolm conspiratorially.

'An' we saw 'im doin' it,' said Big Dave.

'Large as life – and wi' t'curtains wide open,' added Little Malcolm.

'Y'mean a bit of y'know,' said Deke, '...'ow's y'father ... Umpty Dumpty?'

Big Dave looked confused. 'No, nowt like that ... a lot worse than that.'

'It were terrible t'be'old,' said Little Malcolm.

'So come on, lads, tell me straight. What were Duggie doin'?'

Big Dave took a deep breath. ''E were 'ooverin' t'carpet.'

''Ooverin' ... 'ooverin'?' said Deke. 'Y'mean wi' a vacuum cleaner?' Deke was almost apoplectic. 'Bloody 'ell – in broad daylight?' He drank deeply and shook his head in disbelief. 'Lads, ah'm glad y'told me. She's got 'im under t'thumb. Ah'll 'ave a stern word wi' 'im.' He looked at the members of the Ragley Rovers FC propping up the tap-room bar. 'T'football team 'as *standards* – we 'ave a *reputation*... She'll 'ave 'im *washin' an' ironin'* next.'

It was Big Dave and Little Malcolm's turn to recoil. As the eighties progressed, being a male chauvinist was suddenly becoming more difficult. They had survived the first woman prime minister and even the female bus driver in Easington, but this was more than they could bear.

'Anyway, Deke, we thought you ought t'know,' said Big Dave.

'That's reight,' added Little Malcolm.

Deke picked up his tankard and swigged the final mouthful. 'Leave it t'me, lads,' he said confidently. 'Poor kid's gone off t'straight an' narrow. Consider it sorted,' and he walked out.

Back at Deke's home his two eldest sons, Shane and Clint, were about to leave and walk down to the pub.

''Urry up, Nancy,' shouted Shane up the stairs. With his skinhead haircut and a grubby Iron Maiden T-shirt he felt well-dressed for the tap-room of The Royal Oak.

Clint was in his bedroom and winced when Shane called him 'Nancy'. Not for the first time he wished he hadn't got a psychopathic brother. However, he was pleased with his brand-new colourful 'Purple Rain' T-shirt with a picture of Prince on the front, but his *Boy George Fashion & Make-up Book* had provoked serious thought. Experimenting with different shades of eye shadow took a long time. *Life is full of difficult choices,* he thought as he stared in the mirror.

Shortly before eight o'clock Beth arrived at The Royal Oak and was sitting at a bay window table as I walked in.

I kissed her on the cheek. 'White wine?'

'Yes please,' she said and glanced up at the 'Dish of the Day' on the chalkboard. It was fish, chips and mushy peas, 'and the special'.

At the bar I placed my order and Don pulled a pint of Chestnut for me.

'So where's Sheila tonight?' I asked.

279

'Out,' said Don abruptly. It was Friday night and The Oak was busy. 'Gone t'that belly dancing at Nora's,' he said in a loud and slightly irritated voice. The image of the shapely and scantily clad Sheila gyrating her substantial bits and pieces around the floor of the Coffee Shop briefly flickered through the minds of the Ragley Rovers football team.

'There were a lot o' laughin' an' gigglin' an' suchlike when ah walked past,' said Stevie 'Super-sub' Coleclough, 'but ah couldn't see in 'cause curtains were shut.'

Up the Morton Road, Petula Dudley-Palmer was about to leave for the Coffee Shop, and Geoffrey, much to his annoyance, had to stay in to make sure Elisabeth Amelia and Victoria Alice went to bed on time.

'What time will you be back?' he asked not once but twice.

Petula was looking forward to her night out, as it was rare for her to go anywhere with Geoffrey. She had taken advantage of her *Radio Times* Reader Offer and purchased a burgundy velour leisure suit. With its elasticated waist, ribbed crew neck and raglan sleeves, along with her Chris Evert trainers, she knew she looked like a modern eighties woman. She picked up her Jane Fonda ethnic shoulder bag and set off full of anticipation.

In the Post Office, Amelia Duff was sitting behind her counter, sipping tea from her 1935 King George V Silver Jubilee mug, a present from her father, and thinking of Ted Postlethwaite. Last night he had asked her a question, an important one, and she was wondering how to respond.

It was after Ted had fallen asleep that she had looked at his weather-worn face and thought in the stillness of the night that *love is not finding someone you want to live with ... love is finding someone you can't live without.*

Amelia had been the Ragley village post-mistress since 1965 but close friends were few. There were no *confidantes* with whom to share a special secret. She sighed. It was at times like this that she missed her father, Athol Duff, and his quiet manner and good advice. She wondered what he would have thought of the Ragley post-man with his thoughtful gestures and kind words ... and companionship.

Finally, deep in thought, she set off for the Coffee Shop.

By the time Sally and Ruby arrived the place was packed.

Nora stood up. 'Thanks f'comin', ladies,' she said, 'an' please give a weally big Wagley welcome to Bwenda.'

Brenda was wearing a chiffon-topped crop, complete with tassles that seemed to rotate indiscriminately, plus bright purple harem trousers with an elasticated waist that accentuated her prodigious tummy.

'Bloomin' 'eck,' whispered Betty Buttle to Margery Ackroyd. 'Ah've seen some legs in m'time, but them are like tree trunks.'

'An' look at that bra,' added Margery in astonishment.

'Like a couple o' buckets,' said Betty.

Brenda stubbed out her Castella cigar, put on some music that she was reliably informed was popular in a Turkish brothel and began the demonstration.

'It all comes from yer knees, ladies,' she explained, 'an' that meks yer 'ips rotate.'

'She sounds 'usky,' observed Betty.

'Dorothy said she'd 'eard she'd 'ad an operation at back of 'er throat,' said Margery, 'be'ind 'er tonsils.'

'She's mebbe 'ad 'er haemorrhoids out,' suggested Betty helpfully.

Nora and Dorothy were the first to volunteer to belly dance.

'Ah'm not weally sure about wotatin' 'ips,' said Nora. 'Mine can go left an' wight, but not wownd an' wownd.'

As the night wore on the ladies of Ragley relaxed and soon they were all trying to master the art of belly dancing. It was generally agreed that Ruby was a natural and when Sally drove her home our school caretaker was like her old self again.

'Thanks for askin' me, Mrs P,' said Ruby. 'Best night ah can remember for ages,' and she slept the sleep of the peaceful mind.

It was very late when Petula arrived home. The house was dark and she walked quietly into the bedroom. Geoffrey's shirt had been discarded on the bedroom floor.

She picked it up and buried her face in its folds. *A silly habit,* she thought, but the scent always helped her recall happy times when they were first married.

She was surprised. The scent wasn't one she recognized. It didn't seem to smell of Geoffrey any more.

Perhaps I've just forgotten, she thought.

Back at Bilbo Cottage we paid Natasha and I drove her home.

Beth was stirring two mugs of milky coffee when I returned.

'So how are you now?' I asked. We had talked about her initial disappointment at not getting an interview.

Beth smiled. 'I was a bit down,' she said, 'but I'm fine now. It'll happen when it's the right time.'

'Disappointed you didn't go to belly dancing for beginners?' I teased.

Beth smiled and her green eyes were mirrors of my thoughts.

I sipped the coffee. 'This will keep me awake.'

Beth stretched up and kissed me on the lips. 'John sleeps right through the night now,' she said with that mischievous look I knew so well. 'So we could have an early night.'

Two hours later we were both lying naked on the bed. Beth was resting her head on the crook of my arm and breathing softly.

She murmured something.

'What did you say?' I asked.

'I'm just glad you're not a *beginner.*'

Chapter Sixteen

Only a Girl

*School closed today for the May Day Bank Holiday
weekend and will reopen on Tuesday, 7 May.*

*The school cricket team will be playing against
Morton School on Saturday, 4 May. Members of staff
will be supporting the village VE celebrations.*

Extract from the Ragley School Logbook:
Friday, 3 May 1985

It was Friday, 3 May and the swallows had
returned to their familiar nesting places in the
eaves of Bilbo Cottage. The season was moving on
and in the distance a gentle breeze stirred the sea
of grass. I opened the bedroom window and heard
the bleating of lambs while the fragrant scents of a
perfect May morning hung in the air. The woods
were carpeted with bluebells and a thrush with its
speckled breast trilled a song of spring. It was the
end of the third week of the summer term and an
eventful Bank Holiday weekend was in store.

Vera was already busy on the telephone when I
arrived in the school office. 'Yes, Winnie,' she
said. 'That's wonderful news. Come to the WI
tent tomorrow morning and I'll be there to help
you with the display.'

She put down the receiver. 'That was Winifred
Buttershaw, Mr Sheffield,' she said. 'A formid-

able lady ... she was a Land Girl during the war.'

'I'll look forward to meeting her,' I said.

'You certainly won't forget her,' said Vera with a smile. 'She's had an interesting life.' Then she glanced down at her notepad. 'Mr Dalton has offered to help erect the WI tent, I've prepared a note to go out asking for wartime memorabilia and Mr Piercy and Mr Jenkins have volunteered to umpire the cricket match against Morton. So it's good that the school is seen to be supporting the VE celebrations.'

'Thank you, Vera,' I said and reflected on how lucky we were to have such a dedicated secretary.

An exciting weekend was in store. The village was gearing up to celebrate the fortieth anniversary of Victory in Europe Day. On the BBC news we were reminded that on 30 April 1945 Adolf Hitler had killed himself, rapidly followed on 7 May by the surrender of all the German forces in the West to General Eisenhower. The next day, on 8 May, England celebrated Victory in Europe Day. Forty years later, the ladies of the Ragley Women's Institute were unravelling colourful bunting from the wickerwork baskets in the village hall and seeking out old wartime recipes for a few days of nostalgia in the village.

There was a knock on the door. It was Danny Hardacre with his right arm in a sling and his mother looking as crestfallen as her son.

'Bad news, Mr Sheffield,' she said. 'Danny fell off his bike last night. We took him to A & E in York and the X-ray showed a broken collarbone.'

'Oh dear, I'm so sorry,' I said. 'How are you feeling, Danny?'

'It's a bit sore, Mr Sheffield, and I won't be able t'play tomorrow ... but I can clean the blackboard left-handed.' Danny always took his monitor job very seriously.

'Well, perhaps not for quite a while yet,' said Mrs Hardacre.

'Don't worry about that,' I said. 'What is important is that you get better.' Danny was quiet but he was a sensible boy and I knew he understood. 'So what would you like Danny to do today?'

'Probably best he stays with me, but perhaps you could let him take some maths and English home and I'll bring it back next week.'

'That's fine, Mrs Hardacre,' I said. 'Just go into the classroom and help yourself.'

'Thanks, Mr Sheffield.' She paused in the doorway. 'He's so disappointed. You'll need a new opening batsman, I'm afraid.'

And a new captain, I thought.

It was just before morning break that I spoke to Charlotte. She had completed a series of algebraic equations and was standing by my desk as I wrote 'Excellent' at the foot of the page.

'Charlotte,' I said quietly, 'I'm afraid Danny can't play in the cricket match tomorrow. He fell off his bicycle and injured himself. So would you like to be captain?'

Charlotte was disappointed to hear the news about Danny but thrilled to be made captain of the team. 'Oooh, yes please, Mr Sheffield!' It was a joy to see her excitement. 'Can ah tell m'mam? She'll be so 'appy.'

'Go to the office and tell Mrs Forbes-Kitchener

that I've asked you to use the telephone to ring your mother.'

Charlotte was gone in a flash and I was pleased that I had made it a special day for this hard-working and positive girl. The fact that Mrs Ackroyd was the village gossip wasn't uppermost in my mind at that moment.

After morning break our local bobby, PC Julian Pike, arrived to take charge of the first weekly session of Cycling Proficiency. The children were taught to ride safely and look after their bicycles. A certificate and a metal badge was the prize at the end of the course.

He had arrived in his little van and unloaded cardboard traffic lights and old hosepipes to mark out the 'roads'. A row of plastic cones had been arranged so that the children could weave in and out of them. It was serious business, but PC Pike made it great fun.

At lunchtime I supervised the preparations for our games afternoon. Today it included the oldest children in the school, in Sally's class and mine.

Our programme of summer sport had begun well. With the support of a few parents we'd been able to offer a range of activities so that the children could choose their preferred summer sport. I was in charge of cricket with John Grainger, Anne and Kitty Eckersley supervised rounders and hockey, while Miss Flint and Petula Dudley-Palmer came in to support the children who wanted to play a short form of tennis on the playground.

Our cricket team had already been a great

success, probably the best I had ever known, thanks in the main to the bowling of Danny Hardacre and the hard-hitting batting of Charlotte Ackroyd, the only girl in the team. Charlotte could also throw a ball with astonishing accuracy and bowl like the wind. She was the primary-school equivalent of Ian Botham. Best of all, she simply loved to play. They were all looking forward to tomorrow's cricket match against Morton on the hallowed square of Ragley's cricket ground.

Sadly, as always, a few children missed out owing to medical problems. Two letters excusing their children from physical education were particularly noteworthy. The first read, 'Dear Mr Sheffield, Please excuse our Hayley from PE as she has bazookers on her right foot.' The second was almost as graphic. 'Dear Mr Sheffield, Ryan had better miss PE. He had a problem with his chest but we shifted it.'

The games lesson went well and Charlotte managed to hit a ball over the cycle-shed roof. While the children were getting changed afterwards I called in to Anne's classroom.

In the carpeted Home Corner children were busy playing while imitating the tasks of their parents. Madonna Fazackerly and Julie Tricklebank were ironing clothes on the tiny ironing board, Hermione Jackson was preparing a meal and her sister, Honeysuckle, was setting the table. However, little Alfie Spraggon was sitting on a beanbag and staring blankly at the wall.

'What are you doing, Alfie?' I asked.

He continued to stare into space. 'Ah'm watchin' t'football, Mr Sheffield, an' waiting for m'tea.'

It occurred to me that the equality of the sexes still had some way to go in this tiny corner of North Yorkshire. I was about to suggest that young Alfie should help with the chores when Vera looked round the door. 'There's a parent to see you, Mr Sheffield,' said Vera with a wary look. 'I've put him in the staff-room.'

It was George Spraggon, father of Frankie in my class.

'Ah've jus 'eard t'news about Danny,' he said. 'Bad business.'

'Yes, we're all hoping he recovers soon.'

'Thing is, Mr Sheffield, word's goin' round t'village you've made young Charlotte captain o' t'cricket team.'

'That's right, Mr Spraggon, I have.'

He looked aghast. 'So it's true, then?'

'Yes, Charlotte is an outstanding player.'

'So y'didn't think o' my Frankie, then?'

'Frankie is a good player. I'm sure you must be very proud of him and, of course, he's still got another year in my class.'

'Ah've been 'ere in Ragley man an' boy, long afore you arrived, Mr Sheffield,' he said with feeling, 'an' we've allus been proud of t'sports teams.'

'I'm pleased to hear it.'

'But can't y'see, you'll mek us a laughin' stock. Cricket is f'boys an' rounders is f'girls. That's 'ow it's allus been.'

'I'm afraid I disagree. That's why we give boys *and* girls a chance.'

'So y'won't change y'mind, then?'

'No, Mr Spraggon, there's no need. Charlotte is a fine all-round cricketer.'

He turned away in disgust and paused. 'But, she's *only a girl*.'

He left the door swinging on its hinges.

Vera came in and began to prepare our cups of afternoon tea. 'Everything all right, Mr Sheffield? I heard Mr Spraggon's raised voice.'

'Fine, thank you, Vera,' I said. 'Just a misunderstanding.'

'But not on your part,' said Vera with a reassuring smile and I settled down with a welcome cup of tea.

By the open window, Sally was reading her *Woman* magazine. Jane Fonda, the forty-seven-year-old actress with the body of a much younger woman, was describing how to survive the mid-life crisis. Sally sighed deeply and moved swiftly on to Miriam Stoppard's responses to the health problems of concerned readers. Finally, undeterred, she had spent twelve pence on a Cadbury's Skippy bar as her afternoon treat and, following a moment's hesitation, she ate it quickly to lessen the guilt.

It was evening and darkness had fallen on the Crescent. Anne Grainger had found a few items for the Second World War display, including a ration book and John's old gas mask. Then she settled down in her favourite armchair to relax with a good book and a glass of white wine.

Anne had recently joined the Literary Guild Book Club and her first two purchases had arrived recently. For John she had selected *The Complete Encyclopedia of DIY and Home Maintenance,* while for herself she had chosen *The Complete Book of*

Love and Sex. It occurred to her that she might as well make up for what she was missing by reading about it. As usual, John appeared oblivious to everything around him as he immersed himself in his new book.

Meanwhile, the television was murmuring away in the corner, advertising the new series of Thora Hird's *Praise Be!* followed by a reminder of Sunday evening's episode of *Juliet Bravo*, starring Anna Carteret as Inspector Kate Longton. Anne could not help but notice the speed with which John suddenly bookmarked the section on ceramic tiling to ogle at the slim policewoman as she solved another case. It crossed Anne's mind that John's sex drive might be stimulated by women in uniforms and she vaguely wondered if her mother's 1950s nurse's outfit was still in a suitcase in the loft.

On Saturday morning the radios of Ragley were switched on to greet the new day. Ruby's daughters were listening to Peter Powell's Radio 1 show and joining in with Bruce Springsteen's 'Dancing In The Dark'. Anne Grainger had tuned in to David Jacobs on Radio 2 and was humming along to the Phil Collins hit 'One More Night' while Vera, faithful to Radio 3, found Delius's 'Song Of The High Hills' as soothing as her cup of Earl Grey.

When I drove up Ragley High Street the first pink blossom on the cherry trees was bursting into life. I parked in the school car park and walked down to the village hall. It was good to be alive on this lovely day. The month of May was

291

always a joy and the village hall looked a picture with an early-flowering honeysuckle scrambling over the entrance porch.

Inside, Vera was working with a slim, grey-haired lady preparing a display of Land Army memorabilia. 'This is my friend Winnie, Mr Sheffield,' said Vera. 'She was in the Land Army and has brought in some photographs of her time working on a farm in Buckinghamshire.'

I helped them erect the display boards, during which time I learned much about Winifred Buttershaw, who was keen to talk about her life. Winnie, as she was known affectionately to her friends, lived alongside the Ragley sports field in the Hartford Home for Retired Gentlefolk, an imposing red-brick Victorian building. Hidden behind a tall yew hedge, it was set in two acres of attractive private land. In its former glory it had served as a military hospital during the Second World War and here the injured members of the armed forces were nursed back to health.

'I lived in the Park Hill flats in Sheffield,' said Winifred. 'It was the architect's vision of the future – practical, cheap, high-density housing in the centre of a city. It was a utopian dream and modern communal living for the working classes.' Her eyes were shining, the memories vivid. 'They made sure that neighbours stayed together after they pulled down the back-to-back slums and they used the old street names. It was a mini-village. Whoever designed it thought of everything – newsagents, clothes shops, hairdressers, a café.'

'It sounds a good place to bring up a family,' I said.

'It was, Mr Sheffield,' agreed Winnie. 'We learned about friendship, helping each other, and we did our courting there.' Her cheeks flushed at the memory. 'I worked in Dempsey's Shoe Shop and I met my Stanley in The Scottish Queen pub. He was a steelworker and after we were married I thought it was paradise. We had hot water, central heating, three bedrooms – it was like a palace.'

'Good memories,' I said.

She smiled the warmest of smiles. 'There was a name for where we lived.'

'And what was that?' I asked.

'Streets in the sky, Mr Sheffield – *streets in the sky.*'

Across the High Street the first customers were filling the tables in Nora's Coffee Shop and it was clear that teenagers Claire Bradshaw and Anita Cuthbertson had long since left their *Jackie* magazines far behind.

Claire had picked up a spare copy of a *Woman* magazine. It was advertising a good sex guide for inexperienced couples, *Make It Happy* by Jane Cousins. Readers were invited to write to Virginia Ironside to discuss their sexual problems.

'It sez 'ere summat about *vaginismus*,' said Anita.

'What's that when it's at 'ome?' asked Claire. 'It sounds painful.'

'It sez "tensing of the vaginal muscles"' Anita read out. 'Mebbe that's what ah've got.'

'You'll 'ave t'tell me,' said Claire, "cause me an' Kenny 'aven't done it yet.'

'An' ah y'gonna let 'im?' asked Anita.

'Mebbe nex' month, when 'is mam an' dad go

293

t'Skegness.'

Meanwhile, behind the counter, Nora kept popping into the back room to see Desmond Lynam on Saturday *Grandstand*. Nora's pin-up was introducing the Rugby League Silk Cut Challenge Cup Final between Wigan and Hull from Wembley Stadium and she decided to ask Tyrone if he would mind growing a moustache.

Down the street in Old Tommy Piercy's butcher's shop, Betty Buttle's farmer husband, Harry, was delivering his wife's shopping list before catching the bus to Easington market.

''Ere's Betty's order t'collect later, Tommy,' he said.

'So where y'goin' in such a 'urry?' asked Old Tommy.

'Ah'm tekkin m'wife t'market,' said Harry.

'Ah 'ope y'get a good price for 'er,' retorted Old Tommy quick as a flash.

Harry grinned until he saw Betty walking purposefully past the shop window and his smile faded. 'So do I,' he said with feeling.

Old Tommy smiled wistfully. It was a long time now since his wife had died and he had never fancied another woman. As far as Old Tommy was concerned, he was an old dog and it was too late for new tricks.

William Featherstone's Reliance bus was parked by the village green and, in the queue, mothers and children were enjoying the sunshine and in no hurry to clamber aboard. As was his way, William, in his brown bus driver's jacket, welcomed each passenger by doffing his peaked cap and chatting with his regulars.

'That's right, Mrs Whittaker,' he said with a friendly smile, 'it's free for young Sam if he's still five.'

Next in the queue was Mrs Ricketts with six-year-old Billy. She crouched down and whispered in Billy's ear, 'If t'driver asks, tell 'im you're five.'

'Why, Mam?' asked Billy.

'Jus' shurrup an' do as y'told,' ordered Mrs Ricketts.

''Ello, Mrs Ricketts, an' 'ow are you today?'

'Fine thank you, Mr Featherstone,' said Mrs Ricketts as she pushed young Billy up the steps of the bus.

''Ello, Billy,' said William, staring down at the strapping young boy. 'And how old are you?'

Billy glanced nervously at his mother. 'Ah'm five.'

'And when will you be six?' asked William.

Billy pondered this for a moment. 'When ah get off t'bus,' he said. William gave Mrs Ricketts a knowing look and said nothing.

Petula Dudley-Palmer was shopping in Brown's department store in York. She had begun to take Pro Plus tablets. They were supposed to 'give you go' and she needed a pick-me-up. Geoffrey hadn't come home last night. He had said there was a crisis at the Rowntree factory and all the management team needed to be there. 'Trust me,' he had said ... but she didn't.

'I'm not sleeping well,' said Petula to the young assistant in the bedroom department.

'This is t'answer t'your prayers, Miss,' said

Dennis, the trainee of the year. 'It's a Dreamland Electric Underblanket.'

It was a long time since she had been called 'Miss' and Petula smiled at the spotty youth. 'Yes, I saw it in my catalogue.'

'It's gorra padded lining,' he said enthusiastically. 'Jus' feel that.'

'Lovely and soft,' said Petula appreciatively.

'An' it'll warm y'bed jus' perfec',' said Dennis.

'Is it easy to use?' asked Petula.

'Simple as y'twelve times table,' said Dennis, recalling his C grade in O-level mathematics. His mother had been so proud of his certificate she had framed it and hung it in the downstairs toilet.

Petula wished he had selected a better example. She had always had trouble with nine times twelve. It was not the moment to reveal she would have been a non-starter on *The Krypton Factor*.

'Y'jus' set t'independent comfort control,' said Dennis, 'an' Bob's yer uncle.'

'Really?' said Petula, still not entirely convinced.

However, Dennis had saved the best until last. 'It 'as revolutionary safety features – you'll be at t'cuttin' edge of modern living. T'nineties 'as arrived, Miss ... in t'eighties.'

Petula smiled. 'I'll take two,' she said. After all, a spare would be welcome in the guest bedroom. The fact that no one ever came to stay never crossed her mind.

Back on the sports field Tom and I had helped the Earnshaw boys to erect the huge WI refreshment marquee. Don and Sheila Bradshaw set up a makeshift bar on trestle tables at one end and

Vera and a group of WI ladies were preparing their refreshment stall with a Baby Burco boiler plus sandwiches and cakes of all shapes and sizes. The excitement was building.

In the village hall, Winifred Buttershaw was sitting next to her Land Army display with a group of girls from Ragley School, including Charlotte Ackroyd. They were looking at a poster of the iconic image of the Land Girl in her corduroy breeches, green jumper and brown felt hat.

'Girls, during the Second World War two hundred thousand women joined the Women's Land Army and I was one of them,' said Winifred. 'In 1939 we were importing sixty per cent of our food. We had to produce more eggs, milk, fruit and vegetables to feed the nation and many of our male farmworkers had gone off to war. So the female population responded to the challenge.' It was a rousing speech.

Charlotte Ackroyd raised her hand. 'What did y'do before that, Miss?'

'We were typists and shop girls. I was a trainee window-dresser in Busby's department store in Bradford.'

'An' what were it like workin' on a farm?' asked Sonia Tricklebank.

'It was a good life,' said Winifred with a smile, 'although rat-catching and muck-spreading weren't to my liking.'

All the girls grimaced at the thought.

'But I drove a combine harvester and felt very grand,' said Winifred proudly. She pointed to an old, faded pair of brown dungarees. 'And these were made in Leeds at the Montague Burton store, the clothing manufacturer, so we were dressed to cope with the work and the weather.'

'Did it make you a different person?' asked Charlotte.

Winifred studied the intense stare of the leggy young girl and considered her answer. 'They said I couldn't do men's work because I was only a girl ... but I showed 'em.'

The girls wandered off to get some orange juice and a slice of Mary Hardisty's plum cake, but Charlotte hung back. 'I'm playing in t'cricket team wi' all t'boys,' she said simply. 'Mr Sheffield made me captain.'

Winifred smiled. 'Then you must be good, so go out and do your best.'

On my way to join Beth and John in the refreshment tent I stopped to talk to Ruby. George Dainty had brought two folding chairs and a small picnic table and he and Ruby had settled with a cool drink to watch the cricket. As the Ragley children walked out on to the field we joined in the applause.

Deirdre Coe and her brother Stan walked by. ''S'all right f'some,' sneered Deirdre with a fierce scowl in Ruby's direction.

'Who burst your balloon?' shouted Ruby with a speedy riposte

Stan Coe and I had history ... ever since he was removed from the school's governing body. 'You've done it this time, Mr 'Eadteacher,' he sneered. 'A *girl* as cricket captain.'

Deirdre grabbed his arm before I could reply

and they walked off to the beer tent.

'Y'know what she's like,' said Ruby. 'She can 'ave an argument wi'out speakin'.'

'Tek no notice, Ruby,' said George.

'She's a reight frosty chops is that one,' Ruby went on. 'Not a civil word in 'er ... never gives yer t'time o' day.'

'Never mind, Ruby, let's enjoy the cricket,' I said.

'An' 'er brother's no better,' continued Ruby. 'Word 'as it 'e's buyin' land at t'back of t'council estate ... mus'know summat.'

George suddenly looked concerned and gave me a knowing look.

'As sure as eggs is eggs, 'e's up t'no good an' she's a proper 'ussy, Mr Sheffield,' concluded Ruby. 'Ah wouldn't trust 'er as far as ah could throw 'er.'

Judging by the breadth and girth of Deirdre Coe, that wouldn't have been far, but I declined to air a view that lacked true Christian spirit.

The cricket match between the children of Ragley and Morton proved a great success and the umpires, Old Tommy Piercy and Albert Jenkins, did their job with sensitivity and lots of support for the children. The teams were well matched, with the exception of Charlotte Ackroyd, who took five wickets with her fast bowling, made a couple of good catches and, when Ragley batted, she crashed a speedy twenty-five runs to win the game.

At the end both teams were clapped off the field and I spotted Winifred walk up to Charlotte. 'Well done,' she said.

'Like y'said, Miss,' said Charlotte, 'ah showed 'em.'

Back in the beer tent I noticed Stan and Deirdre Coe had made a hasty retreat. Beth had wheeled John's pushchair up to the makeshift bar where Sheila was serving in her skin-tight leather trousers, bare midriff and sparkly boob-tube.

''Ow's young John these days, Mrs Sheffield?' asked Sheila as she poured a glass of white wine and an orange juice.

'Very lively,' said Beth with a grin. 'Into all the cupboards and generally running us ragged.'

Then Sheila pulled a half of Chestnut for me. 'That's t'problem,' she said. 'Babies don't come wi' manuals. Y'jus' go along an' do what y'think is right,' and Beth smiled.

Back in Bilbo Cottage Beth prepared an evening meal while I played with John on the lounge carpet. The television in the corner was advertising this evening's Eurovision Song Contest. Our hopes were pinned on 'Love is' by Vikki, but no one appeared too optimistic. When *The Keith Harris Show* with Orville the Duck appeared, John put down his building bricks, stared in fascination at the green duck and smiled.

It was long after John's bedtime when Beth said, 'Can we talk?'

A little reluctantly I switched off *Match of the Day* with Jimmy Hill and turned to face her.

'I'm going to apply for another headship,' she said and passed over her copy of the *Times Educational Supplement*. She had my full attention now.

'There are a number of really big schools similar to the Scarborough headship,' she said, 'but there's one coming up in York. It's a medium-sized school, so I would stand a better chance. Perhaps I ought to wait for that one.'

'Sounds a good idea,' I said, 'but it's a shame you can't get some interview experience first. That would be helpful.' I looked at the page of headship posts. 'There's a large North Yorkshire school here in Pickering,' I suggested, pointing at the list.

'And an even larger one down in Hampshire,' said Beth.

My heart sank. 'Hampshire?'

'I'm not sure,' said Beth. She looked doubtful. 'The chances of getting an interview are so remote.'

'I agree,' I said. 'The Hampshire one really is a long shot, but they're all for a January start, so if the interview for the North Yorkshire post comes up first they may want to check you out before they shortlist the one in York.'

'I suppose it might work out that way,' said Beth. She was clearly toying with the idea.

'So what do you think?'

'I'm going to keep trying,' she said with determination.

'Good for you,' I said.

'Even though I'm *only a woman*,' she added for good measure.

I just smiled.

It had been that sort of day.

Chapter Seventeen

A Fish Called Walter

Interviews took place today for the post of Class 2 teacher. Preparations were made for the visit to Hornsea by Classes 1 and 2 on Friday, 7 June.
Extract from the Ragley School Logbook:
Wednesday, 5 June 1985

It was a new dawn. Behind the distant hills a shimmering disc of golden light emerged in the eastern sky. The countryside was waking and an eventful day was in store. It was Wednesday, 5 June and interviews for the post of Class 2 teacher were due to take place in the afternoon.

The sun was warm as I drove on the back road to Ragley. In Twenty Acre Field tall stalks of green, unripe barley rippled in the gentle breeze and sinuous shadows danced across the land. Above me the starlings wheeled in close formation and, beyond the tableland of the North Yorkshire moors, the distant hills were daubed with purple heather like the broad streaks of a child's painting.

I parked my Morris Minor Traveller and looked back with satisfaction as the yellow-and-chrome AA badge sparkled in the morning sunlight. Then I paused in the car park and soaked up the warmth. The school looked a picture on this fine morning and the pinks bordering the flower bed outside Sally's classroom were opening up. Across the village green and above the distant pantile rooftops the sharp screaming of swifts could be heard before they swooped up the Morton Road towards the church. It was a perfect North Yorkshire morning and the world felt clean and new.

A group of children whose parents worked in York were always in the playground half an hour before school started. In the entrance porch Sally was working with a group of them, planting trailing geraniums, purple lobelia and bright mesembryanthemums in two large wooden tubs.

Vera looked up when I walked into the office. 'We're all set for the interviews, Mr Sheffield,' she said, 'and the candidates have all confirmed they will arrive in time for lunch.' She looked at her notepad. 'Also, Mr Featherstone rang back to say he'll be outside school in his coach at nine o'clock on Friday for the trip to Hornsea.'

'Thanks, Vera,' I said. 'An interesting few days.'

Sally came in, removing her gardening gloves. 'And the weather forecast is perfect for the rest of the week.'

It was a busy morning. The children were excited about their school journey to the east coast and we spent some time studying road maps of the route and talking about what we might see in Hornsea. Sally had prepared a series of worksheets with information about the planned activities, including a boat trip, seeing the Mute swans on Hornsea Mere and visiting the coastline.

When the bell went for morning break I called

303

in to Tom's class. He had been talking about family trees and the discussion had moved on to grandparents. Tom had followed this up with a writing exercise and he hurried from one child to another to assist with spellings and punctuation. I walked around reading some of the responses. They were all enlightening.

Scott Higginbottom had written in neat printing, 'Grandparents are old people and they don't have any children. They just have grandchildren.' Mandy Kerslake clearly wasn't too impressed: 'My grandad and grandma don't do anything. They just sit at home and wait for us to visit.' Jeremy Urquhart was much more complimentary: 'When they take us for a walk they are different to my mummy and daddy cos they stop next to interesting things like flowers and trees and gravestones and buildings and streets with cobbles and butterflies and robins and those birds that fly dead still over roads looking for mice.'

Charlie Cartwright wrote, 'I like it when my great-grandma helps me read. She never says hurry up, like my mummy does, and she doesn't miss bits out of the story. At night she takes out her teeth and gums and puts them in a glass of water. It must be easy for her to clean her teeth. I wish I could do this, it would be a lot easier than brushing them.'

Katie Icklethwaite was particularly appreciative: 'They never say hurry up and they always button up my coat to the top.' Rufus Snodgrass wrote on a similar theme: 'My grandma reads stories to me lots of times and she never gets fed up. I like Three Billy Goats Gruff and she does the troll really scary. She's better than the telly because she answers my questions.'

Finally, Ted Coggins took a graphic approach. 'Last time we went to visit I saw my grandma's big knickers on the radiator and her teeth and gums were in a big jam jar behind the telly.'

In my class it was just before lunch when Charlotte Ackroyd made a predictable announcement without appearing to look up from the map of Yorkshire's east coast in her topic book: 'Mini Clubman Estate coming up t'drive, Mr Sheffield.'

The first of the interviewees had arrived. It was Ms Pat Brookside.

She was a tall, slim, leggy twenty-seven-year-old blonde who had taught the infant age range for the past five years at Thirkby Primary School. Ms Brookside was a strong candidate who had made the shortlist last year when Tom had been appointed.

Charlie Cartwright met her as she walked from the car park towards the entrance steps. ''Ello, Miss, ah saw you las' year,' he said cheerfully.

'Oh yes?' replied Pat, somewhat confused.

'That were when Mr Dalton 'elped me wi' m'spider 'cause it only 'ad seven legs,' said Charlie with a sad shake of his head. The memory was clearly still sharp and vivid.

'Seven legs?' repeated Pat, none the wiser.

'Yes, Miss,' said Charlie. 'M'spider 'ad lost a leg an' Mr Dalton put 'im back in t'school 'edgerow t'get better.'

'That sounds a good idea,' said Pat.

They had reached the entrance steps but

305

Charlie wasn't quite finished. 'Y'see, Miss, ah love spiders an' worms an' beetles an' frogs an' suchlike ... but spiders are m'favourite.'

He wandered off, content with his life, to practise three-legged racing with Rufus Snodgrass on the school field. Pat Brookside smiled and walked in.

The other interviewees arrived in quick succession. John Birk, a science student from St John's College in York appeared on a motorbike that caused great interest from the children on the playground. Sandra Collins, a recently qualified teacher from a primary school in Malton, bounced up the cobbled drive in a Citroën 2CV with its bungee suspension, while Dawn Freeman, an experienced infant teacher from Easington Primary School, was dropped off at the school gate by her husband driving a swish two-door Opel Manta.

Vera had cleared my desk so that it was as tidy as hers and then borrowed a tin of furniture polish from Ruby's store to restore a shine to both surfaces. Then, in neat alignment, she laid out a manila folder, an A4 notepad and a new Berol rollerball pen for each member of the interviewing panel. This comprised Joseph, as chair of governors; Rupert, representing the rest of the governing body; our local adviser, Richard Gomersall, from County Hall; Anne and myself.

The interviews went smoothly and, as usual, we saw the candidates in alphabetical order. John Birk, with his wavy thatch of uncontrollable brown hair and black-framed spectacles, looked scarily like a boyish version of me when he walked in and Anne caught my eye with a knowing wide-eyed smile. He was keen and articulate and certainly 'one for the future', as Richard Gomersall later described him.

Pat Brookside was outstanding. We had interviewed her a year before but this time she appeared much more confident. She had been on a computer course and her knowledge of the curriculum was good. She offered to support extra-curricular activities and run the netball team if appointed. As a county-standard player herself, this seemed appropriate. At the end of the interview Joseph asked why she wanted to move from Thirkby. 'I've just moved in with a new partner,' she said, 'and he lives in Easington.'

Joseph blinked at the directness of this positive and forthright young woman.

Sandra Collins was another determined candidate. She had clearly formulated a career structure and experience in a small village school was part of that progression before she would move on. I was impressed.

Dawn Freeman from Easington was something of a disappointment. She was simply looking for a change and criticized her current school in a disparaging manner. She clearly believed she would be doing us a great favour if appointed. Richard Gomersall and the Major were unimpressed. However, her knowledge of recent changes in the primary curriculum was very good.

The post-interview discussion centred on two candidates.

'Pat Brookside and Sandra Collins appear to be strong candidates, Jack,' said Richard. 'What do you think?'

307

'I agree,' I said and looked towards Anne, who nodded.

'Two determined young women, what?' added Rupert. 'I like them both.'

'We could do with a bit of stability after Mr Dalton's short stay,' said Joseph, 'so I would favour Ms Brookside.'

'I agree,' said Anne, 'and she has the computer skills we would lose when Tom goes.'

I underlined a name on the list of candidates in front of me. 'So, if we're agreed,' I said, 'it looks like Ms Brookside will be our new teacher.'

Anne stood up and looked at each of us in turn. 'I'll go and invite Ms Brookside to come back in, shall I?'

'Yes please, Anne,' I said, 'and Joseph can confirm that she definitely wants the post ... and then I'll have a word with the others.'

I glanced up at the clock. It was five o'clock; the interviews were over.

Pat Brookside came back in and, as chair of the school governors, Joseph offered her the permanent teaching post to commence in the autumn term.

She smiled and said, 'Yes.'

On Thursday morning I awoke early. The first pink glow of dawn backlit the distant hills in sharp relief as a troubled night became a new day. I should have felt confident, but the experience with Tom had left me uncertain and I hoped we had made the right decision.

I felt more relieved when at 8.30 a.m. I received an unexpected call.

'Morning, Jack, it's Frank here from Thirkby Primary School.'

I recalled meeting him on various North Yorkshire education conferences. 'Morning, Frank. Is it about Pat Brookside?'

'Yes, Jack,' he said. 'Just to confirm, I've spoken to Richard Gomersall and there's no problem about Pat coming to you in September. You've got a very good teacher and I'll be sorry to lose her, but she has personal reasons for wanting to move into your area.'

'Yes, I gathered that,' I said.

'However, the main reason for ringing this morning is that Pat mentioned she heard from the children that you're going on a school trip to Hornsea tomorrow.'

'That's right. My top two classes are going.'

'Well, coincidentally, Pat is from Hornsea and knows the area well. If it's any help I could release her to come with you and it would give you a chance to get to know her a little better. Your call, Jack – I don't mind either way.'

'Excellent idea, Frank, and yes, please ask Pat to join us. The coach leaves at nine.'

'Fine, I'll tell her. And have a good day.'

I rang off.

'You look pleased, Mr Sheffield,' remarked Vera.

'Ms Brookside is coming to Hornsea with us tomorrow.'

'Excellent news,' said Vera. 'Perhaps she can organize the beach rounders. I'm not as young as I was.'

I was first in the staff-room at morning break.

309

Tom had spent twenty pence on his *Daily Mail* and I picked it up and glanced through the diverse headlines.

Terry Wogan's fifteen-year-old son had been found wandering on the hard shoulder of the motorway at midnight suffering from the stress of his O-level examinations. Meanwhile Michael Jackson had bought a new house in California. For £7 million it came complete with a fairytale castle and a railway track from his tennis court to his front door.

By eleven o'clock the sun was shining brightly and Anne had taken the children in her class up the Morton Road, accompanied by Miss Flint, to look around St Mary's Church. Joseph was in attendance and a little self-conscious of the fact that the ridge of his prominent Roman nose had been burnt in the sun.

'What's matter with y'nose, Mr Evans?' asked Billy Ricketts.

'It's all red,' said Madonna Fazackerly.

'Like Rudolph,' added Julie Tricklebank.

'Er, yes, children,' said Joseph. 'Welcome to our beautiful church.'

Alfie Spraggon and Sam Whittaker were soon doing some gravestone rubbings using wax crayons and large sheets of kitchen paper.

'Good to see you working so hard,' said Joseph with a smile of encouragement.

Alfie looked around him curiously at the ancient gravestones. 'Mr Evans ... are there *real* bodies 'ere?' he asked.

Sam's eyes lit up. 'An' can we dig one up?'

Anne came to the rescue. 'Come on, boys, time

to go back,' she said and Joseph leaned against the church wall and sighed.

In my class we were studying the poetry of William Wordsworth. I thought it was going well until Ben Roberts suddenly put up his hand. 'Seems a bit of a shame t'do *poetry*, Mr Sheffield,' he said wistfully.

'Why is that, Ben?' I asked, slightly surprised.

He looked out of the classroom window. 'Well, t'sun's shinin' an' buttercups are out on t'village green.'

There are occasions when, as a teacher, the lesson plan goes literally out of the window. I smiled, made a quick decision and, to everyone's astonishment, made an unexpected announcement. 'Boys and girls, bring your pencils. Sam and Louise, please carry the box of clipboards and follow me.' I picked up a ream of A4 paper and a poetry book. 'Harold, please tell Mrs Forbes-Kitchener we're going across to the village green and then let Mrs Grainger know as well.' He shot off like Seb Coe.

When we sat down on the green Ben plucked a long blade of grass and held it between his cupped hands. Then he blew it to make a sharp whistle and looked around for praise from his audience. I smiled and reflected on my own childhood, growing up on a northeast Leeds council estate. Here in North Yorkshire the joys of the countryside were a blessing for our children, with trees to climb, jam jars of frogspawn to investigate and hedgerows rich in bird and animal life.

'Ah like being outside, Mr Sheffield,' said Ben.

311

'Outside is t'best classroom ... there's no walls.' It occurred to me that he had a point.

The resulting work was a pleasure to behold. The drawings, poems and descriptions of the buttercups, the pond and the weeping willow were of such a high standard I was pleased I had forsaken my original lesson.

That evening Joseph Evans found himself chairing another meeting. This time it was the quarterly meeting of the Parish Church Council. Vera, predictably, was the secretary. The points discussed ranged from the serious to the farcical.

Albert Jenkins noted that the smart new church post box, complete with mortise lock on its cast-iron door, had been fitted to the wall of the church hall as agreed at the last meeting. However, the young man from Handy Andy – the Builder-U-Can-Trust, who had completed the job, had put the new set of keys in an envelope and posted them ... in the new box. Now no one could retrieve them as the box was locked. However, Oscar Woodcock, president of the Ragley Shed Society, said he collected old keys and was happy to spend an hour or two seeing if any of them fitted. Vera noted this down, albeit with gritted teeth.

Gerald Attersthwaite recommended that bat boxes be installed in the belfry 'to preserve these wonderful creatures'. This was countered quickly by the ever-efficient and fastidious churchwarden Wilfred Noggs, who said, 'Beggin' y'pardon, Vicar, but Gerald doesn't 'ave t'clear up the shitty droppings,' and Vera reworded this appropriately for the minutes.

312

Meanwhile, Elsie Crapper had noticed that the photograph of the church on the front cover of the latest *Parish News* magazine was back to front, although in her opinion it looked better that way, and Doris Oates, cook at Morton Manor, complained that the locum vicar's prayers were too long and put the timing of her Sunday dinner at risk.

There was some debate about the annual show, particularly the flower, vegetable and cake competitions, and the forthcoming Live Aid concert on 13 July. It was agreed that the money raised at the show would go towards helping the starving in Ethiopia.

'This Band Aid is on t'same day as our village fête,' pointed out Oscar.

'It's all them rock 'n' roll singers on t'telly,' said Elsie Crapper.

'Like that Freddie Mulberry,' said Oscar, 'an' Status summat and The What.'

'Who,' said Elsie.

'Them ah've jus' said,' reaffirmed Oscar.

'No, they're called The Who,' corrected Elsie.

'Well, it's them ... an' a lot more in t'*Easington 'Erald*. Ah read about it. There were a long list an' they're all famous.'

'Perhaps we can combine the two,' said Vera. 'Then the young folk will want to come along rather than staying at home.'

'You mean use the big television in the village hall?' asked Joseph.

'Good idea,' said Wilfred Noggs.

And so it went on.

Back at Bilbo Cottage Beth was thrilled and we were celebrating. A letter had arrived in the post with a Leeds postmark to confirm she had passed her Masters degree. The graduation ceremony would take place in the autumn.

'All that work,' I said. 'Well done – I'm so proud of you.'

'I'm just pleased and *relieved*,' said Beth and we raised a glass.

Five minutes later she was poring over the *Times Educational Supplement*.

'It's here, Jack!' said Beth excitedly. 'The York headship! I think maybe this was the one Miss Barrington-Huntley was hinting at when she came to see your choir last Christmas.'

I recalled the chair of the Education Committee saying she wanted to speak with Beth on the evening that Rosie Sparrow sang 'Silent Night'.

I leaned over her shoulder. 'So, are you going to apply?'

'Definitely – it's worth a try.'

I scanned the page. 'Then, as I said before, why not go for one or two of the big ones in the interim? The short-listing for the York headship is likely to be the last in the queue according to these dates.'

'I probably wouldn't get an interview, but maybe it's worth filling in an application form.'

'For example, there's a large headship here in North Yorkshire.'

Beth looked closely. 'And that huge one in Hampshire.'

'But that would mean moving.'

Beth shook her head. 'Unlikely, Jack. There's no

chance of me getting a school of that size for my second headship.'

I smiled. 'But if the interview came off it would be ideal experience.'

We finished our celebratory drinks and went to bed early. It was an evening of golden light and a time of peaceful reflection at the closing of the day.

On Friday morning Vera was up early. She read a little more of *The Diary of an Edwardian Lady* over a cup of tea and then looked out of the window. A gardener was clipping a cone-shaped topiary hedge with surgical precision and Vera mused to herself that perhaps the grounds were just too perfect. The rambling blackberry canes and the riot of raspberries in the vicarage garden now seemed like a forgotten friend. There, Mother Nature governed the patterns of plants and winding pathways, whereas here the Major's love of military precision was reflected in the perfect symmetry of the ornamental gardens.

She sighed and prepared for a busy day by the seaside.

William Featherstone was on time as always and we boarded the Reliance bus. I sat behind the driver and across the aisle Vera and Miss Flint shared the other front seat. Petula Dudley-Palmer and Sue Phillips had offered to support and they sat behind me. Sue, as a nurse, took it in her stride to be in charge of the box of sick bags.

In one of the rear seats Sally sat next to Pat Brookside and they were soon engaged in conversation. Pat had seen the Christmas television broadcast and was full of admiration for Sally's work with the choir. However, by the time we were passing through Market Weighton on the A1079, their discussion had moved on to men. Apparently Pat had recently met the man of her dreams, a doctor in Easington. Before we got to Hornsea Mere on the B1244 Sally knew everything about him apart from perhaps his inside leg measurement.

It was a day to remember and one of the happiest school visits I can recall.

We had lunch in the Mere café, where the children in Pat Brookside's group stared in amazement at a glass case on the wall.

'Miss, it's biggest fish ah've ever seen, 'cept on telly,' said Mo Hartley.

'Is it a shark, Miss?' asked Harold Bustard.

'No, it's norra shark,' said Ryan Halfpenny, who recalled fishing trips with his grandad.

'Miss – who caught it?' asked Frankie Spraggon.

'There's a small plaque on top of the case, Miss,' said Victoria Alice Dudley-Palmer, straining to read the engraved sign.

'It's a fish called a *pike* and it was caught almost eighty years ago,' recited Pat, smiling at the eager faces around her. 'It weighed twenty-seven pounds.'

'Just over twelve kilograms,' said the mathematically astute Charlotte Ackroyd.

'More than thirteen bags of sugar,' added Ben Roberts for good measure.

'Well done,' said Pat.

'An' what's 'e called, Miss?' asked Harold.

'Walter,' said Pat. 'He's called *Walter*.'

In their notebooks the children completed writing about the boat trip, sketched the swans, plotted the route from Ragley to Hornsea and drew pictures of Walter.

We finished with games of cricket and rounders on the beach.

'Miss can 'it it further than you, Sir,' said Mary Scrimshaw as Pat Brookside hit the rounders ball with perfect timing, and Pat gave me an apologetic smile.

Back at school we were welcomed like conquering heroes by a large group of parents lined up by the school wall. Pat Brookside caused great interest, as word had got round that she was to be our new teacher.

Mo Hartley was standing at the school entrance showing the Jackson twins the drawings in her notebook. 'Miss Brookside is lovely,' she said. 'She knew a lot about Hornsea. We went to a café and there was the biggest fish in the world there. It was in a glass case and Miss Brookside said it was called Walter.'

The twins were really impressed

Pippa Jackson hurried up the drive and welcomed her daughters.

'We're getting a new teacher,' said Hermione.

'She's called Miss Brookside,' said Honeysuckle.

'That's interesting,' replied Mrs Jackson.

'She starts next September,' said Honeysuckle.

'What's she like?' asked Mrs Jackson.

'She's tall,' said Hermione.

'And pretty,' said Honeysuckle.

'That's good,' said Mrs Jackson. 'But I hope she will be a good teacher.'

'I think she will, Mummy,' said Hermione.

'And why is that?' asked Mrs Jackson.

Hermione and Honeysuckle gave each other that special smile.

Mrs Jackson immediately recognized it.

It was the one they shared when they knew the other twin was thinking the same thought.

'Well,' said the twins in unison, 'she knows a fish called Walter.'

Chapter Eighteen

Mangetout and Marmalade

Pupils' flower paintings will be displayed in the village hall on Saturday, 13 July as part of the Ragley Village Fête.
Extract from the Ragley School Logbook:
Friday, 12 July 1985

A sliver of golden light crested the horizon and dawn raced across the land, touching treetops and caressing the fields. It swept over the village of Kirkby Steepleton, bathing Bilbo Cottage in the sunshine of a new day.

It was Friday morning, 12 July, and Beth and I were in the kitchen reflecting on her interview. Yesterday she had spent the day at County Hall in Northallerton after being shortlisted for the headship of one of North Yorkshire's largest primary schools. It was a rigorous two-day process, but Beth hadn't been asked to return for the second day and the final round of interviews.

'There were six of us,' said Beth, 'including two women, but three men went through to today.'

'Well, you did well to get this far,' I said, 'and you've still got the York headship to come.'

'Yes, in fact as I left Miss Barrington-Huntley said I had done well and made a point of saying she looked forward to the interview for the

319

school in York.'

'That's encouraging,' I said. 'I always did say she thought a lot of you. My guess is they wanted to have a look at you before your next interview.'

After being rejected for the Scarborough headship, Beth had applied for three more and, to our surprise, had been shortlisted for them all. This first attempt had been unsuccessful, but the experience would prove invaluable. The second was for the headship of a huge school in Hampshire, with two days of interviews scheduled to commence on 22 July. The third was the clear favourite – namely, the headship of a Group 4 primary school in York, with interviews at the beginning of the autumn term.

'So let's see how the Hampshire interview goes,' said Beth. 'The good news is I'll be back for the last day of term.'

Beth had been granted leave of absence to attend the interview commencing Monday, 22 July. The following day was the final day of the school year, but we both anticipated she would be back in Hartingdale by then.

'You never know, you might make the second day, and that would be really good experience for the September interview,' I said.

'And pigs might fly, Jack,' said Beth with a smile.

Just before the bell for the start of the school day, everyone had gathered in the office.

'Sally and I are mounting the children's flower paintings on stiff sugar paper,' said Anne, 'and then we're walking round to the village hall with them after school.'

'Thanks, Anne,' I said, 'I'll come along.'

'And I'll help,' volunteered Tom.

'Also, Miss Flint called to say she would offer assistance at lunchtime,' said Vera.

Everyone was rallying round for an important day in the social calendar. The Ragley Village Fête was supported by all the villagers and featured the hotly contested flower, vegetable and cake competitions. Reputations were at stake and there were prizes to be won.

'Marquee's goin' up, Mr Sheffield,' said the ever-vigilant Charlotte Ackroyd.

It was just before morning break and the children were excited. The fête meant candyfloss and toffee apples, donkey rides and prizes. I glanced out of the window. Major Rupert Forbes-Kitchener was issuing orders to his team of groundsmen and, with military precision, the giant tent rose towards the heavens on the village green.

At playtime Tom and I joined in a game of rounders on the field and the children were quick to make comparisons. 'Mr Dalton is faster than you, Sir,' said Charlotte.

'But Sir is better at catchin',' conceded the ever-faithful Mo Hartley.

Meanwhile, in the staff-room, Sally was reading her July edition of *Cosmopolitan* and studying an article entitled 'Sex on the Job'. It read 'Choose your working lover with care'. She glanced across the room at Vera, Anne and Miss Flint and thought, *Some hope!* After putting the magazine on the coffee table, she picked up Tom's *Daily Mail*.

It saddened her to read that the Greenpeace flagship *Rainbow Warrior* had been sunk and Sally wondered if all common sense had finally deserted the politics of France.

At the end of school I loaded up all the children's paintings in my Morris Minor Traveller while Anne, Tom and Sally walked down the High Street to the village hall. Every child in school had chosen a flower and painted it in his or her own inimitable style. It was remarkable to see the progression through the year groups. However, for my part, I simply loved the bright, bold, uninhibited artwork of Anne's reception children.

We mounted it all on the noticeboards on each side of the hall, labelled the paintings carefully and stood back to admire our work. It was a job well done. Tomorrow, families would drift in and out of here to watch the Live Aid concert on the large television set but also to enjoy the efforts of the children of Ragley School.

Tom and Sally drove home while Anne and I called in to Old Tommy Piercy's butcher's shop to buy some bacon and sausages for the weekend. When we walked in Betty Buttle was complaining about the heat.

Old Tommy wiped his brow with the back of his hand and returned to chopping a pound of braising steak. 'There's 'ot and there's 'ot,' he said with a glance out of the window, 'an' this is 'ot.'

He recited this maxim as if declaring peace in our time, and everyone in the queue nodded in subservient agreement. The oracle had spoken. However, we did wonder if we had missed something significant – perhaps a hidden meaning beyond the wit of mere mortals.

On Saturday morning Beth and I drove into York, parked on Lord Mayor's Walk and, after strapping John in his pushchair, walked up Gillygate and into the city to do some shopping.

A Canda jersey-knit dress caught Beth's attention in Woman at C&A. It had black, white and grey diagonal stripes. She tried it on and when she emerged from the changing room she looked cool and elegant and wore it with confidence.

Beth had a Visa card, which I didn't fully understand, and she used it to pay the £17.99. It seemed to be a simple transaction, completed with the minimum of fuss and no money changing hands. Even so, I could never imagine owning one of the new credit cards myself.

In Coney Street we bought a small box on wheels full of colourful wooden cubes for John and a gardening book for me from W.H.Smith. My vegetable plot had improved over the years and I had a bumper crop of early carrots and mangetout waiting to be harvested.

Then we walked up Stonegate and High Petergate to York Minster. There was peace and cool air in this magnificent place. Work was well under way following last year's great fire and soon this majestic building would be restored to its former glory.

'I love it here, Jack,' said Beth quietly.

We stood in front of the stone quire screen fronted by fifteen near life-size statues of the kings of England. Above them a row of angels were playing musical instruments.

'And I love you,' I said. The great windows of the clerestory suddenly filled the nave with shafts of summer light. 'I loved you from the first moment I saw you ... all those years ago in Ragley.'

Beth smiled at the memory. 'You were wearing an old boilersuit and sweeping the school drive.'

John disturbed our peaceful thoughts. 'I think he's getting hungry,' I said.

Beth looked at her watch. 'Let's get back, feed John and then go to the village fête. Also I want to dig out a jar of my marmalade for the competition. It's probably the best I've made.'

I had been putting it on my morning toast for the past few months and hadn't really noticed. 'Good idea,' I said.

'You ought to enter something,' said Beth.

'Such as?'

'Your mangetout look about ready – take a bag of those.'

On our way home we spotted Petula Dudley-Palmer's Rolls-Royce in the car park of the chocolate factory. She had called in with a message for Geoffrey and had seen his new secretary for the first time – a young, dynamic, long-legged beauty. She appeared studied and sure, yet moved with the confident grace of a panther. When Petula spoke to her she was aware of a scent, distinct yet elusive. She knew it ... but couldn't quite remember from where.

Back at Bilbo Cottage Beth put a smart new label on a jar of her homemade marmalade and I went into the garden. It was high summer and butterflies hovered over the buddleia bushes amidst the murmur of the bees that sought their precious nectar.

I collected a handful of my mangetout and cleaned them under the outside tap. Then I put them in a plastic bag, selected a white plate and we set off for Ragley village. The sturdy stems of cow parsley stood tall on the grassy banks and under a primrose-blue sky the shrill screams of swifts were faint in the distance as they swirled around the clock tower of St Mary's Church.

The Revd Joseph Evans was in his cluttered pantry. When Vera had lived there it had been organized beautifully, with serried ranks of fruit in large jars. Now it was in disarray, with a jumble of bottles of homemade wine featuring dubious labels such as 'Damson Delight' and 'Dream of Dandelion'.

However, Joseph was a happy soul and his wine-making gave him great pleasure. His generosity of spirit could never be faulted and it was rare for a friend or clerical colleague to leave the vicarage without a complimentary bottle or two. The fact they never drank it was another matter.

He selected a bottle, put it in his little Austin A40 and set off down the Morton Road to the Ragley Village Fête.

The green was a riot of colourful bunting and lively stalls. In the marquee Vera and the ladies of the Women's Institute were covering the trestle tables with snowy-white cloths and arranging the exhibits for the various competitions. Soon the scent of roses filled the air and, with affected modesty, I handed over my plate of mangetout. I had arranged them in a spiral, like a living ammonite, and interest was aroused.

'Quite magnificent, Mr Sheffield,' said Vera. 'Perfect mangetout arranged with artistry – definitely a strong contender.'

A name card was placed in front of my entry and I went to the far trestle-table where Beth's marmalade was lined up with countless others. 'It'll tek me a while t'taste all these,' said Mary Hardisty. Her husband, George, Ragley's champion gardener, would be judging the vegetables, while the effervescent Miss Gardenia Rose Thyck was already patrolling the contenders for the 'Vase of Sweet Peas' class.

I walked out into the sunshine where Charlotte Ackroyd had just won a prize on the coconut shy and Ben Roberts was spending his hard-earned pocket money in a futile effort to win a goldfish on the hoopla stall.

Meanwhile, the Ramsbottom boys, Shane, Clint and Wayne, were busy down the street in the village hall, where a large television set had been tuned in to the Live Aid concert at Wembley Stadium in London. It was to prove a remarkable event, watched by 1.5 billion people on television and destined to raise over £50 million for those in need in Africa.

Shane was a little worse for wear after a night's hard drinking.

''Ow are y'today, Shane?' asked a concerned Clint. There was some heavy lifting in front of them.

'Well, Nancy,' said Shane with bravado, 'las' night ah were sick as a Cleethorpes donkey, but now ah'm right as rain,' and they set to work.

A lot of the young folk were intending to watch the Live Aid concert with its all-star cast. On a chalkboard at the side of the television, Clint had printed:

Status Quo, Sting, Queen, David Bowie,
Paul McCartney, Elton John, Joan Baez,
Madonna, Eric Clapton, Mick Jagger,
Led Zeppelin, Duran Duran and Bob Dylan.
Plus Phil Collins x 2!

Apparently Phil Collins was to complete the extraordinary feat of performing both at Wembley and then at the American Live Aid concert at the JFK Stadium in Philadelphia, thanks to the speed of Concorde.

I saw Sally and Colin coming out of the village hall with their daughter Grace. Sally was disappointed the Rolling Stones weren't taking part. Long ago, on 5 July 1969, she had been to their concert in London. It had been a tribute to guitarist Brian Jones, who had died two days earlier at the age of twenty-seven, and Sally had shed silent tears. She waved and shouted, 'Good luck with the mangetout,' while Colin merely looked puzzled.

Beth and I stood next to a popular stall called Billy's Balloons, where the stallholder had a novel idea. You could buy a helium-filled balloon for five pence and write on the attached label a message to a loved one before letting it fly up into the sky. We bought one for John, who scrawled a big circle on the card before watching it fly away with wonder in his eyes.

I saw Mo Hartley and her sisters sitting on the grass writing carefully chosen words to their late mother. It was a poignant scene, made even more moving when Hazel Smith joined them and wrote 'Missing you, Dad' with a Berol marker pen before launching a red balloon towards heaven.

Victor Pratt was exhibiting his steam-driven tractor and was proudly polishing it as I walked past.

'Ah've been t'see Dr Davenport,' said Victor.

'Oh dear,' I said, wondering what was coming next.

'Ah went wi' both me 'ands.' He held them out to show me. 'Y'see – they sheck summat rotten. Ah told 'im ah'd got a nervous supposition.'

'What did he do, Victor?' I asked.

''E gave me some tablets t'calm me down.'

'Are they working?' I asked.

'Yes, thanks, Mr Sheffield, but ah can't fry chips like ah used to.'

Poor Victor looked broken-hearted. This was obviously a tough price to pay.

Timothy Pratt had locked up his Hardware Emporium for a couple of hours and, with his best friend Walter Crapper, was looking after the Bowling for a Pig stall. It was proving popular and, according to the scoreboard, Deke Ramsbottom was clearly the one to beat. I felt a twinge of sadness for the unsuspecting little pig frolicking around in its pen and being fed everything from apple cores to candyfloss by the crowd of children.

'Meks m'feel 'ungry,' said Betty Buttle.

'Meks me want t'be a vegetarian,' said Margery Ackroyd.

Outside The Royal Oak Old Tommy Piercy was staring in admiration at his hog roast while his grandson, Young Tommy, carved generous slices for the members of the Ragley cricket team, who were first in the queue.

'Y'can't beat a bit o' pork cracklin',' said Big Dave, licking his lips. 'Ah'll 'ave a bit f'me please, Tommy, and a bit f'my Nellie.'

'And t'same f'me an' my Dorothy,' added Little Malcolm, thrusting forward two plastic plates.

'It would be lovely wi' apple sauce,' said Big Dave.

'An' some o' my Dorothy's gravy,' added Little Malcolm with true loyalty.

Dorothy and Nellie were sitting nearby at one of the wooden picnic tables. Nora had come to join them and they wanted to know how life with Tyrone was progressing.

'This might be t'weal thing, Dowothy,' said Nora, 'an' in m' 'owwoscope it said Awies was wising.'

'That's good news, Nora,' said Dorothy.

'So what yer 'aving Nora?' asked Nellie, getting up with her purse.

'Ah feel like celebwatin',' said Nora. 'Ah'll 'ave a snowball.'

I was brought up not to listen in to other people's conversations, but sometimes it can't be helped. I was inside the WI tent while Sheila Bradshaw was

329

standing just outside talking to Audrey Cuthbertson. They watched their teenage daughters Claire and Anita, down the High Street, walk into the village hall to see the concert.

'They've been friends a long time, Sheila,' said Audrey wistfully.

'They 'ave that,' agreed Sheila.

'Ah think we brought 'em up right,' said Audrey.

'Let's 'ope so,' said Sheila.

Audrey looked across the green. 'At least they 'ad a good start in t'village school,' she said.

'Y'reight there,' said Sheila. 'Ah've allus liked that 'eadteacher. 'E don't jus' teach 'em t'ABCs, 'e learns 'em right from wrong.'

'An' *manners*,' added Audrey, for good measure.

I pretended not to hear but couldn't resist a smile as I studied the class of 'Three Onions' with new intensity.

Meanwhile, Beth was in conversation with Joseph, who was eyeing up the competition in the homemade wines class.

'I've called this "Parsnip Perfection",' he said without a hint of modesty. 'My "Sloe Surprise" isn't quite there yet,' he added pensively. Wherever *there* was, no one dared to ask; but we all knew he meant well and the journey of his wine remained a mystery. What was certain was that when it did eventually arrive in a wine glass it tasted like a mixture of decaying vegetation with a subtle hint of Domestos.

Outside, Frankie Spraggon wanted to buy an ice lolly. He saw Sonia Tricklebank looking in her pink Barbie purse and had an idea.

After scrabbling in Maurice Tupham's garden

he returned to the village green and approached Sonia. He held up a glistening fat earthworm that writhed in his fingers. Frankie was desperate. 'Sonia,' he said, 'ah'll eat a worm for five pence.'

Sonia recoiled. 'Ah'll give you twopence to let it go,' she said with a sense of righteous indignation.

Frankie thought about this. "Ow 'bout for threepence ah eat 'alf an' let t'other 'alf go?' he asked.

Sonia shook her head, walked away and wondered why boys were so repulsive.

Vera and Ruby were standing outside the WI tent in the sunshine and George Dainty was beckoning to them. He had a jug of elderflower cordial and two tumblers. 'I think Mr Dainty would like you to sit with him, Ruby,' said Vera with a smile.

'Will you come as well, Mrs F?'

'Sorry, Ruby,' said Vera, 'I have to help with the arrangements for the judges,' and she hurried off.

Ruby went to sit with George and he poured some cordial for her. Soon they were chatting about old times and the fact that George had retired and returned to Ragley. 'Ah'm pleased you've done well for y'self, George,' said Ruby. 'You allus did work 'ard.'

George's shop, 'The Codfather II', in Alicante had proved a roaring success.

'It were all 'cause of m'batter, Ruby,' he said with pride. 'It were m'special recipe,' he added knowingly, tapping the side of his nose with a stubby forefinger. Then he looked thoughtful and leaned back to stare up into the graceful branches of the weeping willow above their heads. After a while he said, 'Thing is, Ruby ... money don't mek yer 'appy.'

''Ow d'you mean?' asked Ruby.

'Well,' said George, 'can y'recall that Yorkshire miner's wife, Viv Nicholson? She won over 'undred an' fifty thousand pounds on Littlewoods Pools way back in 1961 when a pound were worth a pound.'

Ruby nodded and wondered why George had brought this up. 'Ah remember,' she said, 'she were gonna "spend, spend, spend".'

'That's reight, Ruby, she did – an' what 'appened?'

Ruby shook her head.

'She ended up *penniless*. She couldn't even afford t'pay for 'er fourth 'usband's funeral.'

The sound of a clatter of beer crates came from the open trapdoor that led to the cellar of The Royal Oak.

'Sounds like they'll be settin' up t'bar soon 'ere outside t'pub,' said Ruby. 'My Ronnie would 'ave been first in t'queue.'

''Appen 'e would,' said George with a wry smile.

''E were all mouth an' trousers, were my Ronnie,' said Ruby. 'All airs an' no graces – y'know t'type – but ah still loved 'im.'

'Ah know y'did, Ruby,' said George, 'an' there's nowt wrong wi' that.'

Ruby stared down into her lap and tried to flex her fingers. 'My 'ands 'ave started to 'urt, George.'

'Y'can tell a lot from a woman's 'ands,' he replied, and he stroked the back of her hand, fingertip softly.

Ruby didn't withdraw it.

Joyce Davenport, the doctor's wife, had set up a 'Yorkshire' stall with tea towels, white rose flags and 'God's Own Country' mugs, notepads and pencils. Patience Crapper and Madonna Fazackerly were staring with great interest and Joyce took pity on them. *They probably haven't got a halfpenny between them*, she thought.

'Now, girls,' she said, 'if you're really good then at the end of the afternoon you can come back to my stall and I'll give you a souvenir.'

The two little girls said, 'Thank you,' and ran off. They stopped by the WI tent and sat on the grass. 'What's a souvenir?' wondered Patience.

'Dunno,' said Madonna with blissful ignorance, 'but ah know ah want one.'

'Same 'ere,' agreed Patience and, after spotting a gap under the canvas wall of the marquee, decided this was a more interesting entry point. They crawled through and emerged with dirty knees into a sea of floral dresses, summer stockings, sensible shoes – and tasty things to eat.

In the tent the crowds had cleared and the judges were in attendance. Miss Gardenia Rose Thyck was scrutinizing the flowers and George Hardisty was judging the vegetables while his wife, Mary, Ragley village's champion cake-maker, was sampling the cakes and preserves. Finally she awarded a 'First Prize' card to Vera Forbes-Kitchener's Queen Mother's Cake and a 'Second Prize' to Maggie Sparrow's Never-fail Sponge. Then she moved on to the preserves.

Meanwhile, George Hardisty had placed a

'First Prize' card next to the bunch of carrots submitted by Albert Jenkins and a 'With Merit' card alongside Tobias Speight's 'Peas in a Pod'. He was distinctly puzzled by some of the other entries. There had been a brief hiatus when two small girls were discovered under the table of vegetables ... and they looked very guilty.

Eventually the judges emerged from the tent and the villagers hurried in to see where they had placed the 'First', 'Second' and 'Third', 'Highly Commended' and 'With Merit' cards.

Beth was suddenly animated. 'Look at this, Jack!' she said.

A large white card with gold edging was alongside Beth's jar of marmalade. It read:

1st prize
Beth Sheffield
An outstanding marmalade –
good colour, perfect consistency,
fine texture and excellent flavour.

'Congratulations, Beth,' said Vera. 'A wonderful achievement.'

A delighted Joseph suddenly arrived holding a 'With Merit' card on which the judge had written 'a distinctive taste'. When he saw me he patted me on the shoulder. 'Never mind, Jack,' he said, 'there's always next year.' He pointed to the table of vegetables and I walked over to learn my fate.

Where I had left my entry was an almost empty plate with a single part-nibbled mangetout in the centre. Next to it was a brown card that simply read 'Unplaced'.

The fact it was causing such hilarity among my nearest and dearest didn't help. 'Sorry,' said Vera. 'Apparently a couple of naughty children ate them.'

'Well, I hope they enjoyed them,' I said with feeling.

'Jack,' said Vera quietly, 'the scent of roses lingers on the heart that gives.'

Both chuckling happily, Vera and Beth went to collect their prizes.

Chapter Nineteen

Silent Night

99 children were registered on roll on the last day of the school year. 14 fourth-year juniors left today. 13 will commence full-time education at Easington Comprehensive School in September and 1, Victoria Alice Dudley-Palmer, will begin her secondary education in York at the Time School for Girls. School closed today for the summer holiday and will reopen on Wednesday, 4 September.

Extract from the Ragley School Logbook:
Tuesday, 23 July 1985

It was a new dawn. Behind the distant hills a shimmering disc of golden light emerged in the eastern sky. The countryside was waking and an eventful day was in store. A shaft of golden sunlight streamed into the kitchen of Bilbo Cottage and motes of dust hovered like tiny fireflies. The air was humid and warm, waiting for a breeze ... a wind of change.

It was Tuesday, 23 July, the last day of the school year, and my home was strangely quiet. The usual bustle of activity wasn't there. It was the second day of Beth's two-stage interview and today she would be preparing for the formal interrogation by Hampshire's Education Committee. I didn't envy her and prayed the experi-

336

ence wouldn't prove too stressful.

Beth had travelled down to Hampshire last weekend to stay with her parents in Little Chawton, and John and Diane Henderson were thrilled to have their daughter and grandson to stay for a few days. Apparently our son was enjoying all the attention and, according to last night's telephone call from Beth, looking forward to his first ride on a steam train. Tomorrow would be his birthday, two years old, and I intended to drive down there, making sure I arrived in time for his party.

Beth had telephoned while I was having an early breakfast. 'I'll ring you tonight at seven from my parents' home,' she had said, 'when it's all over – and when I've had time to gather myself and think.'

'I'll still be at school,' I said, 'clearing some paperwork, so I'll take your call there. And good luck ... I love you.'

'You too,' she said and rang off.

I had a bright, determined and ambitious wife and this was her time. It had been a surprise last night when Beth said she wouldn't be travelling back to Yorkshire for the last day of the school year. Neither of us had expected she would be called back for the final selection process. The competition sounded strong, including the current deputy headteacher and two experienced headteachers from Kent and Surrey ... all men. However, Beth had stressed that the post she was keen on was the York headship and her experiences in Hampshire would prove helpful when that interview came around.

As I packed my brown leather satchel, I recalled

a little girl singing 'Silent Night', followed by relaxed conversations over a glass of Merlot with Sarah Mancini. That evening, seeds had been sown and Miss Barrington-Huntley had let it be known that Beth was definitely 'one for the future'. A long career in North Yorkshire beckoned.

It was much earlier than usual when I set off for school. Paul Young was singing 'Every Time You Go Away' on the radio and I hummed along. On the back road to Ragley I pulled in to the side of the road and got out of my car. I paused under the welcome shade of sycamores, standing tall like sentinels, and stood on the moist earth to drink in the resinous scent of the ancient woodland. Beyond the hedgerows swathes of July wheat stirred with a sinuous rhythm in the oppressive heat. The countryside was sleeping, the wind was almost still and the land was holding its breath. Low clouds rolled over the distant hills like a surging sea and the faint echo of thunder rolled over the countryside.

I could smell the rain.

As I drove towards school I experienced that familiar feeling of anticipation. The world beyond the fields and streams of Ragley was changing, but in our tiny corner of North Yorkshire our village was fixed in its own time, steadfast and true, with its church, school and shops. Seasons came and went and our children moved on, but the school remained the cornerstone of our village.

I pulled up outside the General Stores.

'Good morning, Miss Golightly.'

'Exciting times, Mr Sheffield,' said Prudence. 'We're going on holiday for a week in Scotland – up to the Isle of Skye.'

'That's wonderful,' I said.

I glanced up at Jeremy Bear on his familiar shelf. 'And good morning to you, Jeremy.' He was wearing a tartan waistcoat and matching kilt, complete with sporran, plus neat leather ghillie brogues, all beautifully made by Prudence.

'I've never seen him look so smart,' I said.

Prudence beamed. 'Thank you, Mr Sheffield. Jeremy always likes to look the part.'

'Well, have a good holiday, Jeremy,' I said.

Prudence smiled. 'Here's your paper, Mr Sheffield, and best wishes for the last day of term.'

At the school gate Kenny Kershaw walked past and waved. I pulled up and wound down my window. He was a strapping young man now, but I could still see the ten-year-old that I knew when I first arrived at Ragley School. It only seemed five minutes ago.

''Ow do, Mr Sheffield,' he shouted. 'T'school looks fine on a mornin' like this.'

'It certainly does, Kenny,' I agreed.

'We 'ad some good times,' he said wistfully. 'Remember when ah were sick when we went on t'school camp in t'Dales?'

'I'll never forget it, Kenny,' I assured him with a smile.

'Neither will I, Mr Sheffield!' And with a cheery wave he walked to the bus stop.

He was right – memories ... so many schooldays, so many children.

When I parked my car excited voices filled the

air as children skipped up the school drive. I smiled at their love of life and their world of here and now. There were races to be run, trees to climb, streams to dam, secrets to share, friendships to be forged, and I envied their innocence.

On their pathway through life, adolescence was still a distant journey. A six-week summer holiday stretched out before them and their carefree laughter lingered in the air long after they had disappeared from view to play on the school field.

The annual Leavers' Assembly was always a poignant time in the school calendar. The Parent Teacher Association contributed funds to enable each child to be presented with a dedicated book. It was a special moment for the pupil and their parents as they walked out to receive their gift and, as always, a few tears were shed. Major Rupert Forbes-Kitchener did the honours and I almost expected the children to salute when they stood before him.

Charlotte Ackroyd and Ben Roberts, the tuck shop duo, received generous applause. The tall Danny Hardacre gave me a grin and mimed cleaning the blackboard as he walked to the front, and Harold Bustard moved with his usual lightning speed when he was called out. Mo Hartley simply smiled at her father. George Hartley looked down at his clasped hands as the youngest of his five daughters said farewell to her primary school. He wished his late wife could have seen her looking so confident. Little Mo was the image of her mother and he bowed his head for a long time recalling happy days.

They came up one by one: Sam Borthwick, Louise Briers and Callum Myler ... and so it went on. The next step in their lives at the local comprehensive awaited them, along with adolescence, new friends, a host of teachers for every subject, a uniform that would probably fit in a year's time, homework and examinations – perhaps even a new curriculum.

It was different for Victoria Alice Dudley-Palmer. She was destined to join her sister at a private school in York after the summer break, so today she would be saying goodbye to her Ragley friends. In the back row, her mother, Petula, shed a tear, but not simply for her daughter ... there were other concerns.

The Major gave a speech saying he wanted the children to remember the good start they had enjoyed at Ragley School and always to be proud of their village. We finished with our final hymn, 'Lord Of All Hopefulness', followed by our traditional school prayer, read beautifully by Victoria Alice:

Dear Lord,
This is our school, let peace dwell here,
Let the room be full of contentment, let love abide
  here,
Love of one another, love of life itself,
And love of God.
Amen.

It was at times like this that I felt we were more than a school. We were a family.

It was then that Joseph stood up to say a formal

thank-you to Tom Dalton, who was leaving us today. The PTA had bought him a year's subscription to his favourite computer magazine and the staff had purchased a beautiful book about the history of North Yorkshire villages with photographs of Ragley-on-the-Forest, including one of the village school taken in 1946.

Tom responded with a short speech that grew in confidence. He thanked us all for giving him the opportunity to work in Ragley School and reassured everyone that he would keep in touch. This was greeted warmly by all assembled and he shook hands with Joseph. As he returned to his seat he nodded in my direction.

On a lighter note, Shirley the Cook had presented him with one of her excellent apple and blackberry pies and, much to our delight, he immediately shared it in the staff-room during morning break.

Shirley was soon back in her kitchen, topping and tailing gooseberries in preparation for my favourite fruit crumble. The gooseberries were a gift from the bountiful garden of Mary Hardisty, whose husband George had been groundsman when I first arrived at Ragley. We missed him and his dedicated service, especially on the days the county groundsmen team arrived with their functional gang mower, lopped off a few inches of lank grass from our school field before hurrying off to the next school. Times were changing.

It was at lunchtime that I received an unexpected visitor in the entrance hall. Mark Appleby, Rosie Sparrow's father, arrived in his gas-fitter's boilersuit.

'Ah jus' came t'say thank you, Mr Sheffield,' he said and shook my hand.

'We're here to do the best we can,' I said. 'Rosie is a very talented young girl. You must be so proud.'

'I am that,' he said. 'When she sang "Silent Night" on that television programme I could have wept it were so beautiful. It changed my life – brought us back t'gether, so t'speak.' He paused, searching for the right words. 'Ah wanted t'let y'know that Maggie an' me are getting wed nex' month.'

'That's wonderful news!' I said. 'Congratulations.'

'Ah've got a family now an' it's a good feeling.'

'Yes ... it is,' I agreed.

He left quickly, but paused by the entrance door. 'An' if you ever need y'gas boiler repairing, jus' give me a call.' He grinned and left.

I watched from the window as he drove away to his new life.

To the west, in the far distance, there was a rainbow in the sky piercing the dark clouds.

In the Coffee Shop Nora and Tyrone were staring out of the window.

'It's red, orange, yellow, green, blue, indigo and violet,' said Tyrone.

'The colours of the wainbow,' said Nora.

'That's right,' said Tyrone. 'Richard of York gave battle in vain – it's a mnemonic.'

'Is that an orchestwa?'

'No, you remember it by the first letters,' explained Tyrone.

'Ah love wainbows,' said Nora.

'It's a result of the refraction of the sun's rays by light or water droplets,' recited Tyrone in his monotonous voice.

Nora stopped him suddenly. 'Ah always dweamed of a pot o' gold at t'end of a wainbow.'

'Perhaps there is, Nora,' said Tyrone. He held her hand. 'And it's waiting there for you and me.'

Petula Dudley-Palmer wasn't thinking of rainbows. She had returned home, gone upstairs to her bedroom, changed into her rose-pink leisure suit and lain down on the bed. In her *Woman's Weekly* was an advertisement for a seventeen-day discovery holiday in Australia at £1,189.00. *Perhaps it would be good for me and the girls*, she thought.

'Life's not a rehearsal,' her mother had once said to her when she was a teenager. *How true.*

Petula had a tall feather bed with a rift valley of a depression in the soft mattress that exactly matched her prone figure. She lay back and thought of her life.

Geoffrey's shirt lay discarded next to his pillow.

She didn't smell the soft linen any more.

She didn't press it to her face to remember happy times.

The scent that was embedded in the fibres was not hers.

She had remembered.

The scent was the one that lingered in his secretary's office.

At the end of school I said goodbye to the school leavers and watched them walk out of the school gate. The halcyon days of a seemingly endless summer stretched out before them. For children who lived in the here-and-now it was a never-ending pathway.

I walked into the school office and sat at my desk. Vera was busy completing the leavers' record cards ready for transfer to secondary school. In the entrance hall I heard Ruby clattering past with her electric floor cleaner prior to the annual 'holiday polish' of the school hall. Ruby's wedding ring had now slipped down her finger to the knuckle and she twisted it whenever she had a quiet moment. That morning it had dropped off and rolled under a radiator. She had picked it up guiltily and said 'Sorry' out loud. Then she had smiled and muttered, 'Y'daft ha'porth,' and carried on.

I heard her moving the hall furniture – and then to my surprise she began to sing one of her favourite songs from *The Sound of Music*. It reminded me of my first day at Ragley when Ruby sang so sweetly as she swept and polished and mopped.

I smiled and started to wade through the latest North Yorkshire curriculum document.

Tom called in and we shook hands. It was a brief parting. A new direction awaited him, a fresh start – and I wondered if it would include Laura.

Sally popped her head round the door. 'Must rush, Jack,' she said. 'Colin's taking me out for a meal. Ring me if you want anything doing in the holidays.'

Anne came in with the Yorkshire Purchasing Organization catalogue and smiled. 'A little light reading, Jack,' she said. 'Come round for a casserole one night soon and we can catch up with Beth's news. Anyway, thanks again – we've survived another year.'

Finally, Vera tidied her desk.

I was staring out of the window. 'Beth is being interviewed for a new headship,' I said, 'a big one ... down south.'

Vera looked up and nodded. 'Yes, Beth told me.' She picked up her bag and walked to the door. 'Thank you for your support once again, Mr Sheffield,' she said. 'It means so much.'

'The school would be lost without you, Vera ... *I* would be lost without you.'

She studied me for a moment. 'All things come to an end, Mr Sheffield.'

Then she walked back to the window. She put her hand on my shoulder. 'Jack,' she said quietly, 'all we can do is our best while it is happening ... and then look forward to the next adventure.'

Is she thinking of retiring? I wondered.

The school was quiet apart from the ticking of the clock. I decided to go outside for some fresh air and return in time for Beth's telephone call.

When I reached the school gate I stared thoughtfully at the sign fixed to the tall stone gatepost. It read:

Ragley Church of England Primary School
North Yorkshire County Council
Headteacher – Mr J. Sheffield

The letters were fading now and I recalled the first time I had stood here in the late summer of 1977. Then I had been full of excitement and eager for the challenge ahead. This old building with its clock tower and high arched windows had become an integral part of my life. A generation of children had come and gone since I'd arrived – Anita Cuthbertson, Elisabeth Amelia Dudley-Palmer, Ping the Vietnamese Boat Girl, Debbie Harrison the miner's daughter, Heathcliffe Earnshaw, Claire Bradshaw... So many faces ... so many young lives. A generation had come and gone in the ever-turning cycle of village life.

I leaned back against the gate and stared up at the mirror in the sky, but the only reflection was a William Turner cloudscape, a grey wash of turbulence and confusion. Suddenly life wasn't quite so simple any more.

I walked across the green, sat on Ronnie's bench and looked back at the school. Time passed, until a dark ebony sky descended over the vast plain of York. The breeze died and the branches of the weeping willow above me rustled gently before coming to rest in the humid air. It was sultry and overcast and, in the near distance, storm clouds were gathering pace and rolling towards Ragley.

Suddenly the Earnshaw boys approached. Heathcliffe was pushing a wheelbarrow full of empty bottles. ''Ello, Mr Sheffield,' he said.

''Ello, Sir,' said Terry.

'We're c'llectin' empties, Mr Sheffield, an' then we tek 'em back t'Miss Golightly an' she gives us some money.'

'An' a bag o' sherbet lemons,' added Terry.

They eyed up the bench. This wasn't the time to use it as a step-up to the willow tree. They loved to climb up to the top branches and look out on Ragley High Street above the scurrying shoppers and the workers in the fields beyond – to feel the wind trying to pluck you off your perch and to feel that sense of danger and for a few dizzy moments to be king of all you survey.

It was an experience they would share and one that the two brothers would eventually recall in their old age, but not now ... not now.

There was too much living to do and too many bottles to collect.

Alone again, I thought of Beth and our shared journey.

Let us go then, you and I,
When the evening is spread out against the sky...

It was a strange time for my favourite poet, T.S. Eliot, to join me on Ronnie's bench, but his words came into my mind and seemed appropriate. This precious corner of North Yorkshire had been my home now for eight years and I had come to love the ebb and flow of village life. Ragley School was part of the very fabric of my being.

Over the Hambleton hills the rain was beating down like steel rods and smearing the sky in diagonal shafts of grey fury. The arrow on the cast-iron weathervane on top of the village hall creaked and turned towards the west. Clouds were piling up, magenta and indigo, and in the fading light the air had become close and stuffy. An early night was gradually failing over the plain of York and the sky was turning slowly from red to purple and finally, in the distance, to a Stygian darkness.

A storm was almost upon us – a big storm.

I walked back into school, sat at my desk, took out the school logbook, filled my fountain pen with Quink ink and began to write.

The clock ticked on.

It was good to be indoors as the first heavy drops of rain drummed against the windowpanes – a comfortable, secure feeling, warm and cosy.

For a brief moment, between the first flash of lightning and the crash of thunder, all was still. It was as if the world were holding its breath as a dark and silent night settled on the land.

Then the telephone rang, shrill and urgent.

'Jack, I'm back with my parents,' said Beth. She sounded out of breath. 'John's fine and I've lots to tell you.'

'You'll have to speak up,' I said. 'We've got a big storm up here.'

The windows shook. My world was full of electric echoes and the boom of thunder.

'Jack ... Jack,' shouted Beth. 'Can you hear me now?'

'Yes – just. What's the news? How are you and how did it go?'

'I'm fine. It's been an eventful day ... *intriguing*, you might say.'

Lightning forked down to the hills and briefly split the black velvet sky.

'*Intriguing* ... how do you mean?'

349

'Jack, you'll never guess ... they've offered me the job.'

Thunder rolled across the heavens like a giant avalanche.

'What did you say?'

'I have another meeting with them tomorrow morning – things to discuss – I'll explain it all when you come down.'

'Did you say they had *offered you the job?*'

'Yes.'

I sat back in my chair. I had sown the wind ... now I was reaping the whirlwind.

'And did you accept?'

There was a long pause.

For a few moments the storm was still.

In a world of whispers the silence was deafening. Finally she spoke. Her words were soft like the caress of silk.

And in a heartbeat I knew our two worlds had collided.

The publishers hope that this book has given you enjoyable reading. Large Print Books are especially designed to be as easy to see and hold as possible. If you wish a complete list of our books please ask at your local library or write directly to:

Magna Large Print Books
Magna House, Long Preston,
Skipton, North Yorkshire.
BD23 4ND

This Large Print Book for the partially sighted, who cannot read normal print, is published under the auspices of

THE ULVERSCROFT FOUNDATION

THE ULVERSCROFT FOUNDATION

... we hope that you have enjoyed this Large Print Book. Please think for a moment about those people who have worse eyesight problems than you ... and are unable to even read or enjoy Large Print, without great difficulty.

You can help them by sending a donation, large or small to:

**The Ulverscroft Foundation,
1, The Green, Bradgate Road,
Anstey, Leicestershire, LE7 7FU,
England.**
or request a copy of our brochure for more details.

The Foundation will use all your help to assist those people who are handicapped by various sight problems and need special attention.

Thank you very much for your help.